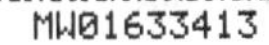

# CLASSIC
## CONVERSATIONS

To request permissions, contact the publisher at acspublishing@hotmail.com

First edition April 2025
Hardcover: 978-1-7383104-6-3
Paperback: 978-1-7383104-7-0
E-book: 978-1-7383104-8-7

Cover art by Cathrine Swift
Interior Design by Cathrine Swift
(@authorcathrineswift)

for the authors who came before us and paved the
road we now walk on,
and for the authors who follow along after us.

never stop writing.

# OFFICIAL READING SOUNDTRACK

Perfect - Ed Sheeran
Which Witch - Florence + The Machine
The Garden / All in the Golden Afternoon - Kathryn Beaumont
(from Disney's Alice in Wonderland)
It Matters to Me - Faith Hill
Think of Me - Emmy Rossum, Patrick Wilson, Andrew Lloyd Webber
(from The Phantom of the Opera)
Haunted (Taylor's Version) - Taylor Swift
Generique - Miles Davis
Rewrite the Stars - Zac Efron, Zendaya
Who's Afraid of Little Old Me? - Taylor Swift
I Guess I'm in Love - Iris Noelle
BIRDS OF A FEATHER - Billie Eillish
I Like You Best - Ella Red
Winnie the Pooh - Disney Peaceful Piano
Strawberry Wine - Deana Carter
Spaceman - Bif Naked
labour - Paris Paloma
To Be Alone - Hozier
Daylight - David Kushner

available on Spotify and Apple Music

# READING GUIDES

Naturally, you're welcome to read the book from beginning to end as prepared, but the table of contents (next page) has been created with intention for easy navigation back to your favourite classic authors and their literary worlds, or straight to discovering new pieces and authors. Should you so ache for a bit more control.

At the beginning of each story you will see a short synopsis for each story to help ground you in each author's unique vision, as well as content warnings, when applicable.

We deal with some rather mature themes in a few of these stories, so please heed the warnings if you are someone who appreciates them.

You are also encouraged by the Classic Conversations team to utilize the official reading soundtrack, (available on Spotify and Apple Music) which has been organized in the same order of the stories. *If reading out of order, please cross reference the playlist with the table of contents as needed.*

We sincerely hope you enjoy your reading journey. However you choose to embark on it!

# PUBLIC DOMAIN NOTICE

If you're holding this book, it is probably because you have a love and appreciation for the classics. Everything we write, read, watch on television or at the cinema, has in some way been inspired by the countless classics. Its unavoidable, really.

This book was created with the intention to celebrate the world of literature, the great authors and works that came before us, and to hopefully introduce potentially undiscovered classic works to new readers.

Every story in this book includes reference to the original creations that are either directly represented or inspired by these works, as we know our world would be nowhere without the art that came before ours, both in and out of this book.

In Canada, the rule is that any book can enter the public domain seventy years after the death of the author. *An exception to this is anything that entered the public domain prior to 2022, when the rule was fifty years after the authors death.* A lot of research was done to ensure that the legalities of this book was done respectfully and above board. If any issues are discovered, please contact Cathrine Swift immediately.

Thank you,

the Classic Conversations authors

# TABLE OF CONTENTS

# CLASSIC
## CONVERSATIONS

# Darcy's Tale

## by Keri Harley

**Literary World**: Pride and Prejudice

Darcy tells his youngest daughter the story of how he met her mother in an effort to redeem himself. Elizabeth helps.

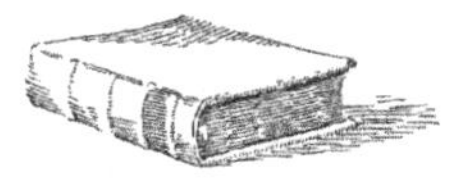

Darcy leaned against the doorframe and watched Elizabeth as she tucked their youngest child, Charlotte, into her bed and placed a kiss into her blonde locks.

"Goodnight, Lottie. Sleep well," Elizabeth crooned.

"Goodnight, mum." As Elizabeth turned to leave, a soft voice muttered, "Can you tell me a story?"

Darcy chuckled, having witnessed this same tactic a thousand times before, and pushed off the door into the room.

"I have it handled, dearest. Go rest," he said, giving Elizabeth a kiss on the cheek before settling onto the edge of Lottie's bed. "Which story shall we read tonight?" he inquired, reaching for the ever-present stack of books on the bedside table.

"We have read all of those. Can't you just tell me a story?" she asked, beaming. Darcy's eyes crinkled at the edges as he laughed.

"What kind of story?" he said, smiling when she put her finger to her chin in thought; the perfect likeness of her mother.

"Aunt Lydia told me the story of how she met Uncle Wickham. Could you tell me how you met mummy?" she giggled, and Darcy had to hold back his disdain for his wife's youngest sister and her utter joke of a husband. Lydia and their five children spent more time in the homes of her siblings than she did her own, and was currently invading Jane and Bingley's home for the summer.

"There is not much to tell; I met her at a country dance where she grew up," he stated, shrugging.

"You met her at a dance and married her, just like that?" Lottie demanded, clearly skeptical.

"That's the long and short of it, I suppose," he said, turning when he heard a hearty feminine laugh behind him.

"I happen to recall there being much, much more to it than that," said his lovely wife from the doorway.

Darcy sighed, resigned to his fate.

"Yes, I suppose there was," he admitted, taking her hand when she came near and giving it a quick kiss.

"Can you tell me the story?" Lottie pleaded, her young features lighting up at once again having successfully stalled her impending bedtime.

"As long as you go right to sleep after, agreed?" he asked, and was immediately met with the bounce of blonde curls as she nodded enthusiastically in agreement, snuggling into the blankets. Elizabeth took a seat in the nearby rocker and reached for her knitting, clearly entertained, as Darcy cleared his throat.

*It is a truth universally acknowledged that a single man in possession of a good fortune must be in want of a wife. Bingley and I had been told this by our own mothers since we had inherited our respective roles, and the pressure to marry and settle down had been growing by the day. I was told of my arrangement to my cousin Anne from the time we were incredibly young, but I felt no affection for her as such, and neither did she. Bingley had no such arrangement, and simply had neither found such a woman that he would spend his life with, nor acquired such an arrangement for his sister—*

"That was due to her affection for you, to be sure," Elizabeth scoffed, rolling her eyes. Darcy's brows came together in a look of confusion as he stared at his wife.

"Surely not; she is like a sister to me as much as she is to Bingley," he sputtered, his distaste for the idea evident. Elizabeth chuckled.

"I assure you, Mr. Darcy, that while she held the highest affection for you, it was not sisterly in the slightest," she corrected. "Or did you not realize she didn't settle for a suitor until after our marriage ceremonies were completed?"

Darcy seemed deep in thought for a moment before giving a slight shudder and turning back to his daughter.

*Bingley and I needed a break from the pressures of our stations and thought some time in the country would do us good. He had friends that notified us of a place for rent that would house everyone, and we set off. Now, I was never one for crowds, but Bingley insisted I accompany him and his sister to the local dance halls, if for nothing other than to get me out of the house – for what were we doing it for if not to have fun?*

*I first spied your mother in a crowded hall, face flushed with exertion and eyes gleaming with mischievousness, for the briefest of moments before she turned away. She was breathtaking then as she is now.*

Darcy smiled at the memory, looking to his wife of twenty years with the same adoration as the day they'd wed. She looked up from her knitting, her eye catching his with the same gleam.

*I had never felt such a pull toward another person, but reminded myself I had a marriage arrangement waiting for me in the city, and I was a man of honor. Bingley was equally as enamored with your Aunt Jane, and was quick to ask her to dance. He has always been easier around others than I, and they spent the evening dancing and laughing – much to the chagrin of his youngest sister, who spent the evening muttering her nonsense complaints in my ear whenever she was near. I made my first prideful mistake when Bingley asked me what I thought of your mother...*

Darcy sighed, watching his wife out of the corner of his eye, and bracing himself for his youngest's judgement.

*He knew the disdain I held for my arrangement with Anne and had told me on multiple occasions I could simply find someone else and tell my Aunt Catherine I was in love, and that would be the end of it. He clearly did not know my aunt well enough, and lucky for him...*

"What did you do?" Lottie asked in a knowing tone, giving him a glare that would rival his Aunt Catherine – though the woman had died before the girl was born. Darcy cleared his throat.

"I said Jane was the only pretty girl in the entire room, and your mother was...barely tolerable," he muttered, flinching when Lottie sat straight up, her eyes wide and her mouth agape. She looked from her father to her mother and back, her outrage a palpable thing.

"I BEG YOUR PARDON?" she exclaimed, looking at her mother. "WHY?"

Elizabeth raised an eyebrow at her daughter's dramatics, her knitting needles clicking away. "You'll have to keep listening if you want the answer," was her only reply.

Lottie huffed, falling back to the pillows, crossing her arms over her chest, and glaring at her father with the fiery passion of a thousand burning suns. "Continue."

*I did not realize until later, when a group of us were discussing various things, that she had overheard me speak ill of her. I deeply regretted it. Her very existence lit up my otherwise darkened world, and I had dulled her light with my lies. I left the hall quickly after that and sulked the rest of the night.*

"What I still do not understand is how you convinced her to marry you," Lottie deadpanned, still glaring at her father with all her righteous fury.

"We never said it wasn't a long story, dear," Elizabeth replied. "Just that it would be told."

Lottie huffed, but waved her hand for him to continue.

He smiled and looked to Elizabeth. "Love? Do you want to take this part? I believe you have things to add," he said pointedly. Elizabeth sighed and set her knitting in her lap, leaning back in the chair.

*First off, I thought him incredibly handsome, yet arrogant. Here came this rich aristocrat who had the gall to call me barely tolerable – and while I was no great beauty like Jane, I knew I was more than tolerable in my own right. After that, with his avoidance of me, I assumed he simply had better things to do, and went about my life as normal.*

*Jane was invited to dine with Bingley's sister the day after they met, and my mother, being the meddlesome creature she is, saw it as an opportunity to force Bingley to spend time with Jane, that would hopefully lead to a proposal. Jane was sent on horseback in a storm and was struck ill as a result, leading Bingley to all but demand she stay until she was well. I, of course, being the only member of the family with any regard for her wellbeing, trudged through the sopping mud to care for her. I am sure I looked a right mess when I was announced, my hem covered in mud and my hair wild from the wind, but since I knew what he thought of me already, I cared not for any opinion other than my own.*

Darcy caught her eye, smiling widely at her.

"You were a wildling, a goddess of nature, a nymph of the forest. I was struck dumb with your beauty," he said, remembering the moment he realized her true effect on him.

"I love you too, dear, but we are telling a story," she said.

*Of course, Jane's illness was mild, but the physician implied she would need several days' recovery before she was able to travel the few miles home. Bingley was overjoyed, but I was reticently dismal. I did not want to spend several days with the prideful, argumentative aristocrats, but resigned myself to their company for Jane's sake – and frankly, it was a break from the normal chaotic nature of our home. I spent my free time taking advantage of the library, reading anything I could reach when the opportunity presented itself. Jane slept quite a bit while ill and I did not want to wake her, so my reading was usually done in the drawing room with everyone else. I learned of Caroline Bingley's affection for your father in that room: the way she would do anything to get his attention, the way she would ask after his sister every time he sat to write his many letters of business, or exclaim loudly how she adored young Georgianna and her accomplishments every time Charles was near. Personally, I believe she wanted her brother to marry Georgianna for whatever reason – but for the life of me, I can't decide why.*

"As if I would have allowed that," huffed Darcy.

*When we finally went home, I swore I would never set eyes on any of them ever again. It was not until my cousin, Mr. Collins, came to visit—*

"Ah yes, Mr. Collins," Darcy declared, holding back a smirk.

Elizabeth just rolled her eyes and continued.

*I came to know he was due to inherit my father's estate, and with not even one of five daughters married, he had come to find a wife among us. Imagine my dismay when my meddlesome mother pointed him in MY direction. He followed me everywhere with his incessant book of sermons. Ugh.*

Darcy erupted in laughter at the look of indignation on Elizabeth's face, wiping tears from his eyes before he took a moment more to compose himself. He took on the mantle of storyteller once more.

*During all of this, whilst listening to Caroline complain and Charles quote trite poetry waxing on the beauty and virtues of Jane, I had about my limit. Caroline suggested going through with the ball Bingley had promised the younger Bennet sisters as a form of entertainment before we returned to London. Seeing it as an excuse to see Jane again, he agreed. I had resigned myself to a dreadful evening, of course, but prepared nonetheless.*

"At least you weren't being charmed by that dreadful snake," hissed Elizabeth, stabbing her knitting needle just a little too viciously into her work, making her drop several stitches.

"What snake, mama?" Lottie asked, her interest piqued at the venom in her usually sweet mother's voice.

"Wickham," Darcy growled.

"Uncle?" Lottie inquired, confused. Elizabeth silenced her with a hand, then stood and paced while she spoke.

*My sisters were overjoyed to have a real ball in Meryton for a change: it had been a while since we had more than a simple country dance, after all, and we went to town for ribbons and things. The militia was in town, and my youngest sisters decided dropping their handkerchiefs for introductions was a clever idea. Wickham was the one Lydia and Kitty latched onto the hardest: he was charming, handsome, and said all the right things. We had no reason not to trust him at first. When he was walking us home, we came upon your father and Bingley on horseback, and Lydia decided to invite Wickham to the ball.*

"I wanted to throttle him; if I hadn't ridden away, I would have," Darcy muttered. "Seeing him with you and the others, after what he tried with Georgianna..."

"I know, love, I know," Elizabeth said, placing her hand on his shoulder.

*After your father had left, Wickham told me the story about how he was cheated out of his inheritance by a man he had loved like a brother. I already had a precarious opinion of your father at that point, and this made me see him as a real villain for the first time.*

"That must be why Uncle Bingley called him a nincompoop," stated Lottie.

Darcy sputtered.

"I've heard him called worse," he muttered, too low for his daughter to hear.

*I knew I had to get Wickham away from the Bennet girls, so I used what influence I had with the militia to have him stationed away from Meryton just before the ball. Your mother searched for him and did not find him. I just followed her around like a lost puppy, but I finally got the courage to ask her to dance.*

"Despite the fact that I was sworn to loathe you for all eternity, and I assumed you felt the same," Elizabeth chuckled, settling back in the rocker.

"Never."

*Dancing with her made the world fall away, and while I was loath to admit it at the time, that was the moment I truly fell for her wit, her charm, her beauty, and her fire. She gave as good as she got, and I found myself looking forward to every spar. I had to remind myself I was a gentleman of honor, or I would have proposed that night and run away with her.*

"No, you would not have. I know you, Fitzwilliam Darcy, and you would have done it properly," Elizabeth said, her knitting needles clicking once more.

"I would have done anything you asked by then; I was yours to command," he declared. "I will always be yours."

*The ball ended, and after much coaxing from Caroline and myself, Bingley packed up the house and we returned to London.*

"Wait, but he loves Aunt Jane. Why would he leave? Why did you make him leave her?" Lottie asked, with tears in her eyes.

"Because while I knew he loved her, I was not sure she loved him as deeply. I was trying to protect my friend," he said.

"You *were* a nincompoop," Lottie said haughtily.

"I was a nincompoop," Darcy agreed. "Dearest?"

Elizabeth did not take her eyes off the work in her hands as she continued the story.

*Jane was heartbroken, of course, but she did her best not to show it. As the weeks went by, she may have started to believe it a little herself. Mr. Collins proposed to me in the most dreadful manner, and I refused him most heartily. It was Mary that held an admiration for the man, not me – but she never spoke up, and my dear, dear friend Charlotte married the insufferable man instead. He took her away all the way to Rosings.*

"Do you regret your refusal, my dear?" Darcy asked after several moments of silence.

"Absolutely not," she said, taking up her knitting and the story once more.

*Jane decided she wouldn't give up on Bingley and went to stay with our aunt and uncle in London to find him. It was dreadfully boring without Jane and Charlotte around to keep me company, so I spent my days mindlessly milling about. I had nothing in common with my younger sisters, and Charlotte was my only real friend, so when she wrote and invited me to Rosings to visit, I took the chance. I assumed it would be a nice, quiet visit with a good friend and her imbecilic husband in a quaint country home. That was my first mistake.*

"Was it, now? That was our first mistake in this whole endeavor?" Darcy needled with a grin.

"Considering the information I was given by that point, yes, I would say it was," she countered smugly.

"If you say so, love," he chuckled.

*Imagine my surprise when there was an invitation to dine at Rosings with Lady Catherine de Bourgh herself. As though that were not intimidating enough, HE also arrived with a full entourage – and while my mother may have had five daughters, we were not truly taught to be proper ladies with impressive lists of accomplishments. We each had something we excelled at or were interested in, and mother allowed us to foster what hobbies we wanted. I play the pianoforte only because your lovely Aunt Georgianna plays so beautifully, and she has helped over the years to teach me to play passably. I have always preferred books to music or drawing or any other ladylike activities.*

"Like Emma with her embroidery, and Amelia with her music," Lottie announced triumphantly.

"Yes, love, just like that. You share your mother's fondness for books and knowledge," said Darcy.

*Dinner was the first civil conversation your father and I had had in months. I was still wary of him after his and Bingley's disappearance from Meryton and all I had heard from Wickham, but I could see the humanity in him as well – and the fact that I was a thorn in his aunt's side tickled me immensely.*

"You were more than a thorn in her side, dearest: you were her worst nightmare," Darcy proclaimed, taking a turn about the room to stretch his legs.

"All right, you tell the story, then," Elizabeth huffed.

Darcy gave a bow, making Lottie giggle. "As you wish."

*I watched her interacting with my friends and family over the time we spent in each other's company, and it stunned me how well she could integrate herself into every aspect of my life so seamlessly. I was right and properly in love by this point and was determined to make her my wife, so when the opportunity arrived that fateful rainy day at the parish, I took it. I laid my heart bare, my reasoning sound in* my *mind. There was no reason for her to say no.*

*Yet, she refused.*

"Mama, what did he *really* do?" Lottie asked, her face skeptical as her tone.

"Told me he liked me against his better judgement, setting aside my station and family, and asked that I end his agony by taking his hand," Elizabeth stated matter-of-factly.

Lottie levelled at her father her most terrifying glare to date, shaking her head in disgust. "Nincompoop," she declared, and Darcy sighed.

"I did not say it was the best I could have done. It was rather impulsive," Darcy admitted, ruffling his hair.

"And I say I am unsure whose proposal was worse: your first, or Mr. Collins'." Elizabeth laughed, sending Lottie into a fit of giggles.

Darcy rolled his eyes and continued.

*Her reasoning for the refusal was sound, of course. I had ruined the happiness of her favorite sister. I was unsure how she had figured it out–*

"It was the colonel of course."

"He always was a blabbermouth," Darcy growled.

*But her refusal made me think. I had never been spoken to in such a blunt manner; rather refreshing, really (it was always one of my favorite things about you, my love). But it forced me to take a step back from the situation and realize I had, in fact, treated her quite poorly on the whole. With that, I wanted to be a better man, regardless of how she would see me from then on. The damage was already done as far as she was concerned, but that did not mean I should not right a few wrongs. I wrote about my side of the transgressions in a letter to her before I went back to London with my tail between my legs, to lick my wounds and do better.*

"You weren't the only one that could have managed it better: I was rather brutish in my refusal," Elizabeth admitted. "I was simply still angry about the news of dear Jane. You had hurt her and in turn could cut me, and I should have simply said I needed time."

"No, I needed to hear it," he said firmly, giving her hand a peck before he sat back down. Elizabeth sighed, collecting her thoughts before she continued the story.

*That letter was a turning point for me. I knew some things had not made sense with Wickham, but finding out he had attempted elopement with Georgianna, and how he was a notorious womanizer and gambler, really made me take things into perspective. I had much to think about as I made my way back to Meryton. It was about when I arrived home that Jane came back from London with aunt and uncle. She seemed in heartier spirits, but I could see she was still hurting. I could not bear to tell her what I knew, as I did not want to open the wounds again. A family friend had offered to take Lydia on a trip to Brighton, and I attempted to appeal to papa to not let her go, but he would not listen – and so she left. Before leaving, aunt and uncle convinced me to spend some time with them in the countryside in Derbyshire, and I inevitably agreed. It was a pleasant trip, to be sure: we got along famously, and it was not until uncle thought to go to Pemberley House that I had my doubts.*

"You came *here?!*" Lottie exclaimed.

Darcy chuckled at her enthusiasm.

"She did indeed, taking a tour of the house with my housekeeper."

"I was told you wouldn't be home!" Elizabeth explained loudly in embarrassment at the memory.

"I rarely was, but I was lucky enough to be home that time."

"You planned it. You *had* to have planned it. It was too much of a coincidence."

"I shall neither confirm nor deny it, and never shall," was all he said.

*The house was beautiful of course – always has been – and it was nice to see what kind of life your father had grown up in. I must have gotten lost along the way and came face to face with the very man I was doing my best to avoid. He somehow convinced us all to stay in town another day and charmed aunt and uncle to the point of questioning my sanity after all the horrid things they had heard about him from me. Then came the letter. I cried for hours when I realized Lydia had run off with that horrid man.*

"That isn't how Aunt Lydia told that part of the story," Lottie explained. "She said she was just so in love with him that they ran away because your papa would not approve, and they couldn't stand not being together."

"That might be the story from Aunt Lydia's point of view…but we'll save the rest of that for when you're older," Darcy said, patting the top of her little blonde head. She made a noise of discontent, but otherwise stayed silent.

*I went home at once and found mama in a right state over the scandal. Her poor nerves: she was inconsolable for days while papa went to London with uncle to find them. We finally received news saying they were found and would be married. Mama's change in mood was almost instantaneous. I could not understand how she could be so happy over the marriage of her youngest daughter to such a man, but she did not know what he had done before, and I did not have the heart to tell her.*

*They arrived not long after the wedding, with Lydia boasting of her "good fortune" to anyone that would give her half an ear. Mama, of course, kept adding to her nonsense all afternoon, until Lydia let something slip she should not have. Your father was the one who found them, paid for everything, and told her not to tell a soul.*

"Well, I could not exactly let her ruin the rest of you with her 'nonsense,' now, could I?" Darcy harrumphed.

"You very well could have. You could have used the excuse to stay far away from all of us," countered Elizabeth.

"I couldn't have stayed away from you if I'd tried." Darcy looked to Lottie.

"Do you remember how I said her refusal made me want to do better?" Lottie nodded. "I wanted to be worthy of the kind of fierce love and loyalty she had for her family. I never expected her to change her mind about me; I simply wanted to be a better man because of my love for her."

"Is that how Uncle Bingley and Aunt Jane got married?" Lottie inquired. Darcy nodded, making Lottie squeal with delight. Elizabeth gave a yawn and waved her hand for her husband to take over the story.

*I had spirited away to London on my fastest horse, determined to find Wickham and force him to make things right. My contacts had found them quickly in a boarding house by the river. To keep the story light enough for you, I will simply say he was given a choice, and made the proper one. They were married two days later.*

*While I was in town, I called on Bingley, who was still woefully depressed over Jane. His sisters had been flaunting eligible nobility around him, and he was having none of it. I confessed my faults, admitted I was wrong, and told him the truth of Jane. He was still scruffed from the week prior, but prepared to return to Meryton. His proposal did not go as planned, but they were happy nonetheless.*

*My aunt was the only hitch in my plans. I should say that blabbermouth Fitzwilliam was to blame. He had let out that I had proposed to your mother, and my aunt heard the gossip, and instead of addressing ME with the news, she travelled to Meryton shortly behind Bingley and myself to speak to your mother, demanding why she would spread scandalous gossip. After hearing of the dressing down the old woman received, I had hope for the first time since that dreadful refusal she might have changed her mind, and I had to know.*

“You could have caught your death walking in the cold night like that,” his wife admonished.

“As could you, my love. Yet fate found us together, and I do not regret a moment of it.”

"So, was that when she said yes?" Lottie piped up.

"That was when I said yes."

*And they lived happily ever after.*

# Out, Damned Spot

## by Julia Jackson

**Literary World:** Macbeth

Before she was Lady Macbeth, Thistle was a farm girl who dreamed of more. A storm brings three witches who foretell the future, promising her a crown in return for blood. And Thistle is willing to do anything to seal her fate.

***Content Warnings:*** *blood, murder, death at childbirth, lust as a weapon, insinuation of father being too close with daughter*

Crimson makes all unclean. The linen of Father's shirt is stained with blood—but how can this be?

The silver devil did it.

Damned washboard.

I bring my finger to my lips, suddenly aware of the sharp pain, and wince at the metallic taste.

Cursed is this life, with its never-ending laundry, collecting kindling, fetching water. Chores from the sun's rising 'til after its setting, making my young skin no longer delicate as a babe's but raw and tender and hurting.

I want more. More than farm life can afford. Yet I continue to wash with my uncut hand, to remove the blood from the shirt. I stare at the red marring the pristine white, a few drops spread with such haste. The yearning wrenches through my insides, but a flutter of my heart screams that

I don't deserve better than this life. For the Fates must know I slayed my mother.

"Out. Out!" The command rumbles from my throat. Useless. Scrub as I may, the linen remains unclean. My eyes prickle and well with tears, feeling that I am failing Father, not able to return the love he has always given to me. The love he craves.

Father deserves better than this, deserves more than the rolling hills of dirt and the small house of stone and mud covered in moss. He is wonderful—stuck with an ungrateful child—and I am undeserving. Though he has given me all of this small part of the world he can offer, I daydream of more. The guilt of leaving in search of a life without chores threatens more tears.

For Father may be cursed, but I wish it were not so—losing his wife and having a daughter unable to manage a laundry scrub board without shedding blood. No sweeter a man in Scotland than he, who could love a daughter as wretched as me.

But he tries. Holds me close on dark nights. Tells me how beautiful I am.

"Out, damned spot!" I cry to the blood, begging it to vanish from the shirt gripped so tightly in my hand.

"What upsets you so, my Thistle?"

Father's warm voice makes me stop cold. My eyes shut, releasing the tear I'd attempted to hold within. I bring my cheek to my arm swiftly to wipe the wet from my eyes before looking over my shoulder at him.

"It is nothing, Father. Just a cut. But it has made a mess of your shirt," I say, forcing a smile as I look at the man I love more than anything. The sun has aged him. Long days farming the land have leathered his skin and wrinkled his brow. He has a slight hunch from bending and picking crops, but his blue eyes are still bright as ever, as if their owner is lost in his youth. He would never leave this place where he loved my mother and raised me—where he put so much of his time and sweat into the earth.

He leans over the basin and pulls my hand out of the water. My stomach aches as I watch the linen float, the crimson like spilled ink, consuming everything.

Water drips onto the packed dirt at our feet, the small, barren plot of land outside the front door of what we call a home. The only space not grown over by crop or thistle, where the wooden barrel collects rainwater. Many storms past filled this bucket, bringing with it more work and painstaking time, which took me only moments to sully.

Father's calloused hands enclose both of mine as he examines the cut. "So much blood for such a little wound," he sighs. "My Thistle, you must be more careful."

I take my hands from his, tucking my long chestnut hair behind my ears. "Yes, Father."

"And worry not of the shirt. It will be covered with muck as soon as I wear it to fight those sheep. They love to kick dirt at me as I shear their brothers and sisters."

I giggle, imagining the scene. His kindness is a blanket, wrapping me tightly despite my misdeeds. Always forgiving, always bringing light to my darkness.

"There's that smile I cherish so. Now, hang the shirt and allow it to dry. I must ready for bed if I have any chance of winning the battle with our wooly friends," Father says. The corner of his mouth lifts to a smile. He kisses my forehead, lingering there as he presses his lips upon my skin, then retires as I heave the sopping mess from the basin.

"No doubt Nicholas will be coming 'round to check on you with this darkening sky," he says once he reaches the threshold, looking back at me teasingly.

"I care not, Father. He is a friend," I call back.

"Poor boy. He is in for a broken heart. You'll forever be your father's daughter." Father shakes his head, but his smile does not fade. He cares only of our happiness, not of others. No matter how much Nicholas has helped us time and time again.

The short wooden door shudders as he crouches and disappears within the darkness of our hut. A plume of dust follows. The mud packed between stone and earth outside the threshold is dry and thirsty for rainfall.

This is the only life I've known: one with Father, through every storm, in this desolate yet beautiful slice of land. Father and his Thistle. Where I have played both daughter and wife.

Though Thistle is not my true name, it is all I have ever been called by. The day I came into the world—as my mother drew her last breaths and blood dripped from between her legs upon the wooden floor—the only solace Father could find was looking out the window at the freshly bloomed thistles surrounding the house.

He held me, a newborn babe cooing ever so softly, while he focused on the flowers of purple. Holding tight to his only happiness left after I took his true love away. Father thought me to be his miracle, but I have never felt like more than the pinpricks that hold the flower of the thistle. The killer of my mother.

Even the neighbour boy, Nicholas—with his doe eyes so in love with me—calls me Thistle. Thinks I like the name. But I don't. It reminds me of all I am not, and all that I am. A disappointment. A killer.

The clouds above swell with fury, grey turning a deep purple, flashes of lightning splitting the menacing air above me. Thunder cracks the sky open so near I feel the rumble of the dirt below my feet. I hurry to the pile of wood that was once a fence to lay Father's shirt on. Perhaps the rain can do a better job at cleansing the blood from it than I.

"Damned!" I cry when a splinter of wood bites into my flesh. It punctures the centre of my palm, and I cannot help but to stare at the bead of blood that sits in its wake once I pull it out. A drop of rain lands on it, and I tilt my head to the sky as though the heavens are opening up to wash away this pain, these stains, this life.

If only it could fill the rain barrel with gold and allow Father and I to create a new destiny.

But I am the spikes of the thistle. Cursed. Unlovable. Poor.

"Thistle! Come out of that rain!" Father cries from inside our hovel of a home.

"Soon, Father!" I yell back to him, straining my voice against the pounding rain and thunder. The door thuds behind him, and I look back to the sky, shut my eyes, and pray.

A flash of lightning knocks me down, so close I could feel its heat. And then I hear laughter. Voices cackling in the distance, the sound swarming around my head while I attempt to stand from the mud. My mousy strands of hair are caked with the mess of wet earth.

I grab onto a fence post and pull, my feet defying me with each slide in the mud they take.

Three figures appear far across the field, from out of the thickest portion of wood, moving with such speed and precision it is as though they are floating towards me.

I freeze, entranced by their beauty. Three maidens with hair so blond it glints like silver. They wear capes over their shoulders, the same colour as the evergreens they just emerged from. As they draw closer, I notice they are bare beneath the capes. The clasps are done up just above the navel, so all their parts are exposed. Breasts white as milk, supple and perfect, peek out from the velvet.

I squeeze my eyelids shut tightly, sure that when I open them again, the beautiful women will be gone. But when I open my eyes, they are still there, closer still. Heading toward me with delicate smiles and a gleam in their bright green eyes.

The tales are true of the sisters three: witches who know of all that is meant to be.

My breath holds still. Their visit must be a blessing.

*A blessing.*

An unsettled laugh cuts through my throat. *No, not for me.* A girl most undeserving. They must surely be bringing a curse.

A hand caresses my jaw, and an inhale catches within my throat. How are they before me when I've barely drawn a breath since they first appeared? They laugh again, circling me, floating a mere hair off the ground. Excitement builds within me, a pleasure I've not known before.

My lips part, ready to speak, but nothing escapes. I lick them and try again. "Who are thee?"

The air around us hums. The rain still pours, yet we remain dry. What witchcraft is this? And why do I enjoy it so?

"Wonder not, little pet," one of the sisters sings with a voice like honey through pink and plump lips, "for we come with good news."

Does she hear my thoughts? My skin feels like ice, prickles running up and down my arms.

Another sister giggles, and I notice the dark beauty mark upon her high cheekbone. "You dream of gold, but it is more that awaits you."

The third girl, identical to the others, runs a hand across her long neck, tracing down to cup her breast. "A woman of power, of strength, and of might. Your beautiful flower is what will set things right."

"I don't understand. Speak not in verse," I beg, spinning around trying to keep pace with them.

"Be as the thistle, your beauty doth glow—" one whispers as she passes my ear.

"—you shall marry a man, if your heart feigns so." Another silver-haired sister brushes a hand across my back.

"For use your words, if you wish to be Queen—"

"I—I will be Queen?" I ask, my heart leaping in my chest. "My head stirs, but pray, tell me more."

"He shall do your bidding, so you will not take the strike." The one with the beauty mark pets her long, thin fingers through my hair, lifting it to get closer to my ear. "The possibilities of being Queen alive if only you give him the knife."

"Who?" I wail, dropping to my knees, begging them. "Who will wield a knife? Is that the only way out of my strife?"

They move to stand in a line, staring down on me, smiling. Their grins grow wider, baring their teeth.

"Please, sing to me thy sweet words once more… that I will be Queen." I arch my back, looking to the sky again, the clouds still haunting and grey.

"Hush. Hush now, child. For your father must not hear the truth of your soul, what you truly hold dear." I don't know who speaks; I only focus on their knees finding the ground so close. One of the witches kisses my cheek.

My teeth clench, growing tired of their riddles and rhymes. "Please."

"Patience, in this moment and the next," one says, taking my hand and reading my thoughts. "You must venture alone along this path, from dust and crops to riches and feasts."

"Use the boy, do so tonight. When the storm ends, there must be the end of a life."

"Death?" I ask, certain I do not understand.

"Before the rain dries this land, thy sacrifice be made." They begin their relentless riddles once again.

One locks her green eyes on mine. "She will do what she needs. Slice through the cord that tethers her here."

They mustn't mean…they can't.

"My father—my father must die?"

"He holds you too close, for this you know. He wants you for his own and will never let you go."

They stand then, beginning to hover once more, and cackle as their eyes glint with flecks of gold.

I stumble in the mud, chasing after them as they take their leave. "No! Do not part. I must know without doubt!"

They move fast across the field, hand in hand this time. I lean on the fence, my head pounding stronger than the storm. How can I be sure what they speak be true? Am I to kill my father? Is this the only way I can have more than all this mud? My hands are thick with it, and hot tears stream down my face. I taste their salt on my tongue as I weep harder.

"Must I kill my father?" I cry into my hands. "As I killed my mother?"

"As you killed your mother?" A familiar voice breaks through the wind. My shoulders pin to my ears, afraid Nicholas heard of killing my father. "Thistle, it was the pains of childbirth. You are not to blame."

"Why are you here?" I wipe a tear from my cheek with my muddied hand. Always dirty. Never clean.

"I came to check on you and your father. This storm was mighty, and I thought you might need help."

Sweet Nicholas. Always so kind. Just like Father.

With a sniffle, I lean into him. His arms wrap around my body, hands clasping at my low back. And then I remember what the witches said.

I was to use the boy.

*Nicholas.*

I tilt my chin up, peering into his slate eyes. "You've always been so sweet to me, though I don't deserve it." My words are true. Nicholas has always loved me, even as children running through the fields and getting lost in the woods together, but I never felt the same. I realise how close I am to him now, our clothes sopping wet, sticking us to one another. This is the closest we have ever been.

"You deserve so much more," he says, and kisses the top of my head. My stomach aches knowing how much he has dreamed for this moment, and yet I am a mere actor playing a part.

I need him more than ever now, for I am unable to do what must be done. My head spins as I accept this all as possibility, knowing that my heart is as blackened as I always thought: cold, and dark, and deadly.

"We should run away," I say, nearly choking on the words. "Together."

Dimples deepen on his face, and I can feel his heartbeat galloping faster than that of a horse in his chest. "What about your father?"

I break our embrace, taking steps backward, allowing the soaked through linen dress to show him all of me, as the witches showed me all of them. They said to use my flower. Is this what they meant? I stand taller, allowing his eyes to devour me. To want me.

"You are right. I must stay here, forever. To help him." I run my hands through my wet hair, moving it to cascade over my shoulder.

"Forever?" he asks, taking a step toward me.

"I don't see how I can leave until he passes." He hesitates, so I continue drinking back the bile that rises in my throat. "I can never be with another until he is...gone."

Nicholas' eyes graze over me from head to toe. I wish he looked not so hungry, but I allow it. Thinking of promised riches. How my destiny will finally take me away from his watchful eyes—the same way Father has always watched me.

Perhaps I will have a castle. And my future King will be fair and true. A throne waits for me to finish these misdeeds.

The witches' words must be true.

The sun is setting, and the rain stops. *Tonight.* It must be tonight.

"Tell me what I must do, Thistle. I have wished for this day. That your destiny would be entwined with mine, that you would ask me to be with you."

I move to him, running a hand down his raven hair. He has grown into a fine young man over the years, but he cannot give me the life I want. The life I need.

So I lie.

"I want to be with you, too." With an exaggerated breath, I begin to cry. He is quick to wipe away the tear, the tear that hurts for fooling him. Using him. "What if I asked you to make a sacrifice? For us."

"*Us.*" He smiles and licks his lips. "What would I have to do?"

I don't want to say the words. I am not strong enough to command this boy to end the life of the person I love—who comforted me through so much I can barely think of it, even now. So close. Always so close.

"If he were… no longer—" My breath is a lump in my throat. "—we could be together now." I fit my hand into his, bring it to my mouth, and kiss his fingers as I look up at him.

Nicholas' eyes search mine, finally understanding.

*Death.* The witches said it. There must be death.

My father must die. At the will of his Thistle.

The night has fallen upon us. "Come," I whisper.

I open the door to the small home—the one I will finally leave behind. For there has been love here, but nothing else. In this moment, I know my choice is right. A woman must do what must be done.

The room is filled with Father's snoring. As Nicholas and I cross the floorboards, I grab a knife from the sill and hand it to him. His eyes go wide before his shoulders broaden and he focuses on my father.

I fall back, staying behind Nicholas, not wanting to see this happen. I don't want this. But if the Fates spun by the weird sisters stand any chance of coming true, this is what *must* be done.

The snoring stops abruptly and I jump back.

Father's eyes remain closed, but he turns onto his back, his chest exposed. An offering.

We pass the stain where my mother bled and died, still a dark mark upon the floorboards. "I'm sorry, Mother," I speak to the only remnants left of her, "and I am sorry, Father."

Father's eyes flash open, blinking at me with the youthful blue that always transfixes me so. "Thistle?" He says, confusion knitting his brows.

This is wrong. All wrong. The witches are evil, not I. They must be. How can I do anything to the man who showed me love and raised me with all he had? The life I dream of is only that: a dream. No dream can truly arrive by means of a garish nightmare such as this.

My hand moves to grab Nicholas' arm, to stop all this. A crown upon my head be damned.

But I am too late.

The knife catches the final remnants of the setting sun flooding through the window as it's heaved into Father's chest. It stays there, sticking out from his heart, while Nicholas trips backwards.

"I—" The boy speaks no more.

I stare down at Father while blood circles the blade, staining his nightshirt. I'd never be able to make that clean. The linen will be soaked with his death forever.

"No." A whispered cry sprung from my lips. "No, no, no."

My hand trembles as it moves to the knife, gripping the handle. With a heaving sigh, I pull it out. Blood sprays my face when Father coughs and says, "Thistle," as his body writhes in pain, crimson dripping now from the corner of his mouth. Blood-stained teeth and lips sputter more blood when he speaks—"Thistle,"—one final time, before he finally stills.

Thistle is not my name. It never was.

Anger burns in my chest. I deserve more. The witches' words but a sweet prophecy I must be happy to heed.

The knife drops from my hand and clinks as it dances across the floorboards.

Father's life is over, and I cannot undo what has been done. I can only be clean. Be free from him. Be free from all.

With haste, I grab the tallow lit aflame, and throw it onto my father. The red-hot flames dance across his body, and the house fills with smoke.

Nicholas is at my side, holding my hand as we look down at the fire that was once my father. "We must leave," he says, coughing against the smoke.

I remember again what the witches said.

That I must venture *alone* on this path.

I've already come this far. What has been done to my father—what has stained this entire place once a home in red—cannot be undone.

I will have my destiny, born from death and flames.

I look into his eyes and smile, trying to comfort him with beauty as the witches did for me. A step closer to him makes his eyes widen. I know the sight standing before him: a poor farm girl covered in the spatterings of her father's blood, surrounded by growing fire.

But he doesn't move or try to make an escape from the thickening smoke when I place a hand on his cheek, offering him a kiss. He leans into it, parting my mouth with a wanting tongue, tasting me as he always dreamed.

I made his dream come true, as he did with mine. I smile and kiss him deeper.

With a tighter grip on the back of Nicholas' head, kneading my fingers into his hair, he groans.

And as his hunger grows, I push him into the burning hell that is the bed where the corpse of my father lay, where my mother's corpse lay before his. Nicholas' screams echo in my ears as he thrashes about, as the flames lick up his clothes, melting the skin off his sweet face. His hands bubble and pop before he finally succumbs to his death.

I run from the place, barking out painful coughs against the night sky.

I don't turn back to see the wreckage, yet I can't ignore the smell of all the mud and muck and flesh and bones burning.

The thought of being Queen someday, alive now more than ever.

As I reach the safety of the dark woods, the last place I saw the witches three, I notice scarlet dripping down my finger once more.

"Out, damned spot!" I laugh.

Then, I lick the blood clean.

# Curious Friends

## by L.E. Tonn

**Literary Worlds:** The Wizard of Oz & Alice's Adventures in Wonderland (crossover)

A series of unfortunate events leads Dorothy of Kansas down a familiar rabbit hole into the vibrant world of Wonderland.

# dorothy

Dorothy awoke with a gasp, the whole room tilted. Familiar, and yet strange. She found herself unable to move. She knew these walls, but the drapes of her windows hung at an unruly angle. Cautiously, Dorothy began to feel for her surroundings to sit herself up. She tried feverishly to blink away the ringing in her ears and the pounding of her head as she steadied herself at the edge of her bed. The sheets just as she remembered, rumpled and cozy, and yet everything felt askew. Where was she? With trepidation, she brought herself to stand unstable on the crooked floor. In this moment, she realised that she had fallen asleep with Toto tucked in her arms. Where had he gone?

In a quiet panic, Dorothy began tearing through her room. Drawers already ajar, she began to toss her things about when she heard his careful whimper from under the bed. *Thank goodness*, she thought, coaxing him out with a balled up stocking. Tucking him back into the crook of her arm, she offered a comforting scratch behind his ruffled ears. Toto's tiny form quaked with fear and Dorothy held him tighter to her chest as she approached the door hanging lazily on one remaining hinge. With Toto in tow, she lifted the precarious door and folded open a world in technicolour.

Hues of inky blues, vibrant and swirling oranges, and rich deep greens stunned her into breathlessness. Everything was so colourful, from the array of flowers to the nearby homes. The grass was so very green, it nearly glittered! Hugging Toto tighter to her chest, she was too distracted to notice the man standing at waist height directly in front of her. Startled by his *hello*, she took in his kind, glossy eyes and immediately thought of her late father. She imagined that this is how he might have looked as a small child. Ruddy cheeks, a bulbous red nose, and eyes illuminated in wonder.

Snapping Dorothy from her stupor, the man began to speak in a voice frankly too big for his little body.

"Citizens of our munchkin land," he turned to reveal a smattering of rather small peers rapt with attention. "Behold, our hero!"

Dorothy was speechless. A hero? Whatever did he mean? She felt assaulted by her new vibrant surroundings. And all of these smiling people! Dorothy was aghast! Where was her family? *This is all just very overwhelming*, she thought.

The man rocked on the balls of his feet patiently allowing Dorothy a moment to process. His gaze darted awkwardly to the cloudless sky and then down to admire the shine of his own shoes twice over before he spoke again. Leaning in to avoid the attention of the crowding munchkins, he continued.

"Allow me to explain without alarming you further," he pressed on tentatively. "You see, you've landed in our quaint town: the land of the munchkins!"

Dorothy's eyes wandered the crowd in confusion as the man signalled Dorothy to walk beside him along a swirling path of gold away from their onlookers. He could tell that she was fraught, so he proceeded with even greater care.

"You see, with your help, the wicked witch who has been tormenting us for years has been eradicated! Isn't this good news?"

His eyes sparkled with reverence pondering his town's new reality, but Dorothy crashed into whatever quiet moment he was having like an overzealous freight train.

"*My help*?!"

She surprised even herself with her outburst! Dorothy nervously fiddled with the tail of her braid and shivered to herself at his brazen mention of a witch! What did he mean *witch*? This was a thing of stories! Surely he was joking.

Dorothy looked down as Toto peered up at her questioningly, as if her wide-eyed pup could offer a word of encouragement at such a time as this.

"We're just so grateful for your…" The man scrunched his nose and gestured back to Dorothy's bedraggled house, "…especially convenient landing?"

It was then that Dorothy saw the crumpled legs of the aforementioned witch and recoiled with a gasp. Could it be that she had squished this woman? And that it was a *good* thing? She still didn't fully understand how her home had even gotten here. She had the thought to pinch herself to check if she was dreaming, but Toto's nervous and gentle nibbles at the inside of her elbow gave her all the clarity she sought.

With a quiet huff, Dorothy resolved that this was all just a little much! She shuddered once more at the sight of the once-witch's legs. She simply needed to find her way home at once.

"Sir, I don't mean to be rude, but I need to find my way back to Kansas!"

The man's next words would crush Dorothy's spirit entirely.

"Kansas?" The man chewed on this word as though he had never even heard it before. "Why, we must be an awful long way from there!"

Dorothy's heart sank deep into her stomach. On such a joyful day for the munchkins, Dorothy wanted nothing more than to be far far away from this spirited place! She longed for the familiar sight of her family's yard. Closing her eyes for just a moment, she recalled the image of a clothesline fluttering in a gentle breeze. The sky a quiet grey cut with fields upon fields of wheat, her safe and placid home.

She could cry! What was she going to do with this little man and her dislodged house? Her gaze fell to her toes, her stockings as tattered as she felt. The man noticed her eyes becoming glossier by the second and jumped to comfort her.

"There there, dear Dorothy! There may be someone who can help you find your way, although it's quite the walk, you know"— the man cheerfully pattered on—"Our committee has been working since your arrival on our plans for celebration! Though, I do suppose that we could postpone..."

There was that scrunchy nose again! But wait, h*ow did he?* Dorothy didn't think that she had offered her name, although maybe she was too frazzled to remember clearly? He *was* altogether a bit strange.

Noticing Dorothy's especially troubled demeanour, the man continued enthusiastically.

"It's settled then! We'll send you to Oz! If anyone can help you, it will surely be the wizard! Although, you'll need some shoes I think!"

Dorothy preened Toto to distract herself. How embarrassing that she hadn't considered shoes! Meanwhile, the man's eyes darted like a busy bee and caught at once on the witch's feet.

"Ah! These will do just fine!" He made quick work of scooping up the shoes.

"But I..."

"She certainly won't be needing them, you know! It's the very least that we can do for your most grand arrival!" He handed the glittering silver shoes to Dorothy. His big, kind eyes sparkled with gratitude as he gestured for her to try them on.

She had never seen anything quite so striking! She carefully placed Toto at her feet and slipped into the shoes one by one. They were a perfect and comfortable fit, although quite a bit fancier than anything she had at home. She wondered if any of her simple brown shoes were even in the house. *This was all just a troubling mess.*

"Now Dorothy, it's imperative that you take your time! The road to the Emerald City is fraught with danger if you're not careful!"

*HA,* she thought! As if she needed any more surprises! The man continued, pointing concernedly to the winding golden road.

"You must follow the yellow brick road at all costs! It will not lead you astray!"

Dorothy had an immediate stomach ache. She crouched to pick up Toto and turned to gaze at the wild and winding road before her, squinting to see if she could see anything resembling an e*merald city.* She took a long deep breath and puffed up her chest as much as she could muster. If this was the way home, she must go.

It was as if this decision had turned the air around her to fizz. She spun towards the man expectantly hoping for more words of wisdom for her journey, but he was gone! What on earth? He was here just a moment ago!

Dorothy felt a chill envelop her and squeezed Toto to her chest.

*Follow the yellow brick road.*

• • •

*One foot in front of the other,* Dorothy thought to herself as she plodded along the shimmering golden bricks beneath her twice shimmering shoes. She had never been further than a few acres in either direction back home, and this fantastical new world before her was just so big! Stretching the full horizon was an endless sky that resembled candy floss. Hues of soft pinks and blues braided into the sparse and fluffy clouds all around her, and the path that lay ahead seemed like it stretched into infinity. Dorothy was overwhelmed to say the least!

Lining the yellow brick road were rolling fields of kelly green, all immaculately kept. She wondered how the fabric of this world was held together, *and by whom?* Everything felt illusory here and she suspected that the closer she got to the Emerald City, the more bewildered she would become.

A niggling fear crept into Dorothy's heart. *How far would she have to travel? Would the night come? What kind of horrible creatures might she meet in the dark??! And would she be alone the entire way? ACK!* She could so easily lose her head if she kept thinking like this! Giving Toto a squeeze for comfort, she resolved to clear her mind by halfheartedly counting the bricks as they touched her toes. *One... Two...* She walked and walked. *Three...*

And walked.

And walked.

• • •

Dorothy had lost all sense of time as she ambled along the golden path distractedly. Toto had gotten antsy so she let him follow closely at her heels. Watching him sniff at the odd wildflower, Dorothy trusted that her sweet and scraggly friend wouldn't meander too far on his own. The two friends had been thick as thieves for years as there wasn't much to do in Kansas, and they both liked to keep to themselves.

Dorothy let her mind wander to the day she had first met Toto. He was all wrapped up in a frayed cheesecloth because their neighbours hadn't expected their own farm dog to bear puppies. Toto's little eyes gleamed an inky black, and his hair was just as mussed as ever covering his tiny folded ears. He was about the size of an apple that day. Aunt Em didn't seem to mind when Dorothy came home with the fresh pup in tow. *There's always work to be done around the farm,* she would always say. Dorothy chuckled to herself. Aunt Em had anticipated Toto to be a better mouser!

Sleepily, Dorothy untangled herself from her daydream and looked around. They must have been walking for hours! Her muscles ached, and she longed to sit down for a short rest. The sky was beginning to darken, and she was still surrounded by fields and fields of green. *I hope we make it somewhere by night fall,* Dorothy thought as she scooped up Toto and picked up their pace. Suddenly the sky plunged into deeper darkness. *How strange.* Night didn't usually fall this quickly! Dorothy noticed that the flossy clouds above had thickened considerably and that the once darling sky was now threatening something sinister.

As if on cue to quell her anxiety, Dorothy and Toto cleared a large hill revealing a golden field of corn just to their left. *Oh thank goodness! Something new!* She was ever so grateful for the change in scenery and hoped that it would mean she was nearing her destination. This was a short lived comfort of course, as the sky began to grumble and spit heavy globs of rain.

Dorothy immediately sought to hide from this intrusive rain storm. She was already so frightened, she didn't need to be wet too! She spotted the tall white fencing along the edges of the cornfields and quickly ran for cover. She pressed her back into the harsh wood and tucked her knees close to her chest, shielding a shivering Toto. The lush leaves that escaped the cornstalks hung lazily over the framing and made an adequate umbrella at least. Dorothy folded up her skirt to further cover her nervous pup and closed her eyes tightly. Toto began to whine.

"There, there, Toto," she cooed at him. "This will surely pass soon!"

She hoped that she sounded more certain than she felt.

It seemed that this exclamation was a challenge that the sky didn't appreciate. As if in answer to Dorothy, a sudden ground shaking crack of thunder reverberated through them both. Head to toe, the pair shook, and Toto yelped in fright. He leaped from Dorothy's arms at once and ran dizzily across the yellow brick road towards a thick and menacing copse of trees.

"Toto!" Dorothy shouted after him, but he was as quick as he was small.

And he was gone.

• • •

Of all the truly horrible things that had happened this day, this was certainly the worst! Dorothy had never felt so helpless and alone. She sprung to her feet, her hair getting tangled in the sopping leaves above her. *Ack,* she thought as she dizzily ran after her furry companion towards the mysterious forest.

"Toto!" Dorothy called, squinting against the pounding rain. "Toto!"

She had thought the storm was scary on the yellow brick road, but the forest brought a kind of heavy darkness that sent shivers down her spine! The trees closed up behind her as though these woods were a gaping and hungry mouth, and Dorothy's gaze shot around in a panic as she searched for her friend. Frightening chirps and wails arose at every turn, and Dorothy's heart pounded wildly as she wandered aimlessly shrouded in shades of black.

Dorothy was rapidly losing hope, when a shot of white fur zipped past her legs sending her skirt aflutter and spinning her around in a frantic circle. *A rabbit? It couldn't be!* She had feared only much meaner creatures in here, so she was momentarily relieved. Without a real plan to find her Toto, she veered to the right to follow what she hoped was a rabbit indeed. With any luck, the rabbit would lead her to her surely frightened pup!

Eyes fixed on the nimble creature, Dorothy was perplexed when the puff of white seemed to disappear into thin air! *What on earth?* Where had it gone? *I can't seem to hold onto anything,* she thought. Dorothy was distraught. She ambled towards the gnarled tree ahead where her only hope had just vanished, and hung her head in despair. Though her view was obscured with heavy tears, she noticed a smattering of hedges and —*wait? Was that a rabbit hole?*

## alice

Alice sat listlessly beneath a lush and sprawling apple tree fidgeting with the petals of her daisy chain. The air was balmy in Wonderland today and the sun dappled the field before her in caramel spots like a funny dalmatian. There was nothing particularly interesting about this day, whatever day it may have been, and Alice was truly bored. It was no sooner than Alicc sighed with disinterest that a sooty looking terrier fell from the sky and plopped into her lap!

"Goodness!" She cried, eyes lazily looking about for the source of the apparently bewinged pup (she found that the English language still beguiled her at moments of surprise). "Wherever did you come from?"

Toto looked up at Alice, his glossy black eyes weeping, his shrunken furry brow scrunched up in tremendous fear. He had just been through a terrible and befuddling fall after all! What an ordeal for such a little thing! Of course, at this juncture, Alice didn't know who was in her lap. Toto, having come from Kansas, said nothing in return and continued to quiver. He was just an ordinary terrier, after all.

"Well, we ought to find you a drink. You must be parched!" Alice offered Toto a comforting scratch behind the ears. It had been awhile since anything truly peculiar had happened around here. Alice was elated to finally have something to do!

## dorothy

Dorothy peered blearily into the rabbit hole and felt her stomach do a somersault. *Could this be where the rabbit went? Perhaps it was following Toto?* Dorothy's head was swimming. She crouched at the edge of the hole and examined it carefully, brushing away stray leaves and brambles. The dark within was even more enveloping than that of the woods around her, and it was wider than a typical rabbit hole. *It couldn't be,* Dorothy thought. She considered for a moment that Toto quite enjoyed the comfort of being in well tucked places, but the thought of her nervous pup jumping down a mysterious hole with no regard for where it might end seemed preposterous!

Dorothy had all but given up hope. *Maybe he wandered back to the yellow brick road?* She turned to look in the direction of the forest's edge thick with twisting branches, and sighed to herself. *What kind of mess have I gotten myself into?* Just then, Dorothy clumsily lost her footing and tipped into the gaping hole.

"—Aaaaack!" Cried Dorothy into the empty forest as the sky began to lift further and further from her reach. She was falling! Before she knew it, the sky had disappeared altogether. Tumbling and tumbling over herself, she whipped her gaze around in a frenzy and felt as frightened as ever. Shelves of books and knick-knacks flopped about in the dizzy air all around her. The rabbit hole had seemed an adequate size for a girl, she supposed, but Dorothy couldn't perceive tunnel walls at all! It was as if she were in an infinite expanse of hazy, swirling purple. *And there was that funny rabbit again!* The bundle of white zipped past at twice her speed. Dorothy found comfort in counting once again. *One... Settle yourself, Dorothy Gale. Two... This simply must be a dream.* Dorothy fell and fell. *Three...*

And fell.

And fell.

• • •

Dorothy awoke with a gasp. *Hmm, how curious.* She found herself in a garden pruned to angular perfection. Bushes of emerald green in tight neat lines with roses exploding from the seams. Both red and pale white roses sprouted from every corner of the garden, and wait—

*Were those ivory roses bleeding with red like melting chocolate?*

Dorothy had never seen a sight quite like it, and she found herself suddenly hungry! The garden was both beautiful and unsettling. As she pulled herself to sit cross legged in the still and quiet garden, she began to hear a distant marching sound. As if by the passing second, the sound grew and grew like the low grumble of thunder! *Not even a moment to sit I suppose.* With increasing impatience, she scrambled up and haphazardly ran towards the garden's opening. Dorothy squinted to see a nearby river's edge and slowed her pace. She turned one last time to look back at the garden. *Finally, a chance to take a short re—*

Suddenly, Dorothy collided with another young girl.

## alice

Alice was knocked clean off her feet into the shallow and reedy waters of the river's edge. The ruffles of her skirt obscured her vision as she reached through the muck to right herself. Had she gotten bigger? (This was a funny illusion of course, her boots were simply above her head, Alice folded up in an amusing "V"). She was sopping wet!

"Toto!" A frantic and strange girl called out from the grass. "There you are!" The strange girl picked up the little pup and he wiggled happily in her grasp.

"Hey!" Alice shot back, popping up to her feet defensively. "That dog is mine!"

Alice hadn't seen anyone quite like her in a long while. The girl standing before her was positively grey. She was rail thin with dark gaunt features, maybe a few years older than Alice. Alice thought to herself that she looked an awful lot like her own sister, if her sister had been drained of all her colours! The girl looked back at her with eyes as big as lemons. Alice thought that it was quite rude of her to just stand there without any explanation after interrupting her new thirsty friend!

"I— I—" The girl held the terrier protectively to her chest. She took a steadying breath and continued. "This is Toto, and he belongs to me!"

She supposed the dog did look the most settled he had looked since his unexpected flight. Alice stubbornly twisted the ends of her dress to wring out the river water she had soaked up like a sponge before answering.

"You know, you really ought to watch where you're going!" Alice was familiar with the hot seething feeling bubbling up in her chest. "Who *are* you?!"

## *dorothy*

With all the trouble that Dorothy had seen today, it still surprised her to be spoken to in such a manner. It had felt like the longest day imaginable.

"I'm Dorothy, and I—" she dug deep for the courage to respond, forcing herself to hold the temperamental girl's gaze. "I don't appreciate your unkindness! It's been a tremendously long day for me, so I think I best be taking Toto and leaving now!"

Dorothy spun on the heels of her glittering shoes, Toto tucked under her arm where he belonged. She was proud of her mettle! Dorothy released the bracing breath she had been holding as she began to walk back in the direction of the garden.

"Wait!" The girl called after her. "Listen, I—"

Dorothy halted, but didn't turn to face her just yet.

"I didn't mean to be rude, I was just... knocked off guard I suppose."

Dorothy tried her best to hold in the smile that had begun to quirk at the edges of her lips. She *had* hit her pretty hard, and she would be angry too if she had just been dunked in a river. She herself was irritated enough having been dampened from the storm. She wondered if maybe she wasn't the only one having a terrible, horrible day.

## alice

"I'm sorry for crashing into you." Dorothy said, visibly softening. "It's just that I'm not sure where I am... and I'm not sure where I was... and I didn't really know where I was supposed to be going... and I had lost my dog... and I—"

Alice thought this girl must be going mad. She would certainly fit right in. The troubled Dorothy had trailed off speaking and was obviously distraught, her eyebrows furrowed as she picked at her fringe. Alice hadn't really ever thought herself to be the comforting type, but she thought she might try. There wasn't much to do today after all!

"I'm Alice! And I'd be most happy to show you around Wonderland." Alice plopped her hands on her waist and beamed a smile as bright and wide as the Cheshire Cat's. She wondered if this came across as soothing or unsettling, but continued gently. "Although, maybe we should take a seat for a while."

## dorothy

Dorothy had been longing for a seat since this whole ordeal began. Alice ushered her to rest beneath the canopy of the largest apple tree she had ever seen. Heavy orbs of red dripped from the branches above, and Dorothy's stomach grumbled greedily. Alice must have heard this because she plucked an apple free in answer and handed it to Dorothy. A peace offering of sorts. The apple was so unusually plump that Dorothy had to set Toto warily at her side so that she could cradle it with both hands.

Between careful bites, Dorothy began to recount to Alice how she had gotten here. She spared no detail about her frightful arrival in the land of the munchkins and the storm that had sent her down the rabbit hole. Alice listened intently. There was a warm and gentle breeze that reminded Dorothy of her home in Kansas, and the sun slipped in and out of fluffy clouds as it set. Toto trotted to a nearby flower patch and rolled around on his backside playfully. *He's very comfortable here,* Dorothy thought. She too was relieved to be able to talk to someone about her feelings and rest for a while.

Of course, it wasn't long before anxiety crept in again. She still needed to find her way to the Emerald City or she would never find her way home. While it was nice to have found a fast friend in Alice, she needed to be realistic.

"Alice, thank you for listening to me. This has been a much needed reprieve, but Toto and I must be going. I'll need to find my way back to the yellow brick road if I'm going to find my way home."

Alice giggled in response, though not unkindly. Regardless, Dorothy felt silly. *This isn't funny.*

"Dorothy, I think you'll find that home is closer than you think."

Dorothy was confused, but Alice continued. "And besides, it's not as though you can shoot back up the rabbit hole from which you came!" Alice laughed cheerfully as a frustrated blush spread on Dorothy's cheeks. This was not helping, and Dorothy felt herself bubbling up like dishwater.

"I don't appreciate you making fun of me, you know!"

## alice

"No, I didn't mean—" Alice sighed. She remembered how overwhelmed she had felt when she had first found this place, and thought she might work on softening her delivery. "I just meant that the rabbit hole is often a one way trip."

Alice reckoned this sounded scarier than she meant it, so she quickly continued.

"What I mean to say is that I myself have been in and out and round-a-bout." She tumbled her hands funnily like a wheel, hoping the rhyme added a comforting whimsy. This type of chatter had grown on Alice; everyone was a bit mad here after all. "And I have found that you're often meant to learn something here before you go."

She took to picking at the surrounding blades of grass to busy her hands and allowed Dorothy a moment to swallow a bite of apple.

"Learn something?" Dorothy set down the half eaten fruit. "But how am I to learn something when I don't know how or why I got here?"

"It doesn't much matter *how* you got here!" Alice answered, tucking a loose strand of hair behind her ear. "Only what you do *while* you're here, I'm afraid."

Alice could see that Dorothy was perplexed by this, so she continued. "As a matter of fact, I once spent an afternoon arguing with a most frustrating caterpillar!"

"A caterpillar?" Dorothy tilted her head quizzically. Alice supposed that Dorothy must not have met any talking creatures yet.

"Yes, a caterpillar! He was big and sleepy and dare I even say... *most* unhelpful!"

"So I suppose you didn't learn anything?" Dorothy responded curiously.

"Well..." Alice tapped her chin as she pondered, a wide grin beginning to form. "I learned to not spend too much time with caterpillars, that's for sure!"

The girls chuckled together until they were in stitches, but a sense of dread quickly overcame Dorothy. She leaned back against the sturdy trunk of the apple tree and closed her eyes. Alice quietly took up space beside her. She patted her lap softly to beckon Toto over. The pair of girls sank into a long and comfortable silence, elbows just touching and tipped against the dependable tree. Toto curled up into a sleepy crescent in the folds of Alice's skirt. The sun began to gently doze over the horizon and Alice let her eyes slip out of focus as she watched the flittering insects mosey in and out of the daisies. The sky was slowly shifting into a bruised plum shade and Alice could hear the breath of the wind as it weaved through the longest wisps of grass. She thought about how frightened her new friend must be feeling and resolved that in the morning, she would help Dorothy find what she was looking for.

## dorothy

Dorothy could simply not believe that she had so easily fallen asleep. As she stirred and lolled her stiff neck left and right, she stared at Alice and wondered how she managed to seem so at ease here. It looked as though she had removed her boots in the night and tucked her stockinged toes under her skirt's ruffles. Her arms were folded in tandem beneath her left cheek, her soft hair spilling over where the grass met the roots of the tree. She looked disarmingly peaceful. Dorothy watched as Alice lazily peeled open into a sprawling yawn of a girl who was comfortable taking up space. *I wonder what that's like.*

Dorothy didn't really have much in the way of company back in Kansas. Aunt Em had been unrelenting in prodding her to get out and make friends. It wasn't as though she was lonesome, it just seemed to Dorothy that things often went wrong. She hadn't made a habit of allowing for newcomers. For the first time, she had the passing thought that she might miss Alice despite them only just meeting.

The sun began to peek at the sleepy girls, and an especially bright ray of light roused a dozing Toto from his curly position. Meanwhile, Dorothy considered what Alice had said the night before. She thought it seemed like nonsense to not bother with the *why* of things, but she longed for Alice's breeziness nonetheless. Dorothy could hear the soft pattern of Alice's slow and even breathing and thought her quite admirable (*and frankly reckless)* to be so relaxed with someone so quickly.

Dorothy looked out at the landscape before her and imagined the dangers that might lay ahead in getting back to her original path. *What if there were wild animals? A lion? Or a bear? And the weather! How will I get by if I stumble into another storm?*

Dorothy felt the waves of her mind toss her asunder as her worries darkened further. *And what if Alice tires of me? I'm all mixed up after all. It's simply safer to be by myself.*

She decided then that she wouldn't burden Alice with her disaster. She was a practical stranger, after all. Thinking better of how rude it would be to leave unannounced, Dorothy decided that she would leave Alice a note. Of course, Dorothy hadn't been carrying a book or a pencil with her. How silly that would have been! She'd have to leave something special to express her gratitude. *I'll have to get creative,* she thought.

## alice

Alice awoke with a groan as the thick afternoon sun lapped over her. She hadn't slept this heavily in what felt like years, and she felt both groggy and clammy from the heat. She sleepily perched herself up on her elbows and began to look around. Alice had been eager to show her new friends around Wonderland, but found very quickly that she had been left alone. She tried to guess at the time. The grass shaded by the billowing branches of the apple tree still felt damp with morning dew, but the sun was high in the baked cerulean sky. As Alice began to climb to her feet wondering what to do, she noticed something glimmering in the grass a few paces away.

Shoes! Dorothy had left Alice her sparkling silver shoes. Did that mean she was in her stockings? The silly girl! Her eyes darted around lucklessly looking for Dorothy and Toto once more. Alice rushed over to pluck the shoes from the grass. She thought that they were a great deal more lavish than anything she had ever worn. She was almost too mesmerised by the sparkle to notice that there was something tucked neatly into the toe of the right shoe. She turned the shoes over in her hands and watched as the slip tumbled free into the tall grass. Alice lowered herself and unfolded what looked like a surprisingly large apple leaf. She could just make out two words scratched into the porous surface:

***thank you***

Alice could hardly believe that Dorothy would have snuck off without waking her! She sat cross legged beneath the tree and allowed a moment to feel sorry for herself. Dorothy had seemed like a promising friend, and she often found herself to be the only half ordinary person here! Moreover, she wouldn't get very far in just her stockings! It didn't take long before Alice was scrambling up to her feet with the curious intention to find her new friend Dorothy. She folded up the note she'd been fidgeting with and placed it in the front pockets of her dress. From her spot under the tree, Alice could see a renewed world of adventure before her. The cobbled lane towards the Queen's kingdom looked more eerie than ever, and the rich surrounding foliage leaned in close to beckon her forward.

*Where would she begin?*

# The True Thief

## by Cathrine Swift

**Literary World**: Robin Hood

The night before her wedding to a Lord, Marion finds herself desperate to escape the new luxurious life she has been forced into without the man she still loves by her side. Will Marion return to Sherwood Forest and find Robin again? Or is her mysterious fate as an unhappy lady and wife forever sealed?

Marion did not do well when she was bored.

So when her lady-in-waiting finally freed her from the ridiculous shoes and corset she had been forced into for the dreadfully dull rehearsal dinner, she nearly leapt for joy. She would have proper, had she the strength to do so. Unfortunately, not even in the loose underdress could she truly breathe.

All evening the silk slippers had pinched her toes, during every tedious speech and lacklustre toast. All while her corset compressed her ribs through bland appetisers and overly salted main courses. Not even being seated at her future husband's side in the romantically lit room had been a relief. If anything, a closer proximity to him caused more distress than she'd felt on all the occasions he'd ignored her requests for a private audience. Or blatantly turned her away during council meetings in recent weeks.

In a dramatic display worthy of the deepest feminine inner turmoil, Marion threw herself across the bed, face down, and screamed rather gutturally into the mattress. After a moment, her lady-in-waiting came to sit beside her, placing a tentative hand on her shoulder.

"Might I be of any assistance?"

"Certainly," Marion answered, voice muffled by the floral bedspread. With a huff, she flopped on her back and pointed toward the ornate vanity in the corner. "There is a dagger in the drawer just over there. Pierce it through my heart, will you?"

Quite used to her lady's increasing hysterics over the last few weeks, Jayne merely sighed, settling her hands in her lap. "How's about you join us tonight instead?"

Marion sniffed and pushed up to her elbows. "Where?"

"The Merry Women are sneaking out to go to the tavern for a few drinks."

The idea of stale mead and live music inspired Marion to sit the rest of the way up. It wasn't a bonfire in the woods like the old days, but it was a start. And she'd grown rather fond of the women who'd joined their gang over the last few years, Jayne in particular – which was why she'd chosen her to act as her official companion when the move from camp had been proposed. Still, what were the chances she could successfully leave the manor undetected?

"There's no way I could go without *him* noticing."

Jayne scoffed. "Everyone in the manor quite expects the bride to be getting her beauty sleep tonight. No one shall be bothering you, especially not your husband-to-be."

There may be truth in that. Ever since Marion had stepped through the gates of the Loxley Estate, it seemed very little thought or concern had been given her way. She might as well take advantage of it, especially if tonight were the last she would spend alone. In a matter of hours, she would stand before Tuck and be married...and God's will be damned, but she didn't want it.

Not like this.

How had things changed so quickly? And so drastically, too?

It felt like only days ago she was out running wild through the woods with Robin and their men. And now here she was, betrothed to the aloof Lord Robert, set to become his wife before next sunset. It might as well be her greatest nightmare. Short of remaining forever under the thumb of her uncle, of course – a fate she'd managed to escape as a young woman. All she'd wanted in her youth, staring out the window of a tower much like this one, was a life of true freedom. To be her own person. To live and love by her own prerogative.

For almost two decades she'd had that very thing, and it had been glorious: better than anything she could have dreamed up in her mind. She and Robin had made a real difference in England – the parts of it they could touch on foot, anyway. Insect-infested tents and squirrel meat dinners aside, she missed her old life. *She missed Robin.* And it was slowly driving her mad that she might never get another taste of it. That she would never again get the chance to sit around a fire, her head on his shoulder, as he and the Merry Men sang.

How sweet their life had been – laughing between kisses as he pulled her up to join the dancing, her skirt hem whipping dangerously close to the flames as he spun her around. Would she truly never join him on a hunt again? Patch his wounds or press her lips to his bruises? Taste fresh spring water on her tongue and breathe the crisp forest morning air into her lungs?

Sadly, no. Not if Lord Robert had anything to say about it, anyway.

Was she truly destined to a life of fluffy pillows and tapestries and boring meetings from now on? It was a crueller fate, for a woman like her, than any jail cell might be. At least behind bars she could hope for freedom. She could plan her escape – but not from this. There might as well be a chain around her ankle. Or her throat. It certainly felt as if there were one around her heart. And despite knowing deep in her soul that she could never leave...nor could she stay and remain whole.

She felt it already; her heart, mind, and soul abandoning her. The normally grounded and firm earth beneath her bare feet was gone, and with it a sense of what it felt like to be inside her own body. To recognize wants and needs and have the strength to carry them out – except for one. Deep in her core remained an inescapable and shrill call, crying out for her to run. And never, ever, look back.

It was a call she could not answer, and one she would have to smother and stifle over time until it was a mere whimper in the back of her throat. Until she learned to walk unbalanced and teetering on shiny satin heels across slippery marble floors.

But not tonight...here, she was being offered a bit of a reprieve. A moment of tortuous salvation. She would be dreadfully stupid not to take it. And of all the things Marion was – skilled swordsman and archer, poet, gardener, and dancer – one thing she was not, was stupid.

"Let us go," she said firmly, and swung her legs over the side of the bed.

Jayne reached for her hands with a smile.

~

*There were eyes on her.*

Marion could feel them boring into the back of her head and making the hairs on her neck stand on end, but she kept a firm grip on the stein and her attentions on the Merry Men and Women seated around her. At least, she tried.

Sneaking out of the manor had been easier than she'd thought, dressed in serving garments and a cape like the rest of the ladies. None of the guards had even bothered to stop and count their group. It was almost infuriating. No one feared her fleeing – which meant Lord Robert had no idea how lost and trapped she had felt these last few months. Or how that feeling had deepened the closer it grew to their vow exchange. Every plea she summoned the courage to speak for a return to her old life had either fallen on deaf ears or been silenced with speeches about duty and honour.

As if he knew the first thing about true honour. Or love. *Or her.*

Outside her thoughts, the strong gaze remained on her; steady and unwavering. Years of running and hiding from the Sheriff and organising raids on travelling nobles had made her hyper-aware of her surroundings, and thankfully it was a skill she hadn't lost in her months as a forcibly kept woman. So, she used it to her advantage now: after spying the dusty mirror in the corner of the room, she shifted her weight for a better view, searching the reflection for a glimpse of whomever might be observing her so intently.

In the corner of the tavern, seated at a table by himself, was a hooded man. All she could make of him was a hunched, broad frame and one gloved hand, fingers loosely wrapped around a drink. Everything else was hidden by cloak or shadow, so much so that she could not see his eyes, nor the direction his face was tilted – but she could *feel* his attention. Clearly, the man wanted to be alone and unbothered given his furtive state of dress and general demeanour; but then, why did he continue to stare?

What did he want with her? Or *from* her? Was he here for her specifically?

Perhaps he was a guard in disguise surveying her every move, sent by Lord Robert to drag her back to the manor? Or was he simply a townsman with a fascination? There was always the unfortunate chance it was more sinister than that. He might be sizing her up as his latest victim for some unspeakable horror...or the Sheriff, seeking final revenge. He'd been missing for months, but coming for her would be a good way to get Robin's attention if that was what he was after.

And here she was, basically defenceless.

Aside from the dagger in her boot, Jayne had convinced her not to bring any weapons tonight, promising it would be just a few drinks and laughs. And for the first couple of hours, that was exactly what it had been: talking about anything, giggling over everything, hiccuping into glasses, and drinking far too much. Then the Merry Men had come through the door – barreled in, more like. At first they'd promised not to disturb, but it only took so long for all the lovesick couples to find their way to one another.

And so Marion had floated back and forth between the two tables of her increasingly inebriated friends, bouncing from this conversation to that, feeling far more like a chaperone than part of the party. Perhaps if she'd been seated at one of the tables and fully engrossed in the happenings, she might not have noticed the man so focused on her. She certainly hadn't noticed him come in.

So far, Jayne had been correct in her earlier assumption, though. No one at the estate had noticed her missing.

Marion scanned the tavern, checking the available exits, sweeping the rest of the busy tables for potential spies or guards. There were two doors, a back and a front, and no familiar faces other than her friends. Could it be possible that she might escape, right here and right now? She had never lived in the forest completely by herself...but she *could* do it. At least, for a time. She would figure it out. She always had, especially since she had not been left with much choice. There would be no asking anyone to come with her – not even Jayne.

All the Merry Women had chosen their partners willingly. And unlike Robin, his men had chosen their women right back. They were all a package deal, and somewhere along the line, she had been gently edged to the side. If it were not for Jayne, she might have lost all hope and connection, but...if they did not notice her, then they might not see her slowly inch her way toward the door. And then, right out of it...

From there, she could run. She could go anywhere. She might not even have to hide. It was possible Lord Robert did not even wish to marry her. He might be relieved to find her missing come morning. There was, however, a glaring problem: the front door was too obvious.

And the back door was right next to the man in the cloak.

At best, he could ignore her completely, and she had nothing to worry about. Or he could attempt to chat her up if she got too close. At worst, he might try and stop her altogether, which would cause a fuss and certainly draw the attention of her friends.

How was it possible that even here, just a few inches from potential, literal freedom, she was just as trapped as she was back at the manor? Unless…there was a chance this man eyeing her up could be used to her advantage. Should he be looking for the courage or opportunity to approach her, whether for nefarious reasons or not, she could enlist his help in her escape. Was it foolish? Insane? Perhaps. But, what did she have to lose? Her life?

She'd already lost that.

Summoning her courage, Marion drained the last of her mead and excused herself from her friends to approach the bar. They hardly noticed, but the stranger's gaze stayed on her every step of the way. When the barmaid had refilled her glass, Marion drank a quarter of it without breathing. Then, she emptied her mind of any fear and turned around. But she didn't approach the tables full of familiar faces. She walked straight up to the man.

"May I?" she asked, pointing to the spot next to him on the bench.

He straightened immediately, on guard. She wasn't sure if he was shocked or terrified, given she still couldn't see his shadowed face.

In a deep voice he choked out, "Uhh, no m-ma'am. I mean, yes…it's free."

"Wonderful." She slid in next to him, sitting closer than necessary to gauge his reaction. He didn't shrink away, but he did stiffen further. "What is your name? I haven't seen you here before."

A practised liar from years of tricks and traps on the road, she said it all with false ease, as though she were a regular here simply flirting with a mysterious stranger. It made him shift away, turning slightly toward the wall, as if attempting to sink into it. The shadows of the dark corner enveloped his upper body even further.

"I…I'd rather not say."

"You've been staring at me for the last hour," she declared casually, swirling the amber liquid she held. "Don't you think a name is the least you can offer me?"

Under the table, his feet shuffled.

"I apologise if I offended you, m'lady."

Marion scoffed. "I am simply a maid from a nearby manor. You needn't bother with the formalities."

The man tilted his head in her direction. "And you needn't bother with the lies."

She sat back a little in the booth, impressed at his sudden brash and bold attitude. "I beg your pardon?"

With the worn leather of his glove still on despite the warmth inside, he gestured at her hands with one of his. "No maid's hands look like that," he declared. "I see not a blemish, cut, hangnail, or speck of dirt. Yours are the hands of a lady."

Marion looked down and frowned at how right he was. She had a few scars here and there sure, but nothing recent. No earth caked beneath her too long nails, no string burn from the bow, or splinters from sanding down the arrows. These, unfortunately, *were* the hands of a lady. Of that there was no denying.

"I was not always one," she admitted, flexing her fingers and then slipping them beneath the table, out of sight. "Well, I suppose I was born one. But becoming one again is a more…recent development."

The dark voice sounded curious. "Your tone implies this is a hardship for you."

"It was certainly not my choice." Briefly, Marion brought her left hand out of hiding, merely to take a long drink, and then tucked it safely back beneath the table.

"Everything is a choice," the man said.

Marion scoffed. "For a man, certainly. For a person who is free, perhaps. But for a woman? A *lady*, as you've identified me as? Never. We have far too many rules, expectations, and demands placed upon us."

The stranger didn't miss a beat, nor did the hardness in his tone waver. "You scoff at your privilege; something others profoundly crave. So much so that many kill and die fruitlessly for it. Do you not find honour in serving people, at the very least?"

Marion gestured to the door, less than ten steps from them. "I served people far more before, out there, than I ever could in a tower, I assure you."

His deep laugh brought goosebumps out on her arms. "Is that so?"

Marion did not do well with being laughed at, and she was quite regretting not just making a run for it.

"Yes," she responded fiercely, shoulders back. "We made a world of difference."

"*We*." The hood nodded slowly. "I see now. This is all about a man."

"Not entirely, and not just any man." Marion brought both of her hands back to the tabletop, desiring the mead far more than she needed to hide evidence that had already been observed.

"Tell me about him."

Marion hesitated, taking a long, deep breath to prolong the memories of Robin – especially the final days, which always brought on agony and longing.

"He was strong. Not physically, I mean. Well, yes, I suppose that, too," she finally said, her voice barely a whisper against the noise of the tavern. It made the hooded man lean a little closer, and she caught the scent of pine and sanding oil on his cloak. Perhaps he was a carpenter, or a hunter. "But...his strength was not in his muscles and hands alone. It was in his eyes and his heart. He acted with courage. Took initiative. When he saw wrongdoing, he acted with everything in his power to correct it. He was a protector, not only of myself, but our entire…family. He brought us together. Supported us. Offered stability and focus despite the rugged, unstructured lifestyle we all lived. He took responsibility for the people he loved very seriously – and what a lot of people that was."

"You especially, I assume," the man said, clearing his throat and shifting on the bench, as though her words made him uncomfortable in some way.

"Some days, I thought so," Marion confessed. "In the end, though, I doubted he even knew me at all. Never mind loved me."

"How so?" The man spoke quickly, as if offended on Robin's behalf.

Marion hesitated with another long, slow sip. "He was everything a man should be, and more. A good and loyal leader, full of confidence and a desire for adventure…And then…one day…"

"You describe him in the past tense. As if he has passed on."

"Not in the sense you mean," she said, fingers tapping against the stein. "But as far as I'm concerned, the man I loved is long gone. I fear I shall never see him again."

"And you are now…with another?" The man gestured to the ring on her left hand and the emerald stone set in the centre of it.

Marion could only nod, eyes focused on the glistening four silver claws of her ring, holding the gem in place against its will. When Lord Robert had presented it their first day at the manor, she had loved it. The stone reminded her of the forest she'd once called home, and she believed it to be a comforting reminder or token: a piece she could carry around with her on the hard days. It was only later she realised it was an unintentional taunt: a flicker of what had been, and what she could never have again.

"And this other man? He is cruel?"

"N-no…not cruel. Cruel I suppose would imply he spoke to me, observed me, or entertained my existence at all. In truth, my soon-to-be-husband does little more with me than a cat does with a mouse on a hot summer day."

"Meaning?"

"Close enough to monitor, but far away enough I don't interrupt him. Or his business."

The man made a move to remove his leather gloves, then seemed to think better of it. "Perhaps he is only trying to protect you. Care and provide for you, as a man should."

Marion scoffed.

"You disagree?" the man dared.

"Hardly." Marion waved her hand. "A man *should* protect, and care, and provide. He should want to and strive to, and do whatever he has to when he says he loves a woman…but is that woman not meant to do the same in return? Are we not to share the privilege and pain of nurturing? Of choosing him right back? He puts me up in a tower to keep me from the sting of arrows and twigs in my hair, but never once did I request such things."

Lost in memories, Marion almost forgot who she was talking to. Or that she was even talking to anyone at all.

"I only wanted him just as he was. Just the way we were," she murmured.

After a long moment, the man spoke again, and she realised she had revealed far too much. And to a stranger no less.

"And how were you?" he asked, dark tone laced with a level of intrigue that surprised her. "What did you love so much about your old life?"

"Everything." Marion's cheeks burned, ashamed at her wistful lilt. "In this life, I shall never stand at his side again. He shall no longer seek me out for advice, and never again shall we make choices together."

"And what of your betrothed? Will he not afford you such things if you asked?"

"He has a whole team of advisors, and I am not even invited into the room."

The man sat tall, his torso still in the shadows, but turned more in her direction now. She could make out the edges of the dark green vest he wore beneath the cloak. The colour always called to her. It was very similar to the bodice of the simple gown she'd borrowed from Jayne.

As though he'd forgotten himself, the man's hands on the table folded into fists once, then twice. He was...angry with her? Annoyed? She wasn't sure, but clearly something she'd said had struck a chord within him. Perhaps it was time she ended the conversation. It was doing little more than upsetting her further anyway.

"Why do you stay?" he asked, voice gruff, words tumbling from his mouth at a rapid pace that made her curious.

"The reason we left this–" She waved at the tavern, but really she meant the entire world as it was. Society in general. "–was because we despised the way things were run: the way things were governed, and the justice system, the taxes, and the use of resources. It was never meant to help. Not built for those who needed it the most."

The hood nodded, as though he agreed. "And now you feel as if you've been thrown straight back into the very fire you believed you'd escaped once upon a time?"

"Yes, and he's left me to burn in it." Marion didn't bother hiding her fury, the familiar anger she'd managed to keep at bay until now rising in her core again. "We saved families, rescued orphans, and personally delivered food to the tables of the starving. Now he'll be signing papers, simply hoping his decrees are put into action."

"Shouldn't you give him an opportunity to try?"

Marion sat back in the booth. "I'm not stopping him. I just don't wish to be a part of it. Not like this. Not where I am separate from him."

"What would you prefer?"

"In the woods we were equals. Partners. The closest thing to a true king and queen there could ever be. But now...he is a lord."

"And you a lady," the hood offered, as though her shackles were the solution.

"That title is a mere ribbon on a box of manure."

The man paused, his fingers tapping on the table. "Your lord and your...lost love...they are the same man?"

The truth she'd been trying to hide from herself all along felt like a slap in the face, spoken so plainly by the stranger. Of course he had figured it out. It was so painfully obvious at this point that her darling Robin Hood, whom she longed for, and the Lord Robert she'd ached to escape earlier this evening, were one and the same. There was no sense in denying it any longer: not to this stranger, and certainly not to herself. She could not protect and defend Robin when he had been the one to break her heart, no matter how much she wished he hadn't.

"Yes." She almost choked on the admission. "When it became clear things were different, my head and heart made a choice. To keep them separate as a way to...carry on. At least, to try."

"Oh, my darling." The man sounded sad, shifting closer to her as he removed the gloves. "If I had known..."

When his voice changed, she noticed it immediately. Even without the familiar term of endearment, she didn't need to see his face to discern who the man at her side had truly been all along. Realisation flooded over her, like someone had dumped a bucket of cool spring water on her head. Her stomach flipped violently as anxiety took root, trying to retrace her steps through everything she'd said. *Not* to a stranger, but to Robin. Robert. To them both. To...the three of them. All the same.

He removed his hood, revealing the handsome face she'd been seated next to at dinner just a few hours ago. The face that had promised her months prior as they stood in the woods amidst the disassembling of their camp that everything would be alright. The face that now looked at her with sorrow and pain. In an instant, she was on her feet, but he caught her wrist, hand bare, the skin-to-skin contact keeping her in place.

"Let go, Rob," she hissed, arrows of rage and hurt shooting from her eyes right for him. "What a ghastly trick."

"Don't run," he pleaded.

"What the hell is this?" She pulled away, but he reached for her again.

"I... I needed to know how you truly felt."

Her raised voice and the spectacle of him holding her hand was beginning to draw the attention of the people around them. She stepped closer to him, wanting nothing more than to give him a piece of her mind before they were interrupted. As it was, John had stopped drinking and was watching them, but he knew better than to interfere unless he was called. As it was, his large hand was on Jayne's shoulder, keeping her in place.

Marion shared a look with her friend, hoping it said she was all right, and then set Robin in her sights, tone merciless. "My words at the manor were not clear enough?"

"You've hardly spoken to me for weeks." He had the audacity to look aghast, which only infuriated her more.

"No. You've hardly listened. Or been in the same room as me."

"I listen a lot more than you realise."

Marion shook him off. "Well then you, *Lord Robert*, are more of a bastard than I thought."

"Is that so?" he challenged, stepping around the table to keep the distance between them lacking. "Do explain."

She huffed a few strands of hair from her face and squared her shoulders. It did little use, as she was nearly a foot shorter than he, but she saw the flicker of intimidation in his eyes all the same.

"It is one thing to be so swept up in your new duties that you do not notice my pain. It is another entirely that you sensed it — knew of it enough to arrange this ruse — and did nothing to aid me."

"What would you have me do, Marion? Have us run off into the woods again?"

"Yes!" She sighed, shaking her head. "I don't know, perhaps! At least...allow me the option."

That made him falter, so much that he took a step back. "You...would go alone? You'd leave me?"

She lifted her chin. "I would."

"You'd die."

He didn't say it like a threat or a warning. There was fear in his voice, and a bit of desperation, but it did little to soften her heart.

"I'm dying anyway. Stuck in the manor with you, like this. I'd rather be strung up by the Sheriff."

If he said anything, she didn't hear it. Her heart pounding in her ears drowned him and everyone else out as she snatched the cloak he'd been wearing from the bench and disappeared through the back door.

~

Breathing heavily and aiming to put as much distance between her and the tavern as she could, Marion got further into the woods than she thought possible before recognizing Robin was indeed following her. Unfortunately, that was also the moment the mead she'd drunk over the course of the night decided to attempt a reappearance.

With his heavy cloak weighing her down, she stopped to rest in a grove of trees, their tops coated in moonlight, and rested her hands on quivering thighs. The fresh forest air coated her stinging lungs and she drank it down greedily, avoiding vomiting up the liquid sloshing around in her mostly empty stomach. Perhaps she should have eaten more dinner.

"Are you all right?"

Marion glared daggers at Robin, who skidded to a halt a few feet away. He wasn't eyeing her carefully in the way that she might be a wild animal to be cautious of, but he certainly looked uncomfortable. When she said nothing, he held his hands up, either defensively or to show he meant no harm.

Too bad the harm had already been done.

"Go away, Rob. I don't want to talk to you. Not now, not ever."

"You have my cloak."

She cast a dark look over her shoulder. "You have many back at the manor. I believe you will survive without this one."

"Yes, well, even with it, I doubt you'll last more than a day or two out here. It's not as if you have your bow."

In one swift movement, she lifted the dagger from under her skirts, showing it off to him. "I'll manage. Perhaps I'll find a team of bandits and charm them into letting me join."

The way his eyebrows knit together communicated quite clearly that he did not even slightly approve of this idea. The types of bandit groups they'd encountered in their years on the run weren't typically the most trustworthy or decent of people.

"Come home."

Not quite an order, but barely a question.

Taking a deep breath, Marion stood straight and faced him. "That–" She pointed in the direction of Loxley Estate, or at least where it might be. She was rather turned around at the moment. "–is not my home."

"We once said that wherever we were together was home. No matter what part of the forest or land or village, as long as we were hand-in-hand–"

Marion screeched, cutting him off. "That was before!"

"Before what?"

"Before you abandoned me."

Robin almost rolled his eyes, but it seemed he thought better of it at the last moment. "I hardly call giving you an entire wing abandoning you." He spoke through gritted teeth.

"I didn't want a wing. I didn't want wardrobes full of gowns or servants to order around. It's disgusting when I am quite capable of taking care of myself. I never asked for titles or riches, or any of the things that have come with this life of yours."

"Of mine..." Robin squared his shoulders and tugged the dark green vest down tight over the white shirt. He looked strange, dressed like a lord in a place where he should be someone else entirely. "It is *our* life, is it not?"

"No."

His face strained, a sure sign he was grinding his teeth. "Be reasonable, Marion, please."

"Just let me go." She shook her head and stepped away. "I'm done."

"What–" He paused, hand outstretched to her, and against her better judgement she waited, her back to him, eyes squeezed shut and willing him to give up.

It would be so much easier if he would give up. Her heart was breaking, knowing it could never have what it wanted to survive. *Needed.*

After a moment, he tried again. "What must I do to get you to stay? Name it, and it's yours."

"I won't stay," she said quickly. Regretting the movement as she did it, Marion faced him. *One more chance...* "...but you could still change your mind and come with me."

"We can't just disappear into the woods the night before our wedding."

"I followed you last time when we had no idea or experience in how to live out here." Marion crossed her arms. "We'll have a better chance lying low if it's just the two of us. I know you don't want to leave John or Will, but–"

Robin closed the distance between them with a few strides, wrapping his hands around her arms. "I...can't."

"You *can.* You just don't wish to."

He sighed. "I wish for us to make the manor our home. To know you have a roof over your head. I want to keep you as safe as I can, and frankly, I want to feel safe, too. We did so much, Marion. Saved and cared for so many people. Slept on the ground, ate all sorts of disgusting things, waited in the rain and the heat and the cold – all to make others' lives easier, so the world felt gentler to them. Now I want the same, and I want it with you. For you, and for both of us."

There was so much sincerity in his voice Marion felt the walls of anger around her heart crumbling, and instinct told herself to rebuild them – but this was the most that Robin had opened up to her in ages and she couldn't risk spoiling it.

"I understand." She said it softly, letting her arms fall and not rejecting his touch when his palms slid down to her wrists. "We deserve a happy ending...I just..."

"Feel guilty?"

"Yes." She sighed in relief, grateful for him putting into words what she'd been unable to. "Why should we get to breathe and relax when there are still so many people out there suffering? What if we can't make a difference inside those walls like we did out here? What if we forget?"

"You won't let me forget," Robin smiled, "and I promise I won't let you, either. Just...give me a chance to try it this way. I still plan on helping as many people as I can. I just also want to lay my head down at night on a pillow that doesn't smell like a horse. And I want to never worry where your next meal is coming from. To make love to you on a bed softer than dirt."

It was hard to argue with his reasons, and perhaps if he'd expressed them to her earlier she wouldn't have acted so rashly. However, even if she said yes to the trial, it didn't solve all her problems. She wasn't made for the life of a noblewoman – but even less than that, she wasn't made to sit still and keep quiet.

"*If* I say yes, I need your word about something."

"As I said, all you have to do is name it."

"If I am to be your wife, that does not erase the fact that we are partners. Equals. I will stand up with you before Tuck tomorrow, but only if you promise to me now that the tower you gave me is not a cage. That I will be allowed to sit in on your meetings, have my voice heard, and be a part of helping the people."

"If that is what you wish, it is yours. I should not have excluded you, my darling. I see that now, and I am so sorry."

"Then why did you do it?" Her sharp tone returned with a vengeance, but she worked to get it back under control. "Why did you think I would want that?"

"I..." He paused. "I assumed you, like me, were tired of our old life. That you wanted more comfort and less responsibility."

"Because that is what you wanted?" she asked softly.

Slowly, Robin nodded, meeting her eyes with an apologetic gaze. "We're so similar, you and I. We've always been, and I admit, I assumed we were on the same page without speaking to you about it. Which was wrong of me."

"I forgive you," Marion said after a moment. "You've had so much on your shoulders...and I knew that. I saw it so clearly and I wanted to help you. It pained me greatly that I could not."

"That I would not let you?" he asked solemnly, and she nodded in response. At that, he grinned hopefully. "So, you'll return to the manor with me?"

"I will."

Reaching up, caressing his face, running her thumb over the beard growing in slowly along his jaw. Since they'd moved, he'd been clean-shaven almost every day, one of the simple but less than subtle changes – like the use of his birth given name over the self-chosen one – that had let her separate the two. But the soft prickles beneath her touch felt familiar: like...home. She almost whimpered at the comfort of his embrace, and no matter how foolish it felt at first, she could admit that *he* was her home: just as much as the forest had been, just as much as the manor could be if they let it. He, Robin, was where her heart was happiest.

Hardly the most independent or self-empowered of thoughts, but she couldn't deny it as their fingers laced together. He stepped forward and she let him lead, her back meeting a tree, his free hand influencing her spine to arch into him. Years of sharing their hearts and bodies with one another had her falling into step easily, like their foreplay was a practised dance she could perform without music. He seemed to welcome her touch as much as she his, pressing entirely against her now, then he lowered his head, lips tentatively finding her throat.

It had been so long since she'd felt this close to him physically, but also more than that. Their last intimate moments together had been at camp; the morning before news of her uncle

Prince John's death spread through all the lands and found them by way of King Richard's men. If she had known that within just hours, her Robin would be regranted his title and asked to return to claim his father's land in Nottingham, she would have held onto him a little longer: prolonged their pleasure, and been more intentional in enjoying each of his touches.

If she could go back, she might have even begged him to run away, deeper into Sherwood Forest, where no one could ever find them. She'd had no reason to believe she would lose him that day, or any day after – but life rarely worked out the way you wanted it to. And promises, while sweet to the ears when made, were no match for fate and everything it had in store.

Still, Marion thought back to that morning in the tent with a smile, surrounded by pillows and furs and the rain-soaked, smoky scent of the world outside. Embraced by Robin's body and the solid earth, she'd laughed between kisses as the Merry Men got to work preparing breakfast a little louder than usual. Perhaps to offer a semblance or modicum of privacy. The canvas never had done much to mask their moans...but was she supposed to hold back? Impossible when he always felt so good inside her, making it difficult to remember her own name, never mind foolish things like decorum or correctness. Besides, he made his fair share of noise and declarations, too. Robin was nothing if not vocal.

The former thief in question brought her back to the present, resting one hand on the side of her face, coaxing her eyes open with a caress of her cheek.

"Where did you go just now? Somewhere far away?"

"A memory."

Whatever mirth or amusement might have been playing in his eyes was replaced with concern.

"A rather good one," Marion said. "I assure you."

His fingers dug into her hips – not painfully, but almost desperately. Like he was afraid she might run off again, or lose herself in the versions of them that used to be instead of their present.

"What you said before at the tavern...did you truly feel I threw you into a fire?"

She remained silent, afraid any further admission would pain him more. Despite months of agony and confusion, harming him was the last thing she wanted. She'd said too much and been too honest at the tavern, and she couldn't take any of it back. She sighed, but no sooner had her eyes cast down than he hooked a finger under her chin and tilted her face back up to meet his gaze.

"I..."

He shook his head when she couldn't find the words. "You deserve more than I have given you, Marion. I know it now, and I shall never fail you again. I vow to you tonight that I shall remain present, listen to and hear you, worship you, and give you security. I'll do everything in my power to prove every day how much I value you. Just as you are."

"You will?"

He nodded, his forehead against hers, their noses brushing. "I will."

Marion took a deep breath, her fingers tightening their grip between his. "Then, in turn, I vow to you that I shall remain by your side. I shall hold you up and inspire you. Keep you steady and warm and comfortable. I shall surrender to you and support you, for all your days. Or at least, for all of mine."

"You will?" he said, echoing her, giving her an opportunity to take it all back or to seal their mutual promises right here and now.

"I will."

She pressed her face into his neck, breathing in the scent of him and the forest – though where one ended and the other began, she never was quite certain. The warmth radiating from his body made her shiver against the cool night air, and she found herself melting into his comforting embrace further.

"You should know," he mumbled. "It was never truly I who was the thief, Marion." His lips caressed the shell of her ear, making her shiver again.

In response, she clung to his vest. "Oh?"

"It was always you. For you stole something no one could ever replace or return. Something I could never retrieve, even if I wanted to." He pulled her hand toward his lips, kissed it, and then pressed it to his body, her palm flat over his pounding heart.

"It might reside in my chest," he whispered, "but this has been yours from the first moment. And it will remain yours until I die. Perhaps even after."

Pushing up on her toes, Marion brushed her lips against his. "I love you, more than life itself."

"And I you, my darling."

# Remember Me

by E.A.M. Trofimenkoff

**Literary World**: The Phantom of the Opera

Love can transcend even the bounds of death. Erik and Christine look back on their life together and the love they have shared over the years. With death looming, it is all Erik can do to hold onto Christine and the pieces of his broken heart as the curtain opens and she softly slips away.

***Content Warning**: grief & death of a loved one*

I trace my thumb over the soft, loose skin of her hand, following the darkened spots of age like a map. Her map. One I have spent a lifetime cherishing. One we have explored together. She has never been more perfect than she is now in front of me, head tilted back, drinking in the late afternoon sun. My angel. I hold her close, but as tight as my grip is, I still feel her slipping through my fingers. No matter how hard I grasp, she continues to fall, to fail, to fade.

The memories of our life together are carved into the lines on her face: the joys in the creases by her eyes, the sorrows in those just to the side of her perfect lips. Her hair, once a waterfall of wild black curls, now sits as a silver curtain over her shoulder. With each rock of the porch swing, the strands fly away, free, like waves of fallen stars. Here, I can pretend the world is as it should be.

"You're staring again, Erik," she says, her voice still soft as a lullaby after all these years.

I place a reverent kiss on the back of her hand, my gaze never straying from her—afraid that if I look away, she may disappear forever. The inevitability of losing her stabs me through the heart, sharper than any blade. I'm not ready to let go. I don't think I ever will be.

"Yes, my love," I whisper into her open palm before brushing my lips over the sensitive skin near her wrist.

She leans into me, resting her head on my shoulder, and I—ever the obliging gentleman—wrap my arms around her, protecting her from the world as I have always done.

"Do you remember the first time we sat here?" she asks.

I nod, relishing the sweet scent of her lavender hair wash and the memory it evokes in my mind.

"You came back to me," I say softly before placing a gentle kiss on the top of her head. "You came home."

My eyes land on the diamond glistening in the sun. The silver metal threads wrap around her finger and hold the gem up proudly for all to see. Mine. Always.

"Christine?"

"Yes, Erik?"

I swallow hard and pull her closer to me.

"Thank you, my love."

She tilts her head to look at me and reaches up to caress my cheek. Her thumb plays over the tender, now wrinkled, skin under my eye, and the landscape of scars that have been there all my life. I lean into her palm, savouring each sensation: equally intoxicated by her presence and sobered by her touch.

"I miss the opera house," she admits, lowering her hand. I lace my fingers with hers on my lap.

She sighs, leaning back into my chest. Her head is heavy, and even as I hold her in my arms, I feel her slipping away.

It's too soon. She can't go. She can't leave me. She can't leave us.

"Close your eyes," I tell her as the first tear falls from my face.

Christine's eyelashes brush against the exposed skin over my heart where my shirt has shifted.

"The audience chatters as the stagehands dress you in a gown of pure starlight," I tell her. "Can you see it? The crimson curtain and golden tassels are the only things separating you from their world. But here, on this stage, the world is yours. The night is yours. And my heart, as always, my love, is undeniably yours as well."

"I see it," she whispers, as if in a trance.

Another tear falls.

"I come to you in the shadows. I see your soul reflected in mine through the mirror. It's just the two of us alone to dance around the flames. And I reach out to take your hand. Can you feel it, Christine? My love?"

"I see you, Erik. I feel you. Please." Her voice trembles. "Don't let me go."

I tilt her chin up and her eyes flutter open. Her once hard gaze is now replaced by soft grey irises. She's slipping. And there's nothing I can do to stop it. No foe to defeat. No war to wage. No price to pay. No time.

No time.

NO TIME.

There was never enough time.

There would never be enough. Not if we lived for thousands of years. Not if we watched a hundred suns be born and a hundred others flicker out. Not if we stretched ourselves to the edge of the universe. There is no place I wouldn't go, nothing I wouldn't do, to keep her here with me. But I can't fight time. If my love was enough to cure every illness and fight every battle, then she would live

forever. But my love is not enough. And I am once again forced to watch her leave—first for a man, and now to the embrace of Death, leaving me helpless, hopeless, and eternally heartbroken.

"The curtain is opening," I tell her through broken sobs. "You can sing now, my angel."

"Remember me..."

~

The scars of my flesh hurt the least.

Monster.

Freak.

Demon.

My life was a symphony of curses and shadows. Until her. Until my angel called to me. Until her sweet voice filled the dark corners of my soul with light and set my heart on fire. Her soft cries through the night resonated through me, shaking my bones until I fell before her on my knees, a penitent man seeking redemption for a life of sin. Never before had I seen my pain reflected so perfectly, as her broken soul called to mine. And I, a man possessed, called back.

Now, only my voice echoes through the darkness. Our strange duet has been reduced to a strangled solo, and I have no intention of singing the aria. I take my leave; let the curtain fall.

It's like stepping back into my life of darkness; back to the nightmare after living a dream for so long. Christine saw beyond my constellation of scars—convinced me I was worth seeing, worth loving. Was she my mask? The thought makes my breath catch. Without her, would the world once again see a beast, or would they look upon a broken man with a shattered heart?

"We're here, sir."

The carriage has stopped. My face is wet from the tears I didn't know I'd shed. I don't want to open my eyes. If I do, I know what I'll see. Or rather who I won't. And I can't bear it.

I twist the rose in my hand and prick my finger with a thorn on the stem. A small trickle of warmth trails down my finger. This is real. This torture. This is Hell.

Just give her back.

Or let me join her.

"Sir?"

I suck in a sharp breath and finally blink away the tears to find the carriage both suffocating and desolate. The bite of the rose is nothing compared to the agony in my heart. Both bleed, but only one shows.

The pale white mask stares up at me as if asking a silent question. It sits heavy in my hand, equal parts foreign and familiar. But I can't do it. I don't want to. I can't hide my face from her, and she would never want me to. I place the porcelain gently on the seat beside me as if laying a babe to

rest. It served me for so long—kept me safe, hidden and sheltered. But I have felt the sun on my face and the bitter sting of the winter breeze. I refuse to throw away those gifts she gave me. It's all I have left of her.

I don't look back.

My steps are heavy through the snow. The carved rocks poke through the sea of white like islands of death, each bearing a name and a story—each life reduced to a small plot of land, marked by a patch of cold stone. I walk over them, treading through the ocean of souls to her.

I kneel and trace the lines of her name.

Christine Daaé.

There was so much more to her than those thirteen letters. More life than the years carved below her name could possibly hope to capture.

I place the flower on the edge of her headstone, the already wilting red rose the only life to be seen in this vast emptiness.

"Christine," I whisper to her, resting my forehead on the frozen rock. "Your voice blesses my dreams, and your absence haunts my waking hours."

Snowflakes dance over my face, catching in my lashes as they fall from the sky like frozen tears from the heavens.

"You asked me to remember you. But you should have known, my love, that I could never forget. Not with a thousand knives could you be carved from my memory. Not with a thousand hands could you be torn from my heart. I am forever yours, my angel. And one day—someday soon, if we are lucky—my curtain will open, and our new act can begin. We've shared this life, and should you wish it, we will share the next.

Wait for me, my love. That's all I ask of you."

# Haunted

## by H. M. Darling

**Literary World**: Wuthering Heights

What if Catherine and Heathcliff had one night where they chose each other? One night to forget about who they were supposed to be? One night to haunt them for the rest of their days?

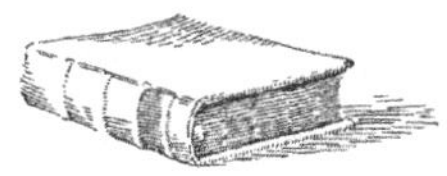

A storm was coming to Wuthering Heights.

Catherine Earnshaw paced before the window in her bedroom, watching the storm clouds roll in and contemplating the day's decisions. They sat deep in her gut, weighing her down and making her feel like she would drown before the first drop of rain reached the moors.

She did not love Edgar Linton. She would never love him. She would never see him as anything more than the sniveling weasel that played ghostly pranks on her while she recovered from her injury at Thrushcross Grange. In and out she'd come from consciousness. Feverish. Broken. Terrified. Alone. In her darkest hour, he reveled in her cries. He'd always seen her as something to laugh at—poor little Catherine Earnshaw from Wuthering Heights. Unkempt without a mother. Wild without a father.

And yet, come what may, she was to be his wife. Their marriage would make Catherine everything she was ever supposed to be. A wife. A mother. A lady.

It was for the best, she thought, as thunder rumbled, shaking the windows. Closer and closer the rain came, though the storm remained a few miles away. She watched lightning flash in the darkening clouds with a frown. Of their own volition, her eyes flicked over the moors surrounding her home. They searched through the gardens, the fields, the stables… and found nothing, as if the one she searched for was a ghost.

She wanted this, she reminded herself, turning away from the window and moving closer to the fireplace. A chill shook her body, and she lowered herself in front of it, her bare knees connecting with the stone floor.

It was she who dared Edgar to propose to her in the first place.

*"If not me, then who, Edgar Linton?"* she'd sneered in his face months ago, after seasons of hints, jabs, and questions—all but begging him to marry her. Catherine would never beg. *"I'm your only option for a wife, if only you'd open your stupid eyes."*

And while Catherine couldn't be sure her words were true, she knew Edgar was her only option. He was her freedom, her way out of Wuthering Heights. And so, as much as she teased and goaded him—for all the cruel things she'd said to him in the years they'd known each other—she never looked away when he called her beautiful, never shied away from his touch, and never argued when he spoke of how much better and *more civilized* Thrushcross Grange was compared to Wuthering Heights. She smiled when she needed to and leaned in a little too close when it was necessary.

Catherine had been working to secure this engagement since the moment she first laid eyes on Edgar Linton. It was everything she needed to become someone... more. More than the wild, feral girl everyone saw her as. More than the mud on her boots, more than the stains on her dress, more than the knots in her braids that never seemed to go away.

If she married Edgar, she would eventually become Lady of Thrushcross Grange. She would have a house to manage, servants to keep her company, and a child or three to warm her womb.

She would never be alone again.

This engagement was everything she'd ever wanted, except...

"Were you going to tell me?"

Heathcliff.

Catherine did not look at him; she did not acknowledge his dark frame in the open doorway to her chambers. He brought the smell of earth with him—the smell of freedom, of so much of her life she was bound to leave behind. Of icy wind and boots slipping in the mud. Of clouds so low one could touch them and laughter as they played hide-and-seek.

In her choice to marry Edgar, everyone got what they wanted. Edgar would get a wife and an heir to what would inevitably become his estate. Her older brother, Hindley, would be rid of Catherine once and for all—the last bit of his humanity washed away so he could finally drink and gamble himself into oblivion. Catherine would finally have somewhere she belonged. Somewhere she was safe.

And Heathcliff...

Heathcliff would lose everything.

Without Catherine to secure his place at Wuthering Heights, Hindley would surely drive him away—as he'd been attempting to do since their father had died. Perhaps the only home he'd ever known would be stolen from him, along with Catherine herself.

She was not blind. She was not a fool.

She knew the way Heathcliff looked at her, the way he'd always looked at her. She was intimately familiar with the darkness in his eyes, the shadow of his attention, the longing buried deep, deep in his soul.

It was for those reasons, and a hundred more, that she refused to look at him or answer his question. She stared into the crackling flames of the fireplace, cringing when another roll of thunder seemed to shake the very ground Wuthering Heights stood on.

"Answer me, Catherine." Heathcliff's voice echoed through her small chambers. The sound of a single footstep made her tilt her head toward him ever so slightly.

"I do not owe you any explanation," she tried to say, but the thunder drowned out her voice. Instead, Heathcliff only heard her final words. "I owe you nothing."

"You owed me this," he sneered, his voice as dark and dangerous as the oncoming storm.

She did not.

She owed him nothing—not an explanation, not a moment more of her time. She did not owe him an apology for discarding the years they'd spent running through the moors, shouting through the fog, and slipping in the dirt—laughing like only children could. She would not apologize for considering the longing in his soul, the desperation she knew he possessed, and then setting it all aside for the more practical option.

Heathcliff would marry her in a heartbeat; she'd known he would since he'd first laid eyes on her as a boy at her father's side. He'd loved her then, and he loved her more now. If she only asked, he would marry her—make her his wife and give her all the children she could ask for.

But he could never make her a lady. He could never give her a proper home over her head or the secure future she longed for.

She would not apologize for breaking his heart, as he never should have given it to her.

"I never thought you wicked, Catherine," Heathcliff rumbled from the doorway. His words struck her deeply, penetrating her heart and forcing a gasp from her chest. Still, she did not look at him; her eyes drifted from the warm, bright light of the fire to the dark, approaching clouds. "Foolish, yes. Uncaring, at times."

Only then did she spin toward him, a snarl escaping her. "Do not stoop to call me foolish. I am no fool."

"And what do you call your engagement, then?" Heathcliff opened his arms wide in accusation, taking another step into her room.

Catherine shrank into herself, glancing behind his hulking figure at the doorway. Of all the times for the house to be devoid of life, it had to be then. She would have done anything for Hindley, Nelly, or *anyone* else to have wandered down the hallway and interrupted the conversation she did not wish to have.

"If not foolish, then what?" Heathcliff taunted.

"Practical," Catherine replied, pushing herself off the ground and smoothing the deep gray of her skirts—so gray they matched the thunderstorm outside.

"Practical?" Heathcliff echoed, tilting his head back and laughing maniacally.

Once, the sound of his laugh would have made her soul soar—it came so few and far between. Tonight, it made her blood run cold.

She had taken everything from Heathcliff, and now she would feel his wrath.

Catherine bit down on her wobbly bottom lip and straightened her shoulders. "Edgar can give me what you cannot."

Heathcliff's laughter ceased. He stared at her, his dark eyes burning into her soul. His chest heaved with his breaths. For the first time, Catherine noticed his shirt was wet, splattered in droplets from the rain. He must have barely made it inside before the storm began. She fought the urge to look over her shoulder and out the window when lightning flashed, illuminating the shadows of Heathcliff's face: the cut of his jaw, the deep bags beneath his eyes, the set of his frown, the endless night in his eyes.

"I would give you everything."

Heathcliff's words carried the weight of the world in them. She knew he was being sincere, that he genuinely believed he could give her anything and everything she wished for.

But that was not true.

Heathcliff was an orphan. He came from nowhere and nothing, existing outside of time and propriety. There was no real home he could offer her. He had no name for her to take as her own. Their children would be nameless, titleless.

Catherine vividly remembered the first time she realized Heathcliff would do anything for her.

They were just a pair of kids, too young to know what the world wanted or who they were meant to become. Too young to care that Heathcliff's lack of parents meant he would always be a shadow and Catherine's lack of a mother meant she needed to work harder than anyone to become someone.

Back then, they'd spent most of their time amongst the weeds and wild grass surrounding

Wuthering Heights. It was before Catherine's father had died, and before Hindley had taken it upon himself to attempt to break Heathcliff's spirit at every turn. They were younger then, perhaps brighter—as wild and unbroken as the moors they played on.

It was a Sunday after prayer service, and Catherine had wandered into the wild land in search of a family of kittens that had resided at Wuthering Heights for a while. Within moments, her boots sloshed in the mud, and her pretty yellow dress was tarnished by the earth. She was too young to care.

*"Where are you going, Miss Catherine?"* Heathcliff had asked breathlessly as he caught up to her, skidding over the wet ground.

She had jutted her chin out and placed her hands on her hips. *"There are kittens out here. I want one."*

Heathcliff had smiled, the challenge sinking deep into his bones. *"Let's find you a kitten, then,"* he'd said.

Together, they'd set off further and further into the moors, calling for the kittens all the way—oblivious to the storm clouds rolling in. And when it had begun to rain and Catherine had slipped and twisted her ankle, Heathcliff had carried her all the way back to Wuthering Heights.

The next day, as she lay in bed nursing her injury, he'd come into her room with a muddy bundle of cloth in his arms. He'd set it in her bed unceremoniously, causing Catherine to curse him for dirtying her sheets.

Until the bundle unrolled, revealing the dirtiest, angriest kitten she'd ever seen.

As the memory coursed through her, Catherine glanced at the black and white cat asleep on the rocking chair near the fire. That cat had been her constant companion for the last ten years, perhaps her only companion—aside from Heathcliff himself.

He would give her everything if he could. Catherine knew that, and she resented it because if he would just let her go, her heart wouldn't be breaking in two. Marrying Edgar would feel easy. Leaving Wuthering Heights would feel easy. If not for Heathcliff, all of this would be easy.

And yet, as she stared at him, studying the grief and anguish painting his face, she felt her heart break.

She had taken too long to respond. Heathcliff spoke again. "Marry me, Catherine."

She sucked in a breath. "No."

Agony echoed through his eyes, and his jaw twitched. "Tell me why you cannot be my wife."

Despite her pain, Catherine felt a flash of annoyance at his persistence. Why could he not understand their reality? Theirs was never going to be a happy ending. They were always going to end in heartbreak.

"I will be Lady of Thrushcross Grange," Catherine began. "I will have a husband who treats me well, a house to run, a family to have dinner with. Eventually, I will have children who will inherit the estate when I am gone."

"Do not speak of him giving you children," Heathcliff growled in disgust.

Catherine huffed. "You asked for the reasons I cannot marry you. There they are."

His eyes darkened and he stepped forward. "I could give you children, if that's what you wish."

A laugh bubbled in Catherine's chest. "Heirs, Heathcliff. You are heir to nothing. Your children will be heir to nothing. My children will not be nothing."

Something broke in Heathcliff then. Catherine watched the anger and anguish in his eyes transform into something deeper and darker—as if he finally understood.

"Is that how you think of me?" Heathcliff's voice dropped an octave, stabbing directly into Catherine's heart. "Am I nothing to you?"

Catherine could not stop her next words. "You are everything to me."

"Then, marry me!" He exploded, rushing toward her and placing his hands on either side of her face. Catherine stumbled backward, though he kept her standing. He shook her as he spoke, though—for perhaps the first time in her life—all Catherine could focus on was the warmth of his callused hands on her skin. "I would love you more in one day than Edgar could in eighty lifetimes. We are the same, you and I. We were always meant to be together."

It was true; Catherine knew it in her heart—in her soul. As much as she did not want to believe it and as much as she knew marrying Edgar to be the proper choice, she wanted Heathcliff. She had always wanted Heathcliff.

When he finally released her, Catherine sank to her knees before him. "It would degrade me to marry you," she whispered, hoping her words would strike true and end this torture once and for all. "No matter how much I wish it weren't true."

She saw it then, the moment Heathcliff broke. The moment all the desperation and longing in his eyes became nothing. She watched the moment he steeled himself from loving her—when he realized all of this was futile and he would never have Catherine the way he wanted her.

They were doomed to haunt each other for the rest of their days, without ever knowing what it was like to be truly loved.

Heathcliff took a step back, then another. Catherine felt her soul deflating with each step he took away from her, turning his body toward the door.

And she knew…

She knew, if Heathcliff made it past that doorway, she might never see him again.

She let him go.

Eventually, his steps faded down the long hallway, perhaps down the stairs. Catherine's chest heaved as she dropped to the floor. Outside, rain pattered against her windows, drowning out the sounds of the rest of the house and making her feel more alone than ever.

The realization sank into her very bones. She had pushed away the only person she had ever loved, the only person who had ever known her as she was.

It was for the best, she tried to remind herself, as sobs racked her body louder than the rolling thunder. Heathcliff could not give her a future. He could not give her a home or make her a lady. Their children would be less than they themselves were.

Their history did not matter. Their childhood together did not matter.

None of it mattered, because it was done. She was engaged to Edgar. She would marry Edgar.

Catherine pushed herself to her feet, feeling as if her legs had gone numb. She gripped the windowsill and pulled herself up as her whole body convulsed with sobs and screams. Heathcliff's departure had torn her soul in half. The pain was unlike anything she had experienced before: raw, unreal, never-ending. It ravaged every piece of her, leaving her veins to burn and her blood to dry up inside her.

Heathcliff had left.

He was gone.

Amid the raging storm, her pain was silent. Not a soul heard her scream.

She gripped the windowsill and peered out into the storm as she gasped for breath. The rain had darkened the land almost beyond recognition, and the world outside had become a thousand torrential shades of gray.

Vaguely, Catherine remembered viewing the untamed land surrounding Wuthering Heights as her kingdom. She'd spent her days frolicking through the mud and shrubbery like she was on a new adventure every day. It did not matter that her boots and dress got muddy, or if she came home with twigs in her hair.

When had her freedom become her isolation?

She stared at the hills then, feeling nothing in her chest for the grass she'd rolled in, the rocks she'd thrown, and the worlds she'd once discovered on the lands surrounding her home. Over the years, as Catherine grew up and learned the reality of what she needed to become to survive, the moors had become less and less of an adventure. They'd become her prison—miles and miles of empty, useless land cutting her off from the rest of the world.

And at the center of it all was a king of nothing.

Catherine saw him then: Heathcliff, without a coat or regard for his safety, standing on the edge of the property. His clothing was soaked, clinging to his body despite the wind rushing through the air. He stood as still as a statue, as impenetrable as iron. Even from afar, she could feel the devastation rolling off him in waves.

Catherine would marry Edgar Linton—that much was inevitable—and their union would set her free.

But just once, she wanted to know what the alternative would feel like.

Catherine's feet were moving before she fully registered what she was doing. She dashed out of her chambers and clambered down the stairs, which were slippery from the rain leaking through the roof. Twice, she almost fell. She slipped several times during her race through the kitchens and hallways on the first floor, tearing her dress and scraping her knee.

Rain pelted Catherine in the face as she threw open the door that led outside. The wind was so cold it sent a chill straight through her bones. Indeed, she could catch a chill after only a moment outside, but Catherine did not care.

If she was destined to become someone else—someone even she was not sure she would recognize—she wanted one more day, one more night, one more moment where she was Catherine Earnshaw, one more moment where she was as wild and unpredictable as the moors.

One more day. One more night. One more moment.

One last time.

She could see Heathcliff, as stoic and gray as their world—as if he were made of the moors themselves. Not an inch of his flesh or clothing moved amid the wind and rain.

Thunder roared overhead when she called his name.

Her hair became so wet that it clung to her jaw and throat as she pushed through the rain. Her skirts weighed her down and slowed her speed. Were her eyes blurry from the tears or the raindrops? She was not sure, and she did not care.

All that mattered to Catherine was reaching Heathcliff for the first and last time.

"Heathcliff!"

Her voice carried to the ghost only a dozen paces from her, and he finally moved, turning toward her with a look of bewilderment. Heathcliff closed the space between them as if it were nothing, as if Catherine had not been fighting for every step.

Heathcliff gripped her shoulders roughly. "Have you gone mad? This storm will drown you."

For a moment, Catherine could say nothing. She gaped at the force of a man above her, blinking rain out of her eyes. Her whole body quivered and her tongue tied itself into knots.

*I'm sorry*, she tried to say.

*I have to do what's best for my future*, she longed to tell him.

*I know you'll never forgive me, but please do not forget me.*

*Kiss me, Heathcliff.*

And even though Catherine couldn't manage a single word, Heathcliff knew her better than anyone.

His mouth covered hers in what would become the brightest moment of her life—the only kiss that would ever make her feel something other than obligation. Heathcliff's mouth was warm and wet, moving feverishly against hers while they clung together in the rain. Catherine thought she tasted whiskey on Heathcliff's tongue and wondered briefly if he tasted the sweets she'd eaten earlier on hers.

Any rational thoughts she might have had vanished as his hands moved from her shoulders, down her arms until they gripped her waist. Heathcliff was a large man, Catherine thought, as he tugged her against him effortlessly; he could do anything with her he wanted.

And for one night—for the first and last time—she would let him.

Catherine would take this night with her to the grave. She and Heathcliff would be the only two souls who knew what was about to happen between them, and it was inevitable that he would leave Wuthering Heights. He would take their secret with him, and Catherine would bury it so deep in her chest that not even her death would uncover it.

She did not need to tell Heathcliff any of this. He knew. He knew just as deeply as she did that this moment—however much of it he decided to take—was all they could ever have.

They could not go back inside. Somewhere in the shadows of the home they'd grown up in waited Catherine's brother, who was desperate for any reason to get rid of Heathcliff. And if Hindley did not see them, Nelly would, and Nelly was the worst gossip of them all.

Catherine began to panic as Heathcliff's tongue explored her mouth. What if this kiss was all they could ever have? What if she never truly knew what it felt like to have Heathcliff's hands on her body and soul?

As if buried in her mind, Heathcliff wrenched his mouth from Catherine's long enough to grab her hands and bring them to his lips. Their eyes met in an eternal understanding for the briefest of moments before Heathcliff scooped her off the ground. Catherine felt weightless in his arms, watching rain drizzle down his face—memorizing every crevice and mark on his skin.

It felt like only a blink of time before the rain was outside and they were ducking inside the barn. Heathcliff set her down haphazardly, pulling the doors shut in a rush.

"Are you sure—" Catherine started.

"No one will find us here," Heathcliff assured her, taking her hand and helping her up the stairs and into the loft.

Catherine resisted the urge to wrinkle her nose at the straw and hay coating the ground and the stench of livestock permeating the air. Rain leaked through the wooden roof in several places, and she dodged puddles while following Heathcliff to the darkest corner.

There, she was surprised to find a small, makeshift bed.

Reality sank into Catherine as she took in the tattered sheets, old pillows, and pitiful stacks of belongings: two books, half water-damaged, a spare pair of boots with holes in the soles, and a trunk the size of a shoebox that must have contained clothing.

She had never seen where he slept before. She had never even thought to ask.

This was Heathcliff's life outside of Catherine. This was what she was leaving him to by choosing to marry Edgar.

A sob built in her throat, and she spun toward Heathcliff with a thousand apologies on her tongue. He would not hear them. His mouth crashed against hers, and he gripped either side of her face with all the passion he was capable of. Catherine let him do as he wished with her, committing every movement to memory. She promised to remember the way he nipped at her bottom lip and the way he sucked on her jaw and throat. She memorized the swipe of his tongue against hers and the scrape of his stubble against her cheeks.

He was everything she could never truly have.

But she would give herself this.

When he laid her back on his bed, she did not complain about the straw digging into her skin. Instead, she kissed down his jaw and flicked her tongue against his lips. When his hands moved to her corset, she sat up and let him undo every string. He undressed her delicately, folding and laying her clothes on a dry patch of hay.

Only when she was fully naked in front of him did he stop to look. Catherine shivered on the bed, jumping when thunder shook the barn, but she did not shy away from Heathcliff's gaze. She let him memorize her, his eyes dragging over every curve of her flesh. It caught at the apex of her thighs, and Catherine's body tensed at the implication.

She remembered a book she had read once, a long time ago. She'd stolen it from her mother's library and pored over the words and images throughout it—images detailing sinful and disgraceful things. As she thought about them then, all she could think was how she wanted Heathcliff to do all those dark things to her.

Ever so slowly, Catherine spread her legs.

Heathcliff worshiped every inch of her, providing pleasure unlike anything Catherine had ever experienced. His lips created art across her skin, and his hands brought a symphony out of her. She lay beneath him, the sound of the storm drowning out any gasps or cries that escaped her.

When their bodies finally connected, Catherine knew there was no moment more right than that one. Heathcliff claimed her body and soul as his own, tarnishing her future. There would never be a moment like that again. Her future husband could not give her that. All the money and security in the world could not give her that.

There was only Heathcliff.

There would always only be Heathcliff.

When it was over, they lay beside each other, listening to the softening storm. Rain still pattered on the barn's roof, but the torrential downpour had ended. Catherine had never felt more alive and yet exhausted in the same instance. She fought to keep her eyes open, startling at the soft thunder in the distance. Lightning lit up the dark just long enough for Catherine to see the ghost of a smile on Heathcliff's face, gone as quickly as it appeared.

"Do you regret it?" he asked her, his voice barely a whisper.

"No," she replied into the dark. "I vow I never will."

Heathcliff drew in a breath. "Don't marry him."

Unlike before, there was no malice in his voice. No desperation. He sounded tired, like he had given up his fight.

Catherine did not have any fight left in her, either. "I have to," she whispered.

Beside her, Heathcliff rolled onto his back and stared up at the ceiling. "I wish I could give you everything, Catherine. I would pull the stars from the sky for you. I would give you the grandest home in England and all the children you could ever want to fill it with." Catherine blushed at his words, tears forming in her eyes. "I would keep you safe, and you could still be Catherine."

She tilted her head toward him. "I will always be Catherine."

He shook his head. "No, you will become Lady of Thrushcross Grange. You will have children and responsibilities, everything you ever wanted. Your boots will never be muddy, your skirts never soiled. You will not search for treasure among the wildflowers ever again. You will never find love amid the thunderstorms."

Catherine drew in a shaking breath. She could not argue with him, because he was right. She had chosen to marry Edgar and give up the side of herself only Heathcliff had ever known—the part of her he loved so dearly. When she was married, she would become someone else entirely. Someone unrecognizable.

"It's the life I want," she breathed, unsure whether she was convincing herself or him.

It was so much easier before she knew what it was like to be touched by him, loved by him. Hours ago, Heathcliff had been a distant impossibility, something she could never truly have. And now she'd had him… and everything was different. She felt homesick for a life she had not yet left behind.

"I'm leaving Wuthering Heights," Heathcliff said. She opened her mouth to protest, but he continued. "It is not my home without you here."

"Where will you go?" she dared to ask.

"Somewhere I can forget you."

Catherine's bottom lip quivered, and her breath trembled as she drew it in. Hours ago, she would have begged him never to forget her, but it seemed forgetting might be the easier option after what they'd done.

"Perhaps in another life," she whispered, unable to finish her thought.

Heathcliff kissed her shoulder, rolling to pull the blanket over them. "Perhaps," he agreed. He kissed a tear off her cheek and then her mouth for the last time. "Sleep, Catherine. I will keep you safe."

Catherine let her eyes fall closed.

~

When she woke, sunlight streamed through cracks in the wooden roof. Catherine blinked a few times as images from the night before flooded her mind. Memories of staring up at a beautiful man as he made her his, of claiming Heathcliff as her own. She drew in a breath, an unfamiliar soreness echoing through her entire body. Slowly, she dragged her hand up her bare stomach, over the curves of her breasts, and up her throat. Finally, she touched her lips, which burned for a kiss she knew she would never feel again.

The realization crashed into Catherine in the same instant she recognized she was alone. She jolted upright, tears welling in her eyes as she looked around the barn loft.

Where the books had been the night before, there was only dust. Where the boots had sat, there was nothing. The trunk was gone. The only blanket remaining was the thin one covering her torso; the others were gone.

It was as if Heathcliff had never been there at all.

Grief slammed into Catherine, and she clawed at her chest as if she could rip her heart out of its cage. Her sobs were as silent and unending as her pain.

He was gone, and he had taken every bright part of her with him. He had stolen her love, her light, her longing for adventure. Her laughter would ring in only his ears. Her touch was burned into only his skin.

Behind, he had left only a shell.

He had left the Lady of Thrushcross Grange—the future Catherine Linton.

Catherine dressed slowly, searching every shadow and corner for a hint of the ghost that no longer haunted Wuthering Heights.

She hoped he would forget her. She wished every piece of Catherine Earnshaw would die within Heathcliff long before he did. If she could not give him peace, he deserved that much.

Meanwhile, he would haunt her every breath. Every sunrise and sunset would be tainted by the reality that she had chosen a life without half of her soul. She would remember, with each child she bore, that none of them belonged to her star-crossed lover. Her house would be lonely without him inside it. Along with the ghost of who she had once been, Heathcliff's phantom would walk beside her every moment for the rest of her life.

That was the choice she had made.

Catherine's boots sank into the mud on her walk back to the estate. She cursed herself for tracking it into the house; it had been years since she'd made such a mess.

"Miss Catherine, where have you been?" Nelly rushed around the corner then, a flurry of skirts and waving arms.

Catherine drew in a deep breath, transforming herself into the Catherine everyone expected her to be. Never again would she be wild, feral Catherine Earnshaw. She was a lady: a member of proper society.

She gave Nelly the gentlest of smiles. "The sunrises are so beautiful after it rains. I wanted to see for myself."

Nelly frowned and stared at the ground. "You have brought mud inside."

Catherine stepped out of her boots. "It will not happen again."

Nelly eyed her for a moment longer. "You do not seem like yourself this morning, Miss Catherine."

She waved the older woman away. "Nonsense, I have never been more myself."

Catherine started down the hall, desperate to be through with this conversation. There was much to be done. She had a wedding to plan. Eventually, she would move to Thrushcross Grange, so she would need her belongings gathered. There was no better day than today to begin.

Before she could turn the corner, Nelly called after her again. "Have you seen Heathcliff? I could use his help bringing firewood inside."

Catherine turned and straightened her shoulders. She felt absolutely nothing when she spoke. "No. I do not know where Heathcliff is."

# Emerald Shadows

## by Kaitlyn L. Hill

**Literary World**: The Hunchback of Notre-Dame

In the shadowy streets of a noir city, Detective Quinn is a seasoned investigator grappling with a troubled past and a corrupt mentor, Captain Lowe. Quinn's loyalty to Lowe, who once saved him from a life of crime, is tested when he crosses paths with Esme Ralston, a captivating dancer wrongfully accused of a series of murders. As Quinn delves deeper into the investigation, he uncovers Lowe's dark obsession with Esme and the sinister lengths he'll go to maintain control. Torn between loyalty and justice, Quinn must confront his own demons and expose the truth, risking everything to protect Esme and bring down Lowe's reign of terror. The lines between right and wrong blur as the city's hidden secrets unravel in this gripping noir thriller retelling.

***Content Warnings***. *suggestion of sexual assault*

Esme Ralston walked into my life like a haunting melody. A dangerous blend of beauty and defiance capable of bringing any man to his knees. Her emerald eyes held secrets as deep as the city's shadows, and every graceful move whispered promises and threats in equal measure. A siren in silk, her voice a husky tune that lingered in a smoke-filled room long after she was gone. In a world of black and white, she embodied every shade of grey. A mystery wrapped in allure. And now, I found myself hopelessly ensnared in her dangerous dance.

I sat across from her, the old rusty lamp above us still swaying from where my giant head had collided with it. It rang like a cathedral bell on holy days. But today lacked any sanctity. The swaying illuminated Miss Ralston's face harshly before receding into darkness. But the shine never left her eyes. That green spark mixed with defiance and vulnerability refused to dim no matter how hard I pressed her.

The night had long settled into its deepest hours when the city's sins festered and thrived. Rain hammered against the windows like a relentless confession. Each drop served as a reminder of the grime and decay seeping through every crack of this damned city. The neon lights outside flickered weakly, struggling to pierce the veil of darkness and storm. My trench coat, draped behind my chair, remained drenched. It clung to me like the weight of every unsolved case. The air, thick with the scent of wet asphalt and despair, mixed with the distant hum of a world that never truly slept.

Inside, the station offered some sanctuary, its fluorescent lights buzzing a harsh contrast to the world outside. But even here, the shadows lurked, hiding truths that no one wanted to confront.

I leaned forward and rested my elbows on the cold metal table, trying to project an air of confidence and control. The clock ticked on, each second dragging me further into the abyss of another sleepless night. "Miss Ralston—"

"We've been at it for hours, Detective. We've learned a lot about each other. You may as well call me by my first name." The huskiness of her subtle, cosmopolitan accent added tension between the dingy walls of the interrogation room.

My cellphone rang shrilly—an unexpected intrusion. I ignored it, but the persistent ringing grew louder. With my jaw tightening, I continued. "*Esme*, this recent evidence is something that could either exonerate you or bury you deeper. It all depends on what you have to say."

*Lies.* The evidence didn't exist, but I'd do anything to help Captain Lowe solve this case—even lie. Morality was a fickle beast that danced just out of reach. I'd always thought I understood the difference between right and wrong, justice and vengeance. But in this city, those lines blurred until they were indistinguishable. And as I interrogated Esme, the weight of those blurred lines pressed down on me. Was I any better than the criminals I hunted, using lies and deceit to extract the truth? Or was I just another lost soul, navigating a labyrinth of moral ambiguity? The rain outside constantly reminded me of the cleansing I sought but never found. And as I watched my suspect, I began to wonder if the answers didn't lie in the law, but somewhere else…

Lowe insisted she'd committed a string of killings in the slums. A horrid place woven into a labyrinth of alleyways and hidden doors, where secrets were traded like currency and the desperate sought miracles. "Tell me about the Court of Miracles," I urged.

Esme's stare hardened. "What's there to say? It's a place where people like me learn to survive. My parents had a deli shop there. Immigrants, like most others. They worked hard to give me a chance. But dancing was my escape from the grime. It brought me to places they could never imagine."

Through questioning the neighbourhood, I had learned they were good people, and that Esme was as colourful and complex as the dance routines that had made her a star. Her talent as a dancer took her to the highest circles of society—a miracle.

Each and every victim was a past lover of hers, and Lowe believed the men were preparing to reveal dark secrets from her past to ruin her career and reputation. Fair. We all had dark secrets we wanted to keep hidden. I would have probably killed to keep mine a secret, too.

A cigarette hung limply between the dancer's full, rosy lips as the faint sound of footsteps echoed in the hallway outside, drawing nearer. Esme and I both tensed, waiting for the door to burst open at any moment. But no one came through. They simply continued past, fading into the distance. The precinct stood nearly empty, but the odd lieutenant lingered around.

Esme returned her attention to her cigarette, struggling with her beautifully sleek silver lighter. As I watched her lipstick stain the butt of the cigarette, a craving washed over my mouth, and I reached for the pack of smokes tucked into my shirt pocket. *Empty.* Before disappointment could crawl through me, a cigarette appeared in front of me, poised between two delicate fingers, perfectly manicured. The harsh illumination of the interrogation room highlighted it like a gift from the heavens.

Lighting Esme's cigarette, I chose to be as blunt as possible. "Lowe thinks you're guilty. I think he's right." She took a long, relaxed drag and exhaled. The smoke curled through the air, enveloping her features. But even the haze couldn't mask the spark in her eyes. They resembled jewels, flecked with gold, holding a wealth of information. Information about the murders, I hoped, as a chill from the cracked window spilled in, mingling with the acrid scent of burnt tobacco.

She studied me just as intently as I studied her. She slid her fingers across her plump bottom lip as the haze moved lazily, creating unique patterns. Her lips curved into a knowing, almost deviant smirk. One I had become very familiar with in the past few hours of interrogation.

"Or maybe he just can't stand that I'm beyond his reach." My gaze held hers, trying to read the secrets she kept hidden behind that smirk. Riddles. She'd been speaking in little riddles the entire time. Sharing enough for me to question her guilt, but not enough to be certain of her innocence. Though something in my gut insisted Lowe had missed something. That the famous dancer wasn't the murderer. The longer we talked, the more I suspected she at least knew...something. "Come on. You don't really believe I'm a killer, do you?"

*Maybe.*

Each victim was male. Aged between twenty-five and thirty-seven. Some were born and raised in the slums, never getting out. Others were affluent men who lost everything and fell into addiction with nowhere else to go. Whether it was a one-night stand, a fling, or a serious relationship, each had seen Esme within their last day alive.

I replied, my voice soft, but laced with a dangerous edge, "The evidence I have…it's compelling. It ties you to each scene and places you in a very precarious position. Care to explain why your name keeps popping up?" My focus darted to the two-way mirror behind her.

"He's back there, isn't he?" The smoke danced between us like a silent challenge.

She meant Lowe. And no. He wasn't. No one was back there at this late hour. Only my scarred face stared back at me. My shoulders hunched over, reminding me to straighten my posture. It proved difficult when exhausted and growing frustrated.

Esme leaned back, the chair creaking under her shifting weight, and crossed her legs—the movement fluid and deliberate, drawing my eyes despite myself. Each subtle shift of her body told a story of survival and grace. "Besides, do you really think I'd be that careless, Quinn? Leaving a trail for you and your puppeteer to follow?"

Her words hit like a slap. But I kept my composure, the flicker of doubt gnawing at the edges of my resolve. Esme's attention shifted to my chest, where I had undone the top button of my white shirt. I adjusted the collar to cover the jagged scar that snaked down my neck. A constant reminder of the fights I'd barely survived.

Each mark on my body told a story, a testament to battles fought and demons faced. But the most wicked scars were the ones that couldn't be seen. Nights spent drowning in whiskey, trying to forget the faces of those I couldn't save. The city had a way of getting under your skin, seeping into your soul until you couldn't tell where you ended and the darkness began. I'd sacrificed relationships, my own sanity, all for the badge I wore. But now, with every drag of her cigarette, I felt a pull—a reminder that maybe, just maybe, there was more to life than this relentless pursuit of justice. But I needed the truth.

"Lowe isn't the one on trial here. You are. And your connection to the victims…it's more than coincidental. Each one of them, former lovers, dead. All roads lead back to you."

Esme's expression hardened, the playful glint in her. eyes replaced by a cold determination. "You're right. All roads do lead back to me. Maybe someone is making sure they do. Someone who can't stand the idea that I rejected them." Her jaw clenched tighter and tighter as she spoke freely, her pitch dipping into a low snarl.

I frowned, my mind racing to keep up with the implications of her words. Or should I say the missing words *between* what she spoke? "What are you saying?" I grew tired of her riddles.

The fluorescent glow revealed a flicker of panic in her green irises. She instantly regretted revealing her vulnerability. "It's late, Detective Quinn. We both know the late hours well, but I'm tired. Physically, mentally, and of this conversation. Might we continue another time?" She snuffed out the cigarette on the metal table, leaving it upright amidst a pile of ashes.

"I'm afraid not."

"If I'm not under arrest, *I'm afraid* you can't detain me." She had a point. I couldn't. But I also couldn't disappoint Lowe. If he came into the station tomorrow morning and I had nothing to show, he'd be furious. Another strike against me. He'd been growing impatient with me for quite some time now.

"Esme—"

"Quinn…" Her lips curved into that deviant smirk, sending an unwelcome pulse through me. She stood, the metal chair screeching against the stone floor. "I'm leaving. Please have an officer escort me to my penthouse."

She certainly did climb the social ladder. But… "You want an escort?"

The smirk faded. "Yes. Please."

My brows furrowed as panic returned to her face. "Who are you afraid of, Esme? Who's making all roads lead back to you?"

Esme ran a delicate hand through her luscious brown curls. They fell around her heart-shaped face as she sighed out of frustration and exhaustion, I assumed. "It's none of your—"

"Sit. Down. Miss. Ralston." I enunciated each word. Sternly. She paused, taking me in. Studied me more intently than before. I was no longer a joke to her. This interrogation struck a personal chord. "I won't ask again." And she did. She returned to her seat, and a gleam shone beneath her eyelids. Fear.

"If you truly believe you're being set up, you need to give me a name. You're clearly afraid of someone. I can help you."

"Help me?" She snapped back at me quicker than an asp. "You cops all think you're holier-than-thou. But you're all pigs." She spat on the ground, revealing a less composed side of her.

"You can trust me."

Esme's composure stiffened. She straightened her spine and pushed her shoulders back, as if preparing for a performance. "Lowe, your captain, don't you think it's odd how things always seem to work out in his favour?"

My heart pounded in my chest, each beat reflecting the growing conflict within me. The man I had idolised, the father figure who shaped my career...

"What are you insinuating?" I shook my head, more to clear the fog of doubt than to refute her words.

Esme's expression softened, the vulnerability creeping back in, tempered by a steely resolve. "You're loyal to him. But Lowe is using you, just like he's used...me. And everyone else he encounters. You need to open your eyes before it's too late."

"Used you?" *What did she mean?*"You suggest you know Lowe...well."

Esme snorted and crossed her arms, accentuating the cleavage of her low neckline.

"I can't help you if you don't tell me."

With a resentful swallow, she leaned forward, her tearful eyes locking onto mine. The intensity of her presence searing through the smoke and shadows. "Do you know why I became a dancer, Quinn?" I kept silent. "When you're a child growing up in the Court of Miracles, the entire world is full of colour. Boisterous life and excitement. Everyone you meet is unique and foreign. But eventually, the Court loses its colour. You realise it's not life people are filled with, but heroin and cocaine. When that day came for me, I sought refuge in the old theatre. You know the one."

"The Eclipse Theatre."

"Yes. I'd explore, run up and down the abandoned rows, draw shapes on the dusty velvet seats, and dance on that stage. It became a sanctuary of my own making. Somewhere the world outside couldn't touch me."

"They bulldozed that place a few summers ago."

"Yes. And the only other place I feel that same sense of peace is on stage, dancing."

"What does this have to do with Lowe?"

"Lowe stole that from me. He stole my sense of peace on the stage."

I leaned in, curiosity piqued. "How did he do that?"

Esme's eyes flickered with pain. "He found a way to control me, to keep me under his thumb.

Every performance, every step I took on that stage. He was there, pulling the strings. Making sure I never felt free. And now, I can't escape the demons anymore."

My thoughts drifted to the gargoyles atop the precinct. Those grotesque stone sentinels perched high above, their unblinking eyes forever watching. In the flickering streetlights, their twisted forms cast haunting shadows, mocking the despair and darkness within these walls. To her, they weren't mere decorations but embodiments of her demons. The ones that haunted every corner of this godforsaken place, especially those who sought justice.

"Esme, what are you saying?"

"It doesn't matter. Please find me an escort, unless you'd like to do it yourself." She rummaged through her designer bag, as if confirming all the contents were accounted for. I couldn't just let her walk away from me, not when I knew she was on the verge of breaking. Esme wanted to leave because she was struggling to hold herself together. For every little bit of her that got under my skin, I was getting under hers, too.

"You want an escort home, Miss Ralston?"

An annoyed sigh rolled up her throat and slipped through slightly parted lips as she roughly dropped her purse on the table.

"Then give me *something* to work with. I can protect you. I can help you. But in order to do so, I need you to help me." The words tumbled out as a plea, betraying the authority I intended.

Esme's lips pressed into a thin line as she glanced away, her fingers tightening into fists on her lap. Silence lingered between us, heavy with unspoken words. She shifted in her seat, jaw clenched, as if weighing the risk of saying too much. Her gaze flickered to the door, then back to me, conflicted. I could see the struggle within her—the fight between her instinct to shut down and the need to share the truth.

Finally, she exhaled, her voice trembling at first. "I'm saying that your Captain Lowe is obsessed. Obsessed with me, with control. He's the one manipulating the investigation and framing me for his own twisted reasons."

My pulse raced. I wanted to close the gap between us and insist she was wrong. Yet, I recalled the look in Lowe's eyes when Esme first waltzed into the precinct. How they burned with an intensity that made my skin crawl. I felt as though I already knew the sinister answer, but I asked anyway, "Why would Lowe frame you?"

She scoffed with a sarcastic laugh and leaned back. Her leg swayed with frustration. Esme was uncomfortable. She didn't want to share that part of her story with me. She didn't want to share any of this with me. Never meant to.

Lowe was the kind of man who filled a room with his presence, a mentor who carved me out of raw ambition and street-smart instincts. He'd molded me, shaped me into a weapon against the chaos of this city. But I couldn't shake the feeling that Esme was right. Somewhere along the way, he had crossed a line—a line dividing justice from obsession. I'd watched him manipulate evidence, bend the law to his will, all in the name of the greater good. Like with the evidence we claimed existed against Esme, but didn't. Each time, I'd turned a blind eye, telling myself it was for the best. But now, staring at the dancer, I wondered if I had become complicit in something far darker than I had ever imagined. Was I still an instrument of justice, or just another puppet of Lowe's, as she suggested?

"If what you're saying is true, then why haven't you gone to the authorities? Why haven't you exposed him?"

She laughed, a bitter sound reverberating off the icy walls. "The authorities? The ones he controls? As I've said, Lowe's reach goes deeper than you can imagine. He has judges, politicians, even some of the press in his pocket. Remember Detective Harris? He was investigating Lowe, and now he's in a mental institution, raving about conspiracies. The only way to bring him down is from the inside. But none of you can be trusted."

"Trust *me*, Esme," I pleaded.

She scoffed and rolled her eyes, pulling another cigarette from the tiled case she held them in, understanding she wasn't leaving anytime soon. "Why should I? I read the papers. Watch the news. I understand exactly who you are to him. You're the least trustworthy."

"Trust me, because I'm desperate to solve this case. I don't make arrests that suit my agenda or Lowe's. I make arrests based on evidence."

"I'm sure that's what Lowe has led you to believe."

"Enough!" I slammed my fist on the table, the metal ringing echoed off the concrete walls. Esme flinched, pulling back from my outburst. I quickly recomposed myself. "I'm sorry. Look, it's true. I crave Lowe's approval. How could I not? He's like a father to me." *Why was I sharing this with her?* "I'll do a lot for his approval. But I'll *never* send an innocent person to jail for him. I still have my morals, Esme."

Taking a thoughtful drag on the cigarette, she studied me, as if searching for my soul. To determine for herself if my morals were as honourable as I insisted. She scanned my face, covered in scars from my troubled youth. As she did so, each scar burned. As if the power of her gaze was opening each to reveal the stories behind them. After what felt like another hour, the panic and fear in her eyes shifted into something hopeful.

"Then help me take him down."

Her words hung in the air, the weight of her plea sinking into the pit of my stomach. I had spent my life fighting for justice, upholding the law, but I approached a crossroads—torn between my duty and the dark truths unravelling before me. This precinct was my fortress. Each corridor a well-trodden path. Every corner echoed with memories of battles fought and lost. Yet the gloom on the walls seemed to shift, morphing into grotesque shapes that whispered of betrayal and deceit.

I took a deep breath, the acrid taste of cigarettes heavy on my tongue. Moments ago, I'd insisted my morality was more important than my loyalty to Lowe. But now that she'd blatantly asked me to betray him, my gut twisted. My voice trembled with the weight of the words, my knuckles white as I gripped the edge of the table. The memory of Lowe's firm hand on my shoulder, guiding me through that first case, flooded back, clashing with the image of pleading eyes in front of me. "You're asking me to betray the man who gave me everything? The man who made me who I am."

Esme's glower softened, her expression tinged with empathy. "Sometimes, Detective, it feels like we're all just ringing bells in a tower, hoping someone will hear our call. You asked for my cooperation. You asked for the truth, Quinn. This is it. I'm asking you to see that. To see Lowe for what he really is. And to help me stop him before he destroys more lives."

The room closed in, the flickering light casting long, sinister shadows dancing along with the turmoil in my mind. I felt trapped. Bound to a life of darkness and isolation. The precinct was my cathedral, a fortress where I sought refuge from a world that had never understood me. As the Eclipse was for Esme. If I sided with her, I risked not only my career but my life. Lowe wasn't just a mentor, he wielded power and connections. The thought of his wrath sent a shiver down my spine. Yet the idea of condemning an innocent woman was a weight I couldn't bear.

Midnight struck and the city's bells tolled in unison—we had a few more hours alone. I stubbed out my cigarette, the ember dying with a final hiss, my resolve hardening. "Alright, Esme. I'll help you. But you need to tell me everything. No more secrets. No more riddles."

A flicker of relief crossed her face, quickly replaced by a fierce determination. "I'll tell you everything I know, Quinn. Together, we can make this right."

I nodded, feeling the weight of our unspoken agreement. The path ahead would be long and treacherous, but with this brave woman by my side, I felt a spark of hope. The truth would surface, and justice would prevail. But first, we had to navigate the dangerous web of deceit that Lowe had potentially spun, each step fraught with peril and uncertainty.

"Is it safe to talk here?" She peeked over a slender shoulder at the mirror, her unease palpable. Esme was right about Lowe. He had eyes and ears everywhere. Out of all the rundown bars and dark alleyways, damn, even my own dingy apartment, this was the one place I knew he hadn't bugged. Lowe would never suspect betrayal right here in his own precinct.

The lights flickered, plunging us into darkness for a brief, heart-stopping moment before they buzzed back to life. Esme's sharp intake of breath broke the silence.

"Yeah, Esme, this is the safest place we've got." I reassured her, though the ticking clock seemed to mock us, each second a reminder that our time was running out.

Esme leaned in, her voice dropping to a conspiratorial whisper as she began explaining her connection to the first victim. We both settled in for the long hours ahead, just the two of us. The fog of cigarettes lingered like the ghosts of our secrets. The shadows lurking at the edges. But now, I had a beacon to guide me. And together, we could face whatever darkness lay ahead.

# Sweet Sorrow

## by Allie Sarah

**Literary World**: Romeo & Juliet

These violent delights have violent beginnings, and family rivalries are no exception, in this prequel. Isabel Ricci gets her first taste of desire when Matteo Capulet shows up at her balcony one night. Her betrothed is away, and Matteo wants nothing more than to win her heart for himself. But a marriage into the Montague family offers nothing but advantages, and Isabel has been taught to place her family above her feelings.

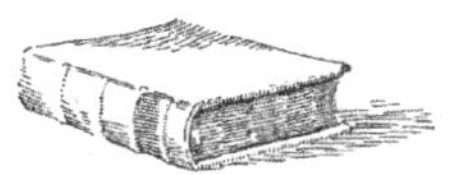

The first pebbles that struck Isabel Ricci's window were unexpected, to say the least. She had been lying on her bed, attempting to read the bore her mother called an etiquette book. Dressed in her nightgown, she had not expected any company at this late hour, let alone a visitor attempting to enter through the balcony.

Isabel glanced curiously at the window before standing and fetching a cloak from her wardrobe. The only visitor she usually received was her sister, who lived in a large townhouse down the block with her husband and twin sons, Mercutio and Valentine. Chiara visited often, but never late at night. With two babies, sleep was both rare and precious.

Isabel crept along the wall as more pebbles sounded against the glass. Was the visitor standing on her balcony, or did they have excellent aim from the courtyard? And was she really about to go outside, dressed in her nightclothes, with no idea whether her mysterious visitor was friend or foe? It would be scandalous if she was caught out at nighttime – shame brought upon her family.

"Matteo!" She gasped upon poking her head through the curtains, spotting the dark-haired boy instantly. Matteo Capulet, a handsome young man she'd daydreamed about more than once, was standing beside her window, currently in the process of scooping up rocks from the gravel.

"Isabel!" Matteo's face lit up as she came into view, a boyish grin taking over his incredibly charming face. It was hard not to be attracted to him, a feat which every single lady who attended tea often failed at. Even Isabel, who had been promised in marriage since birth, caught herself sneaking glimpses at him.

Isabel yanked open the door and rushed onto the balcony, wrapping the cloak around herself tightly. "What are you doing here?" she hissed. "It is the middle of the night!"

"Well, of course it is," Matteo said matter-of-factly. "Do you think I would be here in broad daylight?"

Isabel rolled her eyes, unable to hide her smirk. "What are you doing here at all? Did we not agree to pretend we were not friends?"

Matteo's face fell. "Isabel, I cannot keep doing that," he pleaded. "It breaks my heart to have to ignore you each day. I want to sit by you, admire you across the table, and walk along the pier in the afternoons…"

"No," Isabel cut him off firmly. "You know the rules."

Matteo swallowed and bowed his head. Isabel crossed her arms, hating how this boy had such a pull on her. She had been perfectly happy to be engaged to Damien Montague, planning the wedding that was to happen at the end of the calendar year – shortly after her eighteenth birthday. But then, the Capulets had moved to town and Matteo had begun attending daily socials with the other young lords and ladies their age. Damien, a year older, was off on his travels, meaning there had been no protective lord sitting by Isabel each day.

"I agreed to the rules back when we did not know each other," he argued softly, his voice barely carrying with the evening wind. "I know you now, Isabel. I want to know you more."

"I am engaged!" Isabel exclaimed, the words coming out louder than she intended. "My betrothed will return any day. He is not someone to be messed with, Matteo. The Montagues are a very powerful family."

Matteo's glare hardened. "So, because we have only just moved to Verona, my family has no power here? If it is power you seek, I can give it to you. I will give everything to you, my dear Isabel. We are a very influential family abroad."

Isabel's shoulders sagged, feeling the weight of the world upon them. Her family was counting on this union to restore their dying reputation: to ensure Isabel would live a grander life than the one she currently had. While the Ricci name was not something to be scoffed at, their finances were certainly not what they had been years ago. The Montagues had been eager to arrange a match with Isabel's father, who controlled a large shipping port in northern Italy. Once she and Damien were wed, her family would receive enough gold to ensure Chiara and her sons would be well taken care of, and that their parents could live comfortably for the rest of their lives. In addition, the status boost from marrying into the Montague family was incomparable.

"Power is not what I want, but what I need. My family is here, both current and future. Do you understand, Matteo?"

Matteo was silent for a moment, until he finally said, "May I come up?"

Isabel gaped at him. *He did not mean to enter her chambers, did he?* The sacred space no man dared to even approach – not even her father?

"Pardon?"

"Up," Matteo repeated, moving towards the wall. As Isabel watched, he grabbed hold of the ivy vines and lifted himself a few feet from the ground effortlessly. It did not take him long to scale the four stories and drop himself onto Isabel's balcony, landing a few feet away from her with an enormous grin. "Hi, Isa."

"That is not my name," she said primly before turning around and returning to her bedroom. She made sure to shut the balcony door behind her, but that did not slow Matteo down for a minute.

"It has been six months, *Isabel*, and you still will not hold a conversation with me in public," Matteo argued, pulling the door open and following her into the room. "Wow, this carpet is incredibly soft. What is it made of?"

Her lips curled up. "The engagement bonus my family received from signing the betrothal contract last year."

Along with the giant diamond ring on her left ring finger, the Montagues had handed over a pile of gold when a newly sixteen-year-old Isabel had formally signed the engagement announcement to let the rest of the town know about their betrothal. She and Damien had been informally engaged for years, but rumour became fact even though the ink was barely dry on the parchment.

"You know, my family ran a sheep farm a few generations ago," Matteo pointed out. "All the wool carpets we could ever dream of."

She cast a dismissive glance at him, her breath catching at the sight of his eager gaze. It would be all too easy for her to fall for Matteo Capulet – but alas, she was engaged to a man she had not seen in months. Damien had never been particularly interested in spending much time with her, preferring to lounge in her father's study and discuss business instead. Would marriage be like that with him: long days of waiting for him to join her for dinner and then retiring to separate rooms? She did not want to emulate her parents, but despite visions of romantic walks and hours of entertainment spent with Matteo, Isabel's future was set in stone.

"Do you remember the first words I spoke to you?" she asked abruptly, turning away from him. *Spoke*, because she had seen Matteo walking along the promenade for days, always accompanied by one of his two sisters. They had exchanged formal nods and polite greetings, but it was not until Matteo had appeared at social hour that they had begun to converse.

"You told me you were engaged, and that I would be better off wooing other ladies," he replied.

"And the situation has not changed since then."

"Nor has my response. Do *you* remember, Isabel?" When she did not answer, choosing instead to stare out at the inky sky, footsteps sounded behind her. Matteo's next words might have been low in volume, but he was so close Isabel shivered at every breath he took. "Do you remember what I said?"

"You...you told me star-crossed lovers make the best friends," she said in a shaky voice. Because she could never forget; could never wipe that mischievous grin out of her mind. Matteo had laughed, and a part of her had fallen for him in that moment, before he had sat down at her table and promptly declared the two to be best friends.

All that they had been...and all they ever could be.

Matteo sighed heavily. "I swear on my family name, Isa, I had never intended for things to go this way. But the heart has its own desires, and who am I to deny them? You are a magnificent woman. I cannot say I have ever met anyone as wonderful as you. My day is brightened whenever you are near, and if I am feeling troubled, I know even being in your proximity will lessen my worries. You are my sun, and as with any mere mortal, I cannot help but seek out glimpses – despite knowing the pain it will cause me."

Isabel swallowed, heat flushing through her face at his words. She did not want to admit how he affected her: how her pulse beat more quickly when he was near, or how a mere glance would send tingles through her body. And his words...no one had ever spoken to her with such kindness or such devotion as Matteo had in his eyes right now. Damien had certainly never admired her for her wit and personality: he merely complimented her on her outer beauty.

Still...Isabel's gaze travelled across her room to where a family portrait held a place of pride on her wall. It had been painted mere months ago, after Chiara's twins had been born. In the portrait, Isabel sat between her parents, her mother gazing lovingly at her younger daughter and her father's hand proudly resting on her shoulder. To run off with Matteo would be betraying her parents – her family. It would mean giving up afternoons spent giggling with Chiara, hours upon hours spent in the library with her mother, and even the rare evenings her father would join her by the fireplace to discuss geography and literature and other assorted matters. And as much as her heart sang for Matteo Capulet, that was not a price Isabel was willing to pay.

"You may ask me once again," Isabel said quietly, "but I must request you respect my decision."

Matteo cleared his throat. "Will I get the honour of your gaze, at least, while you reject me once more?"

Isabel lowered her head briefly, surprised at the tears welling in her eyes. It seemed both of them knew how their conversation would conclude, yet were willing to see it through. But if she could not give Matteo all of her, as they both desired, she could at least grant him this one wish.

Isabel lifted her chin, staring directly at his deep blue eyes. Regret and sadness — but also adoration, despite the sombre moment — were reflected back at her, and she could not tell which of them the emotions belonged to. "Ask, Matteo."

"Defy the stars with me, Isabel." His voice was soft, but spoke volumes. "Marry me."

The words choked in her throat, and all Isabel could do was stare at him helplessly. She wanted to scream *yes*, to sing with delight of her love for him. The stars meant nothing when faced with his sparkling eyes, so full of hope and desire she could hardly stand to look at them. "I cannot," she whispered, a single tear falling down her cheek.

Matteo nodded silently. "I wish you best of luck with your betrothed," he said after a few moments. "I will not bother you any longer, as I can no longer be content with mere friendship. I respect your decision – but from this day forth, I will have nothing to do with a Montague, for the pain it will cause me will only multiply tenfold."

"Matt—" Isabel tried to say, but he held up a hand.

"Nor will my children interact with any of yours – and I will educate them from birth of the consequences of falling in love with a Montague." He levelled a solemn glare at her, all the joy wiped from his face. "I have learned not to waste my love on somebody who does not value it, and it is a lesson I will pass on for generations. I could never despise you, but I despise your choice, and your family, and the family you have chosen."

"It is a good lesson," Isabel managed, forcing the words out of her mouth. Matteo was stoic, more expressionless than she had ever seen him, with the light missing from his eyes. "I will teach it to my children as well. Love should be valued, and it will be the greatest regret of my life that I cannot openly value yours."

"Perhaps," Matteo replied, turning away from her. He walked over to the window, glancing down at the street as if preparing to jump. "But perhaps your greatest regret will be only realising the value of love after you have lost it."

Isabel moved forward, but she was too late. Matteo had already swung a leg over her balcony and begun lowering himself down, traversing the ivy easily without giving her a single glance. Once he reached the ground, it was with a ducked head that he continued down the street, without ever knowing Isabel's gaze followed him the entire time he was within her view.

"Parting is such sweet sorrow," she said to herself as Matteo disappeared. Isabel took a step away from her window, closing her curtains with a ferocity she had never felt before. "Good night, Matteo Capulet. That will be all, for we have no tomorrow."

# Mocking Changeling

## by Felicity Devoria

**Literary World**: Jane Eyre

Reader, I married a man with an attic full of ghosts. How foolish I was to think they'd refrain from haunting a plain-faced girl like me. I've spent years running away from the past, but some spirits are slicker than others. Even my forced stint in Wraithmoor Reformatory hasn't managed to shake off this newest pursuer of mine. As night looms closer and shadows start to shift, I wonder: how do you outlast a ghost who seems familiar with every corner of your soul?

***Content Warnings:*** *female rage, violence and physical intimacy, mentions of sexual assault and possible violence to a child, forced institutionalization, non-consensual sedation, and depictions of a historic mental asylum.*

*For the college literature teacher who introduced me to Jane and the Brontës: thank you for not failing me when I wrote an essay on how Rochester treats Jane like a manic pixie dream girl. Please also forgive me for the sacrilegious liberties I am about to take with her story.*

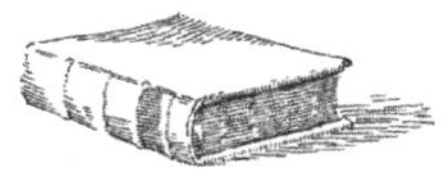

Reader, you can run from ghosts all your life, but you'll never outlast them.

I used to think every home I'd ever known was haunted. When I was a child, I imagined my Uncle Reed tiptoeing just out of sight of his wife's wretched domain. Dearest Helen swept through the halls of Lowood School in search of vulnerable souls to shepherd; she was my guardian angel, I thought, even in death. And the grimmest ghost of all occupied Thornfield Hall.

In my dreams, I'm still cowering against her vicious onslaught.

The trouble starts when those dreams start bleeding out into reality. When those ghosts start blurring the line between night and day.

It's the same scene every night; I'm floating down endless corridors, each one longer than the last. When the lightning flashes—just then, did you see?—there's a snatch of wallpaper I think I've seen before. But in the dark, any lingering familiarity dies. Shadows stretch out into vague shapes of night. Shapes that—if you catch them at just the right angle—play out the worst of your nightmares. Shadow puppets take the stage in a grand menagerie of terrible fates, and the audience? They're laughing at you.

Behind every door lurks a pathway to nowhere. I whisper a little prayer each time I turn a corner. *God, let this be a room I recognize. Let me find a touchstone in this twisting maze. Let me escape.*

My prayers go unheard.

The corridors stretch out far enough to find me running, skirts billowing around my ankles. The wood groans beneath each barreling step. And every time I think I've found the exit, another door knob comes off in my hands.

The greatest scare is always those peals of laughter wafting down the halls. The sound is as familiar to me as the taste of Bessie's cookies, but it only ties my stomach into knots. It used to find me everywhere ... on city streets, in crowded ballrooms, taking centre stage in my sleep.

When my eyes snap open, there's no safety to be found in my surroundings. I wake free of Thornfield Hall but facing imprisonment of another kind. And that's when I see it, standing within an arm's reach of my cell.

A hint of red, a dash of a grimace. Two milky, bloodshot orbs awash in the twilit cellblock. It's far from the first time this mystery intruder has come to watch me in the night. If I were to reach out through the bars—if I was so very quick about it—my fingers might brush against their clothes. I could prove I'm not just imagining it.

But they're smarter than to give me the chance.

There's a bang from down the cell block. Those strange, bloodshot eyes tear away from me, darting to look down the corridor. In a flash of something I can't make out—trailing fabric or a great mess of hair—they flee in the opposite direction.

My heart gallops on with them. As I come to, I realise that none of the homes I've ever known were haunted. My back is aching with the spiritual baggage of every tragedy I've survived: my uncle, my dearest friend, the wife that was my predecessor. My mind is a cobwebbed chamber splitting at its seams. I've been carrying ghostly inhabitants along with me, ready to darken every doorstep I cross. And this new spector—whether otherworldly or decidedly human—has managed to find me despite the groaning locks on every door and gargoyles watching from the façades and mad-doctors hurrying down every hall.

They wouldn't go through that effort if they didn't have something important in mind.

~

There is a certain predictability in being incarcerated. Days pass one after another in a gruelling death march toward no destination in particular. You eat the same food, you sleep in the same cot, and, in the absence of regular sunlight, you invent your own way of keeping time. Which is why most of us stuck in this cell block know Esther is most prone to fits just before daybreak. Only the medicine cart coming mid-morning can sedate her.

The watcher isn't from this cell block.

I'm stirred to get up more by the frigid cold seeping through my dressing gown than by any lingering fears of my pursuer. Not much can shake me these days. There's a simple formula to life here: sleep whenever you can and pass the rest of the time pretending you're still dreaming. Whoever's watching me is going to have to do more than stand in the shadows if they want to see me rattled. As far as I'm concerned, they're just another daydream.

My fingers skim over the surface below me, smooth yet unforgiving. I pull myself up to sitting slowly, in case any rats have found their way into my cell overnight. Move too fast, and you risk sending them all squeaking and running away at once. Better to let them mosey off on their own, none of you any the wiser.

I rub the ache that's screaming through my hip, casting a glance across the scenery. I don't remember deciding to sleep on the floor instead of in my cot. It's yet another entry on the long list of things I can't quite recall. There's a perpetual undercurrent running through the walls here, chugging along beneath our prone forms. It's the murmur of human life that never quite dies down whether it's noon or midnight. It's a chiding hiss in the dark; it's Esther banging on regardless. It's the sort of drudgery you can find comfort in.

That is, until you realise your every movement is being trailed by a shadow other than your own. Then you realise something out of the ordinary is afoot, and you can't tell whether to be terrified or elated. Suddenly, you pace any chance you get. The motions give you an excuse to scan for clues. You lie with your eyes open all night long, pinching your arm to keep yourself from drifting off. Knowing that the moment you inevitably do, the watcher will come around.

I'm usually summoned sometime after taking my morning dose of three brown pills. By that time, it's impossible to say how long I've been sitting in place. A barred window ten or twelve cells down casts just enough light to make out what I think is the building's eastern wall. I stare at the watermarks running down it. They're always changing, traced and deepened each time it rains.

When they call on me, those little brown pills have always made everything go fuzzy like I'm looking at the world through binoculars and my limbs are being pulled on strings. They can try to soften me into the pleasing lady they wish me to be, but they'll never erase how I got here in the first place.

Sometimes I catch my heart committing treason against my head. If only I'd found a way to be content living in London; surely there could have been some joy in raising my children there, even if we were riddled with the plague that is high society. If only I'd put that letter from Wraithmoor Reformatory right back where I'd found it and cast it out of my conscience forever. I would've never had a reason to step foot in Edward's office and learn that Bertha—Edward's first wife—is still alive. I could've birthed little Helen into a family that was splintered but not shattered. Maybe then Edward would've never seen it fit to stir laudanum into my tea when I wasn't looking.

*Such little, inconsequential matters,* my head whispers. Yet my heart knows they were the difference between living my life and losing it.

I've shared a home and a marriage bed and now—most likely—an insane asylum with Bertha, but she remains no more than a stranger to me. If she's even still here, we've been nothing but ships passing in the night. Thanks in no small part to Edward, I'm sure. But are we passing on nights when she decides to take a jaunty stroll through my cell block?

It only makes sense if my pursuer is a woman. The only men who make it in here are guards or mad-doctors, and neither must hide their indiscretions very well. The doctors do as they please, and the guards are impervious to some silly, little reprimand. It's not like anybody comes inspecting when screams echo through an asylum. Who's to say it isn't just the nightly ravings of some patient? Wouldn't it be easier to turn back now, go the way you came? Forget whatever it is you think you heard.

And if the woman watching me is Bertha?

If we met, I think we'd start to piece together all the ways Edward stabbed each of us in the back while wrapping his arm around the other. We'd untangle every lie he's twisted around our graves. And if we spoke—if I heard all the trials she's gone through at his hand—would it put my memories into context? Would I be able to trust my recollections of everything that landed me here?

Would I be able to say I'm not insane and actually believe it?

"Get up," a guard is saying, and I don't remember him opening the cell door. I can't pinpoint the moment I stopped walking on this plane and started running through my memories.

My bones creak like old hinges the whole walk down to Dr. Havenport's office. You'd think the way we all hobble through these halls would suggest a greater need for frequent outdoor time, but you would be wrong. The best-behaved among us are allowed out on the grounds twice a week—still hidden behind a tall fence, of course, lest the rest of the world have to see how we look. But most of us are broken in ways you can't just sew back together again. Only a lucky few are ever going to see unfiltered sunlight again.

Dr. Havenport keeps telling me I'm one of those lucky ones, but I find it hard to count my blessings when everyone keeps insisting I tried to throw my own child into a fireplace.

Never mind that I wasn't even touching the ground when Edward said I did it. All I've got left now are moments here and there, but the last thing I remember … the entire bed was floating as the drugged tea gripped me. Dr. Havenport rushed in, and Edward was crying, flailing, carrying on with those decidedly female dramatics. And if I'd so much as tried to stand then, I would've fallen to the ground. Limp and useless.

My nape prickles as we cross the threshold from the cell block to the innermost halls. The rooms open up, welcoming us to the portion of the building that predates the asylum. The temperature drops a few degrees, and I pull my dress tighter around me, my arms shouldering in as if trying to will my sleeves to tighten, to stop letting the cold air in. If it bothers the nurse and guard, they don't show it. There's always a draft on these higher floors, but it's not the cold that's cutting through me. It's—

I sneak a look behind us. You stop noticing the endless pillars once you've lived in a sullied abbey long enough. The intricate displays of wealth become nothing more than frosting on the backdrop to your foreboding doom … unless you find yourself needing to travel through the shadows. Then all those pillars make the perfect cover to hide from harried nurses and their charges passing through.

The shadow walker thinks she's getting away with it. She's learned to operate outside of her normal parameters. No one looks twice at a nurse no matter where she's headed—they're too lowly to concern oneself with. That leaves the patients. In particular, a patient with a penchant for sneaking out.

There, in one of the pointed arches that line the hall, I see her. Two eyes peer around the corner, checking whether they've been seen, and it's so much like those nights at Thornfield that I want to cry—cry for both the girl losing her innocence and the wife losing her love.

Someone is watching us on our journey to see the doctor, and it's me that their pupils are tracking.

If only she knew I'm watching her too.

~

I enter the office with a lowered head, my mind swimming with questions about my pursuer. If it is Bertha, why didn't she come for me sooner? Why not seek me out during the day instead of lurking outside my cell in the night? But I suppose all my questions now could be answered the same way they were back then at Thornfield Hall. *Bertha is mad,* they all said. *She's no better than an animal.*

Of course, all those people would now say the same about me.

If you had told me years ago that Bertha Mason would come after me again, I would have fled through the country with nothing and no one just to escape her. That simple, plain girl was taken by ghosts and ghouls and mystery pills. Here I stand in her place, harder and rougher and ragged around the edges. I will not stand prim and let myself be haunted so easily. Bertha Mason needn't reveal herself to me. I found out the truth of her once. I will find her again.

Dr. Havenport stands against the edge of his desk, a cigar hanging from his fingers. I'm now familiar enough with him to know this is all for show. He could smoke from a pipe like the rest of England, but how else would we learn he can afford those hand-rolled luxuries?

If Edward hadn't already ruined all men for me, I might take notice of his smart stubble and sharp jaw. There's been chatter amongst the girls about his marital status, but I've been burned before. True insanity is sticking your hand into an open flame twice and expecting it to be more forgiving the second time around.

The doctor pours over my chart as if it's the gossip section of the weekly and he's the meddling mama of three hopeless debutantes. I don't have to lean in to guess what it says. *Patient remains unresponsive to treatment. Isolation, sedatives, and restraints have proven ineffective. Harsher methods should be considered.* It's the same prognosis every week. If I were anyone else, he might have heeded those recommendations by now, but us wives of wealthy men are sometimes shown grace while others face the blade.

Once done, he pierces me to the spot with those hazel eyes. Oh yes, I'm sure the doctor has a blushing bride missing him while he's off at work. Hopefully from somewhere outside these foreboding walls. When he gestures to one of the armchairs facing the desk, it takes me a moment to sit, my knees clattering oddly into position. Sitting in a cold cell most of my days has made comfortable furniture a fleeting memory.

"I think I've hit a breakthrough in your case," he says. His voice flows like warm honey, enjoyable right up until meeting the stinger.

There's a certain game to be played here. When the doctor calls, you do everything up to incriminating yourself before stepping back at the brink. You give and give and give—anything to look promising enough to keep treating—but you never go so far that you've run out of moves.

He stalks closer, taking a drag off the cigar. "Something has been nagging me. You were in the grips of madness that night. Your face, your breathing." He shudders. "Well, you were there, of course. You remember. What a blessing it is that you were found before anything could happen."

I play stupid, hoping it comes off curious, squinting my eyes at him like I'm trying to drag some hidden meaning from his words, delaying the part where I have to respond.

He carries on over my silence. Men have a way of doing that. "But the Jane I witnessed that night isn't the same one I watch stalking through these halls."

I gulp against the pills threatening to crawl back up my throat. "You said I have pet—pur—"

"Puerperal madness," he says with a nod, "brought on by childbirth. I've watched it turn wonderful women into mere monsters." There's a savagery to his voice. "But I fear I might have misjudged you."

I meet his eyes, wondering if he's about to say the words I once dreamed of him saying: *We got it all wrong. You can go home.* At least, I dreamt it until I remembered who my home belongs to.

"There's a little known fact about puerperal madness that we like to keep quiet," he says, his voice conspiratorial. He fiddles with a button on one of his shirt cuffs, that cigar sagging down. "I didn't want to get anyone's hopes up, in case I was wrong. In a small number of women, puerperal madness is more like ... a flash in the pan. There and then gone, lethal as all get out."

"What does that mean for my future?" I hate the hopeful lilt in my voice, but I know I need to play my part if I want any of this to work.

"I think you may be one of those women who makes a full recovery. Your outburst was still worrisome, still dangerous—something we'll always have to be wary of—but nothing that need dictate the rest of your life."

I watch Dr. Havenport evenly. One strange look, one mistimed grimace—could that be enough to scare him out of saying more?

"I am going to tell Edward that you have a good chance of going home. When I heard everything you've been through over the past few years, it became clear to me that something like this was bound to happen. Stress isn't good for gentle ladies like yourself, especially during pregnancy."

My hands clutch for my stomach, and I pray he doesn't notice. My eyes burn. If only he said anything else—

"I want to forge a new path toward your healing," he continues. "In order to move forward, we must look back at what wrong has been done and why you were driven to do it. This flare up of yours was a desperate attempt to process what you've survived in the only way you knew how. We don't need some big reaction to treatment from you now. You've done all the reacting you had left in you."

My eyes bounce around the office, finding anything to look at that isn't this man's face. There's an array of half-drunk spirits on a bar cart in the corner—clinically supported, I'm sure. An especially lumpy chair sits beside it, the uneven upholstery betraying its years of use. On a hook above the desk hangs a collection of keys. A few are ornate, belonging to rooms from before doctors took over the building. The plain ones, a paltry group, must be the master keys.

I look and look until I have no choice but to meet his eyes. "You called me here to discuss why everything transpired that night?" I ask.

There's a twinkle in his expression now. I've finally accepted the bit, now he can hold out a carrot. "I called you here because radical truth telling is the key to finding your vulnerability and stamping it out. It's how we're going to get you home."

My stomach bottoms out at the thought, and this he does notice. His tongue darts over those parted lips. Suddenly he's hurrying to sit up in his chair and look professional. He scribbles something on a notepad. I don't think I've ever seen him take notes before. Still, he's playing coy. There's more he wants to divulge, but he hasn't weighed out exactly which secrets he can give away.

For the first time since coming here, I think Dr. Havenport and I are on the same page.

"If you can be honest with me, we can confirm that it is in your best interest to return. Unless you want another accident like *this* happening again?"

*This* being the supposed attempted murder of my hours-old infant.

"So you're saying you can cure me?" I hope my downtrodden eyes come off demure.

"With the correct treatment, this tendency of yours will be nothing more than a certain vulnerability. If you're reformed, we can monitor that vulnerability. Stamp out any outbursts before they happen.

"All it takes," he repeats, "is radical honesty."

In other words, Dr. Havenport wants me to say I came moments away from hurling Helen into the embers. And I'm going to have to comply in order to get what I came for.

~

Days trickle by, slowly at first but gaining momentum. I spend every waking moment trying to deduce the identity of my pursuer. Her glinting red eyes cut through my every nightmare. All for the best, I suppose. Anything's better than dreaming of that wretched night at Thornfield Hall again. Finding the identity of the perpetrator isn't as easy as just saying it's Bertha Mason hiding under that cloak. There are details to prove: is she still being held here? Is she competent enough to pull off a stunt like this? And then there's finding out exactly *who* she is and where to find her. I haven't exactly gotten a great look at her to go on.

The familiarity of Wraithmoor is why I'm able to pinpoint the few moments a week when my pursuer never materialises. It's during the session time with Dr. Havenport most opposite to my own—an afternoon slot on alternating days. She's one of the *Tuesday, Thursday* girls: the hopeless lot who have been here so long that their sessions tread water, and their names get forgotten, and their time gets tallied in years, not months. They're who I'd be if I didn't give Dr. Havenport a little bit of hope here and there.

If he was concerned about my sudden interest in current events, he didn't show it. He wanted me to look back, after all. All I lost in the transaction was a couple of imitation tears and an admission that Helen wasn't as on purpose as we'd've liked her to be.

My inky fingertips are remnants of the dusty collection of newspapers, but they're nothing compared to the scarlet letter splattered across the complexion of my pursuer. You can hardly make it out when she's relegating herself to shadows and corners. Luckily, there's one tradition in here that pulls out even the most elusive of loners.

Game night is a sporadic event—only happening as often as one of us is able to procure a full deck of cards. It's not that we're forbidden cards—they spare us some luxuries—but keeping a deck full enough to play remains a challenge. But it isn't so hard to swipe stuff from the nurses' station. They hardly look twice if you're not usually the one making trouble.

She keeps her mane wild and long; her arms are fully covered even in the most stifling of rooms. Marie Manx, they call her now. Not an entirely untreatable case, everyone seems to think, if only her husband had any desire to get her back. Wraithmoor may be facing one of its highest occupancies since its formation, but there's never a shortage of placements for unruly wives of uninterested husbands.

When I pull out a crisp set of cards, the table becomes a crowd of grappling hands. One of those hands, sleeve draping past the wrist, moves clunkier than the rest. Mechanical with a certain ticking motion. It takes a second longer for the owner to grasp the edge of a card. Those fingers struggle as they turn it over, their deep red mottling nearly bloody against the fresh white of the card face.

And no amount of unruly curls can conceal the scars that harden with recognition as she surveys her deal.

Bertha holds the only card needed to win the entire game: The Queen of Hearts. In any other game, it would be the luckiest of draws—the kind of feat you die before seeing twice. But Bertha's skin is going grey, cheeks flushed. I can tell she knows I rigged it because she's trying to pull a smile—pretend it was her idea all along—but the smile looks nothing like the unabashed one she gave all that time ago when Edward commissioned a portrait of her for the hearth in their new home. The many years between the painting being hidden in the attic and that attic going up in flames have twisted that smile to anonymity. But time hasn't yet managed to hide the radiance I imagine she was born with.

There's a moment when she's not even sure whether she wants to play along anymore.

Our eyes meet across the table, my crystal clear to her bloodshot. The table splits down the middle in cheers or hollers. Bets are divvied up and cards are dealt again. You can ask the others about that night, if you wish. Their faces will glow with the memory of that one exceptional play that swept the whole game up in it. But no one could tell you that the most exciting game afoot was being played under the table.

~

When she comes for me at midnight, I'm lying on my cot—eyes wide—counting the snores of the sleeper in the next cell over. Her steps are hollow, not unlike those of a dancer; she's used to sneaking around under the cover of darkness.

I rise from my bed at once. There's a flash of silver, and my cell door swings inward. She's careful to hold it just so to avoid that tattletale creak. If she has something to tell me, she doesn't reveal it. Just turns on her heel and levitates down the hall. My feet, plodding traitors behind hers, threaten to give us away with every step.

I knew Bertha had to be well-versed in the secrets of Wraithmoor Reformatory to travel these halls unseen—I guessed she'd had to memorise guard shift changes and untread paths and doors that like to stick in the warm months. It betrayed a level of foresight that challenged everything I'd ever heard about her. But as I trail behind her now, I realise that even my most generous assumptions about her were wrong. This goes beyond mere planning; she's been conspiring long before I got thrown in here. There's no end to the secret corridors and trap doors and hidden entrances in this place. Bertha navigates each with ease. Every time the scenery begins to look familiar, she turns a corner and throws my bearings off their axis once again. It's so silent, save for my shuffling footsteps, that my ears begin to ring. I want so badly to hear Bertha's voice, but I can think of no questions to ask her. My mind is only further disquieted when

I realise I have no idea where she's taking me, let alone why she wants me there. My racing heart forms the driving beat in a symphony of terror. Used to be, I hid under the covers in Thornfield in case she broke into my room in the middle of the night, bent on ending my chances with Edward once and for all. She maimed him, might have done worse to me had she gotten the chance. And here I am following her in the dead of night, completely alone and entirely defenceless.

I shake my hands out, half for something to do and half to hide their trembling. Building up the courage to ask where we're going, I feel a lump in my throat. I try to clear it, but it doesn't work the first time—I'm tamping my throat down, too scared to make a noise—and I find myself swallowing and swallowing against the viscous mass.

Just as I'm about to fall into sputtered choking, a smell hits the air. I cough once or twice. My throat finally clears. Bertha makes no notice of my rasping breaths. She's stopped in the middle of a thin passageway. I follow her eyes ahead. It's a door, but not just any door: there's a small window at the top of it—barred—and beyond …

"We're leaving?" I whisper.

Bertha looks back at me for the first time on this journey. From this close, I can see how her previously sunken cheeks have filled out, how her ashen complexion has caught fire. Back at Thornfield Hall, she looked sick. Spent and spit out. Now when her scarred face works itself into a smile, there's a level of control in her muscles not seen before. She's found greater stability since razing Thornfield to the ground. Like her arson stunt cleared her eyes and her mind, and now the expressions on her face come in concordance with what's inside of her. She might be the first person in the world to nearly burn to death and come out doing better than she did before.

"Only for a time. Thought you might enjoy it out here as much as I do," she says. Her voice is lower than I expected, huskier. I imagine she might have once worked at lifting it so she'd better fit into polite society. Oh, how those old quirks of ours all died when we were sentenced here.

There's a few moments of struggling with the door before its hinges give way. We're dumped out onto a grassy knoll, the hill itself concealing both the door and the corresponding tunnel that connects it to the asylum. My slippers sink into the loamy earth, and my knees shake with every step. That smell from before, it's grass. Sweet and heady and it stretches out before us, acres and acres of blades spitting their fragrance into the air.

When I finally look back the way we came, Wraithmoor is nothing more than a speck of a fortress hanging off a distant cliff. The walls look inconsequential from here, like it's nothing more than the residence of a colony of ants.

"I'm sorry if my spying scared you," Bertha says. She's flung her head back, baring her neck to the sky. Out here in the inky meadows of midnight, the stars sparkle all the more. "I can't imagine what all you've heard about me. My actions at Thornfield, I've been told they were nothing more than ... well, you'll see I'm doing much better now."

"You can speak," I say, blushing the moment it clears my mouth.

"They said I can't speak?"

I glance over her gentle features. It's no secret why Edward was so drawn to her. "You weren't exactly chatty last we met. In fact, you were more likely to growl than talk."

When she laughs, it isn't bitter like you'd expect. Life may have chewed Bertha up and spat her into an unfortunate future, but it hasn't turned her hard and cold. At least, not yet. Her laughter is shrill and intoxicating and utterly infectious. I'm drawn to join her. "Laudanum," she chokes out. "The things it'll do to you." She must see the flash in my eyes, even though it's dark out here. "He slipped you it too?"

The memory of it forces me to look away. "Right after my daughter was born. It made me look—"

"Crazy." She nods. "Strong, that stuff."

We pass the next few moments in amiable silence. I can't read her face, but I think we're both recalling the moment Edward turned on us. How little we expected it from a man like him. How much we'd grown to trust him before that.

"I've spent every single day since I got here wondering how much more of this I can take," I say. She's the first person I've been able to tell. She's the only person who knows how it feels. "I can't fathom how you've lasted as long as you have. I think, before long, I'm just going to snap. Just like that."

"But you know why I've come for you, don't you? You realised I have a plan?"

"I hoped as much."

"It's the same plan I've had since you slept a floor below me, engaged to the very man who was claiming his ... marital pleasure with me each night."

I widen my eyes at her. There aren't many good things I can say about Edward. He might once have saved me from a pitiful life, but the years since have roughened my feelings about him into a point. Sharp and lethal. Yet, I never had to lie scared in our marriage bed. I never had to fear parted thighs and hardened impositions.

"You almost killed him." It's not a question.

She searches for something in my eyes. She's trying to deduce how I feel about the subject, if she should apologise, whether she needs to feign regret. "Almosts are a worthless currency."

I look out over rolling hills and open expanses. "Why not just leave?" I ask, gesturing to the world sprawling out around us. The crickets sing their summer song as if my arms are those of the conductor of a symphony. "Why spend all this time suffering in there when all of this exists?"

"It's too easy." She shakes her head. "It's what he wants. If I disappear, Havenport stops sending him bills. He stops having to look over his shoulder every night. His picturesque future is paved by the fortune he stole from me."

When she sees my frown, she explains, "I was the wealthy one in the pair, didn't you know? Of course not. Why would Edward mention his biggest reason for marrying me? Sells a lot less romance novels, I'm sure."

"So you lie here in wait? You're able to leave, but your morals hold you in place?"

She grasps my hands in hers. The remnants of the burns brush against my palms, scratchy and sickly smooth in equal measure. "If I'm going to take out my revenge on him, I think it's only fair to give you the same chance."

Bertha has thought more about my dreams in the past few months than Edward did in years.

"You don't have to, of course," she blurts out. "I don't mean to force you. It's punishment enough to be stuck in here. The last thing you need is to do something out of ... out of feeling pity for me. It's not too late to go back and pretend we never met."

I position our hands so that our fingers are intertwined, squeezing hers in mine. "What's the plan?"

The way her eyes shine, I can tell the fire has never left her. It's been smoking embers in those amber pupils since that night; it's been stoking itself and burning under her heels, keeping her going, until the glorious destruction can be set ablaze.

Edward's missing hand comes back to me in a flash. Oh, how I cried when I saw it for the first time, cursing the devil who'd harm him when he was so undeserving. All those weeks and months I spent nursing him back to health and convincing him that we could still start a family. I told him those wounds could never define him.

Edward is the blistering, oozing wound souring Bertha's every waking moment. It's time to excise the growth once and for all, cauterise all those infected edges and start anew.

"It's time to finish what I set in motion that fateful night." Her face spells devastation. "We're taking back everything he stole from us. Everything that's rightfully ours."

~

It's no easy task making yourself look feminine and docile while trapped in an asylum. We're not provided with hot tongs to make curls or berries to stain our lips, so I make do with wrapping my hair around the cell bars and biting the inside of my cheek until I draw blood. Beauty isn't a requirement for recovery, but it sure does help when asking to see your husband.

Dr. Havenport's eyes light up the moment I enter. He looks me up and down, that smug smirk coming across his face. I can tell by his expression that he thinks my freshened looks are a byproduct of pills and treatments rather than a tactic of my deception.

The moment I've got him entranced, I let those rolling tears loose. I'm careful to keep it tamped down, closer to blubbering than a full on sob. The last thing I need to do is give him any excuse to think I'm lunatic. Ever the gentleman, Havenport produces a handkerchief and passes it to me.

"There, there," he says. His arm reaches across the desk so he can pat my shoulder. For a mad-doctor, he sure seems out of his element at the slightest expression of emotion. "What's gotten into you?"

"I can't be without Edward a second more." I dab at the corner of my eyes with the kerchief. "The heartache is just too much to bear."

He purses his lips, and for a moment I think he's going to call me out on the lie. Instead, he folds his hands as if in prayer and clicks his tongue. "I'm sure he misses you too," he tries. It's hard for me not to smirk about my apparently passable deception. Is there a wife out there who doesn't go weepy over her husband? The mad-doctors would be hard-pressed to believe it.

I reach towards him, my hands grappling for purchase. When he doesn't take them, I grasp his lapels. "I have to see Edward," I plead. My eyes are swimming with hope. "I can't bear to think that he's upset with me. I need to make things right."

Dr. Havenport clears his throat before removing my hands. "I won't pretend that Edward hasn't been through a great deal of hurt because of you," he says. "Surely, you must know what sort of damage you've caused."

I nod. My eyes find the ground. "I can't imagine what he must be feeling." I'm sure to keep up with the sniffling. "He's been alone with the children for months now. The stress he must have endured without me there ..."

"Mending this rift between the two of you is of the utmost importance," he continues, and I can tell that he's weighing Edward's disdain of me with his honest intention to reinstate me as Edward's proper wife. Even crackpots like Havenport have lofty ideals.

The doctor stands and heads for his medley of liquors in the corner. He pours something deep and amber in a glass, corking the bottle and trying some before turning back to me.

"I will send for Edward at once." His voice grows in surety with every sip. "I will implore him to extend an olive branch. It will be hard, you understand, to put aside the memories of your outburst, but I see no reason the two of you shouldn't try to find what was there once before."

My fingers wipe frantically at the tears lingering on my cheeks. "Thank you, doctor. You have no idea what it means."

"Don't thank me yet. I have said I will try. It will be up to Edward to decide."

"Of course, of course." My lip trembles. "I will pray to God that he can find it in himself to give me another chance. I won't squander it, I promise."

"Good." Havenport nods then. Something steely has gone over his expression. He's lost in thought of how to convince Edward to see me. It's only too easy to stand, the chair squealing across the floor as it's pushed back.

Like clockwork, a great bang echoes through the asylum. There's only a moment to process what we've heard, our ears ringing with the severity of it, before it repeats. In its wake, there's a scream and the scuffle of footsteps. And then, the banging starts up again.

Dr. Havenport should rush for the door at once, knowing that whatever is making that noise is likely the work of one of his patients. Knowing that whoever's in their vicinity—nurses or guards—might need help wrangling them into submission. Help only a doctor with a briefcase full of sedatives can offer. But Havenport is a coward. He stays frozen in place, making no moves toward subduing whatever—whoever's—behind the racket.

To think he sees himself as a hero.

The door squeals open on its hinges, thumping against the wall with the force of whoever's behind it. And there in the doorframe, breathless and fevered, stands Bertha. She's shaking like a leaf, and I can't tell whether it's from the very real nerves of the situation or a pretend display of her fright.

"Doctor," she gasps, "it's Esther."

Everyone in the third cell block knows that Esther is intolerable without her medications. Skip so much as one dose, and she's nothing more than a vehicle for destruction. What a shame those blue pills went missing this morning. No one likes handling those fits of hers.

Bertha crosses the room in an instant, flinging herself at the doctor. "They tried to stop her, but it's impossible. She's too angry—"

"Marie," Havenport snaps. He looks between the two of us, his eyes boggling at the sight of us standing so close together. Surely Edward set some sort of rule about keeping the two of us apart.

I weave my face into a tapestry of horror. "Will Esther be okay?"

"Everyone return to your cells," he commands. And though he's about to face the most dangerous elderly woman I've ever met, something about his face calms. What a relief that these two young women haven't any idea as to the significance of the other.

"At once," he shouts. We hustle into motion just behind him, following at his heels.

Just until he clears the room. Just long enough for him to sprint down the steps to the recreation room, going the opposite direction of the cell block.

We lock the door behind him.

I tilt my chin down at Bertha. "Esther okay?"

"She's been worse." It's not the first time Esther's had an outburst, but it might be the first time anybody was looking forward to the occasion.

Left to our own devices, the room turns into a flurry of activity. My eyes lock on one of the key rings hanging mere feet away from me. The cold of each metal body in my palm is a shock to the senses. I don't think either of us believed we'd get this far. I catch sight of Bertha in the corner. She's rifling through the cabinet of tonics.

"Calomel, rhubarb—"

"We've only got a few more seconds," I hiss.

Bertha goes on mumbling, her hands dancing across the bottles.

Keys in hand, I turn to the next tool for our plan. Havenport is known around here for taking meals in his office. I only hope the nurses aren't so quick about cleaning after him.

"Morphia, camphor—"

My eyes bounce across the room.

"There!" Bertha and I whisper as one. The serving tray sits by the far wall. It's a mad dash with Bertha on my heels, a dark brown bottle clutched in her hand. I throw the napkin covering the meal aside.

*Dear God, let it be anything but soup.*

He answers that one. The plate hiding beneath is smeared with the remnants of a mystery roast. And there, scattered carelessly on the plate—

"Even a knife!" Bertha squeals.

The heavy fork feels foreign in my hand. How long has it been since I took things as simple as cutlery for granted?

Bertha and I swap items—the weight of the bottle making me fumble. It comes inches from dropping, seconds from ruining everything. Bertha pulls the neckline of her dress down like it's nothing. The rosy dark skin revealed there makes my face go heated. I look anywhere else, but nothing could flay the image from my mind.

The fork and knife disappear into some fold or the other in her dress. Like that, we've found everything. It's happening.

But this is too easy to have worked. Too obvious not to get caught.

"Fetch me a dropper," I instruct. I'm standing in front of Havenport's work table in an instant. Her neckline smoothed back to rights, Bertha passes it over. I make quick work of the bottle's contents, pouring a small amount of the corrupting liquid into a tiny vial. This way, we can keep the stash hidden. Once I've got the vial stoppered, I replace the bottle in the cabinet. Not even the most meticulous of doctors would notice anything awry. And the Lord knows Havenport is anything but meticulous. We take a cursory glance over the room—miraculously, it doesn't look like two wild animals were let loose in it—and disappear out the door like we were never there.

There's just enough time to slip into the mass of bodies moving up, out, anywhere to get away from Esther's onslaught. The banging has only gotten louder and more regular since it started. From the sound of it, Esther's making quick work of the shoddy tables we eat on. I imagine her lifting them like they're nothing more than bundles of parchment, shards splintering off against the walls.

We'll have to eat on the floor after this, won't we?

*Not for long.*

There are cheers when we finally survey the damage the next morning. It seems we're not the only ones to find a moment of triumph in the wake of Esther's uprising.

~

Edward Fairfax Rochester stalks into the visiting room of Wraithmoor Reformatory with a satisfied sort of frown and a dark coat buttoned up to his neck, looking stodgier than ever. I peer up into the eyes of my dear husband, and it's the moment I've been waiting months, centuries for. How do you face the man who framed you for trying to kill your first daughter, the baby you birthed and nursed and named after the only friend you'd ever had? *If Helen could see me now ...*

She was the only friend I'd ever had until Bertha sauntered into the cold, dead core of my heart, that is.

It's the moment I practised for every time I caught my reflection in passing surfaces, until I could trust myself to soften all my snarls into smiles.

Edward smiles back, but it's greasy and slippery and piercing me right through my ribcage.

"Edward!" Dr. Havenport crows, standing to greet the man I used to think of as another iteration of myself. The two men shake hands, eager to assert their alliance against the troublesome lady in their midst. "How is London treating you?"

"Much kinder than the countryside ever did," he responds evenly. He's just saying it to hurt me. He's saying it to salt the earth we blossomed in when it was just the two of us out in the woods.

"It seems you and your wife find yourself in similar seasons in life," Dr. Havenport says. His eyes skate over to mine, broaching the subject as delicately as he can. "She too has found healing, though she's found it out here amongst the trees."

I have to stop myself from laughing in his face. The trees at Wraithmoor are no more than backdrops constructed to line the pen they keep us in. They do nothing but cloak the escape routes. Still, I nod. "I find myself much restored by my time at Wraithmoor." When Edward fiddles with the neck of that stifling coat, I continue on. "I've asked Dr. Havenport to invite you to visit because I believe I'm ready to return to my duties."

"Really?" He refuses to meet my eyes. "There was something to that effect in the letter."

"Jane is doing exceptionally well." The doctor looks between the two of us now, his eyebrows raised. He can't figure out why we aren't more overjoyed about our reunion. "I believe she's done her part in acknowledging the harm she caused with her outburst. She is ready to take a new path. A path of atonement."

Edward meets the doctor's eyes, weighing his words. "There is a lot to atone for."

How right he is.

"And there's the crux of it!" Dr. Havenport exclaims, clapping his hands together. "Jane has had to accept many ugly truths, and she knows she must make it up to those she's harmed. But you said it yourself: it can be done. She can redeem herself."

Edward nods, looks out the window. He's always been one to get lost in his thoughts. I follow his gaze. How I long to feel those far-flung rays of sun on my arms, my neck—

Soon.

I stand from the cushy brocade armchair and cross the room to a bar cart, my steps ginger on the plush floor. The eyes of both men trace my every move as I select an ornate bottle and pour two glasses of what smells like brandy. The liquid swishes against the delicate glass, and it's the sound of luxury from a past life. It's oh-so-easy to slip tiny vials into the long sleeves of the dresses we're given for visits. Even easier to undo the stopper and splash the contents into drinks with a practised flick of your wrist. I can't help but be thankful that men's eyes are busy with other matters when a woman turns her back to them.

Who doesn't enjoy that spicy-sweet of brandy—so layered, so cloying—on afternoons spent in warm, sunny rooms? No one has to ask the two men twice. They each select a glass, take a swig of the stuff, and sigh from contentment.

"How long has it been since you've served me a drink?" Edward asks. It's the first time he's addressed me directly. The liquor must already be loosening him up.

"I can't remember," I murmur, eyes down. To anyone else, it might sound like a thinly veiled barb. Only Edward and I know how anxious he was about the difference in class between us two. We both wanted to avoid feeling like master and servant. Edward decided early on that he refused to take any help from me—I wasn't to be caught doing anything a servant might. That included fixing his drinks. It's a rule I followed with pleasure.

"I think you'll find this new Jane will surprise you," the doctor answers. "She needed time to rest. As you said, she's been through more than any woman should."

Edward shuffles in his seat before finally meeting my eyes. They're as dark and clandestine as I remember, and they're—is he tearing up? For the first time since getting here, I consider the possibility that Edward might truly regret his actions. He might be here to apologise, to make happy, and to whisk me back home and off my feet.

Edward has always been a man to do far too little, much too late.

"Dr. Havenport, would you allow me a moment alone with my wife?"

The doctor looks between the two of us. Somewhere in his head, he's reminding himself of the visitation protocol—patients are never to be left alone with visitors. I doubt it's a rule he has to recall very often, considering how few of us have anyone who'd dare step foot here.

He waffles another moment before standing. "Of course," he says, setting his empty brandy glass on the side table with a clink. "I'll be a couple halls down. Please don't hesitate to call if you need me."

I nod my head at his retreating back, hoping I look suitably giddy about my despondent husband taking an interest in me.

The door closes with a click so quiet you'd have to strain to hear it.

"Jane," Edward mumbles, turning that churning sea of darkness upon me. There's something swimming in his eyes that I haven't seen in so long, I almost can't place it. Edward *wants* me.

"Come to me," I whisper.

All the while, I know I'm throwing myself to the rocks the tide crashes against.

Edward's lips are on mine in an instant, plodding and inquiring and heady with that splash of brandy. I spent hours fixing my hair just so, and now it's being crushed against the back of the chair by the force of his kiss. I'll surely look a mess after this. If Edward tastes the blood staining my lips, he doesn't pull back to mention it.

In a few moments, he won't be fit to mention much of anything.

I slide my tongue between those parted lips. I suppose I should be thankful that Edward has always been a capable lover. There was a time before this dreadful place when pleasure was a grace that blessed our every day. How strange that no matter how broken we become, this side of us has always worked.

Edward slides his severed arm around me, holding me against him, while his hand traces up my bodice. His fingers stop to linger over the pleasing swells of my body. His lips are not unlike the beak of a baby bird, picking and pecking until its mother regurgitates everything she has for him. I can tell by the sloppy buzz of his lips that the laudanum is doing its job. Only a few seconds more—

There, under the sound of Edward's groaning, that telltale click.

Edward's hand has ceased its escapades, hovering over my breast. He pulls his head away from mine, and his lips are tinged a carnal red. "There's something here," he whispers, his fingers plunging under my dress. "Something … is it sharp?"

His hands close over a silver handle and pull the knife from my dress, his eyes hazy as he tries to make out the rather dull blade. Just as something surfaces in his mind—which is floating farther away by the second—four tines of a fork find the side of his neck, nestling in at the base of his skull.

He turns and thrashes, but it's no use. He's wedged too tightly between the two of us, and his muscles have forgotten how to escape that rusty old fork.

"Haven't seen you in a while, dear husband." Bertha leans in over his shoulder. If the laudanum hasn't already swirled his vision too far, Edward has no choice but to look into the blistered mosaic of his first wife's face. "I've been in intensive recovery, didn't you hear? I thought for sure my dear husband might check on me, my having been almost flayed to death and all."

Bertha cackles. It's a high-pitched wheeze, not unlike that of a hog. Holding that fork flush to his skin, one of my arms locking him in place, she hastily snaps open the top few buttons of his coat, yanking his cravat away to reveal more of his neck, to give us more purchase on this mortal expanse of skin.

There, lurking on the delicate pane of his throat, is a smattering of love bites. The red marks bloom from skin that Edward was supposed to be saving just for me. He didn't just visit the asylum where he wrongfully trapped his wife with the sole expectation of having his way with her, he came knowing full well his extramarital indiscretions would be revealed the moment he shed his façade. There's a sharp intake of breath. In some vague side of my brain, I realise the sound came from me. Edward doesn't notice, cringing against the shank brandished against him, but I see the sick smile of Bertha's face falter. In one soft moment, her eyes are caressing me with unspoken words of comfort over the prone form of our husband. It's the apology we'll never hear from his lips.

And then that moment is shattered.

I pull the knife out of Edward's hand, his fingers fumbling against mine, but I can tell they've gone numb. It's only too easy to dislodge them. He backs away when the blade reaches his throat, resting just beside the windpipe, and sticks himself on the fork.

Four tiny puncture wounds erupt there, perfect droplets of blood pooling from each one.

"Money," Edward gasps. He tries to gurgle something more, but his lips flop and flub over the words. I remember that fateful night, trying to cry out that I would never hurt Helen but finding my mouth incompatible with speech. Bertha and I don't need to hear the rest to know what he means. If he returns both of our fortunes to us, would that be enough to let him go?

Why does it take being held at knifepoint before a man concerns himself with righteousness?

"Women have other ways of reclaiming their fortunes," I whisper against his cheek.

Bertha grins, her lips brushing against the lobe of his ear. "Everyone knows widows have more fun."

Reader, we murdered our husband in great dredging, hacking thrusts. Mealtimes at Wraithmoor meant wrestling your dinner with sorely lacking tools, and the cutlery fared no better against flesh and fascia. It was slow, dirty work, but Edward didn't give us too much of a fuss.

Everyone knows a body on laudanum sleeps like the dead.

~

The deed done, Bertha and I position Edward so he's hanging half off the couch. Maroon drips from the cream upholstery, and the pools of mortality stain the rug underneath. There's a crunch of cartilage beneath our heels as we back away and assess ourselves.

We're both covered in the stuff, but who would dare suggest us delicate women are capable of anything more than standing rooted to the spot in horror? Who's to say we did anything other than rush for our dear husband in terror, shocked beyond our wits in the moment of his attack?

On my nod, Bertha lets out a bloodcurdling scream. Some little part inside of me knows that sound from a lifetime ago. How many times did it howl down from the attic, that sound of terror caused by a man claiming yet another thing that was never his.

There's a bang at the door, and Havenport lunges into the room. Well, he tries at lunging. His legs have gone wonky and he's put too much power behind the move. His body, listless, collides with Bertha's, nearly taking her down with him. His arms paddle, trying to tread air. At the last second, she catches herself, pulls them back to standing.

The doctor's eyes bulge from their sockets as he takes in the body of the man he thought was such a charming acquaintance only minutes ago.

Edward is sagging somewhere between the couch and the floor. His skin is going yellow, already mottling over.

"You vile wretches!" Havenport hisses. It's hard to make out the words, he's slurring them so bad. "Disgusting whores!"

Bertha salutes, breaking into giggles.

He spits at her then. Rather bold for a man who can't stand on his own, but perfect for two women who are counting on him looking deranged.

I check on Bertha with my eyes one last time. The lights are dimming and the crowd buzzes with anticipation. Bertha and I are about to take the stage for our greatest performance yet.

She smiles at me, taking a hand off the doctor to point outside the windows. *Any minute,* her smile says, *it'll be us two out there.* The movement nearly sends him falling over his feet, but Bertha grabs him. She wrestles him back to standing again. He only needs to be up for a minute more. Once the guards come, he can lie on the floor for the rest of his life, for all I care.

How wonderful would it be if they put him in my cell? Maybe they'd let me lock the door. Maybe Bertha could throw away the key.

We're never touching those cots again. Nobody's serving us slop for so much as one more meal. Someday I'm going to forget that my cell had a hundred and seventeen watermarks and the way baby Helen cried when they yanked her from me.

I take off down the hallways that yawn so wide. My slippers slap against the stone, and the sound echoes like musket fire. "Guards, help!" I screech. "He's gone crazy. We can't stop him!" The navy blue of my skirts billow across the floor, blood seeping from them and getting everywhere. "Someone save us!"

~

**LATER**

Every fine lady who is anybody knows just how important it is to be seen frequenting the Ivory Leaf in times of leisure. The bustling tea room sees its biggest crowds when the weather warms; this particular sparkling afternoon is no exception.

Steam drifts up from the lone cup of butterfly jasmine sitting untouched on the table. It's one of Cecilia Cavendish's favourites, but her acquaintance has yet to show, and she thinks it might be rude to start drinking without her.

Not to mention that she burnt her tongue on the first sip and is doing her best to suck an ice cube in the most ladylike of ways.

The bell over the door tinkles and Cecilia looks up. Maisie Talbot bustles through the doors, settling into the seat across from her. Unaware of Cecilia struggling to swallow an ice cube whole, Maisie orders her usual—an oolong shipped straight from China.

"Gossip pages," Maisie says, procuring the thin sheets of paper from some hidden place on her person. She sets them on the table next to the teacup, but neither girl makes a reach for them. Every lady worth her salt knows the most interesting gossip of all never finds its way into print.

"It's almost time for her to go again," Cecilia murmurs. Her eyes snag on a rather ornate carriage going past the shop with a good crop of horses and a capable driver—a show of great wealth—but the window curtains have been left open. It's too high profile to belong to *her.*

She's the boogeyman of high society.

"Maybe this time the old hag will decide she likes the countryside so much she'll never come back." Maisie's lips quirk up. "Lord knows she's haunted London long enough."

Cecilia shakes her head. "She's never liked the city, not one day of her life. Wasn't that what they said at the trial? She's only here every summer because she knows it drives us mad. She enjoys ruining the social season."

"My brother drove his carriage past her winter estate once," Maisie says, leaning forward conspiratorially. "He said it was dark and foreboding, and ivy was growing all over it like she couldn't pay anyone for the upkeep."

Cecilia finally braves the butterfly jasmine again. It doesn't burn this time. "You know that's not true. She could afford twenty estates if she wanted."

The two girls sigh as one. Oh, to afford such luxuries with no man overseeing the finances.

"It must be lonely out there. She never was allowed to reunite with her children; they won't have anything to do with her now that they're grown. That's enough to say she's guilty, if you ask me. All she has are her servants and that strange housekeeper—the one they say's from Jamaica."

"And the dog," Maisie adds.

Cecilia purses her lips. "Who could forget that dreadful mutt?"

"It's a shame that poor woman is stuck working for Jane Eyre, of all people."

"She must've been fired from too many households to get a placement anywhere else."

The conversation drips off for a few moments, the girls lost in their curiosities. Jane Eyre is the talk of the town—her ritual return each summer season never failing to pique the curiosities of high society—but it's rather hard to keep up the talking when no one has actually seen the woman in decades.

There were those who claimed they caught sight of her, of course, but who could prove it? Only the oldest among them had been alive during the trial, and most hadn't been old enough to be allowed inside. That didn't stop anybody from having an opinion on it, of course. Robert Havenport had died in a facility decades ago, but those that still believed in his innocence lived on.

"Still, she can't be happy out there by herself." Maisie taps her fingers against the side of her teacup. "Can she?"

Cecilia shakes her head, the voice of authority. "She has to be eighty by now—I'd be surprised if she can even get out of bed. No way is she able to visit the Eyre-Mason Academy any more."

Maisie seems comforted by this idea. "They say everyone gets what they deserve. I suppose they're right about that."

When Maisie takes another sip, the harsh smell of oolong wafts over the occupied tables of the shop. It's such a different scent from the green blend the older woman across the aisle is drinking that she crinkles her nose at it. She's dressed in an understated sort of way, wearing one of her usual blue or green ensembles. Never red, never that colour that trailed her when she ran down the hallways screaming her throat raw. She takes another sip of her tea, her other hand busy with a quill and a journal. Most ladies at the shop opt for "light" refreshments, but a platter of scones rests on the table. She shares them with the woman sitting across from her, dressed in the typical ware of a lady's maid. Most of the tea-drinkers have brought their maids with them, but this is the only one to join her mistress. She helps herself to a hearty helping of the scones.

They two women sit in a companionable silence. They look strangely matched if you watch them for too long, but no one ever does. Once a woman reaches spinsterhood, the looks and stares she's accustomed to seem to melt away.

The lady in the blue dress scribbles on. She's working on her novel—the one she hides from even her companion's wandering eyes—and she's gotten to the moonlit meadow. It's the third time she's started it over today, and she resists the urge to tear up this attempt too. She keeps getting stuck on the moment the distressed damsel looks up into the feral eyes of her saviour. The old woman sneaks another glance across the table. That long-ago saviour now pages through a novel, half a scone hanging in mid-air like she's forgotten she's holding it. *Marie Manx,* the author of the novel is called. She's written plenty of romances and adventures, but this new story of hers—she's writing it just for herself.

Her eyes flit back down to the page. *Soft as a lake, surging like the rapids,* she writes. *They're the sort of eyes you find yourself wanting to fall into.* She looked up into them fifty-some odd years ago, and she's been falling ever since.

Reader, it's me. Jane Eyre. Writing in a tea room across from the love of my life, listening to the townspeople wish they could take after me with pitchforks, knowing they'd never be able to find me, let alone take on the both of us.

Not so bad for the plain-faced girl with a head full of ghosts.

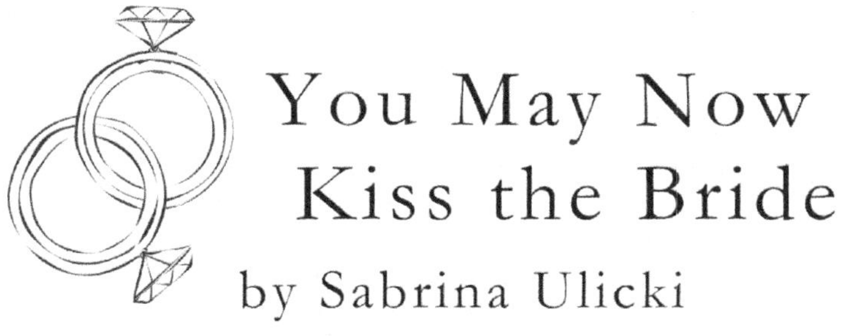

# You May Now Kiss the Bride

## by Sabrina Ulicki

**Literary World**: Anne of Green Gables

When Anne finds her daughter with one leg out of the window, wedding dress on and all, she's unsure of what's going on. The conversation that follows opens them both up to the trials of life, the difficulty of fighting for what we truly want, and the healing beauty of love. Will young Rilla be able to reconcile past and present and say I do? Or will she run into the horizon, forever haunted by her past?

***Content Warnings**: mentions and references of prior loss and grief related to war.*

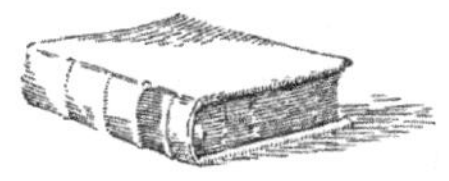

"Bertha Marilla Blythe!" The full name was like a gasp out of my mother's lips, and it was followed by the sound of the door urgently closing behind her. "What in the name of God do you think you're doing?!"

At my mother's intrusion, I stopped cold, one leg dangling out of the window and the white dress bunched up to my knees. I looked at the horizon as if it held all the answers I was seeking, scared to turn around. I had one hand on the windowsill, the other holding the skirts – and they were both shaking lightly as I finally turned my neck to look at her.

For a heartbeat, we stared at one another, my shoulders feeling as taut as my stomach and Mom's expression the picture of shock. Slowly, I angled my body toward the inside of the bridal room, shifting my legs so I was sitting on the windowsill like a proper lady rather than looking like I was about to run away on horseback...*which wasn't too far away from reality, was it?* Not like I'd thought as far as getting onto Dad's horse, but it didn't sound like a terrible option right about now.

"Well, you see..." My voice had an air of casualness I didn't really possess, my heart beating so hard I was sure Mom could hear it from across the room. Her back was pressed against the door, as if trying to keep demons out – or maybe to keep me in. "I was just..."

Mom's eyebrows rose as she made a gesture with her hand to urge me to keep going. "You were..."

"Getting some fresh air?" I finished with a candid smile and a nervous chuckle. "It's just so... stuffy in here."

"Oh, Rilla." My nickname was an exhale that softened Mom's expression. She took a single step into the bridal room. "Talk to me, darling. What's going on? I thought you were so very excited about all this!"

Before replying, I fixed the skirt of my wedding dress, making sure all the delicate embroidered fabric was inside the window. Then, I gingerly lowered myself in, one hand still holding onto the frame as if it were a lifeline. My freshly pink-stained lips parted, then closed. I looked at the large mirror across the room – the one I'd been standing in front of only a minute ago, watching myself on what should've been the best day of my life. My wavy reddish hair was up in an intricate pattern, a few delicate fresh flowers Mom had picked that very morning woven into it; and there was an artificial blush to my cheeks as well as a tiny bit of kohl that rimmed my eyes – which I was sure my beloved would've said looked wonderful on me.

I was the picture-perfect bride I had always dreamed of being. But I couldn't help but look into that mirror and see another life. Another wife-to-be that never was.

Shaking the thought out of my head, I looked at my mother, Anne Blythe, the perpetual image of perfection, the dreamer, the one who had pushed me to pursue this crazy fever dream of mine – who had told me the whole family supported me in this decision and would be here today to celebrate with us. But that was all it was: a fever dream. An illusion. And I couldn't go through with it.

"I can't do this." My voice broke with the heaviness of the admission.

"What do you mean, Rilla dear?" Mom brought a hand to her chest and lowered her voice to a whisper, almost looking scandalised. "The wedding?"

The word felt like a knife right to my chest. *The wedding.* But this wasn't one. This was just a celebration – a mock-up of the real thing. We couldn't walk down the aisle and profess our love in front of the Lord like my parents had before me.

"None of it, Mom. I… I just can't."

The room was small enough that in two or three steps, Mom would've been standing right in front of me; but she stayed where she was, as if her feet were glued to the wooden floor. She shook her head a few times, bit her bottom lip, then closed her eyes tightly and pinched her nose in the same way I remember Grandma Marilla did when headaches became too much to bear – when us kids were driving her crazy with all our running around.

I waited, a knot in my throat stopping me from uttering a single word. *What was there to say, anyway?* I had failed myself, and now I was about to fail the only person in the world that knew how to hold my broken pieces; the one that had kept me sane when I thought I'd lost everything. If Mom wouldn't have come in just then, I would've run away from the one that had made life beautiful again, the one that picked fresh flowers every day because I loved how they smelled, and that cuddled me when tears overtook me.

The one that found ways to make me laugh again when I thought a simple smile was an impossible task.

I was about to break the most noble heart in the world, all because I couldn't kiss the one I loved in front of a crowd. In front of our whole families. *You may now kiss the bride.* The words had haunted me since the moment I'd thought of them standing in front of the mirror.

I just couldn't do it. Not when marrying my beloved meant breaking my own word in front of everyone I cared about. I'd been delusional in thinking this wouldn't chase me, that it wouldn't come back to haunt me. That *he* wouldn't haunt my thoughts.

"Rilla, my dear…if you truly don't want this, I will understand." Mom's words surprised me. I was expecting a reprimand, a confession of how much I had disappointed her, of how unreasonable I was being. Instead, Mom showed me her heart. "I swear I will. I will even run out of that window with you and we can run until we can no more. But…"

Mom took a step forward, standing close enough to hold my hands. Her eyes drifted from mine to the landscapes of Avonlea behind me, to the willows in blossom she loved so much.

"You looked so sure, so happy…what happened? Is this because of what the priest said?" Mom's eyes returned to me, full of worry. "The Lord loves you both as you are, and that priest was an old fool. Or is it a bit of fear just slipping into your core? You know, it's normal," she went on, her voice filling the small room in the way it had so many times over the years.

I was no stranger to my mother's outbursts and never-ending strings of words, but I didn't really mind it now, my mind still stuck on the same daunting words: *you may now kiss the bride.*

"I had a little moment like this when I was about to marry your father, you know," Mom kept on going. "If my dear Diana hadn't been there to talk me out of all my fears, I don't think I would've walked down the aisle. I mean, I didn't think I was beautiful like you are, and I didn't feel worthy. I...I never spoke to anyone about this, but I will if it helps you ease your mind."

I didn't have a chance to say yes or no, or anything for that matter. It was hard to get between my mother and storytelling. And so, as her eyes drifted toward nature again, Mom spoke of her last day as Anne Shirley-Cuthbert. I stood there, my heart beating too fast, my chest feeling like it wasn't getting enough air, and my stomach as knotted as it'd been the last time I'd had bad milk.

"I remember Diana there with me, telling me: 'You always came up with the most amazing tales, your imagination was like no other. But this is real, Anne, this is happening, and you need to live in the now, in the here. Gilbert will be waiting for you at the altar in just a matter of hours...why are you in such a mess, crying all over for this? Isn't this what you always wanted?'

"And it was!" Mom's eyes flitted toward me with a huge smile. "It was everything I had ever dreamed of. I had loved your father for a long time, and not even in my wildest childish dreams would I have imagined a love story like the one we had...and maybe that's why it all felt so unreal.

"Despite my love story with your father being like a book come to life, and my whole life from the point after Marilla and dear Matthew adopted me feeling like the most amazing fantasy tale..." The words trailed off as Mom looked out the window again, as if looking for her old self among the blossoms. “Well, life before that…it wasn’t the best. I had never spoken of the darkness lingering in the depths of my memories – buried under huge willows and flowering bushes.”

We’d heard some of those stories when we were teens, Mom opening up about her childhood in the orphanage and what it’d been like growing up without her parents. We were lucky enough to have a mother that cared and was willing to talk about mostly anything with us, always ready to answer our million questions, always encouraging healthy conversation. But now, as she spoke, a huge part of me just wanted to yell at her to shut up, to leave me alone, and I had to fight that urge. I had to fight the burning heat growing in my chest with every word out of her lips.

“I had covered that darkness with fantasy tales and frilly skirts,” Mom went on, “never even letting my bosom friend Diana glimpse what lurked in the darkest corners of my mind. I’d never let her see the fear, the loneliness…and I had never spoken of my past with her.

“But sitting there, under our willow, and with a soft breeze announcing the return of winter just around the bend, I allowed myself to open up. I told her how fantasy was often a pretty way to forget about the ugliest parts of life. Before meeting Marilla and Matthew, I had never had anything pretty...not physically, nor spiritually. I had no nice dresses or pretty trinkets, no warm homes with delicious meals nor neighbours that baked goods to share when harvest wasn't great. I had nothing. Just my imagination and the confident idea I had once had parents that loved me, and the hope one day someone would be able to love me again."

Mom talked with her eyes glued to Avonlea's greenery, the willows outside gently swinging in the wind. I had heard some of these stories, yes – but I had never seen her talk like this, as if lost in her own memories, her hands bunched up in front of her and her slim body looking smaller than it ever had, like the wind itself could break her if it blew too hard. That was probably the only reason I was able to fight the urge to tell her it was enough. I didn't want to hear how bad everything had been for her, but how perfect her life with Dad was afterward; how after the bad, something beautiful and worthy always came along. I had witnessed a lot of it, after all: I had seen their love first-hand.

But their story wasn't my own. I didn't have their luck; their perfect happy ending. I was cursed. I was a liar. I was about to break a heart.

"I remember how my dear Diana's eyes filled up with tears as I spoke, as I showed her a part of me I had never dared show anyone else," Mom went on. *Did she even remember I was still by her side? That it was meant to be* my *wedding day?* "I was scared Gilbert would one day discover I wasn't the happy girl he had met me as. That he'd glimpse my past in the dark corners of my soul and think I was tainted; I wasn't good enough. I felt like I wasn't worthy of what I had…but do you know what Diana said to me?"

Finally, Mom looked at me, her eyes returning to the present along with the rest of her. I shook my head, the hot feeling growing in my chest taking a monstrous shape.

"No, I don't," I managed to say, the red-hot monster drawing claws and digging through my ribcage, trying to crawl up my scratchy throat.

"She told me knowing where I came from didn't change anything for her. She told me she loved me for who I was and who I've always shown myself to be…and I'm sure it's the same for you. I'm sure Jo—"

"Stop!" I interrupted abruptly, my hand flying out to silence her, to cut the words between us. I couldn't hear that name on my mother's lips. "Stop, Mom. I'm not like you!" I snapped. The red claws opened my throat wide and let everything tumble out. "I'm not brave and love-struck and ready to drop everything for love like you," I said, the words rushing out like an untameable river. "You always talked about your love for Dad and how you would've done anything for him. How he did everything for you, even giving up his job so you could take it when grandpa passed away. How you both gave up so much, but this is different! I'm nothing like you! And I didn't have a hard childhood like you did, mine was perfect!"

"Aren't you? Like me?" Mom looked me up and down as if I were made of glass, and all the hotness left my body in a single breath, leaving me cold and shivering – possibly about to shatter into a million pieces as I saw myself reflected in her eyes. "Of all my children, you've always been the one most like me, Rilla."

*I was, wasn't I?* I was even wearing her wedding dress, tailored to suit my style – less frills and more cleavage.

"Don't think you can fool me; you came out of me." Mom's full focus was on me now. "We've spent plenty of time together, just the two of us as your father worked, and your siblings moved on away from home…it was always us. And I know your heart…"

*She did.* She'd been the one to reassure me my love was valid, that I should follow my heart and accept the proposal. She'd been ever supportive, even now, talking about herself to distract me and get a reaction out of me because she'd always known it was the only way to get me to talk. Anger and frustration were my triggers to let the bottled-up emotions out.

"Even if you didn't have a hard childhood," Mom went on, "you did suffer with loss and…still, I know you'd do anything for love. And I know how much you love Josie—"

"Enough, Mom. Enough." I shook my head, covering my ears not to hear her name. I just couldn't bear it. I couldn't bear the notion that came along with that name, the softness it evoked. It made me want to stay, to hold her, to tell her how much I loved her.

It made me want to be brave, to break all my promises.

Tears clung to my lashes and I tried to keep them in. "You don't know everything, Mom! You don't know how I swore to love another!" As the truth slipped out of my treacherous lips, I brought a hand to them, a single sob shaking my body. Pieces of me were barely held together by a thread. I was coming undone.

"Oh, my dear Rilla…is all this because of Kenneth?"

I shook my head, but my lips betrayed me yet again. "I promised him…"

Mom closed the distance between us then, holding me in her arms as the tears finally broke loose. She held me as she had when I was a little kid, unsettled because I thought the monsters under my bed were as real as the chickens running outside in their coup.

"Oh, child, hush. It's okay, it's okay," she whispered into my hair, her comforting tone the only thing keeping me whole. Despite how much I wanted to yell at her, to tell her to leave me alone, she was the hand weaving that thread holding me together – even if barely.

"No, it's not," I cried, my voice muffled as I buried my face in her shoulder. "When he left…when…"

"It's okay, darling, breathe, it's okay. Here." Mom leaned back to dry my tears with her thumb and then led me to the settee by the wall opposite the full-length mirror – the one that had shown me Kenneth's ghost, his disapproving look tipping me over the edge. "Breathe, Rilla, breathe. I know losing Kenneth was hard on you, but it doesn't mean life doesn't give us second chances..." Mom held my hand in hers, softly. "I saw the way your eyes glinted every time you talked about your friend Josie all those years back, how her support helped you get through your loss..."

"Stop, Mom, please... I... I can't. I just can't." I stood, pacing the small room as Mom watched me from the settee, her shoulders hunched with worry. My hand felt cold; my chest, bare. I looked out the window and the idea of running, of being out in the open, seemed like the only way to get enough air into my lungs. There was not enough in here, so I leaned out the window, taking a deep breath. "I thought...after Kenneth, I thought that was it. I thought I was meant to live without love, like Grandma Marilla did—"

"Oh, no, dear. I must stop you there!" Mom stood up, too, shaking her head with a stern look on her face, her back suddenly so straight she looked much taller than she was. "Marilla didn't live without love; she was filled with it! Not only from Matthew and I, but from the whole community," she said in a stern yet loving tone.

"But she never married!" My voice rose higher than I intended as I turned to her, so I lowered it before I kept going, before I admitted what had been gnawing at me. "And maybe I'm not meant to marry, either...I was named after her for something, right?" I turned to the window again, unable to keep looking at my mother's broken expression. I couldn't deal with the pity I saw in her eyes.

"Yes," Mom replied without pause, and then her voice came closer, right from behind my shoulder. The warmth of her body was like a blanket across my back. "For her love and determination." A hand was gently placed on my shoulder, anchoring me to the bridal room and to the choices I've made. "Not even when she was completely blind was she as blind as you're being right now, my dear Rilla."

Mom's statement paused my every racing thought. Not ever, in my twenty-four years of life, had my mother insulted me like that. And for some reason, it made the gears in my brain stop and start again. *Blind? Me?* She was the one that couldn't see the gravity of the situation.

"Marilla didn't have the desire to marry. You do. You always did. I remember you stealing my wedding dress when you were only seven, pretending you were marrying a prince."

"But I'm not marrying a prince, am I? I'm engaged to another woman. And I'm not even legally marrying, because I can't...so, what's the point? Maybe this is my punishment for not keeping my word. I am not *meant* to marry," I said almost stubbornly.

"Sweety, please." Mom pressed my shoulder, urging me to turn, but I couldn't. "Tell me what you're talking about, exactly. What is this promise you think you're breaking?"

With my eyes on the horizon, I let my mind travel back to another time; to what felt like another life. After all, the landscape outside this window wasn't unlike the one I'd lived by back then.

"Before Kenneth left to join the war, he came to me..." He'd been wearing his uniform, his shoulders so straight as he'd looked me in the eyes, a shy smile playing on his pale lips. He'd been everything I'd ever dreamed of; the boy of my dreams now turned into a man – a man that had to leave and fight a war I couldn't be a part of. The same as my brothers before him, the love of my life was leaving. And I didn't know if he'd come back...but he'd promised. He'd promised he would.

"Kenneth promised he'd come back," I admitted aloud for the first time, the secret of that meeting finally out in the world. "And in turn, I promised I'd wait for him..."

"And you did, darling!" When Mom pressed my shoulder again, I turned to her. "You waited for him. For years." Her hand landed on my cheek, cupping my face as if I were still a little child afraid of invisible monsters.

I shook my head, tears spilling into my mother's palm as every bit of my heart left through my throat. Every word I had never dared say aloud came out in a mess of sobs. "I tried. I tried to, but...he was gone for so long, and when I stopped hearing back from him, when my letters stopped being answered...the Red Cross was meant to be a way to be closer to him, to help in any way I could, to try and do my part when they were leaving their bodies and souls out there..." I took a breath, the image of a completely different face filling my mind now. "I wasn't expecting *her*," I admitted. Josephine had been Kenneth's complete opposite. She was soft where he'd been hard, yet stubborn when he'd been gentle. "I wasn't expecting to find such a good friend, someone that understood me so well, listened to me as I cried about a man I wasn't sure I'd ever see again. And Josephine was there..." Her name had always been a caress on my lips, but it felt like betrayal as I said her full name now in the same way I'd whispered it through the night so many times before.

Josephine Lynde had shown up in my life like a breath of fresh air. When I thought there was no more oxygen, when I couldn't keep going on my own, Josie had knocked on my door – the same where I'd last seen Kenneth – and asked if we needed more nurses to volunteer. I didn't know back then Josie was not only volunteering to help in the Red Cross, but she'd soon be volunteering to be the one carrying me when I couldn't keep going, when the news of Kenneth's death in battle finally arrived and I felt the world was over. It was around the same time Walter had enlisted, and Josie was there to hold me as I prayed with everything I had for my brother to return home safely.

I couldn't put it in so many words, but I knew Mom understood. She had lost Walter, too. And for a long time, she'd thought we'd lost my brother Jem as well. We both knew the heaviness of grief.

"When I lost Kenneth...I promised myself I'd die without my lips ever knowing what a kiss felt like. But...I betrayed him, and I betrayed myself."

Josephine's lips had been a forbidden fruit for the longest year of my life. And if she hadn't been brave enough to kiss me the first time after one too many glasses of sherry, I don't think I'd have ever done it myself. Her lips were soft like velvet, sweet like cinnamon apple pie. They had the most perfect cupid's bow, and I hadn't been able to stop looking at them ever since that very first kiss. But I had never kissed her in front of anyone, only in the privacy of our own company.

*You may now kiss the bride.*

"So, that's why I... I can't do it," I finished.

I couldn't kiss her in front of the whole world and break my promise completely. It was one thing when it was just us, but...I couldn't go on with this farce. It wasn't real. It wasn't right.

Mom looked into my eyes for a moment; searching, waiting. Then, her hands took mine again, and she spoke so softly I thought the Anne I'd known all my life had run out the window and a new one had come in: one that sounded a lot more like Aunty Diana.

"You've been through such challenging times, Rilla," Mom said gently. "And I understand how hard this must be on you. But please, do not think for a single minute God would ever expect you to keep such a promise. Why do you think He put Josephine in your way, huh? If I know Rachel's granddaughter even a little bit, I know she is as hard-headed as her grandma was in some senses...and trust me, she'd have none of it if she heard you speaking like this."

A knock at the door stopped Mom cold. We both looked at the knob, waiting for it to turn. Instead, a cheerful voice came from the other side.

"Is everything okay? Are you ready? Can I come in?"

Mom looked at me with a question written on her face, and when I nodded, she moved to the door and opened it. Diana stood in the hallway with a big smile that dropped the moment she saw my tear-stained face and Mom's concerned expression.

"Oh dear, are we having a situation here?" she asked as she let herself in and closed the door after giving the hallway a quick glance.

"Hi, Aunty." I went over to Diana and gave her a quick hug, unsure I'd be able to hold her properly without breaking into a waterfall of tears again. "Thank you for being here."

"What happened, my sweet child?" Diana took a handkerchief out of her bag and made short work of cleaning my face, as she'd done so many times when I was a messy little kid playing war with Jem and the twins.

"I walked in to find her with one leg out the window," Mom said before I could reply.

Aunt Diana gave her a reproaching look, then turned back to me. With as little words as I could, I told her what had happened, how looking at myself in the mirror had reminded me of the time

I'd stolen Mom's dress – not when I was seven, but when I was seventeen – and had pictured myself marrying Kenneth; how I had seen his ghost by my side, reminding me of the promise I had made. I told her how I'd broken that promise the day Josephine had kissed me for the first time. How I couldn't break it again in front of everyone we both loved, and how it felt like a betrayal.

Diana listened to me intently, her lips pursed into a straight line. When I was finished, she sighed.

"Anne," she said, turning towards my mother. "I think it's time we leave." She said it so softly, for a moment, I thought I'd heard her wrong. But then, she turned to me.

"Rilla, I don't think this is a conversation you should be having with us. This is something you need to talk about with Josephine before you walk out of this room and into the ceremony we've been so carefully planning for all these weeks. You love Josie. Josie loves you. And I know that. You know that. Josie knows that. But whether you're ready to love her openly...that's something between the two of you. No one else."

There were no questions. Just facts. And the words were slow to register, but Mom eventually nodded and moved to the door, her hand levitating over the knob as she looked at me.

"Should I go find her?" she asked, a tentative smile on her lips.

This was it; what I needed. I had panicked myself into a frenzy, but here were the two women that had led every step of my life reminding me of the important lessons we've learned together. Of how communication was key.

My mother had always been open in answering all our curious questions and had even encouraged them. Aunt Diana had been the one I'd confided in when I was scared Mom wouldn't understand my childhood crushes or was scared to share something with her. Diana had taught me some things needed to be brought to my mother's attention, even if I didn't want to; because they concerned her.

As I looked at them, their eyes on me, expectant, I understood these two women not only knew what I wanted, but what I needed: I needed to speak to my betrothed.

No matter how terrified I was of loving her openly, I wanted Josephine to be by my side every day for the rest of my life – that's why I had accepted her proposal.

Diana knew that.

Mom knew that.

And God, I knew that.

But I had let fear get the best of me. I had let the ghost of my past haunt me till the point of submission. Years ago, Josie had taught me I could heal from anything; I was stronger than I gave myself credit for. And life had a way of bringing us what we needed the most. And I needed Mom to weave the thread to hold me in place until Aunt Diana delivered the final knot, reminding me communication only works if your message is getting across...and my message wasn't for my mother or my aunt. It was for my lover.

W*hat had I been thinking?* I couldn't just run away without talking to Josephine, without telling her how I felt, what I feared. She'd been by my side at my worst, so why couldn't I share this one fear with her?

"Go find her," I said, and Mom turned the knob. "Mom, wait!"

I rushed across the two steps that separated us and threw my arms around her shoulders, hugging her as tight as I could with the huge skirts standing between us. "Thank you," I whispered into her ear. "Thank you for everything. And I'm sorry I yelled."

Mom kissed my cheek as I broke the hug and said: "I love you." Then, she was out the door, and I was sure her eyes were lined with tears as she walked down the hall.

"Are you ready for this?" Diana moved over to me and got some powder and kohl out of her bag, fixing my makeup as I replied.

"I think so. And thank you for always having the right words to bring me back to myself."

Diana smiled, put a little powder onto my cheeks, and then kissed me gently so as not to ruin her work. "You know, I didn't even know when I was your age..." She stepped back, looking at me with a fresh bright smile.

"Know what?"

"That I like women the same way I like men," she said simply. My mouth fell open, my eyes adjusting to see Aunt Diana in a light that had never shined on her before.

"You, what?"

Diana laughed brightly, fixing a loose strand of dark hair behind her ear before going on. "I married young. And I loved my husband so very much...but it wasn't until after he passed away I realised there had been many women in my life that had caught my attention in a way...well, less than traditional. It wasn't easy to admit this to myself, but eventually, I guess I fell in love all over again."

"Why is this the first time I'm hearing this?" I asked, trying to think back on the last few years since my uncle had died. I knew Aunt Diana had many girlfriends...*was she in love with any of them?*

"This is not a story for today." Diana shook her head. "I hear steps down the hall, and I'm sure Josephine is just about to knock on the door, so...this is *your* moment. Your moment to figure out what it is you want in life and if you're ready to have it. If you're ready to forget about the rest of the world, about any promises you might've made, and promise yourself now this is who you are; this is who you love. If there's one piece of advice I can give you, it's you should do everything for love, darling. Everything. Real love is hard to come by...and if you don't act on it, it could be too late."

Diana glanced at the door quickly, then looked at me with a worried expression. "But if you're not ready now...you need to tell Josephine. You need to be forthcoming with her and let her know how you feel. She deserves that much."

There was a triple knock at the door and Diana moved toward it.

I nodded, feeling the tears in my eyes as well as the ones stuck in my throat.

"I love you, Rilla." With that, Diana opened the door and squeezed out. I heard her say something, and then a worried voice came from the other side of the door, only a tiny crack allowing me to see some white fabric on the other side.

"Berthie…is everything okay?" Josie asked. "Your mother told me you needed to talk to me before the celebration."

I walked to the door, letting my fingers slip through the small crack as I searched for her warmth. I wasn't sure what I was going to tell her. The promise still hung heavy over my head, but everything Diana had said had also stirred something inside of me, something I'd been trying to push down for a very long time. The moment Josephine's fingers closed around mine, though, I felt grounded. Gravity pulled me right to her and I glued my back to the wall, holding onto her and taking in the sweet smell of her perfume: jasmine and touch of vanilla.

I'd been so stupid to think I could run away from this woman that was the softest breeze of autumn and the flowering buds of spring. Josie wasn't everything I'd ever dreamed of, for not even my wildest imagination could've made her up. It was preposterous such a kind soul could even exist in this war-ridden world.

And I'd been blind to cling so hard to a love I now realised I'd never even known. I didn't know what it felt like to hold Kenneth's hand through the night, but Josephine had held mine for a thousand of them. I didn't even know how he'd liked his coffee in the morning, and yet I had made countless cups for Josie – with just a touch of black pepper and nutmeg to spice life up. I didn't know if he'd snored, but I had woken up laughing when Josie did.

Josie had been there since the day she'd knocked on my door, and she hadn't left my side since. *How could I ever think of leaving hers?*

"I just needed you to know something..." I tried to find the words to talk to her about the promise, about my doubts. *But didn't she know that already?* I had never said it to her in so many words, but she'd been the one to hold me as I'd mourned, the one to dry my tears and make me lemon tea. She'd helped me dress when I didn't have enough strength to do so myself and had cooked me the most nourishing meals to help me gain my strength back. "I know I haven't said it enough, and maybe I'm not always the best with words or the one to show my love as I should...but waking up by your side makes the sun seem brighter," I said, leaning my head against the wall separating us.

It'd been there. It had always been there: a love so strong I no longer knew how to breathe or live without it. I'd always feared putting it into words, so I had never really told Josephine how much she meant to me. I couldn't go through today without her knowing how I felt.

"Every cup of tea is sweeter when you're sitting next to me, our feet tangled under the table. I can talk to you through a whole night, reminiscing on where we've been and where we want to go, and I'd never get bored. Life by your side just looks better, tastes better...and I'm sorry if I don't always tell you these things."

Josephine squeezed my fingers and I heard her clear her throat before she said: "Where is all this coming from, Berthie? Did something happen?"

"You could say so." I chuckled, the notion of running out the window seeming so stupid now. "For the past three years, I've had everything I ever wanted right in front of me, and I feel like I often took it for granted. Took *you* for granted. I don't want to ever take you for granted again..." I squeezed her fingers tighter, wanting to hold all of her, to let my hands travel around her ample hips, to hold onto her waist and stare into her beautiful dark eyes. "This is more than anything I've ever felt before. In you, I found someone worth all the wait, worth every odd look we might get as we walk the streets hand in hand..."

"My love, I'd walk down Main Road and kiss you without a single care in the world," Josie said, her voice full of emotion. *Of course she would.* She'd always been the brave one of the two of us. The strong one. The hot-headed one.

"Can I look at you?" I wondered, my stomach in knots as I imagined walking down the aisle toward her, kissing her in front of all our loved ones. "I need to see you." Something that had felt so scary minutes ago now felt like the highlight of my day, my year, my life. And I needed to see her before we were there; to look into her eyes and make sure she knew just how much I loved her. I needed her to understand how sure I was of this. Of us.

To answer my question, Josie pried the door open. She stood there, her hand still in mine, her eyes lined with tears as she found me looking back at her, taking all of her in. I took a step back to allow her into the room, and she followed me without question.

Josie's dress hugged her every curve in the way I wanted my hands to. It was a glimpse of the breathtaking woman she was, a simple fabric cinched in all the perfect spots, making my eyes water in awe. The white fabric widened just after the perfect curve of her hips, hiding the powerful legs that had held my weight so many times before.

I ripped my eyes away from her waist, her bosom, her perfect lips, and I centred my whole being in her dark freckled eyes as I took a hand to her cheek – to the warm dark skin contrasting so much with the paleness of mine.

"Josie..." Her name was a prayer, a plea for redemption. "I want to kiss you every day for the rest of my breathing hours," I promised. "I want to kiss you good morning as the sun comes up and kiss you goodnight amid the warm sheets in our bed every single night. I want to kiss your forehead when you're being stubborn and kiss your hands as you cook me the most delicious meals. I want this. I do."

As the two simple words stumbled out, their truth grounded me. This was what I wanted. *She* was what I wanted.

"Shouldn't we wait for the ceremony for all these soulful words?" Josie asked, the most beautiful smile tugging her plump lips upwards.

"Don't worry, I can say them again in front of the whole wide world," I said, so sure of this now. "I promise you, here and now, I am yours until the end of our days. And I will say it again in front of all those waiting for us out there, but first…I needed *you* to know it. I needed for it to be just you and me, as it's always been."

My hand trailed up her temple, tangling in her dark curls, and Josie leaned into my touch, her eyes slightly closed.

"I could get used to this," she whispered.

"You'd better." I bit my bottom lip, the daunting words now playing in my mind almost like a joke – or as a statement. "You may now kiss the bride," I said slowly, tasting the words, feeling them to my core.

Josie opened her eyes, laughing. "I think we need to wait a little bit to hear those words, don't we?"

"No. I think I may kiss my bride now, if she's okay with it."

Josie's smile warmed me in such a way I was sure I no longer needed the blush Diana had so carefully applied only moments before.

"She is more than okay with it."

And so I did. I let my lips softly press to hers, tasting cinnamon apple pie and dreaming of home-baked goods for the rest of my life. I took our intertwined hands to her waist and let go of her fingers, tangling myself in the white fabric around her hips instead. One hand in her hair, the other in the small of her back, I pressed her to me, lingering in a kiss that deepened as I forgot everything about the wedding, about the people waiting for us outside this bridal room, and about the people we'd left behind. Future and past were not the matter as I kissed my bride-to-be with my heart and soul, my heart chanting: *I do. I do. I do.*

When we finally pulled apart, albeit reluctantly, Josie's smile was a furnace rekindling my soul after the coldness of letting her go. Her eyes, as dark as night now, glinted with mischief.

"We'd better go now, or else I'm taking you into this room and I'm closing the door behind us," she whispered into my lips, sealing her threat with a single deep kiss.

"I think we've made them wait long enough," I admitted. "Let's walk down the aisle and say 'I do' for the whole world to hear. There will be plenty of time for the rest."

I took Josie's hand and led her out of the room and back into the hall. At the end of it, two figures were waiting for us, and I could swear I saw Diana look at my mother before wiping tears out of the corner of her eye.

"Their friendship gave me hope all those years back, did you know?" Josie's voice was soft, only for me to hear.

"What do you mean?"

Josie looked at me and smiled. "Even if I couldn't have this…if you didn't see me this way…I knew at least I could have you as a friend; we could have a friendship like Anne and Diana's. And, for me, that would've been enough."

I couldn't help it: I kissed her again, just briefly.

"I don't think it would've been enough for me."

# Unwritten Heart

## by Jesica Bavcar

**Literary World**: Little Women

When Jo March decided to write her first romance novel, she thought everything would be smooth sailing. But when writer's block hits and she begins to question her understanding of love, Jo finds herself struggling to connect with the story. That is until Harper, a vibrant artist moves into the same building and quickly becomes Jo's unexpected source of inspiration. As they bond over creativity and shared passions, Jo starts to notice something shifting within her.

Now, she must confront the possibility that the love story she's been struggling to write might not just be fiction—but be her very own.

"No."

Jo scribbled something next to a paragraph before her eyes continued scanning the page from left to right.

"No, no, no, no."

She crossed out a whole sentence, so hard that the pen dug into the paper and left a small hole behind. By the time she was finished, the sheet in her hand was more black than white, full of angry scribbles and questions about her self-worth.

Dropping the pen with a clatter, she leaned back on the chair and frowned at the stack of papers on her desk. They were all in the same state, butchered by the same hand that had given them life.

"Ugh," Jo sighed and closed her eyes. *Why is it so hard to write this scene?* She'd written hundreds of stories in her life —had started when she'd turned seven and hadn't stopped in the past sixteen years. Her computer was full of drafts, she owned an unhealthy amount of notebooks, and people often told her she was talented...but still, somehow, she couldn't get this silly thing done.

True, she was more used to tales of betrayal, revenge, and poison, so this was all new. It was her first time writing a romance. What made no sense to her was that, if she could describe the burning feeling of drinking poison to perfection, then why was it so hard to capture the emotions between the couple in this story? No matter how much she changed the words, they always sounded forced. Hollow.

"Jo?" Meg's voice rang down the hall and, a few moments later, her older sister knocked gently on the doorframe. "Jo, can I borrow your necklace?"

"What?" Opening her eyes, Jo straightened up and turned to see Meg bouncing on her toes. She was wearing a very pretty pink dress; second-hand for sure, but it looked lovely against her pale skin.

"The golden one Aunt March gave you for your birthday last year, the one with the sunflower?"

"What do you need it for?"

"It goes with my outfit." She tugged on her skirt and swayed this way and that, a shy smile on her face. "And you never use it anyway, it's a waste."

"Sure, go ahead." Jo waved a hand, gesturing towards her messy wardrobe, then turned back to her desk. Dropping her head on her hands, she sighed and tugged her hair a little.

Meg hesitated. "You okay?"

"I'm fine, just... stuck."

Walking into the room, Meg glanced over Jo's shoulder at the scribbling mess. "Writer's block?"

"You could say that," Jo scoffed. "I'm writing their first kiss, and it's supposed to be romantic as hell, emotional and grand, but all I write is...yuck."

"Jo," Meg laughed, "I've read the stories you wrote on social issues and injustices and they were amazing. A kiss scene should be a piece of cake for you."

"I know! It's something so simple, but I can't do it! Maybe I'm just a terrible writer."

Before Meg could reply, Amy popped her head around the door, attracted as usual by all the ruckus. "What's going on?"

"Jo is stuck with her novel."

Groaning, Jo face planted over the papers. "I suck."

"You're being too hard on yourself." Meg smiled and brushed Jo's long hair gently. "Romance isn't all about grand gestures. It's about the connection between two people, the small details. Just write what feels natural to you."

"Well, that's the problem, none of this comes naturally. I just don't get it."

Amy let herself in and laid on Jo's bed, propping her head up on a hand. She was chewing gum, and the sound grated on Jo's nerves. "Why don't you write on your computer like a normal person?"

"It's easier to get things going with pen and paper." Jo sighed. "At least usually, it is."

"Just write something like in the fairy tales," Amy suggested, throwing an arm over her forehead and pretending to faint, "when the guy comes and sweeps the heroine off her feet."

Jo shook her head. "I don't want her to be a girl who's simply waiting for her prince charming to come along, marry her, and give her babies."

"Hey, there's nothing wrong with wanting to marry and have children," Meg said, crossing her arms.

"Of course not. It's a perfectly good dream…as long as it's a choice." Leaning back in her chair again, Jo snatched a pillow from the bed and held it to her chest. "But there's still a lot of pressure today for women to do the whole married life, like that's all they are good for. Like, how is the phrase 'stay in the kitchen' still a thing today?"

"Women in the old days couldn't do anything without a husband," Amy pointed out. "They couldn't even make their own money and had to study their whole childhood so they could be good wives and marry rich. It's different today."

"Yes, and it's a huge change, but people still look at you weird if you say you don't want to have children. And I don't want to do that to my character. She's going to be more than just a prop for some guy, but that doesn't mean she doesn't want romance, and I'm doing a piss-poor job giving it to her."

"Jo..." Meg started, but then Beth appeared at the doorway, tilting her head.

"Why are you all huddled in Jo's room?"

"Jo doesn't know anything about romance," Amy said through a bubble she was blowing.

A pillow flew into her face, making Beth flinch and Meg laugh.

"Jo! Ugh, I think I swallowed my gum."

Jo ignored her. "I'm just having a hard time describing the attraction between characters."

Beth walked in gingerly and leaned against the wall, her hands behind her back. "Well, you live in New York. Everywhere you look there are new people and stories to tell. Why don't you draw from that? Go to the park, watch some couples interact."

"I don't know if that'll help." Jo bit the tip of her ink-stained finger. "I tried using couples from movies and books as inspiration, but what I come up with...it doesn't feel real. If I don't believe in what I write, who will?"

Her sisters looked at each other, but before any of them could interject, Jo pushed her chair back and started pacing. "Everything I come up with feels fake. Like, what does..." Pausing in front of her desk, she grabbed one of the sheets and read, "'...his broody eyes darkened' even mean? How can eyes get darker?"

"Oh, I know!" Amy jumped up, sitting on her knees and bouncing on the mattress. "You know when a guy looks at you in that particular way, like his head is tilted down," she did this herself, acting it out as she talked, "and his eyes are all serious and it's like that 'you're mine' kind of thing."

Jo made a face and pulled back. "Ew. I thought we agreed women aren't men's property."

Amy sighed and dropped back on the bed. "See? You don't understand romance at all."

"Then how would *you* go about it, smartypants?" Jo crossed her arms. "Without being all...weird and creepy."

"It's not creepy!" Amy huffed, offended. "Love has to be passionate. When you like a guy, you want to spend all your time with him, get to know everything about him and show him every part of you." She tugged on a strand of blond hair and looked out the window. "You want to know what his lips feel like."

"Gross," Jo deadpanned, then turned to Meg. "Meg, what do you think?"

Meg blushed and looked away. "I think Amy has a point." Jo started to protest, but Meg kept talking over her. "I also think love is kind. Like Mr. Brooke."

"Your teacher?" Beth raised her eyebrows, and Amy's eyes widened. Meg's cheeks were bright red now.

"He has a way with his words, and he's such a gentleman." Meg looked down, but a small smile tugged on her lips. "He knows how to listen and makes me feel seen. It's hard to focus on studying when he's around."

Jo and her younger sisters were silent, staring at Meg. They'd never heard her talk about a man like that, let alone her teacher. Meg loved her classes as much as Jo loved writing, and she couldn't remember a time when any guy had kept her mind from focusing on her stories.

"I like him, okay?" Meg blurted when the pressure of her sister's gazes became too much.

"Oh, you *like* him," Amy drawled, smiling wide. "You want to marry him and make pretty babies with him?"

"Shut up!"

"I think love can come in many forms," Beth interrupted the imminent argument with her quiet voice. "Mr. Laurence is very kind to me, but I don't see him that way."

"Thank God," Amy interjected. "If you fell for Laurie's grandpa..." She shivered from head to toe.

"I like going next door to play the piano and listen to Mr. Laurence talk about his daughter, but it's more like a familial bond."

Jo pondered all this for a moment. Out of everything her sisters had said, she could only relate to Beth's experience. She'd never felt what people said she was supposed to feel. That was part of the reason why she was working on a romance novel. Loneliness gripped her heart sometimes, along with the desire to experience something like the great stories she read, but she'd never felt that way about any man she'd met. She didn't get it. If she could write about it, maybe she could understand it.

Or maybe she was broken.

Shaking her head, Jo went to the door. “Forget it. I’m just gonna go for a walk.”

“Are you going out looking like that?” Amy pointed out. Jo looked up and touched the old hat she was wearing. It looked straight out of 1860s men’s fashion and she loved it, but it wasn’t something she wore outside. Taking it off, she threw it somewhere on the pile of clothes in her wardrobe and walked out.

It was nice sharing an apartment with her sisters while they all studied their respective careers, but sometimes she felt like she was the odd one out. She didn’t have Meg’s patience, Amy’s appeal, or Beth’s politeness. She was loud, and fierce, and rough, and all the things her Aunt March said men didn’t like in a woman.

The hallway outside was quiet and Jo sighed as she got into the elevator, pressed the button for the lobby, and tapped her foot impatiently.

Suddenly, a loud bang startled her as someone slammed into the closing doors, forcing them open again. Jo jumped, her heart racing, but quickly relaxed when she saw who it was.

"Teddy!" she exclaimed, punching him lightly on the arm. "You scared the shit out of me!"

The boy grinned, rubbing his arm in mock pain as he joined her in the elevator. He leaned against the wall beside her, that familiar glint of mischief in his eyes. "Sorry, Jo. You looked so out of it, I couldn’t resist.” The doors finally closed and, as they began their descent, Teddy bumped his shoulder against hers. "What's got you so lost in thought?"

Jo groaned. "Just this scene I don't know how to write."

"Wanna go back to my place and play Call of Duty till you forget about it?"

"I don't think that's gonna help," Jo laughed, shaking her head. "But thanks for the offer. I'm going to clear my head for a bit, if you want to join?"

"Well, someone's got to keep you from running into lamp posts." Teddy nodded solemnly and Jo smiled, punching him again.

"Thanks, Teddy."

The doors dinged and opened. As they were about to step out, Teddy noticed Mrs. Higgins, an old lady from the second floor, shuffling in with her small dog. Taking a step to the side, he put an arm out to hold the doors open for her. Mrs. Higgins looked up, surprised, but smiled when she saw Teddy.

"Thank you so much, dearie," she said, walking into the small cubicle. Then she noticed Jo, and a knowing smile spread on her face. "Off on a date, are you?" she asked, her voice warm and teasing.

Jo rolled her eyes. "Again, Mrs. Higgins, we are *not* dating."

"Well, honey, what are you waiting for?" The old woman gave her a sympathetic look, smiling like old people do. "If you don't hurry, that train will leave the station."

The doors closed on her and Jo rubbed her temples. "Why do they always say things like that? I'm twenty-three, it's not like my life will end tomorrow."

"I think she just wants to help, you know? Offer her *elderly* wisdom," Teddy joked.

"Well, *her* advice on relationships won't help me write my novel," Jo grumbled.

The breeze outside was a welcome change from her stuffy room. Jo breathed in deep, her thoughts travelling far. Her parents were an exception, but people had always tried to tell her how to behave. They wanted her to wear pink dresses, play with dolls, and be all proper. But Jo had always been on the wild side: she loved climbing trees, sitting in weird positions that were not "ladylike", and playing football with the boys.

As she got older, the talk about boyfriends and dating only got worse. She remembered the first time she'd told Aunt March that she didn't want to get married or have kids. The old bat had been scandalized, and had simply said Jo was too young to understand what she was saying.

"Where to now?" Teddy asked, following after her.

"Anywhere is fine."

They lived on a quaint, relatively quiet street—for New York, at least. Jo loved that it was lined with trees, the greenery offering a stunning contrast against the brick walls and endless lines of cars parked by the sidewalk. It provided the perfect backdrop for aimless strolls.

As they walked, Jo glanced at Teddy, at the way he smiled and brushed his long black hair back against the wind. She knew women fell at his feet and that he'd dated his fair share of girls, but she'd never thought of him the way everyone expected her to. In her eyes, Theodore Laurence was just a friend, the raucous neighbour who had one day moved in across the hall and accepted her for who she was, tomboy or not.

"Hey, you're a guy," she said suddenly.

Teddy raised an amused eyebrow. "Thanks for noticing?"

"How would *you* describe love?" Why hadn't she thought of this? She'd always been more in line with Teddy's thinking than her sister's. His perspective would surely help more.

Teddy paused, looking up at the blue sky. He took a moment to reply, and Jo waited while they strolled down the sidewalk. "Well, love is...when you can't stop thinking about someone, right? Like, you see them, and your heart just...skips. And you want to be near them, make them happy, be better for them. It's like...everything's brighter when they're around. You know?"

Jo stared at him for a moment, trying to process what he'd said. It made sense, in a way…but also, it didn't. She'd felt something like that for her friends and family, so what was the difference? Also, she couldn't relate to the idea of love as some all-consuming force, and the words felt... distant, somehow.

"I'm a hopeless case, aren't I?" she whined.

Teddy laughed. "Honestly, I'm still trying to figure it out myself. I used to have a more selfish look on this whole thing, more focused on what *I* wanted." Glancing back at their apartment building, a small smile tugged one corner of his lips up. "I'm sure that, when the time is right for you, it'll all make sense."

Jo wasn't sure what he meant by the right time, but she sure hoped he was right.

A few days later, she still hadn't made any progress. She'd spent hours at the park, people-watching until she feared someone might mistake her for a stalker. She'd read books and wrote, wrote, wrote —yet every piece of paper became a crumbled corpse in her room's cemetery. It was clear she was out of her depth and, as she trudged back home after a long day at uni, the thought crept into her mind: maybe she should just give up.

The idea resounded in her brain constantly, and she was so distracted that, as she got off at her floor and toyed with the keys in her hand, she almost tripped over something.

Stopping in her tracks, she found piles of boxes stacked by the door of apartment 6. The door was open, and she could hear movements and straining coming from inside. *Someone must be moving in*, she thought, her curious eyes scanning the belongings. A large easel caught her attention. Jo took an unconscious step closer just as a girl walked out, brushing the back of her hand over her slightly damp forehead. She halted when she noticed Jo snooping around, and a wide smile spread across her face.

"Hey," she greeted.

There was a dimple on her cheek. Her pale pink hair was cropped short on one side, with soft waves cascading over the other. She wore baggy jean overalls with nothing but a tight crop top underneath, revealing the skin along her sides. Her eyes met Jo's and, frozen as she was, Jo fumbled and dropped her keys.

The girl laughed. "Sorry, didn't mean to startle you. I'm Harper."

"Hi, um..." Jo hurried to pick them up, heart jumping and mind scrambling for words. "Welcome to the building."

With that, she turned on her heel and almost sprinted back to her apartment, sparing only one swift glance over her shoulder before closing the door behind her. Leaning against it, she let her head thud back on the wood and stared up at the ceiling.

*What was that?*

Logical thought had left Jo's brain and, in its place, all that was left was *Wow*. Harper was cool. There was a carefree aura about her, something Jo admired, and her smile was pretty. She had no idea why her heart was pounding so hard. Perhaps it was just that the new girl seemed so daring. Perhaps Jo wanted to be like her, just a little bit. Trying to figure it out, she stood there until Meg found her and frowned.

"What happened?"

Jo blinked, still trying to process. "A girl moved in."

Meg's frown deepened. "And?"

"Oh, I saw her," Amy chimed in, coming from her room with a backpack in hand. "Aunt March would hate her."

Jo rolled her eyes. "Aunt March hates everyone who isn't conventional. She's been very clear about it whenever I'm around."

"That's not true," Amy said, defending her. "She's just pragmatic. She only wants to help us make good money, like she did."

"Yet she won't say where she made her fortune," Jo retorted, igniting the old-time question she and her sisters loved to discuss every now and then: what kind of job had Aunt March had?

"Maybe she's a mafia boss," Amy ventured.

"She certainly looks the part."

"I wouldn't like to make her my enemy."

"Do you think she's ever had to kill someone?"

"That's rude," Beth interjected, her soft voice cutting through their banter.

Amy ignored her and turned to Jo with a teasing grin. "So, why did the new girl scare you?"

Jo stiffened. "What? I'm not scared."

"Well, you sort of look out of breath," Meg pointed out.

"I'm fine," Jo insisted, though her voice wavered slightly. "Just thinking about stuff."

"Okay..." Meg said, unconvinced. She exchanged a look with Amy before adding, "We're heading out for a bit. We'll be back by dinner."

As her sisters grabbed their bags and left, Jo found herself alone in the quiet apartment. She considered crashing at Teddy's place, the usual refuge when she needed to escape her thoughts. But, deep down, she knew she was just running away.

Sighing, she resolved to give her story one more try. If the words didn't flow, she'd put it on hold. A vague idea lingered in her mind, something she couldn't quite grasp yet. Putting on her old hat, she settled on the couch, notebook in hand, when a sudden knock on the door interrupted her thoughts.

Jo tugged on the doorknob and there stood Harper, all bright smiles and blue eyes. "Hey, sorry to bother. You wouldn't happen to have a cup I could borrow, would you? I know mine are somewhere, but I checked through every box and couldn't find them."

Jo blinked, momentarily caught off guard by Harper's presence. Her hair was tousled, and there were paint smudges on her jeans that she hadn't noticed before.

"Oh, sure!" Jo replied, shaking off her surprise. "Come on in, I'll grab one for you."

She led Harper inside and rummaged through the kitchen cabinet. Harper's eyes followed her every move, and Jo's heart did that weird fluttering thing again.

*What is wrong with me?*

She was used to people looking at her weirdly, but she wasn't usually affected by a stranger's judgement.

"That's an interesting hat," Harper commented. There was no contempt in her voice though, just a warm interest that puzzled Jo.

"Oh." Looking down, she toyed with her favourite mug, the one that had a flowery J on it. "You might think it's silly, but I wear it whenever I write. Sort of like a ritual."

"Not at all." Harper nodded, her expression understanding. "Helps you get in the zone, right?"

"Yes!" Jo exclaimed, a small smile forming on her face. She handed over the mug, worrying her lip. "Sorry, I don't think I introduced myself earlier. My name's Josephine, but everyone calls me Jo."

Harper eyed the mug, her grin widening. "Yeah, you seemed to be in a rush. It's nice to meet you, Jo." Her gaze drifted around the apartment, pausing on the scattered notebooks, pens, and books. "So, you're a writer?"

"I try," Jo huffed. "I'm working on a novel right now but, honestly, it's been more of a struggle than I'd like to admit."

Harper chuckled. "Yeah, some days are like that. You can't get your hand to capture what's in your head, or your head simply won't cooperate."

Jo glanced at her, surprised by how easily Harper seemed to understand. "Yeah..."

Sensing her confusion, Harper pointed at the paint on her clothes. “I’m an artist.”

*Of course*, Jo thought, remembering the easel she’d seen before. Leaning her hip on the counter, she crossed her arms. “What do you do on those days? I’m working on a scene that refuses to cooperate with me."

Harper laughed and took a seat at the small kitchen table. "I know the feeling. Sometimes I’ll start a painting, and it’ll just...not work. It’s like the idea is there, but the feeling is missing."

“Exactly!” Jo relaxed a little, the feeling in her chest easing up. "It’s weird, right? I mean, we’re supposed to be creative, but sometimes it feels like creativity has its own mind."

"Totally," Harper agreed, her eyes lighting up. "But I think that’s part of it, you know? The struggle is what makes it meaningful when it finally clicks."

Smiling, Jo sat across from her. "I guess you’re right. Maybe I’m just too caught up in trying to make it perfect."

"Perfection is overrated." Harper rolled her eyes playfully. "It’s the messy, imperfect stuff that usually ends up being the most interesting."

That struck a chord in Jo. She’d always been a perfectionist, quick to criticize not just her writing, but her appearance and personality as well. Harper’s words knocked on the walls Jo had built over the years and made them shiver. It was as though she acknowledged the vulnerability and said it was fine.

Of course, she knew logically that Harper wasn't trying to be so deep. Still, she liked it—the way Harper seemed to understand without even trying.

They fell into a comfortable silence, both of them seemingly lost in their own thoughts. After a moment, Harper cleared her throat. "I don't want to take up more of your time. Thank you for this." She cradled the mug between her hands and smiled softly. "I promise to return it soon."

"Sure, take your time," Jo replied, deflating a bit.

She couldn't quite explain it, but she didn't want Harper to leave. She was finally feeling inspired again, and she knew part of that spark had something to do with Harper. Amy was majoring in fine arts, but she and Jo didn't always see eye to eye. There was something refreshing about talking to someone who understood her creative struggle so well.

As Harper moved toward the door, Jo suddenly blurted out, "Wait."

Harper turned, curiosity in her blue eyes.

Jo hesitated for a second, then took a deep breath. "I know this has nothing to do with painting, but...would you consider reading my story? I think your perspective might help."

Harper's face lit up. "I'd love to. Why don't you come over this weekend? I'll actually have a place for you to sit by then. We can drink tea and commiserate over our artistic frustrations."

Jo chuckled. "Sounds good."

Harper gave her a final smile before heading back to her apartment, leaving Jo feeling lighter and more hopeful. Maybe the creativity wasn't gone after all—maybe it just needed a little nudge in the right direction. As the quiet in her apartment settled in, Jo grabbed her notebook and her pen started flying across the page.

On Saturday, Jo stood in front of Harper's apartment, shifting from foot to foot. She held her printed chapter against her chest and knocked on the door, a knot of anxiety tightening in her stomach. But when the door swung open, all her nerves seemed to melt away.

Harper appeared, a paint brush tucked behind her ear, purple and orange streaks smudged across her face. It was fascinating, and for a moment, Jo just stood there, taking in the sight of her. Harper tilted her head with a curious, amused expression, and Jo blinked, snapping out of her daze.

"Hi," Jo finally managed to say, her cheeks warming up.

Harper laughed; a warm, infectious sound. "Hey, come on in."

Inside, Jo was immediately struck by the apartment's artsy vibe. It was colourful and bright, much like Harper herself. Plants adorned the corners, and vibrant paintings covered the walls. The sofa, rug, and even the wall by the window were a mix of turquoise, yellow, and orange. A few boxes were still scattered around, but the space felt well put together, cosy, and full of personality.

"Your place is beautiful." Jo turned in a slow circle to take it all in. "How did you do this in such a short time? My sisters and I took a month just to buy a table."

Harper shrugged, smiling. "I already lived alone before moving here, so I pretty much know what I like by now."

As Harper's gaze landed on Jo, her stomach flipped. It was the first time she'd shown her work to someone outside her sisters or Teddy. The thought was both exhilarating and nerve-wracking.

"So, tea and commiseration?" Harper raised an eyebrow, a playful grin on her lips and Jo laughed as she relaxed some.

"That would be nice."

"Go settle in my study. I'll be over in a minute," Harper said, gesturing toward the end of the hall.

Jo nodded and made her way down the hallway. The door was slightly ajar, and when Jo pushed it open, her breath caught. If she'd thought Harper's living room was colourful, it was nothing compared to the explosion of hues in her studio.

Paintings of all sizes filled the space—hanging on the walls, propped on easels, and tucked away in organizers. Jars of brushes adorned a well-used worktable in the centre of the room, paint streaks splattered across its surface. A colour chart hung on the wall, alongside cases filled with acrylic paints and coloured pencils in every shade of the rainbow. Sunlight streamed in through the French windows, casting a warm glow over a vase of flowers, illuminating the petals in a stunning display.

Jo walked over, curious, and saw Harper had been painting that vase. Her strokes were bold, unapologetic, but soft at the same time, making the colours mix in a way that brought the whole thing together.

"It's a bit of a mess, but you can sit wherever you like."

Jo turned to see Harper at the door, smiling and holding two steaming mugs. She smiled. "This is nothing. You should see my room whenever I'm editing a story."

Harper tilted her head. "Why's that? You don't work from your computer?"

"I like the feel of pen on paper." Jo stroked the first page, a familiar, comforting feeling. "And sometimes my room gets so full of paper that there's barely any space to walk."

Harper nodded toward the stack clutched in Jo's arms. "Were those part of the decoration?"

Jo sighed, glancing down. "No, these haven't gotten to that stage yet." She frowned as frustration reared its head again.

"That's okay," Harper said, her voice gentle. "You can take it one step at a time, no?" She smiled, and the pressure between Jo's shoulders eased a bit. Harper's gaze shifted back to the papers, and she lifted her chin slightly. "Mind if I take a look?"

"Yeah...yeah, of course." Jo slid them over to her and moved to sit across the table.

Taking a sip from her tea, Jo hummed and tried to distract herself by admiring the beautiful room around her. But every time she heard the rustle of pages turning, she couldn't help but glance back at Harper, her heart beating a little faster.

Harper sat casually, holding Jo's story in one hand, elbow propped on the table. A strand of pink hair fell over her face, but she didn't seem to mind. With her free hand, she flipped through the pages and placed them upside down on the table as she read. Occasionally, she picked up the mug and took a sip of warm tea, her heart-shaped lips gently brushing the rim. It took Jo a moment to realise Harper was using the mug she'd lent her—the one with the letter "J."

"This is not bad," Harper said when she was done.

"But?" Jo prompted, sensing it. Harper bit her lip, hesitating, and Jo nodded. "It's okay, you can say it."

"I may be mistaken, but it feels like you wrote this because someone told you that's what you were supposed to write." Jo deflated, and Harper sent her a small smile. "Don't get me wrong, some phrases here are gorgeous, but others feel like...like they are lacking a deeper meaning." She paused. "Sorry, maybe that was..."

"No, no, it's fine," Jo said, though she hated hearing that her work seemed shallow. "It's exactly what I thought, but I don't know how to make it better. The stories I've read are amazing, but mine feels a little flat."

"That's because you're trying to write someone else's version of love instead of your own," Harper said simply.

Jo frowned. "What do you mean?"

"You're probably getting inspired by novels you've read or movies you've seen, right?" Jo nodded, and Harper continued. "That's absolutely fine, but it kinda sounds like you are writing about something you don't feel, or don't understand."

The room was quiet as Jo pondered on this. Dust particles floated lazily through the sunrays, and Jo watched them move about like they didn't have a care in the world. Finally, she turned back to Harper, waiting patiently.

"To be honest, not understanding love was part of the reason I started this in the first place."

"Art helps a lot in getting to know yourself, doesn't it?" Harper ventured, guessing it on the first try once again.

"Usually, it does," Jo huffed, and Harper laughed.

"Love comes in many shapes and forms." She tucked the loose strand of hair behind her ear, and a beaded bracelet in tones of pink, yellow, and blue tinkled on her wrist. "It's different for everybody. Maybe you just need to find what love means to you."

Her words resonated in Jo's mind and echoed through her body. She hadn't thought about it like that: like she'd been trying to see the situation through someone else's lens. Or pen.

"Not sure how I can find that out though."

"Well, I can't tell you that," Harper said, grabbing a brush and focusing on her paint. "But you're welcome to come and write here whenever you want. A change of space might help."

Jo smiled. She could feel creativity bubbling underneath her skin; it was in every corner of this room and it seeped into her, warming her like the tea she'd just had.

"I would like that very much."

Over the next few weeks, Jo spent most of her free time in Harper's studio. She barely even wrote in her room anymore. Harper's apartment grew more lived-in, the boxes now gone and replaced by the signs of Harper's life: photographs with friends, books being read, blankets crumpled on the sofa.

Jo's novel followed a similar path—slowly filling up with life. Bit by bit, the story began to take shape, images forming more vividly in her mind and words flowing with less resistance.

As she wrote, Jo and Harper grew closer. They talked about everything: art, love, their passions. They always sat on opposite sides of the table, Jo with her pen and notebook, and Harper with her easel and brushes. It was nice, just like when she'd first met Teddy, but different. Being around Harper felt easy and natural, like they had always known each other. Jo found herself wondering…why hadn't she ever met any men like this? It would be so easy then.

One particular afternoon, Jo was sighing and tapping her foot, mentally juggling words that refused to fit together. "How's that going?" Harper asked, glancing up from her easel.

"I'm getting there. I changed most of the beginning to be honest, and the emotions sound more…real. It's the physical scenes that I still have trouble with."

"Why don't you take a little break?" Harper suggested. "C'mon, I want to show you something."

Intrigued, Jo put her pen down and walked around the table to see the piece Harper had been working on during the past three days.

"What…what is this?"

Jo's heart thudded against her ribs as a warm, tingling sensation spread from her chest to her fingertips. She reached out, wanting to touch the painting, but not daring to.

It was a portrait of her. In it, Jo was looking out the window in the study, her face tilted up and eyes closed, enjoying the sun. It had Harper's particular style: all warm colours and vivid brushstrokes, but what truly caught Jo off guard was the expression on her face.

*Is this really how Harper sees me?*

Harper shrugged. "You've been a good inspiration."

Jo glanced down and their eyes met. Up close, she could see all the shades of blue in Harper's gaze—pale like a summer morning sky near the pupils, deepening to a vibrant azure around the edges. There was a quiet intensity in those eyes; a depth that made Jo's breath hitch. Her heart fluttered in a way she couldn't quite explain, and Jo couldn't help but notice Harper's eyes weren't broody, but warm, happy, inviting.

Realizing how silly that sounded, she cleared her throat and took a step back. "You're so talented."

"You are too, Jo. The physical part of a relationship can be in the small things. When you're with that person, you notice the little details. You watch their hands," she said, turning back to the painting and adding some finishing touches. Jo's gaze followed Harper's hands, moving so delicately with the brush, each stroke a soft, fluid motion from her wrist. "Their expressions, their movements, their mouth."

Each thing she mentioned, Jo's eyes admired: Harper's serene face while she did the thing she loved most, her mouth as she spoke. Her chest burned, the weight of the conversation settling on her. It felt like she was on the verge of something major, something so big that it would change everything, and she wasn't sure she was ready for it.

"I... I should go," she said, her voice a bit strained. "I've got some things to finish up."

"Jo—"

Scrambling to grab her things, Jo rushed out of there before Harper could say anything else. As she stepped out of Harper's apartment and closed the door behind her, she took a deep breath, trying to calm her racing thoughts.

*What was* that*?*

Jo rushed back to her apartment, her mind a whirlwind of thoughts and emotions. Over the next few days, she locked herself in her room, determined to write her confusing thoughts into oblivion. She tried to focus on her manuscript, but the more she wrote, the more distracted she became. Words blurred on the page, and her protagonist's once-grey eyes had inexplicably shifted to blue. His movements, once rugged and spontaneous, now seemed delicate and measured. The heroine's newfound fascination with his laughter and the sound of his voice only made her think of sunny studio rooms and black tea.

It left Jo confused and grappling with feelings she'd never considered. She read and reread her novel many times, spread her manuscript across the floor, and saw all the details laid bare for her, the details that pointed out her main male character resembled Harper more than she'd ever realized. Things the heroine hadn't paid much attention to before—the way he smiled, the softness of his hair, the tenderness in his gestures—all seemed to mirror Harper's features.

Frustrated and overwhelmed, Jo paced the room, trying to make sense of everything.

"Hey, Jo?" Meg called, knocking lightly on Jo's door before stepping in. "You've been stuck in here a lot lately." Her tone was laced with concern. "And you're going to carve a path on the floor with this much pacing. What's going on?"

Jo looked up from her scattered notes, her heart pounding. She hesitated, struggling to find the right words. "I…I think…" she gulped, her throat suddenly dry. She met Meg's gaze, her eyes wide. "I think I like Harper."

As soon as the words left her mouth, Jo knew them to be true. Every new feeling, every small thing she'd noticed about Harper, the details she'd never cared about with anyone else, they all came to light when she thought about Harper, and she *relished* them. It was both liberating and terrifying.

Her struggles with the couple in her story, her difficulty connecting with the views her sisters and Teddy had shared…everything made sense now. It was because she'd never felt something like that until now.

Meg's expression softened, and she stepped closer, placing a comforting hand on Jo's shoulder. "It's okay, Jo. Figuring out your feelings can be confusing, but it's a good thing."

Jo glanced up, tugging on a long strand of hair. "Do you think she likes me?"

"Jo." Meg laughed, her amusement catching Jo off guard. She covered her mouth with her hand, her eyes twinkling as she couldn't stop.

"Well, there's no need to be so rude about it," Jo grumbled, stung.

"No, no," Meg said between laughs, her voice softening. She took Jo's hands in hers. "Jo, she's asked you out for coffee how many times now?"

Jo froze, her mind going blank for a moment. "But...but that was just to talk about art or...to hang out."

"Oh, my dear sister," Meg said with a fond smile, "you can be so blind sometimes. Doesn't she still use the mug you lent her? After all this time?"

"Oh my God." Jo raked her hands through her hair. "Meg, I've been avoiding her for days. All this time. I didn't know...I couldn't make sense of it, and now..." She bit her lip, the weight of her emotions crashing down on her. "What if she thinks I hate her?"

"Well, there's only one way to find out, isn't there?" Meg gently tugged on her hands, dragging her out of her bedroom. "You don't have to confess your feelings, but clearing up any misunderstanding is a good place to start."

She was right. Jo knew she was, but as she opened the front door to leave, a wave of fear crashed into her.

*What if everything goes wrong? What if this is all just a big mistake?*

"I still don't think I want to get married," she blurted, frozen at the entrance.

Meg rolled her eyes. "Jo, you're asking for some time together, not her hand. Get to know her more, start there and see what happens."

*Right, small steps.* She could do that. Besides, she was finally starting to understand this thing everyone talked about, discovering her own way of seeing and feeling it. It would be stupid to stop now just because she was scared.

The hallway stretched out before her, seeming longer than ever. She adjusted her clothes nervously, her heart pounding with each step she took. Jo stopped. What if Harper didn't want to see her anymore after she'd run away?

She thought of Harper's confident gaze, her focused expression while she painted, her calm demeanour which contrasted so nicely with Jo's chaotic personality. She thought of her warm smile and her comforting presence. Then, Jo kept walking.

She hesitated in front of Harper's door, staring at the patterns in the wood and the shiny number 6 that glinted back at her. Taking a few steadying breaths, her hand trembled as she raised her fist.

*Knock, knock, knock.*

# Bloodlust & Betrayal

## by Cortney Murchie

**Literary World**: Dracula

A modern reimagined, retelling of the classic Dracula. Jonathon Harker, hired by Count Dracula to help him with the procurement of an estate, starts to develop feelings, although engaged to a woman. Together, they form an emotional and intimate relationship, bringing Jonathon to the realisation that he was missing something in his life. When Mina, his fiancée shows up, his world is changed. But is it for better, or worse?

***Content Warnings**: Sexually explicit scenes - MM/MMF/MF, Explicit language, Mental Health - Anxiety, Illness, Blood, Praise/Humiliation kink, infidelity*

*2, May 2024*

Jonathon

Everything Mina does is grating on my nerves. I'm irrationally short with her and as guilty as I feel, I can't stop myself from acting this way. It's been a couple weeks since Dracula reached out to me regarding an estate purchase. Ever since then, I have developed these feelings I cannot explain, so instead of handling them in a healthy manner I'm just pushing the one good thing in my life away — my fiancé. Who knew an unexpected email would change the entire trajectory of my life? I leave tomorrow for Bucharest, and I need to remind myself to be nice and try to enjoy tonight. How terrible is that? I have to talk myself into being nice.

I hear the door; Mina must be home from work. Part of me was hoping she would be going with the girls to the pub afterward. Maybe I can just stay in my office "working". "Jon, I'm home," Mina yells in the distance. "I brought dinner. Come eat!"

My stomach rumbles at the mere thought of food. I hope she picked it up from the new Indian place down the road. Perhaps I can get out of this mindset and actually enjoy our night together. Mina is amazing – I just don't know what's been going on with me lately.

Immediately when I reach the dining room, I'm annoyed. The smell of Thai from our favourite place wafts up. Mina stands there beaming, as if I'm the best part of her day. Why isn't she mine? I sit down, trying not to show my emotions as she places the containers on the table.

"I was thinking, since you leave tomorrow, maybe we can watch a movie and go to bed early." She says this with a look in her eyes that lets me know exactly what she's implying.

"I don't know, Mina. I have to leave early and I'm already exhausted," I say while ensuring I am not making eye contact. Maybe I can get her to drop it.

"You don't leave that early, Jonathon. It's been weeks. Come to bed with me."

I finally look up and see the desperation in her face. *Fuck.* I don't want to do this. I don't want to hurt her, but not one ounce of me wants to entertain this right now.

"Listen, I'm not in the mood. I have a lot going on and I just want to get a good night's rest before I leave. Can we just drop this?"

I watch her process what I'm saying and see the change in her emotions.

"*Can we drop this?* It's been weeks. You don't talk to me; you don't touch me. What are we anymore, Jon? I don't know what's going on with you, but I won't just sit by and wait for you to figure your shit out."

She storms out of the room, and I hear the front door slam a moment later.

*Great.* I guess there's no need to pretend to have a good night. I got my wish. An early night – with thoughts of Dracula invading my brain.

*3, May 2024*

I sit anxiously at Euston Station, waiting for my train to depart for Bucharest and listening to the hustle of the station while smelling the mixture of coffee and baked goods blending with the scent of human activity – but also the hint of metal mixed with the acrid scent of exhaust from the trains. This is my first time leaving London, let alone travelling on a train, and I am on my way to meet someone I have corresponded with for weeks. I am intrigued by the mystery of this man, Count Dracula. There's just something inviting about him. What began as a simple inquiry regarding a real estate procurement has escalated into personal discussions. I don't recall when this change happened, but we had a strong connection and I was so comfortable speaking with him, which made me anxious. I have been engaged to Mina for six months, and it feels almost adulterous how I have been confiding in Dracula.

I strum my fingers on my briefcase while waiting to board and realise I will be alone with my thoughts for the next 2,100 kilometres. Never in my wildest dreams did I consider I would be anxious and confused about a man. I had always considered myself entirely heterosexual, and had never been attracted to another man – until now. I don't even know what he looks like, and here I am, with thoughts I really shouldn't be having while engaged to a woman.

The fight Mina and I had before I left is still replaying in my mind. We've never fought this much before, and I know I am to blame. I have distanced myself when she asks about work or this upcoming trip. She had initially wanted to come with me, as she's always wanted to travel to Romania, but I quickly shut it down, knowing I hurt her feelings. Add in the guilt of denying all her sexual advances lately, blaming it on exhaustion or stress, and I feel like the world's worst fiancé. With building guilt, I send Mina a text to let her know I'm okay.

Jonathon: *I've made it onto the train fine. I'll call you in the morning.*

Mina: *I miss you already. Are we ok? I love you.*

I immediately put my phone back into my pocket.

How am I supposed to respond to that? "Yes, we are okay. I just may be having feelings for my client."

*4, May 2024*

I wake, startled from sleep, not quite remembering where I am and uneasy. Almost morning: I consider going to the cafe to grab an espresso. I am going to need it today. We should arrive in Budapest shortly, and I need to do some work for the estate. I have this sinking feeling something terrible will happen; I just can't put my finger on it. I feel as though I am being watched, and the sleeper train's unsettling eeriness makes me uncomfortable. People should start waking shortly, and to avoid being subjected to small talk, I make my way to the cafe before it becomes too busy.

Once I have returned to my seat, I open my laptop to start working when I find myself distracted and drawn to rereading emails from Dracula. I have that undeniable flutter in my stomach, and I curse myself for feeling this way. I haven't even met the guy: I have no idea what he looks like, and here I am, acting like I have my first crush. I start getting that unease creeping in again, and I wish I knew what was setting this off. Perhaps it's just first-trip jitters.

Budapest comes and goes as if it were just a blip on my radar. I've managed to get all the work I can accomplish until I arrive done, and caught up on all pertinent messages. Finally, setting my email to out-of-office, I settled in for the remainder of my ride to Bucharest. Alone with my thoughts, I can't help but daydream about this man I'm suddenly infatuated with.

*5, May 2024*

Ah, Bucharest! It's been a long trip, but I am almost to my final destination – of course, after I meet Dracula's driver somewhere around here. Passengers are de-boarding, and I can sense the tension immediately. I take my phone from my pocket and stare at it, willing myself to text Mina. I start to type out a message that I've arrived safely, but I still haven't responded to her last text and I am not willing to unpack that by messaging her now. I sigh and put my phone away, looking up and trying to find the source of my unease. There was a couple sitting near me I had seen a few times along our trek, and they kept eyeing me suspiciously. Huddled together, I see them watching me now and talking. Before long, the woman comes up to me. "Excuse me, sir, but you're not going to see the Count, are you?"

*Well, that's strange*, I think. "I am indeed. Why do you ask?"

She must have seen the sign for my driver before I did. How else would she know who I am going to see?

The woman looks dreadfully shocked. "I'm sorry, sir, but I must warn you – there are rumours about the Count, and you seem like an awfully nice man. I wouldn't be doing my due diligence if I didn't try and convince you not to go. They call him the son of Satan, and it's been said the rash of missing girls in the area are because he drains them of their blood and drinks it." The woman looks pale, almost frantic.

I can't help but chuckle slightly at that thought. "Well, ma'am, I do not know the Count well, but I can assure you from my interactions with him thus far, he seems very friendly and courteous. That is not at all what you would expect from someone so evil-sounding. I'd say that they are just that: rumours."

Shaking her head, the woman retreats as I finally come upon the driver holding a sign reading *Mr. J. Harker.* Such an odd interaction that was. I shake my head, trying to clear the hilarity of the entire situation.

It's a quiet drive to the castle — nearly three hours to think to myself and spike my anxiety, wishing I brought something to settle myself. The driver doesn't say a word, staring at me periodically through his rearview mirror. One would say it's almost like he has something to say; he doesn't want to overstep, perhaps? As it gets darker, I think about the woman at the train station and where these rumours she heard could have started. Blood-draining? Was this woman seriously trying to insinuate Dracula was a *vampire*?

The thought is completely unbelievable. Vampires don't exist; they are completely fictional characters made to scare children or glamourize the occult. I cannot believe I am even thinking about this...but if he were to want to bite me, I think I would let him.

*What is going on with me?*

## Dracula

I pace around the front entrance of my home, anxious for my visitor to arrive. *Why am I feeling this way?* My heart feels as if it is going to pound right out of my chest, and that if anyone were to walk by, they would be able to hear it beating so hard. It's usually not in me to care about the rumours swirling around about me being a vampire – but for some reason, Jonathon's opinion matters to me.

Our conversations over the last few weeks regarding my estate purchase have been some of the most refreshing I've ever had. I felt a connection I didn't even realise I wanted, much less needed.

I know my life is the hot topic of conversation around here, making me out to be this blood-sucking monster out to steal their women – and they are partially correct, but they have never even given me a chance. Hence my desire to move to London and start anew.

Jonathon seems to get me. I think that is what drew me to him in our conversations to start with. He seems so kind, so genuine, and entirely thoughtful and considerate of others. I don't have a lot of experience forming meaningful relationships in adulthood, and I have recently found myself craving it: craving the connection I have found in Jonathon – or at least I hope it's real, and I haven't just been reading into it.

I find you never really understand people's intentions anymore; there seems to always be an ulterior motive. Or maybe my past has just given me trust issues: it's entirely possible. For some reason, with Jonathon, I can see a future, and it scares me. His heart is so open, so kind. I hope it's that way when he gets here. I'm so in my head right now – maybe I need a drink to calm my nerves. Thinking of that, I should also pull out the other decanter for Jonathon. Imagine if I served him mine accidentally? That would be beyond mortifying. "Welcome to my home, and here's some blood-spiked whiskey for you to enjoy."

I groan internally. Where did Albert put the other decanter? I need to do this now before I make the mistake, given the current state of my mind.

I never told Jonathon of my disease. It never came up, but to be honest, I was also trying to avoid it. I've let people think what they will about me forever: my aversion to sunlight, and the fact that it appears I have fangs...I laugh internally. I understand why they would jump to the conclusion that I'm a vampire. If I were in their shoes, I would likely think the same thing. I know the rumours about draining women of blood; that I am stealing the local girls for nefarious reasons and corrupting them so no other man will touch them. I do indulge in the local women: they're curious, and I'm a man with needs. Some are willing to offer up their blood to me, but I never take it without consent. I just have them sign a non-disclosure agreement, as I don't like to share my personal life with others – instead, I let them think what they want and keep to myself. I grew up in fear of what people would think knowing I have porphyria. It's not as prevalent as it once was, and not much is known about it – unless, of course, you're a medical professional or someone suffering from the affliction.

There is no cure for me: I came to that realisation at a young age. Thankfully, I can keep the symptoms of my malady mostly at bay, for now. London should be good for me. With a high sensitivity to light, I prefer when it's overcast or I stay inside to avoid the pain. I come across as this enigmatic man, and so studious, but in reality I am a borderline hermit who avoids smiling to hide the *fangs* created by the disease.

The more I keep contemplating what this means, the more nervous I am for Jonathon to show up.

"Fuck," I curse as I fist my hands in my hair and pace. How do you explain to someone that you essentially drink blood as a way to keep your ailment at bay?

It's then that I hear the unmistakable sound of a car door. Whipping around on my heels, my heart speeds up as I internally scream, "He's here."

*...he's here.*

## Jonathon

Shutting the car door behind me, I stare up at the house – or rather, the castle – in front of me. It's beyond me why Dracula would want to leave this for an estate in London. I'm so mesmerised I barely register the driver walking past with my bags and in the front door. No time for my nerves: I take a deep breath and steel myself to meet the Count for the first time.

As soon as I walk in, I take in the depth of the foyer, the dark bannisters of the impressive staircase, the dark marble flooring, and the deep red of the heavy curtains. For being so darkly decorated, it's welcoming and comforting and not at all as ominous as one would think. I casually walk the entry, running my fingers along the table bursting with beautifully fragrant bouquets of dahlias, hyacinths, and calla lilies.

Adjusting my posture and fidgeting with my cufflinks, I smooth down my outfit, hoping the butterflies in my stomach calm down.

It's then I feel the undeniable awareness of someone's eyes on me. I turn slowly to see him standing on the stairs. He's more than I could have ever imagined, and I feel as though I have stopped breathing to take him in.

"Hi," I almost whisper, standing so still it's as though I'm afraid he will disappear.

"Hi to you," he says as he walks slowly down the stairs toward me, not once taking his eyes away from mine. My heart is beating incredibly fast. I can't take mine off him, either, watching him slowly descend the stairs while running his fingers down the bannister with the most intense eye contact I've ever been entranced by. I think unabashedly that I want it to be me he's running his fingers along. I knew we had a connection, but this – this is unexpected.

*What should I do next?* Do I shake his hand? That seems...wrong. It seems too formal in this situation – but an embrace? Is that too intimate? Why does he seem so calm?

Finally making it to the bottom of the stairs, I'm sure he can hear my heart beating out of my chest – and I still haven't moved.

His stride towards me is purposeful and confident – the exact opposite to how I am feeling – and his smile is genuine and entirely disarming.

"Jonathon, it's so nice to finally meet you in person," says Dracula. It takes me a moment to register that he is speaking to me, and I stammer out my words.

"Yes – you as well. It's nice to see you finally...I mean, meet you finally. Although I am seeing you...never mind, you know what I mean." I nervously chuckle.

"Shall we retire to the study for a drink and get business out of the way?" He's smirking while he speaks, I'm sure realising my mortification as he walks out of the foyer to what I am assuming is his study. I can't help but watch him walk, trying not to be too obvious. *Please don't let him realise I can't take my eyes off of him.*

In the cozy ambiance of the study, my eyes dart around the room, taking in the bookshelves filled with volumes spanning various genres and eras. It is a sanctuary of intellect and taste, yet calming with the light emanating from the fireplace in the corner.

Dracula is leaning casually against the desk, pouring what appears to be a whiskey for me – and possibly red wine for himself? His fingers toy with the rim of the glass as he swirls the deep red liquid inside without really drinking it and hands the other glass to me. Although I cannot help but take in the magnificence of the room, I find myself flicking my eyes towards Dracula more often than not, watching him with a mixture of curiosity and uncertainty.

His posture is effortlessly composed as he rests one hand on the desk while gazing steadily at me, watching me closely to see what I am going to do next. The air of calm assurance he maintains starts to soothe my unease – either that or the drink I have polished off so quickly. With each sip, I feel my nervousness slowly start to disappear, my body relaxing. Before I know it, I find I have wandered over to the desk and I'm standing directly in front of him. With the intense look we are sharing, I feel we are forging a bond that goes far beyond the mere sharing of a moment. I feel as though something more profound is taking shape.

"So, the estate." I clear my throat, unsure of how to even converse with this man, but I know I have to say something. He stares at me, with a smirk and a raised brow – almost as if he is baiting me.

"Yes, the estate. What do you need me to do?" His voice has almost a growl to it. I can feel my knees going weak. This man is trouble.

"Um, we should…I should…I mean, I brought the paperwork."

I am horribly embarrassed as I lay the paperwork on the desk, reaching around him and smelling how fucking delicious he is: like cedar and smoke. Any intelligence has left my brain and I'm making myself look like an idiot.

"Well, Jonathon, let's take a look, shall we? Get through this…paperwork."

He hasn't taken his eyes off me. I can't help but notice the way he's leaning back against his desk, the way his hand is gripping the pen. I can't help but fantasise about the way he would grip me. I swallow, feeling like my heart is in my throat, the anxiety bubbling up.

Without even realising I am doing it, I find my fingers are entangling themselves in his. I'm taking comfort in the heat of his hand and the warmth from the drink that is helping give me the confidence I need to do this.

In the quiet intimacy of the room, my emotions are hanging palpably in the air like a delicate, unspoken melody. Dracula slowly starts leaning toward me, his movements gentle yet purposeful as he closes the short distance between us. My breath catches in my throat, heart racing, and I feel an anticipation as our lips draw nearer.

As our mouths finally meet, it is a meeting of souls and not merely physical touch. The kiss is a gentle exploration of emotions long left unspoken as the outside world fades into insignificance. I've entered the uncharted territory of new beginnings as I find solace in his embrace.

After the kiss, we remain close, our foreheads touching gently and savouring the closeness and shared vulnerability of that intimate exchange. Our entwined fingers feel like a silent promise of more moments like this, where my heart could find refuge in his presence.

Sharing the breath between us, I feel myself melt into him, not knowing what to say – just needing to touch, to become closer. It's as if my clothes are suddenly too tight, too stifling.

"Fuck, Jonathon, what are you doing to me?" I can't comprehend the words Dracula is saying to me right now. What am I doing to *him?* What about what he's doing to *me?* With his lips to my ear, he murmurs, "I've been thinking about this for weeks."

Before I can even question what he is talking about, I feel his hands on my waist, expertly making quick work of my belt and zipper before my pants hit the floor. There's no time for words as his mouth crashes against mine. Suddenly, the desk is cleared in one swift movement, everything crashing to the ground.

~

*What am I doing?*

I watch Dracula standing in low-slung pants, feeling myself harden with thoughts of last night. It's as if he can sense what I'm thinking as he shoots me a sly smile, pouring our coffees, leaning against the counter, and pulling me to him. It might seem greedy of me, but if I could keep him and Mina both, I don't think anything could make me happier. A breath away from his lips, I'm suddenly startled as Albert, the house manager, comes rushing in, panting.

"Sir, you have a visitor."

And just as he finishes his sentence, Mina charges into the room.

It is as if time stands still: Dracula with his hand on my waist, and Mina with her eyes darting between it and my face, trying to understand what she's witnessing.

"Oh!" she exclaims. "I didn't realise I was *interrupting* something."

I can feel the heat rushing through my face, horror evident. How does one explain to their fiancé that it was a one-time thing and didn't mean anything? Especially since I wasn't even sure if that was the truth. Dracula made me feel things last night I didn't even think possible. I don't know if I can feel those things with Mina.

"Mina, I wasn't expecting you. What are you doing here?" I ramble as quickly as possible, stepping back from Dracula. I am anxious about how to handle this and unsure of how she is really feeling.

"Well, Jonathon, that is quite evident in the state you both are in." Short in tone, she's angry. I can't blame her.

"When I didn't hear from you, I worried. I thought coming to surprise you would help ease your anxiety, but now I can see that you were fine. You were just *busy.*" She scoffs. "Little did I know what your idea of being busy would be."

I step toward her. I'm unsure what to do or say that won't cause irreparable damage. I do love her. I just...I don't even know. This is all so new to me, and I'm struggling to distinguish my potential love for her and certain lust I feel for Dracula.

Mina and I stand there, not touching, just staring at each other. There are so many unsaid words between us, and so many that need to be said.

"Well, then, who would like some breakfast?" Dracula breaks the awkward silence as he grabs the pot of coffee and walks over to the dining table. Sitting casually in the chair, the Count has effortless confidence in him as he sips his coffee, watching how we will react.

"Mina – how about you come sit, love? We can discuss the situation at hand." He uses his foot and pushes the chair out toward her.

Mina can't stop staring at him, either, while she grabs the back of the chair, the cup of coffee he has poured her, and sits.

"So, you're the reason Jonathon has been so distant."

I groan internally, standing in the middle of the room and unsure of what I should do. Do I sit? And if I sit, do I sit next to Mina? Or do I sit next to Dracula? The man was inside of me last night, and here I am contemplating where to sit.

"Mina, darling, I fear I may have been the one stealing his attention. It was not my intention, and I do not intend to take him from you. I do, however, believe there is something here. Perhaps we could see if all of us could find some...common ground?" Dracula shifts his gaze between Mina and myself, and I feel a blush creeping into my face. It's almost as if he can read my mind.

Mina stands abruptly, turning to face me. I'm unsure how to read her emotions. I cannot tell if she is angry or intrigued at this moment, but my heart breaks thinking that I could possibly have hurt the woman I love.

Seemingly out of nowhere, Dracula comes up behind me and grabs Mina and I together with force. I can tell from the look on her face that he had her entranced with his gaze as he leans forward and licks up my neck, eliciting an unintentional moan from me as Mina's cheeks turn a pretty shade of crimson.

Without him even voicing it, I know what is happening. Am I ready for this? Am I prepared to explore this with both of them? My legs feel wobbly, knowing that this *is* what I want. I want to watch

him with her. I want to see him bring her to ruin like he did to me just hours ago. I want to explore this between the three of us.

## Dracula

I don't know where this need came from, but seeing this woman walk into my home and interact with Jonathon, I need to know what will happen here. I need to see how she will react to my feelings with her fiancé, and I would be remiss to ignore how strikingly beautiful she is. I need to feel her skin, to run my fingers through her hair, to taste her. I am completely captivated. This woman is trouble. From the moment I laid eyes on her, I could sense there was going to be something between us – hoping it would be between *all* of us. Together, perhaps everyone could be happy. Together, they could destroy me. I already know I will do whatever they want: they own me.

As I plan to bury myself inside her and feast on her blood, I remain uncertain whether I intend to shred her into fragments literally or figuratively. I've only just crossed paths with the girl, yet I feel the pull she has on me – on both of us. She exudes a kind of sexual curiosity that will be fun to explore and see what I can bring out of this innocent little thing.

Making our way into the bedroom, I back her towards the bed while silently gesturing for Jonathon to sit before spinning her around, causing her to stumble and get exactly where I want her: bent over, with her hands on my bed. Bringing my hands up her thighs and under her skirt, I feel exactly how soft she is and think about all the deliciously vile things I would love to do. I hook my fingers in her panties, dragging them down slowly and realising just how wet she is. Her smell alone is intoxicating, and I plan to spend some time enjoying the taste of her – but I can't wait. I need to feel her around me.

Sliding my pants off while gazing down at Mina, I see Jonathon in my periphery sitting in the wingback chair, looking for any emotion showing me he isn't okay with this. I thank the universe when he stares back at me with approval and lust in his eyes. Who knew my room was set up so perfectly for this?

I push into her slowly from behind, spreading her legs further apart, making her squirm and whimper with just a hint of pleading in her voice.

"That's a good girl," I growl. Now that I am fully seated in her, I wait for her to adjust to the fullness. "Take from me what you want, Mina: what you need."

She moans, back arching as she licks her lips, staring straight at Jonathon as he watches us, stroking himself. Fuck, she's like a craving I just can't sate. Together, both of them could mean the end of me. They have brought me to my knees, like an itch that needs scratching and nothing but them can reach. I wrap my hand in her hair, pulling her neck to the side, lips brushing her ear.

"Is this what you need, baby girl?" I rasp into her ear. "To get fucked while your fiancé watches you?"

I chuckle darkly, knowing this is precisely what they both need. I realised then that this is also what I need. I don't need to drain them; I need to feel both of them clenching around my cock as I feast on them. I need the look of hunger on her face as I start pounding into her in a rhythm I can tell is bringing her close to the edge.

Jonathon finally cannot take it anymore and climbs onto the bed, purposeful in his pursuit. Maintaining eye contact with me as Mina looks between us, I can tell what it is he's after. I grab Mina by the chin and whisper into her ear, "Be a good girl and show me how much you want him."

## Mina

Resting my hands on the countertop, I stare at myself in the mirror.

"Get yourself together, Mina."

I don't recognize the face staring back at me: hair dishevelled, lipstick smeared, and marks on my neck, chest, and arms. I don't know what came over me or how I feel about it. Shouldn't I be the least bit upset? Not only did I just watch my soon-to-be husband be with another man, but I liked it.

Rubbing my hands over my face, I think about the fact that I also joined in. Finally, a minuscule amount of guilt creeps in. Is it considered cheating if your fiancé is there during it, and also participating? I have so many thoughts and questions racing through my mind – but first and foremost, I want it to happen again.

*What does that say about me?*

I can't stop thinking, though – what does this mean for our future? But more importantly, does it even matter?

Before tonight, Jonathon was the only man I had ever been with, and I would not complain in the least – but I never knew it could be like that, and I wouldn't even call our sex life vanilla. Maybe it was, though. Remembering the way his hands felt caressing my skin, I feel my arousal dripping down my leg. Who knew I would like being called a good girl as much as I did? Watching Dracula's eyes darken as he growls it in my ear makes me question exactly what I *am* into.

I've been standing in this bathroom long enough that I am sure they are starting to wonder where I am. I splash some water on my face, staring at myself in the mirror and trying to muster the courage to step back out there and face the reality of what we just did. What *I* just did.

"It's now or never, Mina." I stare back at myself and shake my head. If I want to face this head-on and continue where we left off, I have to just jump head-first into the deep end here. Taking a deep breath, I decide to just do it.

Opening the door, both of their heads quickly turn to me. Jonathon is still lying in bed with the sheet covering just enough to make me groan while biting my lip. Thoughts of what we did and what I want to explore more start invading my thoughts. I want to crawl into that bed and sink myself onto him. I feel other eyes on me as Dracula stands nearby with his arms crossed and a whiskey in hand.

Slowly, without breaking eye contact, he gently places his drink down. I walk confidently over to him, watching his eyes darken and his pupils dilate, showing me just the effect I am having on him. I push myself against him and look up, and he immediately starts backing me against the wall. His hand comes up to caress my cheek, then trails down for him to press deliciously against my throat. He stares into my eyes and asks, "Have you been a good girl?"

A moan quietly escapes from me and my eyes close as I feel myself needing to please him, to have him dominate me. Opening my eyes again, I see Jonathon has made his way over to us and stands behind

Dracula – hands on his shoulders, sliding down to his biceps with heavy-lidded eyes, and I know this is where I want to be. This feels right, and I just need to let my body take over and stop getting so in my head. All I want and need for now is the two of them.

## Jonathon

Crashing onto the bed in a mess of tangled, sweaty limbs, the three of us lie there trying to catch our breath. The smell of sex is heavy in the air, and the lust is still palpable. I don't know if I will ever tire of the beauty we have created between our bodies. I don't know if anything else in my life has ever felt so right – but what the three of us have created goes far beyond just the physical. Even if we wanted to, I do not believe we would be able to go our separate ways. It is as if the universe brought us together for a specific reason.

With Mina between myself and Dracula, our legs all still entwined, Dracula props himself up on his elbow, looking toward us.

"I have something to tell the two of you," he says, with a look of trepidation.

*6, August 2024*

It's been some time since we left Dracula's castle and the estate sale in London was finalised. Mina and I remained with him the entire time. The three of us are intrinsically entwined now. We sold our place in London and moved into the estate with him. It just seemed right.

London seems to be perfect for him – and for us. After he explained his condition to us, we knew we would stick by his side through it all.

We even share our blood to help keep his porphyria at bay – which, if I'm being honest, has been integral in our more...intimate moments.

Mina and I decided to put our nuptials on hold for the time being. We would love to find a way to include Dracula. The three of us did a small, intimate ceremony together, binding ourselves to one another as a commitment to our relationship. There is no doubt in our minds that we will share our lives together as one. Mina has even started hinting at expanding our family. Currently, we are researching more regarding Dracula's condition and what the chances of it being passed on would be. For now, we are enjoying each other thoroughly, physically and emotionally.

Who knew an unexpected email would change the entire trajectory of my life? I could never have seen this coming, but I also wouldn't change a single thing about what happened. It led us to one another and created a beautiful life for the three of us.

# Thanks For Noticin' Me

## by Kassandra Jackson

**Literary World**: Winnie the Pooh

For Tigger's birthday bash, Eeyore takes on the task of making balloon animals to save the parade, despite feeling unsure of himself and his abilities.With the help of his friends, they create a colorful parade that symbolizes their community and Eeyore discovers a new sense of belonging among them.

A box of knick-knacks was left to the side at the start of a fun celebration, and although Eeyore was never interested in parties, he became curious as to what he would find. Party hats, candles, streamers, and noisemakers overflowed as he looked inside. Deflated orange balloons with black stripes caught his attention. *Tigger's Birthday Bash* was written in colorful font at the front of each balloon.

While Tigger bounced around greeting all of his guests, Piglet frantically ran straight for Eeyore. "Oh d-d-d-dear, this is awful Eeyore, just awful!" a little wide eyed Piglet exclaimed.

"What happened Piglet, is everything alright?" Eeyore asked nonchalantly.

Piglet's urgency intensified. "It-Its just Christopher Robin said the balloon artist has not shown up to the party yet and the balloon animal parade is going to happen after we cut the cake! What are we going to do?"

Christopher Robin made his way towards Eeyore and Piglet, determined to fix the issue and chimed in, “Piglet’s right Eeyore, we must figure out a way to continue the balloon animal parade for Tigger!”

I only have one made,” Eeyore said, feeling down about his friend's birthday bash.

Christopher Robin was surprised; he had no idea Eeyore could make balloon animals. “Eeyore, this is incredible! We can turn this party around and make it in the nick of time for the parade. Wait here, I know just what to do.”

While Christopher Robin went to speak with their friends, Piglet offered his help to Eeyore. He was determined, and wanted to do his very best for Tigger.

“I don’t know what I am doing," Eeyore admitted. He knew how to make one or two, but not enough for a full parade.

Piglet jumped eagerly at the idea of helping.

“Don't worry Eeyore, I will help you. After all, what are friends for?”

Not wasting any time, Eeyore began teaching Piglet how to create balloon animals.

Christopher Robin walked over to Pooh who was helping himself to the snack bar. Mini honey pots, cupcakes, popcorn, candy, and other yummy snacks were spread across the table in a great wilderness display.

“Wow, Rabbit, what a terrific job! Tigger will love this!”

Feeling proud of himself, Rabbit gave Christoper Robin a wide smile back and laughed. "Heh, thank you. If only Pooh would stop eating the honey pots, we would have enough for everyone."

"Oh Pooh, you silly old bear, you can have all the honey to eat after the party." Christopher Robin giggled.

"But this honey is the most delicious honey I've ever tasted, and it's because Rabbit whipped it up this morning." A hungry Pooh said, scraping every last bit of honey his little paw could manage.

"Say, Rabbit? Pooh? Do you mind helping Piglet and me assist Eeyore on making more balloon animals? I think with all of us together, we can make it in time for the parade," Christopher Robin counseled.

"Sure thing," Rabbit replied, feeling confident it would work.

"Will there be honey after?" teased Pooh.

Rabbit smirked. "Of course."

Overhearing the conversation, Owl, wise and old, came swooping in with suggestions and ideas. "Perhaps we can all pitch in and create different balloon animals, from any color or sizes. It will be fun to do it together!"

"Tigger will be so surprised when he sees everything. Let's do it." Christopher Robin beamed.

Making their way towards Eeyore and Piglet, Christopher Robin noticed all their hard work.

A tiny elephant had been crafted by the smallest hands.

"Piglet, I think your elephant is magnificent!" cheered Christopher Robin.

"A symbol of strength, community, and familial bonds," explained Piglet, feeling so proud of what he had created.

"Don't pay any attention to me." Eeyore said in a gloomy tone.

"And I'm so impressed with your wolf balloon, Eeyore. You both did a wonderful job," Christopher Robin encouraged.

"I suppose it's great to travel in packs," Eeyore replied.

Although Eeyore was feeling unsure about his abilities, he still wanted Tigger to have the best party ever. He knew a wolf would be a perfect fit for the parade. As wolves rely on each other for survival and cooperation.

Piglet turned to pat Eeyore on the back for a job well done. "Thank you Piglet," said Eeyore.

After spending most of the morning preparing for Tigger's parade, Christopher Robin, Eeyore, Piglet, and the rest of their friends sat around each other to sing *Happy Birthday* to Tigger. They also ate delicious carrot cake, courtesy of Rabbit.

"Mmm, sweet scents of honey float through the air," Pooh bubbled.

"As you requested Pooh, here is more honey," said Rabbit, handing the golden pots to his fluffy friend.

Christopher Robin made a toast, "Happy Birthday, Tigger, we love you!"

"Ooo-hoo! And Tigger loves all of you," the bouncy Tigger squealed in excitement.

"Ohhh-kayyy, it's time for the parade," Eeyore said as he walked over and picked up his balloon to start the parade.

He made a bland expression, which Christopher Robin noticed.

"You saved the parade, Eeyore, I knew you could do it."

Eeyore's ears perked up slightly.

"Ooo-hoo! Yeah, it's the best balloon parade ever! And it wouldn't have happened without you." Tigger bouncing up and down with absolute glee.

"Well I didn't do it all by myself," he said humbly. "But it's nice to know I helped."

Tigger placed an arm around Eeyore. "That's what makes it so special—you all made it together."

As the friends gathered to walk in the parade. Eeyore felt warmth in his heart, with his friends by his side. He might have started out unsure of himself, but with everyone's support, something wonderful had come to life.

Eeyore stood in the center, surrounded by his friends, with a sense of accomplishment. He knew that he'd always have a place among his friends no matter what.

"You know something Eeyore," Piglet added, "if you weren't you, then we'd all be a bit less we."

With a small contented sigh, Eeyore grabbed his balloon and turned to follow his friends. He marched down the path feeling lighter than he had in a long time.

# Death Among the Berries: A Strawberry Festival Mystery

## by Paula Phillips

**Literary Worlds**: various classic mysteries

Strawberry Fields is bustling with its annual Strawberry Festival. Villagers and visitors alike gather to enjoy the festivities, including strawberry picking, pie-eating contests, and local crafts. Among the guests are Miss Jane Matthews and the renowned detective Harvey Phillips. On the second day of the festival, tragedy strikes. The body of Mr. Henry Blake, a local landowner and the festival's main sponsor, is found in the heart of the strawberry fields, his basket of strawberries spilled beside him. The cause of death appears to be a blow to the head with a heavy object.

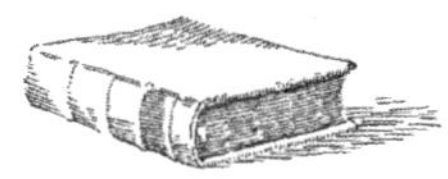

*Dear Harvey,*

*As I write this letter, I hear congratulations are in order: I recently read in The Paragrapher Press that you had a murder in your apartment building. That poor Mrs. Ernestine Grant, shot in a lover's quarrel! I am sure her husband is happy you managed to solve the crime and prove his innocence, but I guess not so much when he discovered his wife was having an affair with Captain John Hastings. I read John thought he had gotten away with it and was almost ready to board the plane at Heathrow Airport and head to New Zealand. Your keen mind and sharp eye, as always, have brought justice to the forefront. Bravo, my dear Harvey!*

*I can only imagine the scene: your neighbours in shock, the police fumbling for answers and there you are, with that little glint in your eye, piecing together the puzzle with grace and precision. I've always admired how you manage to find the truth hidden in the tiniest of details. Mrs. Grant's lover thought he was clever, didn't he? But he didn't account for the brilliance of Harvey Phillips. The way you deduced his guilt from those subtle clues it's nothing short of masterful.*

*But enough about that sordid affair. I know how much you love to have a bit of downtime between cases, and ever since I moved to Strawberry. I have been wanting you to come and visit me. You will love the fresh country air and the smell of strawberry fields. This coming week is the beginning of the annual Berry Festival, and the week is filled with fun events and laughter. The whole town just comes alive for the event, and I feel it's the perfect opportunity for you to stay with us.*

*The Berry Festival is truly a sight to behold. There are strawberry-picking contests, jam-making competitions, and even a parade with floats adorned with the finest berries. The local farmers showcase their best produce, and there's a delightful fair with games, music, and dancing. I can already picture you, my dear friend, strolling through the fields, marvelling at the abundance of berries, and perhaps even sampling a few.*

*I have organised and prepared my spare room for you to come and stay. It's a cosy little room with a view of the strawberry fields, and I've stocked it with all your favourite comforts. I've even placed a few of those delightful Belgian chocolates you're so fond of on the bedside table. The quiet serenity of Strawberry is the perfect antidote to the hustle and bustle of London and the aftermath of your latest case.*

*I must admit, I'm rather excited about the prospect of showing you around my little corner of the world. The village is charming and picturesque, with its quaint cottages, winding lanes, and friendly locals. You'll find the pace of life here quite refreshing, I'm sure. And the festival is just the icing on the cake.*

*One of the highlights of the festival is the grand feast held on the final night. The entire village gathers in the town square and long tables are set up, laden with the most delicious strawberry-themed dishes you can imagine. From tarts and pies to salads and soups, it's a festive delight. I've reserved two seats for us so we can enjoy the food and the company of my wonderful neighbours.*

*I know how much you value your solitude and the quiet time you need to reflect, so I've made sure to arrange a few peaceful spots where you can retreat to whenever you feel the need. There's a lovely little garden at the back of my cottage, with a bench under an old oak tree, perfect for sitting with a good book or simply enjoying the tranquillity. And if you're feeling adventurous, there are some beautiful walking trails through the countryside, offering stunning views of the rolling hills and lush fields.*

*My dear Harvey, I cannot tell you how much I am looking forward to your visit. It's been far too long since we've had the chance to spend some quality time together, away from the demands of your cases and the distractions of the city. I'm eager to hear all about your latest adventures and to catch up on all the latest news. And I know the people of Strawberry will be just as delighted to meet you as I am to have you here.*

*Please let me know when you plan to arrive so I can make the necessary arrangements and ensure everything is perfect for your stay. The festival begins in just a week, and I do hope you can join us. It would mean the world to me to have you here, sharing in the joy and the celebrations.*

*With all my love and fondest wishes,*
*Miss M.*

~

*My dearest Miss M,*

*Your delightful letter has brought much joy to my heart. Indeed, congratulations are in order, and I am most grateful for your kind words regarding my recent case. The affair of Mrs. Grant was indeed a tragic one, and while the truth has been unveiled, it leaves behind a trail of sorrow. Captain Hastings, in his desperation, underestimated the powers of observation and deduction. It is always a poignant reminder of the frailty of human nature.*

*Your vivid description of the scene warms my heart: the police baffled as ever, the neighbours' faces painted with shock, and there I was, piecing together the fragments of a broken tale. The details, subtle yet telling, always reveal the truth. Hastings believed he could escape, but justice has a way of catching up. As for Ernestine's husband, I hope he finds solace in knowing the truth, though it is a bitter pill to swallow.*

*But enough of that grim business. Your invitation to Strawberry sounds like a balm for the soul. The fresh country air, the scent of the fields, and the promise of your company are all too enticing to resist. The annual Berry Festival, with its vibrant activities, sounds utterly delightful. I can already picture the joyous atmosphere, the laughter, and the warmth of the community.*

*The idea of strawberry-picking contests, jam-making competitions, and a parade with floats adorned with the finest berries brings a smile to my face. I must confess, the thought of sampling the local produce is quite appealing. Your description paints a picture of a festival brimming with life and happiness a perfect antidote to the recent darkness.*

*Your preparations for my visit touch me deeply. A cosy room with a view of the strawberry fields, stocked with my favourite comforts; including those delightful Belgian chocolates sounds heavenly. The thought of such tranquillity, contrasted with the hustle and bustle of London, is indeed appealing.*

*I am looking forward to exploring the charming village. Its quaint cottages, winding lanes, and friendly locals will be a refreshing change. The slower pace of life, away from the demands of my cases, is something I cherish. And the festival, as you rightly said, will be the icing on the cake.*

*The grand feast on the final night of the festival sounds like a truly memorable event. Long tables laden with strawberry-themed dishes, the entire village gathered in the town square, sharing in the joy of the celebration it will be a delight. I am grateful for the seats you have reserved for us; it will be a wonderful experience to enjoy the festivities together.*

*I also appreciate your thoughtful arrangements for peaceful spots where I can retreat and reflect.*

*My dear Miss M, it has indeed been far too long since we have had the opportunity to spend quality time together. Your letter has stirred a longing in me to catch up on all the news, to share our latest adventures, and to simply enjoy each other's company. I am also eager to meet the people of Strawberry and to experience the warmth of their hospitality.*

*Please consider this my formal acceptance of your kind invitation. I shall make the necessary arrangements and plan to arrive in time for the festival. It would be my great pleasure to share in the joy and celebrations and to bask in the tranquillity of your lovely home.*

*With all my love and fondest wishes,*
*Harvey*

*P.S. Do let me know if there is anything specific I should bring along or any special requests you might have. I want to ensure that my visit is as pleasant for you as it will be for me.*

~ ~ ~

Harvey Phillips, with his customary elegance, stepped off the train at the tiny station of Strawberry Fields. The platform, like everything else in the town, was immaculately kept, with flowerbeds of marigolds and geraniums lining the edges. Their vibrant colours were a cheerful contrast to the pale morning light. He paused for a moment, taking in the scene with a satisfied nod. His vacation had begun.

Harvey was dressed impeccably, as always, in a dark grey suit tailored to perfection. His bowler hat sat neatly on his head, tilted just so, and his neatly groomed moustache quivered as he took a deep breath of the fresh countryside air. The aroma was sweet and earthy, a heady mix of blooming flowers and ripening strawberries that grew abundantly in the fields surrounding the village.

As he walked down the platform, a porter rushed forward to help with his luggage. Harvey handed over his suitcase with a polite nod, and together they made their way to the station's exit, where a small crowd had gathered. The people of Strawberry were clearly excited about something, but Harvey, ever the observer, quickly remembered Jane had mentioned his stay coinciding with the annual festival as he saw a large banner being strung across the village square reading "Welcome to the Strawberry Fields Annual Festival!"

A smile tugged at the corners of Harvey's mouth as he surveyed the scene. The village was just as Jane had described it in her letter: a picture of rustic charm, with its narrow cobblestone streets, thatched-roof cottages, and ivy-covered stone walls. In the distance, he could see the famous strawberry fields that gave the village its name, stretching out like a lush green carpet dotted with red jewels. The festival preparations were in full swing. Stalls were being set up along the main street selling everything from strawberry preserves and pies to hand-knitted scarves and locally crafted trinkets. The air buzzed with the hum of cheerful conversation, punctuated by the occasional laugh of a child or the bark of a dog.

At the heart of the village, dominating the square, stood a grand old oak tree, its branches heavy with leaves. Under it, a makeshift stage was being constructed, likely for the various entertainments scheduled for the festival.

Harvey noted the attention to detail in every aspect of the preparations. Everything was being done with care and precision, a reflection of the pride the villagers took in their community.

Waiting for him near the oak tree was his dear friend Miss Jane Matthews, her familiar figure easily recognisable even among the bustling crowd. She was dressed in a simple but elegant outfit suitable for the countryside, her white hair neatly pinned beneath a small hat. Her bright blue eyes twinkled with warmth as she spotted Harvey and waved him over.

"Harvey, how lovely to see you again" She greeted him with a smile as he approached.

"Miss M," Phillips replied, bowing slightly. "The pleasure is all mine. What a charming village you live in. It is exactly as you described it a true picture of English tranquillity."

Jane chuckled. "Yes, Strawberry does have its charms, especially this time of year. The festival is always a highlight such a delight to see everyone come together. I do hope you enjoy your stay."

"I have no doubt I will," Harvey said, casting another appreciative glance around. "And I must thank you for your kind invitation to stay with you. It is a rare treat to experience the countryside in such a way."

"It will be lovely to have you," Jane replied. "I must say, Harvey, your visit has caused quite a stir in the village. It's not every day we have a famous detective in our midst. But I do hope you'll find the peace and quiet you seek."

"I am sure I will," Harvey told her, though there was a glint of curiosity in his eyes. "But I must admit, I am intrigued by this festival. It seems there is much to see and do."

"Oh, indeed," Jane said with enthusiasm. "There's the strawberry picking, of course, and the pie-eating contest is always a crowd favourite. The local crafts are quite lovely, too – I'm sure you'll find something to take back with you as a souvenir. And tonight, there's to be a dance in the village hall. Quite a lively affair, by all accounts."

"How delightful," Harvey said. "And what of the people? They seem a cheerful lot."

Jane's expression softened as she looked around at the villagers, many of whom she knew by name. "Yes, they are good-hearted people, though, like anywhere, we have our share of little dramas. But nothing that can't be solved with a cup of tea and a chat, usually."

"Ah, the wisdom of the country," Harvey said with a smile. "But come on, Jane let us not keep you standing in the street. Shall we make our way to your home?"

"Of course," Jane agreed. "My cottage is just a short walk from here. I do hope you'll find it comfortable."

The two set off down the cobblestone path that wound through the village, passing by the cottages with their neatly trimmed hedges and colourful flower boxes. The sound of birds chirping filled the air, adding to the idyllic atmosphere. As they walked, Miss Matthews pointed out various landmarks: the old church with its ivy-covered bell tower, the village green where the children played and the local pub, The Red Lion, which was already doing a brisk trade with festivalgoers.

Finally, they reached Jane's home a charming little house nestled at the edge of the village. It was exactly as Harvey had imagined a picture-perfect English cottage, with roses climbing up the walls and a white picket fence surrounding a small but well-tended garden. A stone path led to the front door, which was painted a cheerful shade of turquoise.

"Welcome to my humble abode," Jane said as she opened the door and led Harvey inside.

The interior of the cottage was cosy and inviting, with low wooden beams, floral wallpaper, and a crackling fire in the hearth. The furniture was comfortable and well-worn, with an air of quiet elegance. Harvey noted the many small details that spoke of Jane's character -the neatly arranged bookshelves , the embroidered cushions and the vases of fresh flowers that adorned the tables.

"Please, make yourself at home, "Jane said, gesturing for him to take a seat. "Would you care for some Earl Grey?"

"That would be most welcome, thank you," Harvey replied as he settled into an armchair by the fire.

Jane bustled about the kitchen, soon returning with a tray laden with a teapot, cups, and a plate of homemade scones with cream and strawberry jam made from the local fields. As she poured the tea, Harvey glanced out the window, which offered a view of the fields in the distance. The sight was peaceful, a patchwork of green and red stretching out under the clear blue sky.

"This really is a beautiful place, Jane," Harvey said, accepting the cup of tea she handed him. "I can see why you have chosen to make it your home."

"It is," she agreed, sitting down opposite him. "Strawberry has a way of growing on you. The people, the landscape it's a little world unto itself."

They sipped their tea in companionable silence for a moment, each lost in their own thoughts. Harvey's keen mind, however, was already at work, observing, analysing, and filing away details about the village and its inhabitants. Though he had come for a vacation, he could not entirely suppress the detective within him.

"You mentioned earlier your friend Mrs. Edith Pickering invited you to the festival," Harvey said, breaking the silence. "Is she a long-time resident of Strawberry as well?"

"Yes, Edith and I have been friends for many years," Jane replied with a fond smile. "She moved here shortly after her husband Lawrence passed away, she found the village to be a place of solace, I believe. She lives just up the road in the old manor house. Quite a grand place, though she doesn't make much use of it these days. Edith is rather private, you see, but she has a good heart.

"I'm sure she'd be delighted to meet you," Jane said. "Though I must warn you, Edith can be rather... eccentric at times. She has a keen interest in the supernatural, you see ghosts, spirits, that sort of thing. Quite harmless, of course, but it does lead to some interesting conversations."

This piqued Harvey's curiosity as his eyebrows lifted in mild surprise. "How intriguing. And does she believe her manor house is haunted?"

"She does," Jane replied, with a twinkle in her eye. "Though I've never seen any evidence of it myself. Still, it adds a bit of mystery to the place, don't you think?"

"Indeed," Harvey said, smiling. "It seems Strawberry Fields is full of surprises."

The afternoon passed pleasantly, with Harvey and Jane chatting about a variety of topics, from village gossip to the latest detective novels, like their current favourite The Never List by Koethi Zan. Harvey found himself enjoying Jane's company immensely her sharp wit and keen observations made for stimulating conversation, and her gentle manner was a welcome change from the more intense personalities he often encountered in his line of work.

As the day wore on, the sun began to dip low in the sky, casting a warm golden light over the village. The festival preparations were nearly complete, and the first few visitors had begun to arrive, eager to partake in the festivities.

The evening air in Strawberry was filled with the scent of ripe strawberries and the buzz of anticipation. The quaint countryside town was ready to kick off the annual festival, and the first event was set to begin tonight at Edith Pickering's grand manor house. Edith had opened her lavish ballroom for the occasion, transforming it into a warm and inviting space filled with the aromas of traditional English fare.

Harvey Phillips, ever the meticulous man, was adjusting his tie in the mirror of his guest room at Edith's home. Miss Matthews, always practical and with an eye for detail, was fastening a delicate brooch to her collar, the final touch to her ensemble for the evening.

"Ah, my dear Miss M," Harvey remarked, his voice tinged with amusement, "it seems we are to dine in the company of some rather intriguing characters tonight."

Jane smiled knowingly as she smoothed out her dress. "Indeed, Harv. Edith has gathered quite the assembly. It's not often one finds such a mix of personalities under one roof."

As they made their way downstairs, the pair could already hear the hum of conversation and the clinking of glasses coming from the ballroom. Edith stood at the entrance, greeting each guest with her customary grace and charm. Her silver hair was pinned neatly in place, and she wore a dress of deep burgundy that complimented her stately demeanour.

"Jane. Harvey." Edith beamed as she saw them approach. "I'm so glad you could join us. The festival simply wouldn't be the same without the two of you."

"It is our pleasure, Edith," Jane replied warmly. "Your home looks as lovely as ever."

"Merci, Madame Pickering," Harvey added, with a slight bow. "I have no doubt this evening will be most enjoyable."

As they stepped into the ballroom, the grandeur of the room took their breath away. The long dining table was adorned with crystal candlesticks and gleaming silverware. The aroma of freshly baked shepherd's pie and roasted vegetables filled the air, mingling with the sweet scent of the trifle being prepared for dessert. Edith had spared no expense in ensuring her guests were treated to a meal that was both comforting and exquisite.

The guests were already seated, each lost in their own conversations. Harvey and Jane quickly observed the varied group, each with their own stories and secrets – some of which were already the talk of the village. Jane wasted no time filling her old friend in.

At the head of the table sat Henry Blake, the wealthy landowner whose presence seemed to command attention. His stern expression and sharp eyes gave him an air of authority, and it was clear that he was used to getting his way. Henry had a reputation for being harsh and unyielding: a man whose wealth and power had afforded him little need for compromise.

Next to him was his estranged wife, Alice Blake, a woman of striking beauty and icy demeanour. The tension between the two was intense, and it was no secret their marriage was a fractured one. Alice had been the subject of much gossip in the village due to her affair with local artist Jason Dowling, who also happened to be the festival's designer. She sat in silence, her eyes downcast, as if trying to distance herself from the man beside her.

On the opposite side of the table was Tom Radley, a rugged local strawberry and dairy farmer and single father, as his wife Maggie had died from breast cancer a few years earlier. Harvey noted Tom's broad shoulders and weathered face which told of a life spent working the land. Tom had a longstanding feud with Henry Blake over land rights, a dispute that had simmered for years and often flared up in public. Tom's daughter, Lily Radley, was also present though she sat quietly, her eyes flitting nervously between her father and Henry. Lily worked as a maid for Henry and Alice Blake, a position that placed her in a difficult situation given the feud between her father and her bosses.

Further down the table was Michael Hart, a charming and smooth-talking strawberry vendor who had a stall at the festival. Michael was known for his easy-going nature, but there was a steely determination behind his smile. He, too, had recently a business disagreement with Henry Blake over the price of strawberries, and it was clear the two men were not on friendly terms.

Patricia Turner, Strawberry's very own gossip queen and local old biddy, was seated near the centre of the table. She was a small, wiry woman with sharp features and a tongue to match.

Patricia took every opportunity to share the latest rumours and secrets she had gleaned from her daily rounds in the village. Her eyes glittered with mischief as she whispered to the guests on either side of her, no doubt spreading the latest juicy titbits of scandal.

Finally, Constable James Howard, the local policeman in charge of security was seated at the far end of the table. James was a steady and dependable man with a strong sense of duty and a deep commitment to the community. He had been tasked with ensuring the safety of the festival, a responsibility he took very seriously.

As the dinner progressed, the conversation flowed, but beneath the surface, tensions simmered. The strained relationship between Henry and Alice was apparent to all, and Tom Radley's animosity toward Henry was barely concealed. Michael Hart's charm did little to mask the underlying resentment he felt towards the wealthy landowner, and Patricia Turner's incessant gossiping only served to fan the flames of discord.

Jane and Harvey exchanged knowing glances as they observed the dynamics at the table. It was clear each guest had their own motives and secrets, and the potential for conflict was high.

The delicious shepherd's pie and decadent trifle did little to ease the tension that hung in the air.

As the evening wore on, the atmosphere in the ballroom grew heavier, the weight of unspoken grievances pressing down on the guests. It was a gathering that promised more than just good food and pleasant conversation; it was a meeting of conflicting interests and unresolved disputes.

After dinner, Edith stood and thanked everyone for attending, her voice warm and inviting.

"I hope you've all enjoyed the meal" she said. The festival is just beginning, and I'm sure we're in for a wonderful time over the next few days. But tonight, let's raise a glass to the spirit of Strawberry Fields and the joy of coming together as a community."

Glasses clinked as the guests joined in the toast though some with less enthusiasm than others. As the evening ended, Harvey and Jane knew the events of the night were only the beginning. The festival might be a time for celebration, but it was clear that beneath the surface, tensions were building, and it wouldn't be long before they reached a boiling point. Little did they know at the time that the boiling point would be reached by the second day of the Strawberry Festival and result in one of the guests that very night being murdered.

*Day One of the Strawberry Fields Festival*

The sun shone brightly over the quaint countryside town of Strawberry, casting a warm and golden glow over the bustling festival. The air was thick with the scent of ripe strawberries, mingling with the sweet and savoury aromas wafting from the various food stalls. Laughter and the cheerful chatter of villagers filled the air, creating a harmonious symphony that echoed through the fields. The annual festival had begun, and it was a day for joy, indulgence, and community.

Harvey Phillips, his attire impeccably neat despite the casual setting, strolled alongside Miss Jane Matthews and Mrs. Edith Pickering. The three companions had spent the morning

exploring the festival grounds, delighting in the sights, sounds, and tastes the event had to offer.

"Ah, Jane and Edith," Harvey began, adjusting his hat to shield his eyes from the sun. "It is indeed a pleasure to experience such a charming festival. The ambiance, the atmosphere it is truly phenomenal."

Jane Matthews smiled gently, her keen eyes observing everything around her with quiet curiosity. "Strawberry has always had a special charm during the festival, Harvey. It's a time when the entire village comes together, and the joy is always buzzing like bees. Though I must say, there's something in the air today a certain unease, perhaps."

Edith Pickering, a sprightly woman with a warm smile, nodded in agreement. "I feel it too,

Jane. It's as if the air is charged with something more than just excitement. But let's not dwell on that now. We're here to enjoy ourselves, and there's so much to see and do!"

The trio wandered toward the food stalls, where vendors offered a mouthwatering array of themed delicacies. Edith insisted they try the shortcake a festival favourite made with freshly baked scones, cream, and strawberries so ripe they practically melted in your mouth.

"Oh, do try this, Harvey," Edith urged, handing him a piece of shortcake. "It's simply divine."

Harvey took a delicate bite, his eyes widening with appreciation. "C'est magnifique, Edith. The combination of flavours, the freshness it is perfection on a plate."

Jane savoured her own portion, nodding in agreement. "It's the little things like this that make life so delightful. And the strawberries this year are exceptionally good, don't you think?"

As they continued to stroll, they came across a pie-eating contest. The sight of villagers young and old eagerly devouring strawberry pies brought a chuckle from Harvey. Edith, always one for a bit of fun, encouraged Jane to participate.

"Oh, I couldn't possibly," Jane protested, though her eyes twinkled with amusement. "But you, Edith, would be splendid at it!"

Edith laughed, waving her hand dismissively. "I think not, Jane. But let's watch and enjoy the spectacle, shall we?"

They found a spot near the front, and Phillips, always attentive to detail, noticed the gleeful determination on the contestants' faces. It was a light-hearted competition, but even so, the intensity of the moment was not lost on him. He observed the crowd, his sharp eyes picking up on subtle cues, nervous glances, forced smiles, and a tension that seemed to hum beneath the surface of the festivities.

When the contest ended, the trio continued their exploration, stopping to admire the various crafts and goods on display. Local artisans had set up stalls showcasing everything from handwoven baskets to intricately carved wooden figurines all themed around strawberries, of course. Harvey found himself particularly taken with a set of strawberry-shaped teacups, their delicate design and vibrant colours catching his eye.

"These would make a charming addition to any afternoon tea, don't you think, Jane?" Harvey asked, holding up one of the teacups for her to see.

Jane examined it with a discerning eye. "They're lovely; you should purchase them as a memento of your visit."

Edith, meanwhile, was drawn to a stall selling strawberry preserves and jams. The vendor, a cheerful man with a big grin, offered samples on little slices of bread. Edith tasted one and declared it the best she'd ever had, promptly buying several jars to take home.

As the day wore on, the sun climbed higher in the sky and the festival reached its peak. The main event, the "Strawberry Fields Parade," was about to begin. Villagers and visitors alike lined the streets, eagerly awaiting the procession of floats and performers that celebrated the town's rich history and bountiful strawberry harvests.

Harvey and his companions found a spot with a good view, and soon the parade began, as floats adorned with strawberry-themed decorations rolling by. There were dancers dressed as strawberries, children wearing strawberry crowns, and even a giant strawberry balloon that floated high above the crowd. It was a spectacle of colour and joy, and for a moment, the unease that had lingered earlier seemed to dissipate in the warmth of the afternoon.

But as Harvey watched, his mind couldn't shake the feeling something was amiss. There was tension in the air, a sense of anticipation that went beyond the festival's excitement. He caught a fleeting glimpse of a shadowed figure in the crowd someone whose presence seemed out of place among the revelry. The figure disappeared just as quickly, leaving Harvey with a nagging sense of foreboding.

As the parade ended, Edith suggested they take a break and enjoy some of the festival games. They tried their hand at strawberry picking a game where participants had to pluck as many strawberries as possible within a time limit. Edith was surprisingly skilled, her nimble fingers working quickly to gather a small basket full of strawberries. Jane and Harvey cheered her on, their laughter mingling with the sounds of the festival.

Next, they visited the ring toss, where Edith won a small stuffed strawberry for her efforts, and Harvey attempted the themed trivia quiz, impressing the quizmaster with his vast knowledge of horticulture.

But as the day began to wind down, the sense of tension returned stronger than before. The sun dipped lower in the sky, casting long shadows over the festival grounds. Harvey noticed some of the villagers seemed more subdued, their earlier cheerfulness giving way to quiet conversations and furtive glances.

Jane, ever perceptive, caught Harvey's eye and nodded slightly. She, too, had noticed the shift in the atmosphere. It was as if the festival were a stage, and the actors were waiting for the next act one that promised to be far less joyous than the day's festivities.

As the last of the sun's rays faded into twilight, the trio decided it was time to head back to Jane's cottage. The walk back was peaceful, the sound of crickets filling the evening air. But even in the tranquillity of the countryside, the unease lingered.

Back at the cottage, Edith bade them goodnight, leaving Harvey and Jane to their thoughts. They sat in the cosy living room, the warmth of the hearth a stark contrast to the chill that had settled in Harvey's mind.

"Tomorrow," Harvey said quietly, "we must be prepared, Miss M. I fear the festival may have been the calm before the storm."

Jane nodded, her expression thoughtful. "Yes, Harvey, I believe you're right. But for tonight, let us enjoy this moment of peace, for we may not have another."

And so they sat in silence, each lost in their thoughts, the quiet of the evening a fragile barrier against the uncertainty that awaited them in the days to come. The Strawberry Fields Festival had been a day of joy, but the undercurrent of tension hinted at darker things to come.

*Day Two of the Strawberry Fields Festival*

The villagers and visitors were already bustling around as the sun rose on the second day of the festival eager to participate in another day's worth of events. Children laughed as they ran through the fields, baskets in hand, while the adults indulged in the festival's many offerings.

Amid the cheerful atmosphere, Mr. Henry Blake was found lying lifeless in the heart of the fields. His body was discovered by a young couple out for an early morning stroll. The couple's screams alerted others nearby, and soon a crowd had gathered around the grim scene.

Harvey Phillips was quickly on the scene, along with Jane Matthews. But now, faced with the body of Mr. Blake, his peaceful retreat had turned into a crime scene.

Mr. Blake's basket of strawberries lay tipped over beside him, the red berries scattered across the ground. Some were ripe and juicy, while others were still green and unripe: a curious detail that caught Harvey's attention. It was unusual for someone as meticulous as Mr. Blake to pick such a mix. Harvey bent down to examine the basket more closely, his sharp mind already working to piece together the clues.

"Peculiar," Harvey said, addressing Jane as she stood beside him, her face a mask of concern, Don't you find it odd our dear Mr. Blake would gather such a strange assortment?"

Jane nodded thoughtfully. "Yes, indeed, Harvey. Henry Blake was known for his keen eye in the fields. He would never have picked unripe strawberries unless something distracted him – or perhaps he was in a hurry."

As the two detectives pondered this first clue, Constable James Howard arrived to secure the scene. He was a young man, clearly out of his depth with such a high-profile case in the usually quiet village. Grateful for the presence of the two renowned detectives, he quickly welcomed their help.

As the investigation commenced, Harvey and Jane began to gather information from the villagers. It wasn't long before they came across their first suspect: Alice Blake, Henry's young and beautiful wife. A pearl necklace belonging to her had been found near the body, half-buried in the soft earth.

Alice was shaken when questioned. Her eyes were wide, and her hands shook as she spoke. "I don't know how my necklace ended up there," she stuttered. "I was wearing it earlier, but I must have lost it. I swear I had nothing to do with Henry's death; even though he was a bastard at times, I still loved him!"

Harvey observed Alice carefully, noting the way she avoided meeting his gaze. "Madame Blake," he said gently, "this necklace was very dear to you, non? Surely you would have noticed if it had gone missing."

Alice hesitated, her voice barely above a whisper. "I was upset last night. Henry and I argued...about money. I stormed out of the house and went for a walk. I must have lost the necklace then. But I didn't go near the fields, I swear!"

Harvey exchanged a glance with Jane, who was quietly observing from afar. Alice's story seemed believable, but there was something off about her demeanour. Still, they couldn't jump to conclusions just yet.

The next person of interest was Tom Radley. Tom had been seen earlier that morning wearing muddy boots despite the dry weather. When asked about it, Tom appeared nervous.

"Those old boots? I was just checking on my crops near the river," Tom explained, a bit too quickly. "Nothing suspicious about that."

Jane raised an eyebrow. "But Mr. Radley, the river is quite a distance from the fields, and your crops don't require much attention during the festival, do they?"

Tom flushed and looked down at his boots, his hands fidgeting. "I might have taken a walk closer to the fields, just to clear my head. Henry and I had a bit of a disagreement yesterday, but I would never harm him."

Suspicious, Harvey made a mental note of Tom's muddy boots, especially since the murder weapon a heavy stone covered with blood had been found near the river. The timeline of events was becoming clearer, but there were still too many unanswered questions.

As they continued their investigation, they came across Lily Radley. The young woman had been seen earlier with tear-stained cheeks, her usually bright outlook replaced with one of sorrow. When asked about her tears, Lily hesitated before responding.

"Henry was a kind man," she said softly, her voice trembling. "But he was also very strict. He disapproved of my relationship with Michael Hart. We had a terrible argument the night before, and I was so upset. But I would never...I couldn't have..."

Lily's emotions were raw, but there was no direct evidence linking her to the crime. However, her connection to Michael Hart raised further questions.

Michael was a charismatic man, well-liked by the villagers. He claimed to have been at his stall the entire time, selling his goods to festivalgoers however, no one could confirm his whereabouts during a crucial 15-minute window around the time of the murder.

When Harvey and Jane approached Michael, he greeted them with a broad smile. "Ah, the famous detectives! I suppose you're here to ask about poor Henry's death. Tragic business, that."

"Indeed, Mr. Hart," Harvey replied, his eyes narrowing slightly. "It seems no one saw you during a key moment this morning. Can you account for your whereabouts?"

Michael shrugged casually. "I was at my stall, as I said. Maybe I stepped away for a moment to get some water or speak with a customer. Nothing unusual."

Harvey was unconvinced. Michael's alibi was flimsy at best, and his carefree attitude did little to change their suspicions.

As they gathered more information, the name Patricia Turner kept coming up. Known for her love of gossip, Patricia was always keen to share the latest news, whether it was true or not. When the detectives spoke with her, she was eager to share what she had seen.

"I knew something was wrong when I saw that mysterious figure lurking around the Blake estate the night before the murder," Patricia said, her voice filled with excitement. "They were dressed all in black, creeping around like they didn't want to be seen. I thought it was strange"

"Did you recognise this figure, Mrs. Turner?" Jane asked.

Patricia shook her head. "No, it was too dark. But I'm sure it was someone who had no business being there."

Patricia's account added yet another layer to the mystery. Who was this mysterious figure, and what were they doing near the Blake estate the night before Henry's death?

As the day wore on, Harvey and Jane retreated to her cottage to discuss their findings and create their makeshift murder board. The clues were beginning to form a picture, but there were still many loose ends to tie up.

"The strawberry basket, the necklace, the muddy boots, Lily's tears, Michael's alibi, and Patricia's gossip they all point to different motives and opportunities," Harvey said.

Jane nodded in agreement. "Yes, but the key will be separating the truth from the lies. The villagers may not be telling us everything – but eventually, the truth will come to light."

Harvey smiled, his eyes twinkling with determination. "And we shall find it, Jane. Together, we shall uncover the truth behind Mr. Blake's untimely death. The culprit will not escape justice."

As the festival continued around them, the two detectives knew the peaceful façade of Strawberry had been shattered. But with their combined skills, they were confident they would soon bring the murderer to justice. The game was afoot, and nothing would stop them from solving the case.

The night was quiet in Strawberry, save for the occasional rustling of leaves in the gentle breeze and the distant hoot of an owl. Inside Jane's cosy cottage, the atmosphere was

anything but serene. The sitting room had been transformed into a war room of sorts, the walls now lined with notes, photos, and bits of evidence pinned to a large corkboard. At the centre of it all, Jane and Harvey worked side by side, their sharp minds cutting through the fog of confusion that had settled over the village since Henry Blake's murder.

Jane, with her knitting laid aside, sat in her usual armchair, her eyes flickering over the murder board. Her understanding of human nature, honed over decades of observing life in small villages like Strawberry, had given her a distinct perspective on the case. She knew the key to solving Henry Blake's murder lay in understanding the complex web of relationships within the village.

Harvey, with his immaculate moustache and impeccable suit, was the picture of concentration. His methodical approach, rooted in logic and meticulous attention to detail, was already bearing fruit. He was standing before the board, carefully rearranging pieces of evidence, his mind working through the puzzle one piece at a time.

"Jane," Harvey began, his voice soft yet commanding, "we must consider every angle, every possibility. But I believe we are closing in on the truth. The physical evidence is starting to tell us a story, one that involves more than just a crime of passion."

Jane nodded thoughtfully, her eyes narrowing as she considered the relationships in the village. "You're right, Harvey. People are rarely as simple as they appear. I've always believed to truly understand a crime, one must first understand the people involved their motives, their secrets, and their fears. And in this case, it's clear the relationships between Henry, Alice, Jason, and Lily are more complicated than they seem."

Harvey glanced at the photo of Henry Blake, pinned to the top of the board. "Henry Blake was a man of means and influence, but he was not without enemies. He had discovered his wife Alice's affair with Jason and was planning to divorce her. With the prenuptial agreement in place, she would be left with nothing. That, I think, was the catalyst for everything that followed."

Jane's lips pressed into a thin line as she considered Alice's position. "Alice was desperate, afraid. She stood to lose everything if Henry went through with the divorce. But she wasn't the only one with a grudge against Henry, was she? Lily...poor Lily. She harboured a deep resentment against Henry for the way he treated her father, Tom."

Harvey nodded, his eyes sharp as he began connecting the dots. "Lily was close to her father, and when Henry humiliated him and pushed him out of the business, it left a scar on her heart. She had kept that resentment buried – but such feelings often fester, and in moments of anger, they can erupt, with devastating consequences."

Jane's gaze drifted to the photo of Lily: a young woman with a sad, determined look in her eyes. "Alice confided in Lily, didn't she? Perhaps seeking sympathy, or perhaps hoping Lily might offer her a solution to her dilemma. But instead, she unleashed a storm that had been forming."

Harvey's eyes narrowed as he tapped a finger against the photo of the stone found near Henry's body. "Lily, in a moment of impulsive rage, struck Henry with the stone. She may have intended only to frighten him, to teach him a lesson – but in her anger, she misjudged her strength. Henry fell, his skull fractured, and the life drained from him in an instant."

Jane shuddered, imagining the scene. "And Alice...she arrived shortly after, didn't she? Seeing what Lily had done, she must have been horrified. But she would have quickly realised if Lily were caught, she would be ruined, just as she herself would be ruined if Henry's plan to divorce her became public. Desperation drives people to do the impossible."

Harvey turned to Jane, his expression serious. "She decided to cover for Lily. The necklace found near the body it was Alice's, was it not? She left it there, hoping to divert suspicion, to make it look like a crime of passion committed in the heat of the moment by someone else."

Jane nodded slowly, her mind racing as she pieced together the final details. "Yes, and she would have counted on the village's natural inclination to gossip to suspect someone like Jason, or even a spurned lover, might be responsible, just like your case back in London. It was a clever move, but ultimately, the truth has a way of bubbling to the surface."

Harvey stepped back from the board; his hands clasped behind his back as he surveyed their work. "But the truth, Jane, is not enough. We must have proof of something that will hold up under scrutiny. We need to find the stone Lily used, and we need to confront Alice and Lily with what we know. They will try to deny it, but I believe the weight of their guilt will force a confession."

Jane sighed; her heart was heavy with the knowledge of what was to come. "So much pain, so much suffering all because of pride, resentment, and fear. But you're right. We must see this through to the end, for Henry's sake and the sake of justice."

Harvey gave her a reassuring smile, his eyes softening with understanding. "You are a kind soul, Jane. Sometimes the pursuit of justice requires us to face uncomfortable truths. Let us prepare for what must be done."

The two of them worked through the night, refining their theories, gathering the remaining evidence, and planning their next steps. As dawn broke over the fields, casting a pale light over the village, they knew the end was in sight.

*Day Three of the Strawberry Fields Festival*

By the time the sun had fully risen, Jane and Harvey had everything they needed. They would confront Alice and Lily that very day, and by evening, the truth would be known to all. It was a sad victory, one tinged with the sorrow of knowing the lives of everyone involved would be forever changed. But it was justice nonetheless, and as they left the cottage to face the new day, Jane couldn't help but feel a deep sense of gratitude for the partnership she had found with Harvey Phillips. Together, they had uncovered the truth and brought justice for a man whose life had been cruelly cut short.

The sun was setting over the fields as Jane Matthews and Harvey Phillips cornered Lily and Alice in the quaint sitting room of Jane's cottage. The evidence was overwhelming the fragment of fabric found at the scene, the overheard argument and the letters hidden away in Alice's drawer.

"Lily," Jane began, her voice gentle but firm, "you knew we would find the truth eventually. The evidence speaks for itself. You were at the scene the night of Blake's murder."

Lily trembled, her eyes darting between Jane and Harvey, searching for an escape and finding none. The weight of their combined gaze bore down on her until, with a broken sob, she collapsed into a chair. "I didn't mean to," she confessed, tears streaming down her face. "It was an accident. He...he threatened me, and I just...I just wanted him to stop."

Alice, standing beside her, seemed to shrink into herself, her face pale with guilt. "I helped her," she whispered. "I covered it up because I couldn't bear to see her life ruined. I thought...I thought we could keep it hidden."

Harvey nodded. "The truth always finds its way to the light, Alice. It is better this way."

As the Strawberry Festival continued, the shadow of Henry's murder lingered in the hearts of the villagers.

The next morning, Harvey and Miss M parted ways at the train station.

"The Case of the Missing Will calls me back to London" Harvey said. They exchanged a look of mutual respect, knowing Strawberry would never quite be the same again.

“Till next time, my Miss M,” said Harvey fondly as he stepped onto the train and tipped his hat at her.

# Mary and Dickon and the Garden of Fools

## by Angelika Miria

**Literary World**: The Secret Garden

In a familiar, secluded garden, a tender moment is shared, and an ache of longing for love is shared. As they reflect on their bittersweet pasts, Mary and Dickon navigate the fragile territory of first love, discovering that even the smallest acts of care hold the power to mend hearts and nurture hope.

***Content Warnings:*** *themes of loss, grief*

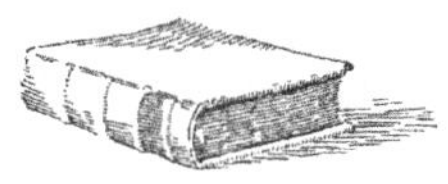

Within the walls, partially adorned with luscious green vines, surrounded by rose bushes and English lavender, upon a rustic white swing, young Mary and Dickon hold but the tiniest Blue Tit with the faintest beat of a heart within the palm of their hands. Their gaze solely peering into the suffering bird when Dickon breaks his concentration on the suffering avian and glances up at Mary when he inhales a thin breath.

*Dickon:* "Mary, do you ever miss your parents?" He began.

*Mary:* "If you're wondering if I miss the people who were too busy focusing on their lives that I had merely been a trinket of faint amusement to them, then yes, I do, and I believe a part of me always will." She responded matter-of-factly.

*Dickon:* "But how Mary? How does one miss those who have left them as if they were merely an object of observation and not something made of their own flesh and blood?" He was cautious with his reply, his words filled with a deepening sorrow.

Mary, finally lifting her eyes to meet Dickon's, inhaled sharply.

*Mary:* "Is that not the most amusing part Dickon? You can be mistreated, forgotten, and neglected by the ones who brought you here and yet, once they are gone, you seem to only recall the faintest of good days with them, as if the ones who hurt you, no longer have the power to do so and they in turn become helpless. My mother brushed my hair after the maids bathed me once, she seemed lost in her own thoughts, somewhere up there in her own mind, and I wondered if she thought about how it felt to brush my hair; the child she bore in her womb for so many months. She looked into the mirror at my reflection and her eye sparkled just for a fraction of a second, oh, but Dickon I knew if she could have done things differently, she would have. When the cholera consumed the vibrance of their existence, it was that singular image that had sewn itself into the very back of my eyelids. Sometimes, I wonder what it's like for them under there, or up there somewhere with the stars, or if they are here with me in such a place like heaven."

Dickon pondered what she had revealed to him.

*Dickon:* "Before we started to play together, I had heard stories of how wretched you had been. What changed?"

*Mary:* "I have thought about how I behaved when I lived in India and I know I was angry. The only love I wanted was from my mother and father, and if I couldn't have that, then it didn't matter what they brought to me; the servants, nothing was enough, I wanted more, to fill a void I presume."

*Dickon:* "I think I understand. But again, what changed?"

*Mary:* "Knowing that they weren't here anymore. At first I thought I drank poison and I too had died. From the entire voyage to England it all felt like a dream, or maybe I too was dead, I couldn't be certain. When I arrived here, I knew this wasn't my home, I thought someone would come for me and bring me home and maybe Mother and Father would be alive, and well, maybe they needed this break to start fresh, and I allowed the anger to swallow me like a disease. Yet, each day I awoke, I was still in the same room, in the same bed. It was your sister who, through her kindness, through showing me that there was more to this place than I could have dreamed, opened senses and feelings I hadn't been privileged of feeling before. Then you happened."

Dickon took a breath in as his chest warmed and ruby flowed into his cheeks, his smile was meek.

Dickon cleared his throat, perhaps she didn't mean what she said in the same way he would have.

*Dickon:* "What did my 'happening' do exactly dear Mary?"

*Mary:* "It made me love Dickon, at least that's what I think this is, when your chest seems tight and your sternum feels weak when the person isn't around, but just a small appearance that they make sends every atom in your body into a frenzy. Sometimes Dickon, I picture how it would feel to be held by you, and if you love me, because I haven't felt love, but what I feel with you, the kindness you show me, I can't help but think that for the first time, I am loved."

Dickon removed his right hand from beneath hers in which they still cradled the bird, and he effortlessly and ever so gently brushed her cheek.

*Dickon:* "Mary, I think I have loved you my whole life."

*Mary:* "Well don't be a fool Dickon, you haven't known me your whole life." She answered with embarrassment and a taste of sarcasm.

*Dickon:* "I didn't need to Mary, but my heart beat to a feeling I didn't recognize before, and when I saw you, I understood that it was the same beat, I recognized that the feeling was tied to you. So, yes Mary, I think I have loved you my entire life. May that be only fourteen years, but it is the entirety of my existential life this far."

Mary smiled, and her eyes glistened with the reflection of the light against the fluid that had built up like a filter over her iris'. She sniffled.

*Mary:* "Do you think he'll be alright?"

They looked down at the bird.

Dickon leaned over and placed his lips against Mary's. He left them there, close enough only to feel the tingle of atoms yearning to touch each other, before he softly spoke, "Mary, everything in this garden lives, it never dies. Even if he remains within these walls, we have everything we need. I love you Mary Lennox and you love me and there is nothing that cannot survive through that. Everything this love touches will live forever."

Mary closed her eyes and pressed her lips against his and he kissed her back.

*Mary:* "No matter what little bird, you will always live forever."

# I Do Believe in Falling Stars

by Maddi Neuenswander

**Literary World:** Peter Pan J. M. Barrie

Tinkerbell and Captain Hook help Wendy become a true feminist icon and confront Peter Pan about his chauvinistic ways.

***Content Warnings**: domestic violence, emotional abuse*

*To all the boys I've ever dated who underestimated me, and to all the friends who only ever wanted me to be exactly what they wanted. I hope you have the life you deserve.*

I'm half concealed by leaves as I watch Peter's hand slam into the girl. The purple shadow of what will be a bruise covers her cheek and eyes like a mask. She flinches back, eyes wide. His face contorts in anger, and his mouth opens and stays that way for a long time. Grief covers her expression, and tears gather in her eyes. I zip into his face, my hands at the ready to say what's on my mind.

They say I sound like bells, but I imagine bells just can't describe my angry words. My hands snap at the air with a force so unlike me, even I'm surprised. But Peter isn't listening.

He never does.

I kind of understand. I don't like listening to someone when they're essentially yelling at me either. But this is important! Didn't he ever learn that hitting is wrong? I mean, I know his whole thing is that he doesn't grow up, but you'd think he'd at least learn some manners or something.

So, maybe my next move is petty, or out of line, or whatever. But, if Peter won't listen, I know exactly who will.

The pirate is difficult to find, but he's eager to listen when I do. I tell him all about the girl—*was her name Wendy?*—and how Peter tries to tell her who to be.

He uses one hand to reply. "Sounds to me like this Wendy girl needs saving—from herself just as much as anyone else."

I think my next words *would* sound like bells as my hands dance in the air. "Yes! But how do we get her away from him long enough to see it?"

We hatch a plan.

A foolproof plan.

A plan so foolproof only I could twist it around into failure.

It isn't hard to get her alone, seeing as Peter leaves her alone most times to do all the mothering she traded her dreams for. It is on the beach we find her—stringing together the holes in the Lost Boys' socks.

"Wasn't it only days ago you told Peter it is your dream to become a music instructor?" My hands are a frenzy in front of Wendy's eyes. "Why would you silence your dreams for him?"

But she ignores me just like Peter did, only swatting at the air to be rid of me. I try again, flipping my hands smoothly in her face. Again, she ignores me. My signing becomes frantic, angry. Why won't she look at my hands? Doesn't she know my hands are stronger than my voice ever could be?

Hook is, as always, comforting to me in my defeat, watching the whine of my fingers with rapt attention. "I'm sorry, Tink."

"She wouldn't even listen, Hook! I mean, how rude is that?"

*Whatever, time for plan B.*

It begins with my bad attitude smoking even hotter than it was a minute ago.

"Don't worry, Tink," Hook says with gentle hands. "I'll talk to her. I mean, at least I can't do as bad as you did."

My outstretched tongue bids him farewell as he smirks down the sandbar to the water's edge. I watch from the branches while he approaches her. She's sitting—I mean, pouting—on the beach, working grains between her toes and adding salt and sadness to the sea. Hook leans back against sand pressed hands next to her, and they become two statues framed against the finest grains for a long time. Long enough that the sun has moved across the sky before either moves.

Hook turns to face her, the profile of his face etched with concern. My heart pounds against the bones in my chest when he makes his fingers dance in front of her face. My chest stills when her face squishes in what could be confusion or maybe even disgust.

*A quick breath in before I do something reckless.*

I take a grand aerial loop to land on Hook's shoulder. I definitely don't sound like bells now. My signing is too frenzied and sharp to be anything but rage.

Wendy's lips move around words I can't hear. I think she's trying to say the music sounds upset. *What music?*

Hook slices the air with his namesake to stop me.

His signing is slow and smooth, as always. "She doesn't understand sign language. We have to reach her another way."

My tongue pokes out at him, but my eyes throw daggers at her as I move from Hook's shoulder to a small rock half buried in the sand. "How will we communicate with her, then?"

"I have a plan."

I watch him open his mouth. Once. Twice. Three times. Then he pulls a stick through the sand to leave behind long, looping lines. A heavy breath follows my throat. Wendy studies the lines with watery eyes. Meets Hook's. Flicks her eyes to me.

I meet her gaze until Hook's hand flaps for my attention.

"She likes music. You sound like bells. If you sign to her and make it sound lovely, she might listen."

I roll my eyes. "How do I make it sound lovely if I can't hear it?"

"Happy thoughts, Tink."

So I sign happy thoughts about following my dreams and living a life I love. I sign about my love for the island and nature and tinkering. But I stop when Wendy starts to cry and furrow my eyebrows at Hook.

He pushes his hands at me, his thumb pressing into his hook.

So, I pick back up again about how happy sunrises make me. And how I love my job and the smell of salt on everything, everywhere.

She pulls a stick through the sand, and Hook interprets for me. “Music is all I’ve ever wanted. And children. I guess feeling wanted made me forget.”

Hook urges me to continue with his thumb again. My hands tell the story of the first time I discovered what my wings could do. What a day that was! So maybe my bells sound like freedom now.

Wendy scratches a message into the sand again. And Hook interprets for me. “I don’t want to give up music, but Peter is a good friend to me.”

It is as if Hook ate something disagreeable. His sour expression lingers as he drags his hook through the sand, and his frustrated fingers say, “Would a good friend require such an expensive sacrifice of you?”

She watches the tide wash over his rebuttal and drags her own into the freshly damp sand. “Peter may be selfish, but he saw me when I was looked over by everyone else.”

The tide washes her message away three times before Hook scratches out a response. “He had eyes to see you, but that doesn't mean he has the heart to keep you."

Wendy turns her eyes to the sea and writes without looking at her words. "I thought he was protecting me."

"And why does he think you need protecting?"

I watch a swallow travel down her throat. "He said I have been told lies of the most diabolical sort."

Hook smirks just slightly and digs into the sand again. "And what lies are those?"

"That I want to teach music." She writes her response into freshly wet sand.

"How is that a lie? It's all you've ever wanted."

Wendy shrugs. "He says I need to stay in my lane."

Hook's forehead crinkles with confusion as his fingers continue to interpret for me. "What lane?"

She pulls her shoulders to her ears again. "I don't exactly know, but he made it sound like I shouldn't have dreams, because I'm a woman. I guess that means my lane is in the home or something."

Hook gets to his feet and paces down into the shallow kiss of the ocean. He stands there for a long time, the water washing in and around his ankles before he returns. But he doesn't say anything. Only loops his arm around Wendy and pulls her into his side. When they pull apart, his tunic is wet.

I fly onto Wendy's shoulder and nuzzle against her cheek. We may speak entirely different languages, but I hope physical affection is one anyone can understand. She doesn't flinch me away, so I think my message is clear enough.

And then I get an idea. A brilliant idea.

"Let's kidnap her," I sign at Hook.

His eyebrows sink on his face. "Why?"

"Peter won't accept this betrayal. So we need to do something drastic. Obviously, it won't be a real kidnapping, but she can play along for the sake of her freedom."

Hook furrows his face into a knot as he scribbles something to Wendy in the sand. She writes something back.

For the first time, I have to remind Hook to interpret for me. "She has some things to say to the boy."

"I never said we had to gag her," I say, my hands almost deflated.

Hook and Wendy write back and forth for a while, and I feel as useless as a one tined fork during the exchange. But then Hook shoots me a thumbs-up, and we separate.

Wendy and Hook stay on the beach, and I fly off to alert Peter and the Lost Boys. By the time I've found them deep in the heart of the woods—playing some kind of chasing game—Wendy screams, and the plan begins.

Peter looks frantic, afraid, panicked. "Where's Wendy?"

*So now Peter wants to talk to me.* "On the beach."

"Is she alone?"

I shrug, holding up my hands in mock ignorance. "I don't know."

"Come on," he says. "Let's go save her."

I smirk and fly in front of him to warn my newest friend of his arrival.

Hook is winding a rope around Wendy's arms and shoulders when I get back to the beach. He winks at Wendy, and she starts to cry.

Peter glowers hotly at the two of them and points his wooden sword at Hook. "Let her go, you scoundrel!"

Hook makes a face to mock the boy, but before he can say or sign a witty comeback, Wendy speaks up, "I want to go with him."

Peter digs the toes of his shoes into the sand and meets her eyes with an intense fire blazing in his. "Anyone who's a friend of this *criminal* is no friend of mine. Explain yourself."

She doesn't respond, only looks up at Hook. I fly in his face, only far enough away to ask him if I need to get Peter alone. Hook waves me off, pointing to a printed message in the sand.

"Read it and weep, Pete." My hands almost glitter with sarcasm as Wendy leads Peter to the note she's scribbled into the sand.

Peter rushes over, knocking shoulders with the pirate on his way. His face falls, and he turns it weepily back to Wendy. "I haven't stifled you. I've just shown you who you are."

"No, Peter," she says, swallowing hard. "I am not an unpaid servant. I am not a mother to these Lost Boys. Or even to you. I am more than this contrived life you've cooked up for me. I want to teach music. I want to raise a family. *My own family.* I want to watch the sunrise over the

Thames. I want to open Christmas crackers with my parents, and I want to sing carols at Sunday services. I want lace handkerchiefs and frilly dresses, and I want shoes with polish. I want bigger things than the minimised dreams you convinced me were mine. If I am too big for you, it only means I have outgrown you. Your size is the one that is wrong."

I open the pouch at my side and sprinkle Hook and Wendy with glittering golden dust. They rise into the air, and the three of us take to the sky.

Wendy's tears join the ocean as we fly. I sign as big as I can to give loud bells to the air. And when we land on an island far away, she folds into herself and sobs into the sand. Hook pulls his arms around her in a platonic hug. I land on the crease between her neck and shoulder to provide what little comfort I can. Hook's hand against Wendy's back interprets her words to me:

"I don't know where I'm going anymore. Peter was my North Star." Wendy's blue eyes search his.

He tucks a loose strand of hair behind her ear, and his mouth moves with the first words I think he's ever said. "Stars always fall, Wendy. But you are your own True North."

# A Lonely Woman's Retribution

## by S. Victoria Nakamun

**Literary World**: Carmilla

On a carriage ride to a ruined castle, Laura and her father hear the tale of the death of their friend's daughter at the hands of a mysterious villainess thought to be a vampire. But as the story unfolds, so too does the truth about Laura's partner, Carmilla, whom she shares a secret romance with. Laura then confronts a choice; to face the truth of her lover's nature and save herself, or embrace the darkness hidden within both of them.

***Content Warnings**: Violence, Cannibalism, Sadism, Sexual Content*

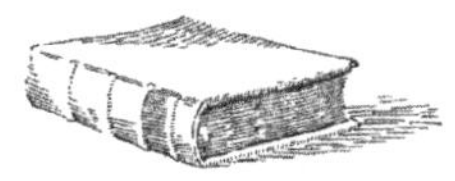

I had thought in my girlhood that our afternoon rides to the ruined castle of Karnstein held the greatest promise of pleasure. It was the furthest I had gone outside of the manor-house I lived in with my father and his madams after the death of my mother, and the rare adventure was one I revelled in. I believed this until the day our dear friend and guest, General Spielsdorf, joined us in the carriage; his navy eyes swimming with grief, sunken with an exhaustion heavy enough to drown them. His hair was slicked with the greyness of an age that betrayed his own, and the thinness of the great general's frame was enough to shock my nerves into silence. He was meant to arrive weeks ago, his first and only explanation rife with salacious details of his late ward's death: a beautiful young woman I never had the pleasure of meeting. It was a shocking discovery when his letter first arrived, but the incessant ramblings of the general's words made the situation that much more curious. And here he was, joining us on the journey to the ruined village, with the story to tell.

“There is a creature responsible for the death of my dear girl– one that indulges in the most preternatural temptations and lust. There is a demon in need of expulsion in retribution for what they have done.” The general’s voice was vicious with rage. I avoided making contact with the fire in his eyes, for I knew what they saw when they looked upon me. “And I know who this monster is.”

“Go on, General. You have a story you wish to tell us,” my father interjected. I focused on the ridges beyond the carriage window as the castle came further into view. The sky was the colour of an old bruise, looking just as unforgiving.

“It began with an invitation from my dear friend Count Carlsfield...”

He described the grand trappings of a ball thrown by the illustrious count that lived only a few days' ride from our home. But his recount of meeting a mysterious young woman, Millarca, in the hands of an identically esoteric countess, brought me to attention, for the description of the girl’s indefinable beauty and charm struck me as deathly familiar...

I bit my tongue until I tasted metal, using my silence as a shield against the horror of his words.

“The young girl’s horse had fallen with her on a recent hunt, and her nerves had not quite recovered. The dear countess, who revealed herself as the girl's mother, relied solely on my chivalry to take charge of the young woman in her absence; something dire had revealed itself, requiring her immediate attention. And I realise in hindsight just how disastrous this decision was."

Only months before the carriage ride, a visitor had blessed me with her presence in an event not unlike the one that had brought the general and Millarca together.

The possibility of speaking with someone new had thrilled me beyond belief, throwing me in a fit of elation unlike anything I had encountered. After the general's letter first arrived and bore the terrible news, the grief of a girl I had never known was more distressing than I had once known loss to be— it was the removal of a possibility that was more than I could bear. The long nights in the seclusion of my room returned to the indefinite, the conversations with my madams and father forever to remain the only tempers to cross my tongue. The confines of the manor had left me defenceless against the terrors of loneliness, and the fresh prospect of company thrust me into the hands of my beloved.

My Carmilla.

Her eyes were pools of dark richness. Her features were crafted with the highest degree of elegance, the smoothness of her skin a moonlit pond of desire; a temptation I couldn't fathom until I saw her lying in her chambers after the accident. Her movements were languid and enchanting in the way they wavered; the anticipation of what she might do, of where she might touch, was tantalising, yet unbecoming of my lonely girlhood. But most importantly, she was the perfect image of a woman who once visited me in dreams; the face of a hidden desire finally actualized. She grasped my hands with a tenderness that stayed with me after the first night, one that meant true companionship as she whispered: "Good night darling; it is very hard to part with you, but good night."

My beloved was no Christian; I knew that now. I had never seen her do her nightly prayers in her time with my father and I, nor had she joined us when we prayed. She was irritatingly private, but I did not wish to know her as much as I wished she would know me.

The General continued, revealing further details of the guest whose arrival had begun the failing and demise of his dear ward. My father remained attentive and grew more apprehensive as the details multiplied. Millarca awoke late each morning after being seen perusing the gardens beneath moonlight in a way that resembled sleepwalking. She was often seemingly trapped in a trance; not unlike his ward, who had soon begun to feel the effects of the mysterious illness that took her. And at the height of her illness, she had experienced dreams that reminded me of the ones that visited me since I was a young girl.

Dreams with the spectre of Millarca at the foot of her bed, in the form of a black creature, lunging for her throat. The strangling touch of a hand, the embrace of lips against her neck...breaths against the thin paraffin of my skin. The general's story grew more difficult to listen to with each recollection, as though he had found the treasure of my memories from where I had hidden them. I avoided his eyes as he described the symptoms: a languid greyness of the face, recalling the sensation of a large pair of needles entering her breasts, and the final falling of unconsciousness. I shuddered, if only to think of my beloved behaving this way with anyone but I.

It gave me no pleasure to hear a recounting of the very story my beloved had disclosed to me only days prior, on the same day the general's letter arrived. But the terror it created was no longer one of supernatural horrors, but one of that creeping clutch of isolation I had so long been inflicted by. That was the only sickness I cared to be cured from, and his threats toward her were also toward the one beacon of my happiness.

"I pray to God vengeance for its crimes can be achieved by a mortal arm," the general finished, his voice gravelly with the graveness of a dire task. My father, gentle man though he was, flashed a horrified look at him.

"What sort of retribution?"

Every muscle of the general's neck tensed as his eyes found refuge in mine. Then, he growled his terrible declaration: "Hacking off the head of the devil, splitting it in twain, and burning its corpse."

The ruined village was the only whisper of civilization close enough to the manor-house to visit. The endless days of isolation left my heart a hollow waste of what once was, much in the same way the village stood now. My father told stories from the reaches of Upper and Lower Styria, Moravia, Silesia, Turkish Serbia, Poland, and Russia that would lead one to believe in the power of revenants, and the village surrounding the ruined castle of Karnstein was the proof of their abilities. Many centuries before, the sleeping monsters were said to have ravaged every man, woman and child within the village, fulfilling their wicked desires with blood, drinking their vitality, and leaving no one living behind.

The creatures that once ravaged the village were unlike my beloved; she was tempted not by vanity or the languor of life, for her exhaustion matched mine. She slept until the late afternoon and recovered only by the light of the nascent moon. Each of my frustrations were quelled by the sweetness of her words and the way she rubbed her sculpted features into my hair. She was neurotic at times, exacerbated by passion, and didn't wish to hold me for fear of confinement.

I was lulled from my nightmares by her presence. I was haunted by the image of robbers and maniacs entering the house, blood staining the white of her nightgown; the terror of harm extended to her. But when she visited me, in the same way she had comforted me in the nightmares I had as a young child, it was a comfort that remained beyond the confines of sleep. I believe now she had extended beyond the space between dreams to reach me, sharing every part of our minds when the night grew dark and everyone else drifted away.

But I was no fool. I knew there was no coincidence that I had soon after begun to experience symptoms of an illness for which I had no accounting: the exhaustion, the puckering greyness of my skin, the nightmares of bloody spectres and robbers in the night. All of it weakened me greatly, but my mind was never dulled. My father knew all too well, and in his grave concern welcomed the general in– not despite his ramblings, but because of them.

"My daughter's physician believed I was in need of a conjuror at the end of her life, not a doctor. It was quackery beyond anything I had heard: the idea of her afflictions being the consequence of a vampiric infection!" The general's eyes had saddened again when mine returned to the carriage wall, my hands twisted around each other as tightly as one might press against a wound and my chest rife with the pounding of a heart in terrible distress. He had found my eyes in that moment, and I stifled a gasp at the smallness of them: the water that pooled around the black pits was like a warning of oblivion.

It was then my father had grabbed my hand– the tender touch of a man who knew the same loneliness but had nothing to stave it. He had no one but me and my madams since his own beloved's death; a woman I had barely known and never understood, his sorrowful eyes an imminent reflection.

"It will be alright, Laura."

His grip held me gently, the look behind his eyes grew more frightened with each revelation of my situation, knowing now what I had known already; I was the subject of an infection, but greater than the one they claimed to describe now. Mine was the same as his, and I wanted nothing more than to be cured without remorse.

The general then spoke only to me as the carriage finally arrived at the castle, his voice a tonic of desperation and despair, and said the piece my father and I would undoubtedly carry until my death: "But into what quackeries will not people rush for a last chance, where all accustomed means have failed, and the life of a loved one is at stake?"

It was no longer my wish to see my beloved in the castle as intended– the midday plans of a picnic in the ruins were squandered by vows of retribution. The fire in the general's eyes burned only for a creature that carried her name, held her figure, spoke her words. He would take her from me if she gave him the chance, and the only wish I had would be to have the chance to steal her away before harm befell her.

The old Gothic features of the castle were mesmerising to behold as we stepped through the gates; nearly enough to grant me respite from the troubling thoughts the general had brought on. The dusty stone corridors and curling ivy strangled every remaining column. The wind slithered through every vulnerable crevice and produced a melody of eerie gasps through the vacant halls, converging to create a melancholic air that reminded me of my previous solitude. Such a horrible recollection those times were—before the carriage accident, before the mysterious visit of the elegant countess and her daughter. The circumstances of our meeting mattered little to me now, and I felt infinitely grateful for them the moment my eyes met hers across the castle hall.

I could have called out to her from my place beside my father, if not for the terror that would soon befall us. She caught it first, of course: the incoming threat of the old general wielding nothing more than a huntsman's axe. I nearly screamed at the horrible sight, though it is quite easy to find humour in it now with how obscene the general was. He was deep within his grief, his mind so clouded by the same dusty air that filled the castle he could no longer think without being reminded of what once was; so troubled with regrets he could think of nothing more than retribution. Justice. As though either of those things existed when my beloved lived as she did.

She caught the attempt on her life with a single hand, holding the general's axe stiffly above her head before it could make contact with her skull. He screamed and shouted something profane; not that those were the things I remembered. Only the look in her iridescent eyes struck deeply enough to become ingrained in my fading vision, even now, at the edge of knowing. She was a mirror of my fear, her eyes wide and white at the scene: my father and our guest luring poor Carmilla to her murder– and I, standing at their side beyond the arch of the doorframe. Her strength granted her sanctuary from the old man's attack, but there was none to aid my betrayal. And with that, she was gone.

So I ran.

The objections of my father and the general were sparse in the shock of the situation. They so reasonably believed I had run to another part of the castle in fear, with the hope of finding some respite from the terror of the moment. Their hopes remained only in finding me again, so they might draw me close and comfort me in the way I had been comforted as a child, when the dreams of maniacs and robbers grew too real to bear.

But that was far from my destination, and far from my desires.

I ran to Carmilla. Millarca. Mircalla.

My beloved.

~

I find her in the woods between our two manors, pale from fear and frozen from the exhaustion of her feat. I know she caught my presence far before I got there, listening to my panting breaths and the foliage crunching beneath my boots; my skirts snagging against bushes, caressing my calves, begging for my surrender. Desperate not to let me go. She is prepared for my arrival, and I to confront my terror.

I don't realise the shift in the day until I behold her eyes again– we are under the light of the crescent moon in the clearing she inhabits, the iridescence reflecting off the porcelain of her skin like a lighthouse beacon calling me to shore. The more superstitious of my madams, Mademoiselle De LaFontaine, believed the moon to bring out madness; but the lick of lunacy is one I very much like. I welcome the moonlight with beckoning arms, for I know who I welcome into my bosom.

I meet her with my arms outstretched, fleeing toward her despite the objections of my weakened body. I imagine being enveloped in her sweet scent; the soft strokes of her glowing hair against my flushed cheeks, safe at long last. But that is not what I find when I meet her at the foot of the black-ink pond where she found her rest.

Her boots aren't caked in mud like mine are, nor are her skirts tattered from the spikes of the foliage. Her eye sockets are deep and hollow pits, drained by exhaustion. Her radiance melts off into the water in the form of the moon's reflection, the pale glow gone dim on her skin. And her pink lips, the keepers of her endless secrets, are pursed in a fine line, sealed in anger against me. My panting breaths thin as my nerves fatten, and I drop beside her for respite from my own exhaustion.

"Thank God you're alright," I pant, but she hardens, water pooling in her eyes.

"Did you know of your guest's intentions?" Her voice is frost on spring grass, suffocating the hope in my veins. My fists clench together nervously, resisting the urge to hold her.

"I…I did."

She wails a single sob, clasping a delicate hand over her mouth and turning away from me. "Did my story not beget your sympathies?"

The sound is a horror to hear, but the pain she feels is beyond that. I want nothing more than to make it end.

"I thought his threat to be the words of a madman! The ramblings of a father in grief! I did not think…"

"That is all it takes to be driven to murder, Laura!" She wails before finding her breath again, her voice wavering with sorrow as she confesses: "A fresh loneliness…a lost love."

The pain that struck her shakes me deeply, and my mind begins to reel with cursed thoughts of her previous affections. My voice grows quiet, as though the accusations come from a distant onlooker.

"The general sought revenge for his ward, and that entailed your murder. He knew well enough to accuse you."

"You don't think me a monster, do you?" she cries, her eyes filled with growing desperation. She sits up in her resting place, still unable to stand. "My candour has never faltered – not from you."

"You told me it was a necessity: that your hunger drove you to such horrors. But you loved her." Her face becomes a well of sorrow at the accusation, enough to nearly make me falter in my anger. But I persist. "The hunter feasts on the animal for his meals, not his love. In the eyes of God, that is the work of a demon."

"Do not wound me like this, Laura. I am no demon!" Her troubled eyes grow wider as I find myself drawing closer. "Did I not tell you why I am in this prison? Why I must take from those who have?

"Because I have not! My means of life were stripped from me upon my death all those centuries ago; and the mother who took me, stole me from my coffin, and traded me like coins..." She grabs my hands the moment I kneel close enough to her. "Do you wish for me to degrade into nothing?"

Her touch was the water on my slate, washing away the accusations with the promise of more. "I have never wished for that."

"Then you must understand." She gives it to me as she lifts her hand to cup my cheek, her frail grasp never faltering in its tenderness. I fall into it, pressing deeper into her embrace. "I do this for you. I do this for us. My only light, my brightest ray of– "

I cannot help but touch my lips to hers, trembling with a desire once held only in my dreams, and fall deeper into the pool. I taste the juice of her power, the tart sweetness of a currant coating raw teeth. She kisses me hungrily, lapping at my lips with an unfounded strength, growing with each indulgence.

We kiss until I lick iron. When I pull away, I feel the prick of flesh tearing from my lips. I cry out and press my hand to the wound, wetness slipping between the pads of my fingertips. She licks her red lips with alluring delight before taking my fingers to them, sucking off the blood with greedy laps. She smiles, her pointed teeth gleaming.

"Do you fear what feeds me?"

I begin to stammer, her words stirring me from my terrors and further toward a familiar heat. "What is your sentence if you should not feed? Can an immortal consciousness be slain with a huntsman's axe?"

She wraps an arm around my waist, her voice dropping to a whisper as she pulls me closer. "There is a great loss; a loss of myself, a loss of my movements and my thoughts." Her finger trails down my neck, tracing my chest with a feather's stroke. "My only means of loving you."

I gasp at her touch, growing more delirious with every decedent stroke. "That is what I truly fear. But why must you stray to others?"

She catches the hiss of jealousy I had been so eager to restrain and places a kiss against the softest flesh of my neck.

"It is my fidelity that troubles you..." she murmurs into my skin, a breath of burnt sugar and fresh iron. "But it should not. I beg of you, my dearest, grant me the love I feel for you; endless, untainted, beyond the limits of the holy and the rights of men. Cure me of this infliction, this weakness of my restraint. Let us fall asleep again, and live where no one else may touch us."

I press my neck harder into her lips, but they pull away, leaving me yearning. Her eyes catch mine in a watery embrace.

"But if I am the monster you believe me to be, perhaps it is my retribution if you should not."

The sounds of hoofbeats echo through the quiet of the night, bringing to the paleness of her face an even greater aura of fear. She closes her eyes, turning me away in the only way she can. "Bring me to the axe if I cannot have you."

I gasp between our lips, the sound snapping me from my trance. "They're coming for us."

She opens her eyes as though waking from a pleasant dream, the danger in my voice neglected the moment she beholds me. I clasp my hands against her jaw, eyes wide and insistent. "You have to run."

She says nothing, and I think she is listening to the movements of my familiars– but she shakes her head. "I will not go. The strength to do so has left me."

I clench tighter around her face as my desperation grows. "You must! They know how to destroy you; you cannot survive another encounter."

She takes my hands with a tenderness that causes them to tremble. "I cannot live without you."

"Then we'll go together. *Please.*"

She drags my hands back down and sinks to the ground, resigned to watch the sky. "I cannot protect you like a father, nor sustain you like a mother. You will die in the world I must run to."

My mind begins to race with the night's damnations: a lonely past renewed by her murder, or a future of anguish at her side. My throat begins to close around itself, terror wrapping around my neck to strangle me.

"I cannot be without you!" I cry. "I would rather throw myself on a pike than be without!"

Her eyes flick toward me, unmoving as she is, and I throw myself into her chest as I sob, drowning out the sounds of our imminent doom approaching. I fight through future visions of an axe splitting the soft skin I am nestled into, my cries echoing off her body. I cry until she whispers in my ear, as she did on our first meeting:

"Then let us live in dreams."

I choke back a sob as I listen to her softened pleas.

"If there is a night I cannot have you, let it not be this one." I pull away as she strokes my cheek, a tear falling with her fingers. "I shared you in my mind, and now I need your strength, your body. I need you."

My lip throbs from the pulses of pain my body gives me, and I still feel the weakness she spoke of festering within. She exists beyond the limits of my own life; she could be with me for as long as I grant her a taste, and I want her forever. I want to prove my devotion– enough to make her stay beyond the confines of a mortal life, beyond the confines of God and His plan.

I thought of my poor father and the reflection in his eyes when I looked at him. His loss would be a great one; a canvas painted over white. A life cored as you would an apple. I only hope he will know pain enough to run away from this place, to finally find his own cure.

Like I have.

The pain dulls instantly as the pools of her eyes envelop me. "I revel in your desires, if it is me at the end of your lips."

I turn her head back toward me and lay myself down at the touch of her lips against my skin, my body laid bare for her to indulge in. Her kisses are gentle despite the heat my body gives off, trailing down the places exposed by my gown.

She tugs, then tears into the fabric with a strength that continues to grow with my offering, and I revel in the feeling of her consumption. She savours every inch of me with her mouth, her long fingers trailing around my waist, pulling deeper, deeper,

deeper.

The loneliness of my girlhood is nothing more than a dream in the promise of her presence, and I want nothing more than to serve her in the same way she served me. My solitude was my fever, infecting me with a sickness she cured the moment she found our humble manor on the edge of civilization.

And so I will do the same.

Her lips find the space between my breasts and press deeper into my skin. I shiver with anticipation, knowing her intentions, and accept her final plea: "Let me taste you."

I gasp at the spikes of pain thrusting deep into my breast, gripping her shoulders with a harsh strength, still pathetic compared to her own. She holds me down, her hands finding my thighs beneath my skirts and squeezing until white spikes stab through my vision. I feel the hot trails of my juices trickle down my bosom, the sucking of my sacrifice into her irresistible mouth. My eyes move to the sky above, the curling moon like her smile at the sight of me: breathless, beautiful, glowing entirely for me.

I heard the distant rumbling of horses through the treeline I ran from: the shouting of men and their hopeless cries for my return.

They will find us, and I fear they will do so before my beloved has the chance to bring me to my unconsciousness. She licks away the retreating lines of my blood, gathering every part of me before it disappears.

I feel the black water of the pond envelop my senses, starting from my boots, up my legs, and toward the growing heat of my panting breath. The warmth of the water swirls around my body, flooding me with peace. I drift beyond the lull of sleep, beyond the confines of a dream, and into a place entirely new.

This was the altar of her love, the dais of her desire, where only I belonged.

*Cure me.*

~

Carmilla will never awaken from the fantasy of her delicious indulgence of Laura's essence, taking enough to strip the light from her eyes. Her mouth wraps around her breast as her blood thins, feeding like she could still provide.

The departure of her countess always left Carmilla with a need for sustenance unlike that which satiated the living: she needed blood. But more importantly, she needed lust. A power strong enough to let her feed upon the vessels of her affection, and deep enough to let them satisfy her. She found it in Laura's desperation: her need to be consumed driving Carmilla to act. The frenzy of her desire, drawn from an insatiable need and unholy agenda, finally delivered her to the madness her countess had warned of.

Laura was meant to be different. Carmilla had fed upon the girl for months before, tastes which sustained her for only short periods. The strength she gave her was unlike any of the other girls, but she needed *more*. She needed Laura's fears, her joys and obsessions, the desires that drove her. She was a sustenance Carmilla could never fully envelop in the way she wanted to; not before tonight.

Now, beneath the light of the moon and the threat of her own demise, she finally drained the ichor from Laura's veins, gulping down her decedent juices like the fruit would never run dry – until it did.

Grief was not the affliction love gave to immortal beings. When Laura's weightless form falls slack in her arms, Carmilla's teeth nip and gnaw at the skin that remains. Tears of pale white strip away, filling her mouth like the fuzz of forbidden fruit, and she grows starving for more.

*More!*

Sheets of skin peel like a delicate peach, revealing the tainted yellow fat above the flesh. And the pit nestled in the centre, though no longer beating, beckons to her teeth to tear through more, more,

*MORE OF HER SWEETNESS!*

The hard white hollow of her bones glistens in the light, encasing the viscera like jewels in a cage of silver. Her fingers find the remaining warmth of Laura's body tantalising, a reminder of the pleasure she gave her lover when they entered her. She does so for a final time, pressing the pads of them through her chasm, squelching through the organs that resided there.

She tears, then takes bite after delicious bite: power caught between her teeth; dripping down her throat and past her lips; spilling onto her clothes in thick, syrupy drops. She chews, then chases each taste with another gulp, feeling every true part of Laura in the confines of her body– the last embrace she'll ever give.

When she finishes, the night air strangled with the scent of sugar and entrails, Carmilla swallows a final time and beholds what she has done. Sinewy shreds are left dangling from the legs, the chest but a chasm, what it held now stuffed in the stomach of her beloved; the womb which Laura might finally understand. Strands of honey gold are clumped together on her head, her face gone as grey as the satisfied moon.

Carmilla, too, wanted to be cured of the illness that afflicted her– a desire she didn't ask for, driving her to horrors she had no choice but to sustain. She was created by a monster that loved her, and she dreamed her hunger would one day be satiated if she loved what fed her enough. She dreamed she could finally flee the weakness of her damned life; that she might finally feel how it was to exist without the burden of hunger and to be powerful enough to destroy whatever might threaten her.

But it was only a dream, and the power she sought in Laura's bones never came; her deceit and the sacrifice that came from it fruitless.

The clearing is silent save for Carmilla's whimpering, bloody tears dripping in streaks as she claws through the remnants for more (as if she left any part of her to smile again, the hand her father had clutched stripped to bones in her frenzy, her mind hollowed to a chalice from which she hoped to drink).

What a sight for her encroaching hunters to behold: a demon, knowing they are damned, clutching the remains of their last victim with the tenderness of love.

Let the retribution for this monster come.

She is not the only one.

# Achilles' Final Judgement

by Shanni Pinkerton

**Literary World**: the Iliad, classic Greek mythology

After his prophesied death in the Trojan War, the hero Achilles is brought before the judges of the underworld to determine the weight of his deeds in life.

***Content Warnings**: themes of death and grief, mentions of violence, and war, brief descriptions of gore*

*Goddess, sing the rage of Achilles, son of Peleus,*
*which brought countless woes to the Achaeans*
*and sent the souls of many brave heroes to Hades,*
*their bodies made into a feast for dogs and crows*
*all to carry out the unfathomable will of Zeus.*
*-The Iliad, Book 1, Line 1*

*   *   *

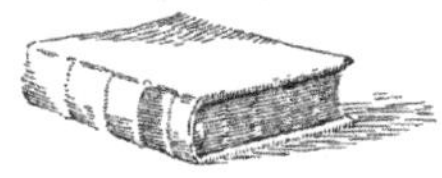

The arrival of Hermes in his role as psychopomp always heralded a judgement of circumstance. With the war at Troy reaching a frenetic, bloody peak and Olympians involving themselves on both sides, it was becoming a more common sight. Heroes' souls had been dropping into the Underworld at the same rate flies had come to the plains of Ilion in the world above to feast on their scattered corpses. Even still, the soul Hermes led today was particularly consequential. The shades of great heroes had become standard fare in the underworld, but this hero was in a league of his own.

Despite the warrior's renown, there was nothing glorious about the state of his spirit. His limbs quivered, the taut muscles straining against nothing, flexing so hard it looked as though they'd snap. He remained on his hands and knees in the centre of the judgement chamber, bowed and bloody, looking liable to retch at any moment. He clung to the rock, frozen in the haggard state he'd spent his waning final days.

The shade hadn't met the eyes of any of the figures assembled around the edge of the water that cut his lonely, circular dais off from the judges and the Gods that surrounded them. His position had nothing to do with deference to the divinity of those gathered. Indeed, the dead mortal did not even seem to register they were there.

In the soft gloom of the vaulted chamber, a huge number of chthonic deities had gathered to observe the judgement of the hero. It was strange for so many immortals to take such keen interest in a human death, but this was no ordinary human.

The judges of men – Minos, Rhadamanthus, and Aeacus – sat on the imposing thrones that jutted out into the waters on stone platforms, set equidistant around one half of the circle. Only two noises could be heard in the cavernous room: the soft lapping of the offshoot of the Styx which encircled the stone isle, and the ragged, rasping breath of the soul who sat upon it. The whispers about the hero had come to a full stop, and each God's gaze slid away from the man whose soul was to be venerated or condemned. All eyes were on the couple who had appeared on the bank of the Styx opposite – all eyes, of course, except those of the soul awaiting judgement. He continued staring into the dirty space between his hands, shaking and dripping blood onto the grey rock beneath him.

The King and Queen of the Underworld were especially resplendent in contrast. Hades looked solemn and stoic in rich, pitch black robes, with Persephone radiating her irrepressible essence of life on his arm in a chiton of deepest purple trimmed with floral embroidery. Twin crowns rested atop their heads; the intricately wrought circlets of obsidian and platinum studded with tiny, sparkling flowers of diamond, amethyst, and topaz that flashed even in the gloom. The assembled gods all bowed their heads in deference to the Underworld's rulers.

"Lord Hades!" Minos called. "It is not every day you and our gracious Queen attend the judgement of a mortal soul."

Hades rested his hand atop Persephone's, looped over his arm, and said, "It is not every day judgement is made on a hero such as him."

Persephone said nothing. She stared at the shade curled in on himself at the centre of the cold stone plinth with her brows knit together.

Hades nodded to Aeacus, directly across the water and dais from them, and the judge sat straighter, voice booming throughout the chamber.

"So begins the judgement of Achil les, son of Peleus, General of the Myrmidons, called Aristos Achaion."

The spirit of the greatest of the Greeks hardly seemed to register the address. He curled his fingers into the fine layer of dirt atop the stone, cracked and bleeding nails dragging furrows in front of him.

Aeacus spoke again. "Let us review the deeds of Achilles. Bring forth the waters of mem—"

He was cut off by a bloodcurdling wail from the back of the hall. A flurry of movement came from one side of the room, where the assembled gods were being pushed to the side, the shriek as powerful as the distraught sea nymph forcing her way through their number.

The nymph's blonde locks lay in tangles across her narrow shoulders. Tears streaked her face, leaving shining trails over pale skin marred by the red blotches of drawn-out crying.

"My son! My sweet Achilles, my golden one." A sob burst from her, echoing obscenely across the chamber. "What have they done? What have they done to you, my shining boy, my—"

"Thetis. You've found your way into the Underworld, yet again." Hades' tone was as carefully neutral as his face, but ire sparked in his wife's eyes.

At his words, the nymph whirled towards him. "Hades. Give me my child. Let me take him; let me carry his soul beneath the sea. He is not made for your dour halls of ash and sorrow: he was meant to be immortal. He should be a god as I am, he—"

"Your son is mortal, Thetis. Despite your attempted interference." Hades' glance fell to the waters of the Styx before them, where the nereid had dipped her infant son so many years before to burn away his mortality. It had very nearly worked.

Thetis shrieked, raking her fingers through her hair. "This is a gross injustice! To have my son stolen from me as a pawn in the games of gods, to watch my own divine blood fall to sword and rot and decay among human swine, for you to dare keep me from my child—"

"Thetis, please." Hades pinched the bridge of his nose. He looked exhausted.

"Let me take him, Hades. Give me my child. I will keep him close to me always, place him among the pearls and jewels of the sea. Please. Please. Please." Her begging continued, the pitch of each 'please' rising higher into a horrible new round of keening.

"I cannot, Thetis. You know I cannot." Hades set out his refusal firmly, but in a tone that was gentle and soft, nearly sad.

This softness did nothing to ease the grieving mother's frenzied state. "You deny me? You dare deny me? I will bring the wrath of the sea to your realm! You will drown as I drown now in my sorrow. I will have him!"

Horrified gasps ripped through the crowd around the nereid as she stepped out into the Styx, the waters foaming and thrashing around her thin ankles. Gods recoiled from the spray that rose up as she began striding towards the dais where her warrior son's shade sat.

"Enough Thetis." Persephone's voice echoed around the chamber as she picked her way towards the water's rocky edge, and the distraught nymph. Thetis froze unnaturally in the middle of the stream, but the water kept roiling around her feet. The Styx was bottomless, but the nymph was a daughter of the sea, and she stood up to her calves at the churning surface of the river.

Persephone continued, "There will be no war between the realm of the dead and the ocean. My Lord and I will forgive you these transgressions, recognizing despair makes us...foolish. You know he cannot go. Every mortal must be judged upon their death, and he is mortal." The Queen lowered her voice and reached towards the goddess from the bank. "Come out of the river, Thetis. Don't make his death any more of a spectacle. Let him rest peacefully."

Thetis' nose wrinkled, lips curling back to reveal her teeth in a near-feral snarl as she recoiled from Persephone's offered hand. She couldn't move far, though: she was rooted to her eerie station in the river, unable to move any closer to the spirit on the rock.

"Release me at once, Kore. I won't be hushed and consoled by a childless bride of death. By you, a lifegiver who cannot bear life herself. A—" Her string of insults cut off abruptly as her lips turned grey and clamped shut. She fought to open her mouth and continue, but instead of hurling curses, silence and smoke dribbled down her front and dissipated on the surface of the Styx.

Hades looked fit to murder, but Persephone remained placid. She stepped out into the water as well, a bridge of blooming vines growing from the barren shore to keep her above the whirling river. The queen shot a look back at her husband when she reached Thetis, and the power binding the nymph's tongue waned. She continued sobbing. "We are not your enemies, Thetis. He does not have to remain lost to you forever, but you must allow his judgement to pass. There is no hope of reunion until he is at rest, and even then, that remains at our discretion." Her tone was low and calming, even if she couldn't keep the hint of a threat from her last statement. "The hall of judgement is no place for the grieving. You can rest in the palace until this is over, or—"

"I will remain." The puffy circles beneath Thetis' eyes threw shadows across her beautiful face, but she no longer looked ready to call down watery retribution on the realm of the dead. She even let Persephone take her hand.

"Hypnos?" Persephone called. The god of sleep stepped to the edge of the water, waiting in the patch of flowers that had sprung up to carry the Queen over the turbulent river. His calming aura reached the goddesses as they returned to shore, and the thrashing of the Styx ceased. "Remain with her, please."

Hypnos guided Thetis to a rock. She sat, the exhaustion of grief washing over her in the sleep god's presence.

"Take comfort, Thetis," offered Rhadamanthus. "This should be brief. Your son died a hero on the field of battle. Certainly the gloried isles of Elysium will welcome him with no hesitation."

"I wouldn't make any promises," Hermes had remained in their midst, wearing his armour and keeping uncharacteristically quiet until now. He looked dusty and travel-worn – a tall order for the god of travellers.

Hades quirked an eyebrow, and Hermes shook his head. "The end was… ghastly."

Silence hung in the wake of Hermes' words, and the God of the Dead looked over the shade with renewed scrutiny.

"Enough speculation. Continue with his judgement. Aeacus?"

"Very well, my King." Aeacus inclined his head. "Bring forth the waters of memory."

The goblets appeared in a gust of mist, along with the slim columns of rock they rested on. The contents swirled and rippled, a potent mixture of the underworld's rivers with just enough of the Lethe's waters to pull memories from the final ingredient: a drop of the mortal soul being weighed. The judges and rulers of the Underworld drank deeply, draining the dancing liquid inside. Smaller cups appeared in the divine spectators' hands, and they too gulped them down, eager for a voyeuristic glimpse into the deeds of the hero before them.

The effects were instantaneous, and in a split second, the gods and judges experienced a melange of moments from Achilles' life:

> Achilles, a chubby-legged toddler with golden curls, races across the sand to Thetis, waiting in the surf with open arms. He

shrieks and giggles as she spins him, kissing his forehead.

Achilles, a laughing child climbing a tree with another boy, offers a hand to pull his friend higher. They hide among the branches, playing games and sharing secrets for hours.

Achilles, struggling to maintain a stoic face as a seer relays a double-edged prophecy: he is destined to become an unparallelled warrior and hero, but his life will be cut short barely into the prime of adulthood.

Achilles, in his father's palace training grounds, sparring with a group of much older boys. He beats them all soundly without breaking a sweat, and turns to grin at the dark-haired boy watching him.

Achilles, a golden-haired youth with a bow strung across his shoulder, walking with the same dark-haired boy next to a broad-chested centaur. They pause in a forest clearing to peer at the stars. The centaur gestures broadly at the constellations and begins lecturing. Achilles slips his hand into the other boy's, squeezing tightly, faces tilted to the night sky. Neither lets go.

Achilles, fully grown in armour wrought by Hephaestus himself, leading the Myrmidons in fierce battle. City after city is sacked, no foe able to stand against the might of Aristos Achaion.

Achilles, shining golden even among the most celebrated heroes of his age, shouts at the King of Sparta, and overturns a table in his fury. The dark-haired man steps from the group of soldiers and grabs Achilles' shoulder, whispering into his ear. Achilles turns and storms from the tent. The man and their retinue follow.

Achilles, bent double over the lifeless body of his dark-haired companion, agony etched on every line of his frame. Someone tries to pull him away; the force of Achilles' answering shove sends them flying to the ground. Achilles presses his face to the lifeless man's chest. Blood from the gaping spear wound in his companion's stomach smears across his golden curls.

Achilles, eyes red-rimmed and crazed, slaughters his way through countless Trojans. Blood and viscera spray off his sword as he cuts foe after foe down with brutal slashes. He screams for Hector, prince of Troy, over and over until his screams are raw. The Prince answers his call; the combat is brutal. Both heroes fight with ferocious skill, but Achilles is undone, ruthless. He runs Hector through and drags the Prince's lifeless body back to camp behind his gore-splattered chariot.

Achilles, merciless and unfeeling, rides before the walls of Troy with Prince Hector's body trailing behind his chariot, bouncing off each rock. He carries on this way for days. No Greeks will meet his eye; no soldier calls him brother. Golden Achilles is sequestered in his tent, alone but for two corpses and his grief.

Achilles, broken and hollow, lets the pleading of King Priam atop Troy's gates – begging for the return of his beloved son – wash over him. Some final frayed cord in his heart snaps. He cuts the ropes that bind Hector's mutilated remains and leaves the Prince's body to his family and burial. He barely registers the arrow that flies, guided from Prince Paris's bowstring by Apollo himself, and sinks into the vulnerable flesh of his heel. One strike is enough. When Achilles falls, the last word he whispers – a name – is carried away on the wind.

The crowd of gods didn't move. They hardly breathed. The excited fervour of witnessing the judgement of as great a hero as Achilles had dulled, replaced by palpable discomfort. Many more memories had revealed snapshots of the hero's life, but his grisly final days seemed to linger in the chamber, stretched long and ugly before them.

Finally, Rhadamanthus said, "Lord Hermes spoke true. The man dishonoured himself and the soldiers he led."

Murmurs of agreement cut through those gathered, and Thetis's breathing hitched. Hypnos moved closer to her at the tilt of Persephone's chin in the nereid's direction.

"Much violence is done in battle. Will we condemn him for the same prowess that made him great?" asked Minos.

"Violence in the heat of battle is one thing; the desecration of a body over the days that follow is another. Two shades barred from entry to the Underworld for days, without proper burial—"

Hades cut Rhadamanthus off. "Both shades are accounted for in our realm. The proper rites were completed for Prince Hector of Troy and Patroclus both."

The movement on the dais was so fast all three judges startled in their thrones. Achilles' head shot up, and the golden warrior's sharp stare bore into the King of the Underworld. The shade still didn't speak, but it seemed Achilles was at last aware of the gathering of gods around him.

A goddess in leather armour bedecked with knives scoffed. She leaned against the chamber wall behind Minos with a knee propped up, one side of her mouth curled in a sneer.

"Something to add to the proceedings, Nemesis?" Hades rubbed his temples.

Nemesis strode forward, uncrossing her arms and squaring her shoulders. "This hand-wringing insults me. Everyone is comfortable with revenge from a distance. Now you've borne witness to the truth of vengeance up close, and you fret and squabble about customs and honour. You would all do well to remember: revenge is poetic, but it is not pretty. Not neat. Great love sundered by war demands great vengeance. That is what carried your actions, is it not?"

No one had directly addressed Achilles thus far. Sluggishly, his gaze slid from Hades to Nemesis, and he nodded, tight-lipped, at the goddess of vengeance. The golden-haired hero looked around those assembled, throat working furiously to swallow. He stood with surprising fluidity but froze for a moment when his gaze caught on his mother, who began weeping anew. He looked at each judge, then at Persephone, and finally, he addressed Hades.

His cracked lips parted, and his hoarse whisper hissed out a single name: "Patroclus."

Hades studied him, face unreadable. "His spirit rests in my realm. I can tell you no more."

Achilles took the gentle statement like a blow to the gut. He crumbled back to the stony earth, weeping into his hands. His sobs bounced off the walls of the chamber, echoing off the waters of the Styx in an eerie, dissonant echo of his mother's cries.

"He will be given a final reprieve, yes?" Persephone whispered over her shoulder to her husband. She had returned to his side on moss-silenced feet.

Hades' expression softened for a flickering moment as he looked at her and murmured, "You know he will, love."

Persephone's eyebrow rose. "Not his final statement. A reprieve."

Understanding dawning, Hades nodded and turned back to the judgement. The hall had fallen into chaos.

The divine around the edge of the Styx buzzed like a hive of insects, small groups breaking off to whisper and hiss. Nemesis and Rhadamanthus had begun arguing loudly, and the sound coupled with Achilles' cries and the fresh wave of keening from his mother, bouncing off the stone walls in a heinous cacophony.

Hades sighed and snapped his fingers. Silence slammed down, and the deities gathered around the water froze. Time stilled in the chamber as a column of thick grey smoke and shadow engulfed the platform, where the spirit knelt alone.

* * *

Achilles choked out a final sob before the change overtook him. A plume of smoke burst from the smooth, swirling wall of grey that blocked the rest of the chamber from view, and Hades and Persephone stepped onto the dais. A lifetime of deference to the gods was powerful enough to cut through his grief, and Achilles shifted from his slumped posture into a bow of supplication.

"Lord," he rasped. "Lady."

A hand came to rest on his bowed head. "Drink, Achilles. You're a mess." Hades offered a small cup brimming with a sparkling golden elixir.

Taken aback by the casual offer, Achilles lifted his head to see Persephone settled on a settee with her elbows resting on her knees, her chin in her hands as she looked him over. Hades stood above him with the proffered drink, and the barren rock around them now boasted two plush benches facing one another. The stone under his knees was now a soft rug he was dribbling blood all over.

"What—"

"Drink." Hades pushed the cup into his hands and moved back. Achilles obeyed, gulping the effervescent contents. His wounds closed over, and the pallid cast left his skin.

"Consider this a breath before you give the judges your final statement," Persephone said, "without the circus beyond adding their racket. A very small respite." She gestured to the seat across from her. Achilles staggered to sit, still breathing unevenly.

Hades slumped on the settee next to his Queen. He pulled both hands over his face, long fingers coming to rub both temples. "Always so dramatic; always with the cavalcade of rituals and rules. Death is hard enough on mortals; it does not need to be this over the top." The God of the Dead spoke to no one in particular, with the long-suffering air that could only come from aeons of immortality. Persephone patted his knee, gem-encrusted rings glittering with the movement.

"The Fates hate when we do this, so I'm afraid it must be kept brief. We can give you but a moment." She swept a graceful hand, and a solid shape filled the empty space just beyond the impromptu seating area.

Achilles fell off the couch in his haste to reach the shade that appeared on the dais. Patroclus rushed forward to meet him, and the men crashed into one another in a furious embrace. Achilles' hands, predestined for the sword and spear, were not gentle where they gripped the back of Patroclus's tunic. In answer, Patroclus wound an arm low around Achilles' waist, the other hand tangling in his blonde curls as he pulled the warrior to him, bodies and foreheads crushed into one another. Achilles' tears poured freely down his face, but he kept his gaze intent on Patroclus' dark eyes. They shone, but Patroclus had settled into death and could not cry.

"Why, love? The prophecy was clear; your death following Hector's. Without avenging me, you could have lived—"

"I died when his spear took you."

"Achilles—" But Patroclus was cut off in his admonishment by Achilles' impassioned kiss.

The men remained entangled in their embrace, and the gods on the settee finally looked away from the reunited shades. Hades took Persephone's hand. She nodded, the two exchanging a warm smile.

"Achilles. Patroclus." The Queen of the Underworld stood, and the lovers parted. Barely. "Your rulers are moved by your ardent devotion. In the eyes of your Queen, the depth of your love exonerates you of your final transgressions. We extend our favour to you, and—"

Her declaration was interrupted by Hermes popping through the wall of smoke that wreathed the dais, brushing lingering tendrils of shadow off his armour.

"All right, how is this ending, boss? This is gonna end like we want it to, right?"

"**HERMES!**" Persephone and Hades shouting in furious union was as jarring as a rockfall, shaking the floor and rattling the Underworld around them.

"What? I can see when you two do this! You know that! They can't see your little tricks out there, but I can!"

"Will you please," Persephone snipped, "give the boy's death a moment of proper solemnity?"

"Seph, you know I hate waiting," Hermes whined.

A small smile twitched across Patroclus's lips, and Achilles caressed his cheek.

"On my mother's fields, I will throw you into the pit, Hermes. I really will."

Hermes threw up both hands in surrender, "Okay, okay, I'll go. But you owe me all the details the next time I'm here."

"Scarper off, Hermes," Hades growled. He was massaging his temples in earnest again.

"Got it, yeah." Hermes turned to leave, but jabbed his thumb over a shoulder at Patroclus. "You know the Fates hate it when you do that, right?"

"Hermes..." Persephone's curls began to float off her shoulders in an unseen breeze, and

Hermes shrugged, disappearing as quickly he'd come.

"Our authority has been sufficiently undercut for one day, I think." Hades rose, taking a flask from within his robes and offering Persephone a sip. Her hair returned to its usual sleek tumble as she took a hearty pull.

"Right. Our boon," she said, returning her attention to the dead heroes, "can be used to overturn the ruling of the judges – but then gods will talk, and I will never, ever hear the end of it from your mother. And if she petitions Zeus and he chooses to shuffle you between the underworld and the sea, our hands are tied."

"Would you like to spend half of your eternal afterlife in Thetis's kelp garden?" Hades asked Achilles drily. The warrior shook his head, brow furrowed.

"Exactly," the goddess continued. "So, if you are able to convince them with your final statement that your actions were justified, your judgement may go as you hope. You will be reunited with your love and carry our favour forward into your afterlife. Is this clear?"

Achilles' face twisted as he bit his lip, but he nodded.

"Most gracious dread lady," Patroclus asked hurriedly, "I ask not for further favour, but please...if he is not judged wanting...will his mother still be barred from him eternally?" Patroclus kept his eyes on Achilles, whose anguish at the threat of another separation was clear.

Persephone regarded the dark-haired man who remained cradling his lover's soul and said fondly, "I, too, suffer from the overwhelming affection of a divine mother who would cause destruction at our permanent parting. In any part of the realm, excepting Tartarus, we will work to accommodate Thetis's devotion." In an audible aside to Hades, she added darkly, "Not that we can keep her out, anyway."

Hades inclined his head "I cannot hold the others frozen in time any longer. Patroclus must return to his place of rest, and you to your weighing."

Patroclus dragged his hand through Achilles' hair and gripped his chin gently. "No matter what their decision, our souls are bound as one. No matter what."

"Always," Achilles breathed, and kissed his lover once more. When their lips parted, the warrior's eyes shone with determination.

* * *

At another snap of Hades' fingers, everything resumed in fits and starts. Patroclus disappeared and Achilles stumbled without his presence, but the hero remained standing as the smoke cleared, whisking the makeshift room away with it. Hades and Persephone returned in a juddering flash of shadow to the edge of the water, where they maintained their regal posture as the din of the gathered crowd crescendoed like it had never stopped.

"Enough," Persephone's command cut through the chaos like a whip. "This unseemly spectacle must cease. Let us hear Achilles' final statement."

The judges spoke in a single voice that boomed around the chamber:

**Speak to your deeds, Achilles, son of Peleus,**
**Hero among heroes and Greatest of the Greeks.**
**Consider the weight of your life and actions,**
**Your final words will condemn or redeem you.**

Achilles stood with his shoulders thrown back and eyes clear. His voice restored, it rang through the room in the clear, direct tones of a general.

"You seek to weigh the soul of Achilles, promised as hero and leader of the Myrmidons. That hero you have gathered to judge is not the soul who stands before you. That hero died on the plains of Troy long before my body was struck by the arrow. His soul was taken by the spear of Hector, alongside the soul of valiant Patroclus – my steadfast companion. The best of me died along with him.

"Prophecy foretold my birth and death. My valour and courage were gifted to me by the Fates and steered by the gods' unknowable will. Heroism was my ordained birthright, but my heart and soul remained, as any mortal's, mine to do with as I wished. They remain now, as they did in my days among men, with Patroclus.

"I will not pretend my actions in my final hours were not my own. I shamed my divine mother and my house with my most base impulses, giving in fully to the rage and despair of the revenant I had become." He found Thetis among the crowd and held her eyes. "I beg forgiveness for the pain I have caused you, and for the pain I caused the Prince of Troy's noble father and loving wife. For this, I am sorry. What I cannot apologise for is the vengeance I sought when all light and hope was drained from the world, the most worthy parts of my soul with it.

"If you find the remaining husk of my spirit wanting and choose to cast me into Tartarus, I am prepared. My final, black days with the living were stretched into tortuous years of agonised fury; in this, I have felt the bleak grip of Tartarus. The rending of my soul as my love was torn from me dealt me a harder punishment than any violence I have known.

"Should you condemn the tattered scraps of my soul you weigh before you, know you chose to condemn not only my worst aspects, but those heroic pieces of my soul that remain entwined with the shade of Patroclus, at rest in the Underworld. His soul, too, will be condemned to the pain of our separation, and you will punish his honourable spirit for his continued fidelity and love.

"I am responsible for my transgressions. All I ask is you weigh them against the parts of my soul that already rest in the Underworld. Weigh the wrath of my vengeance against the boundless force of my love. I swear by all the power of the gods: you will not find it wanting."

A pregnant pause blossomed in the wake of Achilles' speech. He watched as the judges exchanged slow, measured looks, then risked a glance toward the rulers of the Underworld at his back. A small smile played at Persephone's mouth. Hades winked at him.

"Achilles, son of Peleus, General of the Myrmidons, called Aristos Achaion," Aeacus began, "we have measured your actions against the fate that was spun for you. No part of your soul has been found wanting. Your shade will rest as you have demonstrated it should: entwined with its matched half in the hallowed fields of Elysium."

With the decree set, the waters of the Styx began to rush toward a fresh crack opening in the cave wall. A shallow white boat docked against the small stone isle, and Achilles stepped aboard.

The last the divine audience saw of the greatest of the Greeks was his broad-shouldered silhouette against the peaceful glow of Elysium – and beyond, the spirit of Patroclus, awaiting his lover in paradise.

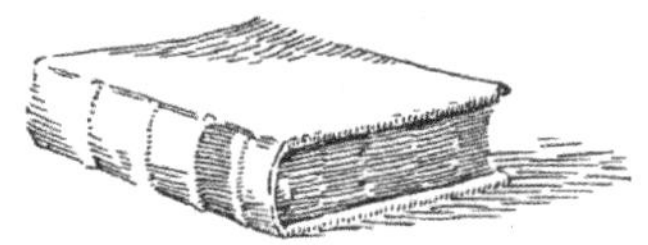

# ABOUT THE AUTHORS

**Keri Harley** (she/her) is a mother of two incredible humans, a gargoyle, and a four-legged behemoth. She enjoys reading, baking, gardening, plotting world domination, and snacks. Currently has a high-fantasy, high-steam novel series in the works, that will hopefully be done before the end of the world.

After a near-fatal car accident, **Julia Jackson** turned to writing as part of recovery and now crafts chilling stories that strip away the masks women wear, revealing emotional depth and damage. Julia has had more surgeries than Frankenstein, is a creature of the night like Batman, and creates memorable heroes and monsters of her own. She studied English and Arts Management at the University of Toronto and is an alumnus of Adrienne Young's Writing with the Soul. Julia teaches mindful writing at Kristin Dwyer's Breaking the Story Retreat, as well as to the online writing community. Her writing is featured in Gone by Morning, an international horror anthology. When Julia is not writing, she works as a Communications Officer.

**L E. Tonn** (she/her) is an aspiring multi-genre fiction author and musician from Edmonton, Alberta. She owns a music studio in the heart of Spruce Grove and has a passion for her work in music education. She also is currently working on her second studio album! In her spare time, she loves to read, craft and diy, and binge video games. She also co-runs a book themed YouTube channel, Crows Before Bros, with her best friend Randi! Classic Conversations holds her second published short story, and she can't wait to continue finding herself as a new author.

**Cathrine Swift** writes multi-genre fiction and poetry that pulses with cinematic emotion. Sometimes steamy, always inclusive, her stories explore found family, identity, empowerment, and healing. She believes love, in all its forms, deserves to be seen.

Beyond writing, she's a lifestyle & wedding photographer, book doula, and co-host of *The Energy Within* podcast. She's building a thriving community of writers through *Abundant Artists*, empowering creatives to rise together.

When she's not lost in fictional worlds, she's homeschooling her daughter, dreaming of NYC, or indulging in her love of fandoms (Marvel, Star Trek, Star Wars, Doctor Who & more). Her heart beats swiftly—for stories, for words, and for love itself.

**E. A. M. Trofimenkoff** (she/they) is a Lord of the Rings and cat enthusiast from Southern Alberta. When she's not doing research, writing papers, preparing presentations or teaching chemistry, you can find them writing fiction (obviously), binging TV shows with their partner, re-reading The Hunger Games for the 30+ time, or pestering one or more of their four cats. If it's not any of the above, she's probably sending memes.

**H. M. Darling** (she/her) is a fantasy and paranormal romance author who writes to make you feel. Her writing journey began as soon as she was old enough to hold a pen… and the rest, as they say, is history. She has a Bachelor's degree in English Literature and Creative Writing, and she uses it to write books full of fantasy characters and villainous love interests, topped off with lots of spice. H.M. Darling lives and burns in Arizona with her partner and two overly-spoiled cats named Tobey and Rory. When she is not writing, you can find her listening to Taylor Swift or reading a book off her never-ending TBR list. Learn more about H.M. Darling and her books at www.hmdarling.com.

**Kaitlyn L. Hill** is an emerging author in the realm of dark fantasy romance. Inspired by her love for the fantastical and the mystical, Kaitlyn explores the darker shades of fantasy, where forbidden romance and unearthly beings intertwine. She's known for passionately embracing darkness, and not-so-happily ever afters, and giving a voice to individuals who feel misunderstood and invalidated.

Kaitlyn currently lives in small town Alberta with her dogs, Molly, and Hades where she climbs mountains, enjoys nights out on the town, and cozy campfires. You can follow Kaitlyn's writing story and personal life on Instagram @kaitlyn.l.hill

**Allie Sarah** is a New Jersey based writer currently studying creative writing and business. When not working on her next book, she can usually be found obsessing over Broadway musicals, beading for her Etsy shop (The Shop of Starlight), or curling up under blankets with a romance novel.

**Felicity Devoria** is an emerging author committed to writing stories filled with sexual tension or murder. Ideally, both. She is currently pursuing an MFA in popular fiction at Emerson College. By day, she works at a museum and a library. By night, she is haunted by what she should've said in that argument three years ago. Her supportive family and yappy dog tolerate her presence in the American Midwest, where she can be found curled up with a good book or a terrible slasher movie. If your friends also say you have bad taste, check out @FelicityDevoria on Instagram.

**Sabrina Ulicki** is a writing coach, freelance ghostwriter, and author from Buenos Aires, Argentina. But before that, she was a biology student, a waitress, a factory worker, a pole dance instructor, a restaurant manager, a secretary, a world traveler, and so much more.

Nowadays, she lives with her two cats, Naila and Solcito, and enjoys lifting weights, crocheting, reading like there's no tomorrow, scuba diving, hiking, changing her hair like it's a religion, drinking coffee, caring for foster kittens, and pottery classes. When you're neurodivergent and queer, there's no end to how many hobbies and interests you can have—and the best part is being able to pull them all into the writing craft!

Sabrina wholeheartedly believes in magic, romance, modern witchcraft, and that kindness can still win.

**Jesica Bavcar** has always been drawn to storytelling, whether through poetry, music, or the intricate dance of romance and fantasy. She was only a little girl when she first found her creative spark through poetry and music thanks to her grandmother, who through encouragement and inspiration, introduced her to the magic of words.

Originally from Argentina, she spent a few years in London, perfecting her English and soaking up the city's literary charm. Now, when she's not weaving love stories, she's working behind the scenes as a ghostwriter and consultant, a role she's embraced for over five years. She's currently working on a celebrity romance novel that blends fame, passion, and the price of love, so even though this is her first official publication, it will certainly not be the last.

Influenced by her wild imagination and life experiences, **Cortney Murchie** loves to explore the depths of emotion and the unconventional.

When she isn't lost in her writing, you can find her nose buried in a good book, watching hockey or spending time with her favorite people – her twins.

Cortney pours her heart and soul into every piece she creates and has been writing from a very young age. She likes to take her readers on a journey through shadows and light and reflects on the complexity of human nature and the beauty you can find in the darkness.

**Kassandra Jackson**, is a special effects artist based in New Jersey and WNY, bringing 14 years of expertise in film and television. Specializing in monsters and gore, She has always had a passion for crafting terrifyingly realistic creatures, wounds, and prosthetics that bring cinematic nightmares to life.

Picking up reading again was something she took on in 2023 and since then she's made amazing connections, friends with the reading community and authors alike. So much so, she decided to take a stab creating a short story with Classic Conversations.

**Paula Phillips** is a passionate bibliophile and dedicated bookworm based in Tauranga, New Zealand. A lover of all thing's literature, Paula is known for her keen eye for literary gems and her ability to discover hidden treasures in both new releases and timeless classics. Whether it's a gripping thriller, a heartwarming memoir, or a thought-provoking piece of literary fiction, Paula's diverse reading tastes make her a trusted resource for book recommendations. Her love for books extends beyond reading, as she enjoys sharing her literary insights with others through reviews and online platforms.

In addition to her love for reading, Paula has a deep interest in writing. She frequently explores her creative side through short stories and writing online articles. When she's not reading or writing, Paula enjoys exploring local bookstores, attending literary events, and engaging in thoughtful discussions with fellow book lovers.

**Angelika Miria** is a Canadian and Serbian author from Brampton, Ontario. She began her love of reading and writing at the tender age of five. Since then she's published multiple novels and poetry books. She is not only a writer but Alternative Medicine Practitioner, Kickboxing Instructor, dance teacher, and dancer. She spends her days with her three children, husband, and cat and enjoys activities of every season.

**Maddi Neuenswander**, an international bestselling author from Logan, Utah, believes in the healing power of stories, and her stories prove her passion for disability inclusion and education. Readers who enjoy fantasy with relatable characters will love her unique combination of wit and whimsy and fall in love with reading all over again. You can find her on Instagram (@writermaddineuenswander) or her Facebook page (Maddi Neuenswander).

**S. Victoria Nakamun** is a full-time psychology student with a special passion in writing queer-oriented fantasy and horror stories— if there's not at least a little bit of gore or sapphic yearning, they didn't write it. They live in Sherwood Park, Alberta with their partner and two cats. Other works include the first of a queer fantasy series When Two Roads Meet. Classic Conversations is their second anthology.

**Shanni Pinkerton** (she/her) is a multidisciplinary creative who is passionate about the power of storytelling. She shares that love in her work as an author, actor, and drag performer, and nurtures it in others as a theatre and language arts educator.

Shanni has had a lifelong fascination with Greek mythology, and reflects on timeless themes like grief, love, and power through her myth reinterpretations. 'Achilles' Final Judgement' marks her second published story, expanding on the exploration of the underworld she began in 'Heat Wave', her contribution to the Sweet Bitter Love anthology.

You can find more of Shanni's work on stages around Edmonton, AB, with geeky improv company Sorry Not Sorry, and online as cosplayer Skeleshan.Creative.

Made in United States
Orlando, FL
27 April 2025

60830088R00252